Looper

A Novel by Ann Bakshis

Published by Ponahakeola Press, 2018
Typeset in Avenir Light, Avenir Heavy, and PT Mono

For Aunt Jeanne, who always encouraged me
to keep writing.

Table of Contents

One

Working in the grove is the only time I get to be outdoors. I've never been past the high concrete walls that encompass the property. I don't even remember what the front door of the main house looks like, as it's been years since I saw it. Leaving the orphanage is highly restricted by the government. There are only two ways to leave: when you turn twenty-one and are allowed to reenter society – or what there is of it – which is by permit only, or in a body bag. That's happened here too many times for me to keep count. There are a few who try to escape, finding weathered holes in the wall, but they only get so far before they're shot by someone patrolling outside. I've only met one person from the world beyond our walls, but that's when he brings me work. The only other people we see are the staff, many too old to still be alive or too mean to reside with the regular population. The headmaster doesn't even pay us a visit. The only time you see him is when there's a new arrival, but no one new has shown up in the last several years.

The temperature has been steadily falling each day as winter approaches, but that doesn't stop those in charge from making us work outside. The crops have stopped growing, but there's more in the grove than just vegetables. Our job for the week is to work on the carriages that run along the cable lines through the city. Maintenance workers would typically enter the back of the grove, dragging in the rusty, derelict cars and placing them under the pavilion off to the left of the entrance. We're tasked with scraping off the rust, sealing holes, and repainting the cars black. The government is too stingy to buy new carriages, or even upgrade the ones they do have. We're taught at an early age that surplus is bad, everything has a purpose no matter how old or trivial, and ornamentation and frivolity are only for the deserving. Those of us who live in the Outer Limits are subjected to these rules and regulations on a daily basis. If it's repairable, fix it. If it's too damaged, destroy it. No wants, no desires, and no dreams are the daily opinions fed to us.

My hands freeze as I wait by the back door for the workmen to bring in our workload for the day. The wool hat on my head is too small and my gloves have no fingertips. My clothes are thin, like me, full of holes that I don't have time to repair, and dingy. We're allowed to thoroughly wash our clothing, and ourselves, once a month. Each person is assigned a specific day and mine is tomorrow, but I'll probably be stuck working and not get a chance to clean up. At the moment I'm the only one outside, which is typical. I'm the first one out and the last one in. I'd sleep in the grove if they'd let me, as I hate being stuck in that big house with so many callous people. I share a room with four others, or at least I did. Now it's just Brink and me. The others were moved to second-level housing when they turned twenty-one. We all came to the orphanage when we were young, some only a few weeks old. I've been here since I was three. I'm told my parents were killed in an industrial accident down at a smelting plant across town. That was sixteen years ago, so I have no memory of them, which is probably beneficial since I don't have any attachment to the life I may have once had.

Lil comes bounding down the dirt path from the house. She's always a little too happy for my taste, so I try to avoid her when I can, but it's hard when she practically stalks me on a daily basis. Why she likes me, I don't know. Her blond hair is cut short and well-hidden under her hat. She never misses her day to do laundry and to shower. I've missed three in the last four months.

"Vernon isn't here yet?" she asks, jumping to a stop next to me.

"He's late, as usual," I respond sharply.

"Brink's been looking for you since breakfast."

Great. What does he want now?

Brink and I share a room, but I know he wants to share a bed. I've been avoiding him the last several weeks when I can, now that it's just the two of us. I've been hiding in the grove since early morning. I try to eat breakfast before everyone else gets up, so I don't have to deal with their horrible attitudes. The cook, Tilda, allows me to slip in and grab what I want before the others come down. She's the only nice person on the staff, at least to me anyway. She can be rough and grouchy with the others, but somehow I've managed to get on her good side. I'm not sure how I did it, but I try to do everything I can to keep it.

The double doors covering the back entrance squeak open as Vernon begins pushing a carriage through. Lil takes one side and I take the other, trying to keep them open. The doors are dead weight, since they're constructed out of thick wood secured poorly by rusted bolts inside crumbling bricks. It's amazing these doors have lasted as long as they have.

"I have two more that need repairing," Vernon hisses. He's missing several teeth, so it always sounds like air escaping when he speaks.

The carriages are hanging from a cable that stops under the pavilion. Normally they're electrified by the cable but once they're taken off the main circuit, such as the line in the alley behind the orphanage, you have to manually push them. They're bulky, awkward, and sharp. I pull the one Vernon is pushing, taking it from him so he can move the other two inside. I lock it down at the far end of the pavilion, and Lil locks hers next to mine, with Vernon bringing up the rear.

"When do you need these by?" I ask, knowing the government won't want them idle long.

"Three days," Vernon replies, wiping his hands on a cloth he keeps tucked into the pocket of his filthy overalls.

"That shouldn't be too bad," Lil says, "if we can get the others to help."

I stifle a laugh, since I know that'll never happen. Since the headmaster hasn't been around, many of the others have gotten used to doing nothing. Most of them spend their time lounging around the common room watching television, or tormenting the staff. We did have a governess once, but she vanished one night, and no one knows if she left voluntarily… or not. Citizens do have a habit of disappearing during the night, but it's never spoken about. If someone is gone the following morning, everyone has to act as if they never existed to begin with. Those occurrences have now become more legend than fact, but the others like to speculate on who'll be next.

I turn to Lil and ask her for the scraper as Vernon leaves, locking the gate behind him. The car in front of me is almost rusted through in the floor. I spend most of the morning scraping away the rust, trying to get to the clean metal below before I begin making repairs. I break for a small lunch that Brink brings down to us.

"I was wondering if you were out here," he says, handing me a sandwich and thermos.

"Someone has to get these fixed," I say, snatching my food before he can pull it away like he usually does. "I don't want any Aedox raiding us. Going through their torture once is enough."

Brink smirks and retreats to the house.

The Aedox are the security forces of our ruling city, Tarsus. They closely monitor everyone in the Outer Limits, and if we're not performing to their high standards we're put through a series of punishments. The easiest being locked in a room without any windows for hours, to the harshest, being burned. Thankfully, I haven't had the worst chastisement, but I haven't just had the easiest either. It took a couple of times for me to learn that I wasn't in control of my life, and my body bears the scars from that.

After I finish eating, I remove the badly damaged floor from the carriage and solder a new one in place. It takes me all afternoon to buff out the rough metal, so it's dark when I start spray painting. Lil barely made a dent on the one she was fixing, which means an early day for me tomorrow. My hands are covered in black paint when I finally stop for the night. I've missed dinner, but Tilda has a plate for me in the kitchen. She and I eat together. She could eat with the other staff, but she's as much a fan of them as the rest of us.

"It's your day tomorrow," she says, after sipping her coffee.

"I know, but with all the work out there my shower and laundry aren't going to happen."

"Max, you have to take some time for yourself. Your clothes are so dirty they can walk themselves out the door."

We both laugh. I know she's right, but with two more cars to be repaired and no one doing a damn thing except me time for myself doesn't exist. Not even for one day.

Tilda finishes her soup, then leans over to me. "Before you go to bed, leave your clothes in the basket at the top of the stairs and I'll wash them for you."

"You'll get in trouble if you do that."

"By who, Headmaster Edom? He hasn't been here in ages."

I thank her by helping with the dishes. I head upstairs and gather my clothes, changing into a black tank top and shorts to sleep in. I don't have to worry about Brink walking in on me, as he's too busy downstairs staring at the television like everyone else. The one respite we're given is entertainment from Tarsus in the form of a television game show called the *Litarian Battles*. The one problem is it's the *only* show ever on, it continuously runs non-stop, twenty-four hours a day, and people can't stop watching it. The game consists of young men and women competing against each other in simulated battle, and all for the chance to live in the utopian city of Icarian. No one knows exactly where it's located, or even if it actually exists. The government only allows those who prove themselves worthy in the *Litarian Battles* to go there, and they never seem to return.

During the selection, all current contestants wear the most ridiculous clothes ever created. For the women, their outfits can consist of brightly colored skirts over patterned leggings, crop tops with short sleeves in various colors, or thin fuzzy sweaters, and all with glitter-coated hair in non-natural colors. The men wear brightly-colored pants, white shirts, and flashy vests. During the game itself the outfits are uniform in their design.

I've never been interested in watching the stupid show. Brink can't get enough of it, which is fine with me because it keeps him out of our room. Lil is indifferent like I am, but she does watch it every so often.

I drag my clothes out of the room, dumping them into the basket by the stairs. A few minutes later, Tilda comes and picks them up. The shower will have to wait, though. We're permitted to have a slight, short bath, but no full washing until our designated day. Since the lone communal bathroom is empty, I take the opportunity to scrub my hands and fingers. I wash my face, getting behind my ears, and brush my teeth. I wish I could wash my hair since it's getting tangled from lack of care. I've managed to get it grown out to my mid-back, and if I had to cut it off I would be furious. It's the one possession that's truly mine. Vanity isn't tolerated in the Outer Limits, but no one else here has long, straight, raven-black hair and blue eyes like me.

When I'm back in my room, I lie on my bed and stare up at the dingy-gray ceiling, its plaster peeling in chunks. It's too early to go to sleep but there isn't anything else to do, so I turn off the lights with the switch by my bed. My eyes are barely closed when the door flies open and the lights flash back on.

"Maxy, you missed it," Brink says, storming into the room.

"I keep telling you to stop calling me that," I say, picking up my pillow then dropping it over my head to block him and the light.

He pulls the pillow off and practically jumps onto the bed. "They're going to pick two people from the Outer Limits to compete in the *Litarian Battles*."

I start shoving him off but he's a lot stronger than I am, so I don't move him at all. "Why would I care? It's a stupid show."

He pulls the covers over himself and wraps his arms around my waist. "I hope it's me."

"So do I, since I'd love to have a room to myself." I jab him in the ribs with my elbow, but it doesn't do any good. "When is this supposed to happen?"

"Tomorrow, early afternoon."

Great, I'll be the only one working tomorrow.

He starts caressing my arm, so I hit him in the stomach, which causes him to stop but only for a few seconds. "Come on, Maxy, if I'm chosen you may never see me again."

"That works for me." I take my heel and kick backwards, hitting him in the crotch.

He lets go and rolls onto the floor, moaning. I turn the lights off, but I don't close my eyes. This has become almost a nightly ritual between the two of us, and he's never going to learn that I'm not interested, but unfortunately there aren't any open beds other than the two in our room, so I'm stuck with him for the moment. I'll be glad when he turns twenty-one in a few months, then he'll be given a permit to move into second-level housing. I have two years to wait before I get mine, then I can move from one nightmare into another.

I'm up before the sun is. Tilda has breakfast waiting for me in the kitchen along with my clothes, freshly laundered. I eat quickly, as I want to get a jump on the work since I'll be the only one out there. I put on my winter coat, hat, and gloves while Tilda cleans my dishes. She moves breakfast to the dining hall for everyone else as I go out the back door. I check the carriage I worked on yesterday, making sure the new floor adhered properly. I have to finish painting it before moving on to the next one. I find a couple of more rust spots that need treating by the cable attachment, but those are easily handled within a half-hour. The second car needs minor repairs, mainly the gears need to be oiled. I paint over the spots Lil scraped yesterday, but I decide to wait until after lunch to work on the third carriage.

My hands are frozen when I walk into the kitchen, but Tilda isn't there. I exit into the large foyer and cross over to the common room. Everyone, including the staff, is surrounding the large television hanging on the far wall. I locate Tilda huddled in a corner squeezed between two other staff members.

"Why is everyone in here?" I ask quietly when I reach her.

"They're choosing the new contestants," she whispers.

Why does this matter to everyone? It's just a stupid show. Nothing but a game.

I've only viewed a few minutes of it, and I can't see what the appeal is with watching others fight in simulated battle. No one dies, or gets hurt; they only rack up points, which doesn't mean anything. Normally the contestants are volunteers, young adults between the ages of twenty and twenty-five, from the city of Tarsus. I don't ever remember a time when someone from the Outer Limits was allowed to participate. The *Litarian Battles* have only been around for a little over five years, but have been so ingrained into our daily lives that it seems like it's been on since life began.

"I hope everyone is excited about this as I am," the announcer says through speakers over my head. I can't see the television itself, so I have no idea what the man looks like or even how the selection process is being handled. "The two new contestants from the Outer Limits are Lil Jasper and Drake Kelly."

The front of the room erupts in joy for Lil while I retreat to the kitchen with Tilda to help her prepare lunch, but she won't let me near the food until I shower. I roll my eyes and head up to the communal bathroom. In order to access the lone shower stall, we're all given a code to enter into the keypad by the glass door. The code only works on the day you have permission to use the stall. A freshly cleaned towel hangs on the other side of the door, along with a small bottle of soap. I close the door, making sure it locks, take off my clothes, and step into the hot water. The shower is timed, so the clock above the spigot begins to count down from ten minutes. I wash quickly, since I want to enjoy just standing under the clean water.

"Max, you in here?" Lil calls out.

"Yes."

I can't see her, but I know she's probably jumping towards the stall. "Did you hear? I got chosen to be in the *Litarian Battles.*"

"Good for you," I say, trying to sound sincere. "How soon do you have to be in Tarsus?"

"They're sending a couple of Aedox over in the next hour. I have to go pack, but I wanted to say goodbye to you while I could."

"Good luck. I hope you do well."

"Thanks."

The main door closes behind her as I decide to do another quick wash, the timer running out just as I finish. I wrap myself up in the towel, pick up my dirty clothes, and go back to my room. Tilda placed the basket on my bed, so while I'm looking for something to put on I'm also putting them away in the small dresser at the foot of my bed. Lunch is ready when I get back downstairs, but I still eat in the kitchen with Tilda.

I spend the rest of my day rebuilding the third carriage. I've created a metal shop behind the pavilion where I keep scraps, cutting machinery, and all my tools. No one else goes back there, so I doubt anyone has even noticed it. If I need more supplies, I usually let Vernon know on the days he comes by to drop off work. I have just enough material to get the third carriage operational, but I'll need more paint and metal sheets if I have to make any other major repairs. I clean up my mess, trying to get everything sorted for Vernon when he comes to pick up the cars tomorrow. I know he told me I have three days, but the government counts them as the day you get the workload as day one, and the day it's due as day three.

I stick my hat and gloves in the pocket of my coat when I enter the kitchen, which is quiet. There isn't anything on the stove or in the oven even though dinner is normally served at six, which is in a half-hour. I hang my coat on the hook by the back door and go into the dining room, which is also empty.

Why do I even bother looking? They're all in the common room now that Lil is in Tarsus. She's probably being placed into the game tonight.

When I get to the common room, Brink is the only one there. His back is towards me and he's sitting rather still. The television is actually off, which isn't normal. I cautiously step into the room, constantly checking over my shoulder, but I'm not sure why. Brink is awake, as his eyes flutter when he notices me, but he doesn't move. In his hands is a small device I've never seen before and I try to determine what it could be. It resembles a trigger used on some of the Aedox bombs, but there hasn't been any violence in the Outer Limits in months. At least not by its citizens anyway.

"Brink," I say, slowly stepping towards him.

Sweat beads his brow, soaking the brown hair that hangs slightly over his eyes. "I can't move," he says calmly.

"Where are the others?"

"I don't… I can't."

The lights in the room go off and I'm thrown to the floor. My arms are secured behind my back, my legs are bound, and my mouth gagged. I recognize the Aedox uniform even if I can't see their faces. The three blue stripes along the sides of the gray pants gives them away. Another one approaches Brink, pressing a button on the top of the device in his hand to turn it off.

"The after-effects will wear off in an hour," the man tells Brink.

"What are you going to do with Max?" Brink asks, his voice shaking.

"She'll be back soon, Brink. We just need to borrow her for a little while."

I try to scream but I'm hit in the head, which shuts everything out.

Two

When I wake, I'm in my bed and Brink is sound asleep in his. My muscles ache and I feel groggy, but not I'm not sure why. I toss the covers off, swing my feet onto the floor, and try to stand. The room sways violently in front of me, forcing me to sit back down. When I push myself off the bed, pain shoots through my fingers and I scream, waking Brink. He's next to me in seconds, helping me back into bed. I slowly look down at my hands and notice they're scarred with intricate lines, from the tips of my fingers and all the way down to my wrists.

"What did they do to me?" I cry, tears running down my cheeks.

"Let me take a look," Brink says as he gently cradles one of my hands in his palm. The flesh is red hot, almost blistering. The scars appear to be healing, but they still look fresh. "Try to bend your thumb."

I do and it's excruciating.

"Don't move. I'm going to get Tilda."

He runs out of the room, but it's almost ten minutes before he returns. Tilda isn't looking too well herself as she kneels down in front of me and exams my hands.

"What happened last night?" I ask her, almost pleading.

"I'm not sure. A man came to the door just before I was to start dinner. He had several Aedox with him, or at least they were wearing the uniforms of the Aedox. He made all the staff go into the cellar, while the Aedox escorted everyone else to their rooms."

"Except me," Brink says, sitting down on his bed.

"Why not you?" I ask.

Tilda looks up at me, fear in her eyes. "They were looking for you," she replies, trembling.

The room turns cold, so Brink goes to my dresser and grabs a sweatshirt, wrapping it around me. I try to recall the events from last night, but all I remember is seeing Brink sitting in front of the television, motionless.

"Why? Why me?"

"I wish I knew," Tilda says.

"They had me hold a paralyzer. It keeps the body from moving but you can still talk, hear, and see. I heard someone tell the Aedox I was your roommate, which is why I was chosen. I think if Lil was still here it would've been her."

"Any idea what they did to you?" Tilda asks, gingerly placing my hands in my lap.

"I don't remember any of it. How did I even get back here?"

"I can't tell you," Tilda says. "We weren't released until a short time ago. Brink was passed out in the common room, so a couple staff members carried him up here." She stands, brushing the wrinkles from her skirt. "I'll be back in a moment, as I have some burn cream that might help."

I lie back down, shoving my feet under the blankets as Tilda applies a heavy ointment to both of my hands after her return. It stings at first, but then turns soothing. She slips a pair of gloves on to protect my skin and orders me to stay in bed. She says she'll have Brink take care of the carriages when Vernon arrives this morning. Brink helps tuck me in, a concerned look etched on his face.

"No sexist comments today?" I ask, trying to break the anxiety that's filled the room.

"No, Max, that won't happen anymore. I'm sorry I acted that way. I'll bring you breakfast," he says, closing the door behind him.

What happened that changed Brink so much? This isn't like him. He's been harassing me since I came of age, which was when I turned eighteen. I wish I could remember last night.

Tilda is the one who brings me breakfast, not Brink since he's outside tending to Vernon. She has to hand-feed me since I can't hold anything. It's now that I remember the supplies I need, so Tilda says she'll send a message to Vernon later in the day. I don't like lying around not being able to work. It's been a long time since I wasn't occupying myself with some sort of labor out in the grove. After a couple of hours I can't take it anymore and attempt to get dressed. It's painful, but I manage.

Most of everyone else is grouped around the television when I reach the bottom step. Several staff members are milling about, but I've never understood exactly what they do in the orphanage. Tilda isn't in the kitchen, which I'm glad about since she'd be scolding me for being out of bed. I put my coat on and struggle to get my hat over my head. I leave my gloves in my pockets since I'm still wearing the ones Tilda provided me earlier. Brink is fiddling with another broken-down carriage when I step outside. Luckily there's only one today.

"What are you doing out of bed?" he asks when he sees me.

"I'm bored."

"So? It's not like you can do anything out here."

I squat down on my knees next to him, looking at the door panel of the carriage Vernon dropped off. "You'll need to scrape that rust spot before you patch it," I comment.

"You know, I've done this before believe it or not," Brink replies as he sets down the wrench to pick up a wire brush and begins to scrub the small spot. "How are the hands? Is the ointment helping?"

"A little. The pain has subsided some, but it still hurts to bend my fingers." I stand and walk around the carriage, checking for other spots that may need tending to. "Do you really not remember last night?"

He continues to work as he answers. "I just didn't want to worry Tilda because I know she's close to you," he says, stopping to look up at me. "They threatened to kill everyone if I gave any hint to you that Aedox were there. The staff and everyone else were already secluded when they said that to me, so none of them know."

"Did they say anything else?"

"Only that they were specifically looking for you." He begins scraping again then stops, but he doesn't look at me this time. "They knew who you were… where you were. They didn't ask us any questions, they just ordered the others to their rooms and kept me in the common room. It wasn't a usual raid. There was something different about it."

I'll say. Normally those they remove aren't ever returned. So, why was I?

I go over to a workbench by the carriage, my hand hovering over the tools. I bend my fingers slowly and notice they're not as stiff or sore as earlier, but the flesh still burns when I attempt to grasp a screwdriver. I shove my hands into my pockets to keep me from temptation.

"Why the change, Brink?" I ask, turning towards him.

He's in the midst of spray-painting the freshly scrubbed spot on the door, so he has to lift his mask up before he can respond. "Does it matter?"

"Yes, it does," I respond.

"Why, Max? You've always had disdain for me, so why would you suddenly care if I actually behave more civilized toward you? Is there something so wrong with me showing some kindness and consideration?"

"I guess not," I say, kicking the ground in front of me as he returns to working. "I was just wondering, since it's a complete alteration to your normal personality. Sorry I asked." I go back into the house and spend the rest of the day lying in bed.

Tilda applies more cream to my hands just after lunch, then again after dinner. The burns have almost healed and the pain is substantially less, but the joints are still stiff. She has me do some exercises to prevent my fingers from completely hardening on me. I turn in early, but I can't sleep. I've tried not to think about what happened last night, keeping it as far from my mind as possible, but now that I'm trying to sleep it's all I can think about.

Why would they do something like this to me? What purpose is there? I'm the only one who works hard in this place and they choose to maim me?

Sleep finally finds me, but it seems like moments later my bed is shaking. I try to open my eyes, but they're covered. I begin to panic when something is placed on my abdomen, preventing me from moving.

What is Brink doing? I thought he was done with these games.

"How are the hands?" a deep male voice asks, but it's not Brink.

Fear takes over, but I can't feel it since I'm paralyzed. I'm able to hear and speak, but not move.

"They hurt," I respond, trying to keep the shakiness out of my voice. I don't want this person to know I'm terrified, otherwise they might take advantage of that.

"We'll give you something for that," the man replies.

I sense movement next to me, but I can't feel anything.

"That should help," he says a few minutes later.

"Why are you doing this to me?"

"Patience, Max. You'll soon know why."

The door shuts and the room becomes quiet. A few moments later, the lights are turned on as Brink rushes into the room. He removes the item, a paralyzer, that's on my stomach after deactivating it by pushing the button at the top. It's the size of an apple, completely constructed out of metal, and glows blue when it's in use.

"Are you all right?" he asks, removing the cover from my face.

"Yes, I'm fine."

"You won't be able to move for an hour, so there's no use in trying."

"Where's Tilda?"

"She's been removed."

"What?" I shout, trying to move my head but I can't.

"She was taken just after dinner. Two Aedox arrested her and a new cook is already in her place, who's as nasty as the rest of the staff."

"Did they say what Tilda was charged with?"

"You know they would never tell us. Did they do anything to you?"

"I have no idea. They asked how my hands were, so I told them about the pain and they said they gave me something to help."

Brink picks up my arm and gingerly removes the glove. The hand is completely healed of the blisters, though I still have the incision marks. Those are probably permanent. He checks the other hand and finds it's also healed.

"We'll have to wait until you can move to see if your joints still bother you," he says as he gets ready for bed. He makes sure the blanket is tucked around me before getting under his covers and turning off the lights.

The hour seems long as my body slowly restores to normal. When the feeling returns to my hands I try to bend the fingers, discovering they move with ease as if nothing happened. I'm about to tell Brink but I hear him snoring, so I settle myself further under the covers and fall asleep.

I hate eating breakfast with the others, but since Tilda is no longer in the kitchen I don't have a choice. Once the dishes are cleared I head outside. Brink joins me, which is very out of character for him, and the two of us finish the repairs on the carriage. Vernon picks it up just before lunch and drops off a couple of printing press machines. I ask him about the items Tilda was going to tell him I need, and he says he'll have them for me tomorrow.

I haven't worked on a printing press in over two years. Vernon didn't say what was wrong with them so I take the housing cover, a big metal plate that's awkwardly placed on the side of the bulky contraption, off the motor first. One of the belts that transfers the power from the motor to the gears has snapped. I look over the rest of the machine, noticing the injectors feeding the ink to the main print plate are clogged, and that the casing for the plate is cracked. Very little is distributed in print form in the Outer Limits, so for one of these machines let alone two to have this much damage done, the government is going all out to lecture us about something.

"This one's in the same shape," Brink says, pointing to the other press. "Wonder what they've been up to for both to break down at the same time."

"Who cares, let's just get them fixed."

I have to dig through the junk pile in the back of the grove to come up with two belts, both being too big. I measure the old one and cut the other two to length, then melt the ends together over a small smelting pot I use for soldering. While those cool, I remove the injectors from my machine while Brink removes the plate casing. He'll have to build a new one, so I tell him where the parts are. He drops the plate next to me, casing and all, before going into my metal shop to get the material. As I dig out dried ink from the tubes, scraping it against the workbench, my eyes catch the single word raised on the plate: sartneP. I realize the letters are backwards, so they'll print correctly on the paper. I remove each individual section of the plate and arrange the letters, so they'll display as if printed: Pentras.

What does that mean?

Brink comes up behind me, looks over my shoulder, and reads the word. Neither of us has seen it before or even knows what it stands for, if anything. It could be just government jargon that's only known to the Aedox, which is common. Brink constructs the new frame, slips the pieces of the plate back in, and attaches it to the machine. It takes me till almost nightfall to clean out the injection tubes. Brink has both plate frames and belts back in before I'm done. Dinner is being served when we enter, so we don't have time to clean up before eating. My hands are thick with ink, which I get all over the bowl and utensils. The new kitchen woman isn't happy with me and berates me in front of everyone for being so unsanitary.

When I'm done eating I scrub what I can from my hands, brush my teeth, and head off to bed. Brink is sound asleep when I enter. It's not like him to be in bed this early, let alone not watching the *Litarian Battles* like everyone else. He's been a completely different person since the other night, which has me concerned. No one can change that quickly or drastically without some kind of intervention, or threat. I don't know if I completely believe him when he says nothing else happened.

My mind is moving at such a rate that it's preventing me from sleeping. Normally I don't have insomnia issues, but the last several nights have been awful. I push the covers off, slip on a pair of socks since the worn wood floor is cold, and head downstairs to the common room. No one else is around, but the television is on regardless. I find myself walking to the tattered floral couch at the front and sit down. The older man on the screen is standing in the center of a ring as he speaks into a shiny old-fashioned microphone that's dangling from the ceiling. He's talking about an upcoming event composed of some of the more experienced players associated with the game. His pencil mustache twitches when he smiles. His greased-back hair shines from the lights above his head, but it accentuates his receding hairline. His suit is form-fitting, a black jacket neatly closed with a sparkling pink necktie and matching pocket square.

"Yes, children, this event is touted to be the most daring of its kind," the man says enthusiastically. "An experiment the government has decided to conduct on our little community: an opportunity for one lucky winner to govern the new collective being constructed next to Tarsus."

I can hear the audience clap with excitement but I can't see them which makes me question their existence.

"This new utopian communal will be named Pentras, but before we can allocate the correct players for this event each of our current contestants much reach a point level of 50,000 or higher in order to compete." Sounds of disbelief pour from the speakers hidden in the ceiling. "Now, children, this isn't an unheard of number for our contestants to reach. Only once has this ever been accomplished, and that winner is living a life of leisure, relaxation, and happiness in Icarian."

The cameras pan out, showing the speaker not in the center of a ring but in the middle of a large room full of high-backed seats in neat circular rows around him. Four tiers of them, all filled with young men and women dressed in the most outlandish clothes I've ever seen. In front of each of them are small screens jutting out from the back of the seat in front of them. I'm disgusted with the display, so I turn it off.

"Hey," says an angry voice behind me. "We were watching that."

I turn and notice a couple of the others lounging in the chairs behind me, so I flip the screen back on and go to my room where sleep continues to elude me.

I'm up before the sun. As the days grow shorter there's very little light outside in the morning and evenings, which makes working all the more difficult. I decide to skip breakfast and head right for the grove. Now that I know what the words on the plate mean, I wonder why they'd be printing such propaganda in the Outer Limits. That sort of task is usually done in Tarsus since marketing of that kind isn't permitted here, as it would lead us to have desires and aspirations.

The only thing left to do on the press machines is to work on the ink injectors for the second unit. They're not as clogged as the first one, so it doesn't take me as long to clean. Brink doesn't come out to assist but he did most of the work yesterday, so I'm not mad that he's not here. I'm looking for a wrench in my shop when the back gate opens and six Aedox with heavy rifles march through the grove, heading towards the back of the house. I tuck myself deeper into my shop, trying to stay out of their line of sight. The kitchen woman opens the door, almost like she's expecting them. Shouts from inside seep out into the cold air and Brink is thrown out the back door, landing hard on the frozen ground below the steps.

"Where is she?" one of the Aedox screams at him, kicking Brink in the ribs.

"I told you I don't know," Brink replies, curling up slightly to protect himself from another possible blow.

The Aedox points to two others and they begin to tear apart the grove. Brink is being pulled to his feet and shackles are placed around his wrists. The gate squeaks as Vernon walks in, an expression of shock on his face. The Aedox who was questioning Brink marches over to the elderly man, grabs him by the shoulder, and shoves Vernon down onto his knees.

"Caretaker," the Aedox begins, "where's the orphan known as Max?"

"I haven't seen her, sir," Vernon replies, pain creasing his weathered face. "This is my first visit of the day. Have you checked inside?"

The Aedox takes his rifle and hits Vernon in the face with the grip, breaking his nose. "Don't get smart, caretaker, or you'll share the same fate as her."

What the hell did I do? I've been obedient, serving, and quiet. Why are they looking for me?

I catch Vernon looking in my general direction and the Aedox follows his gaze, spotting me amongst the scraps. I bolt up but my shoe catches on a loose nail sticking up from the makeshift floor, preventing my escape. I fight with the Aedox when they try to touch me, but it's not a smart move. I'm hit in the back, knocking the air out of my lungs, then shackled and marched towards the back door of the house. I'm shoved through it with Brink behind me, and we're escorted to the foyer. Everyone has gathered in the common room to see what the commotion is about, but none of the staff asks any questions about our arrest. They simply open the front door and allow the Aedox to take us.

Three

Two carriages wait in the middle of the brick-paved street. Brink and I are placed in the back of the first car since two of the Aedox will be in the front. The carriages can only carry four people, so the remainder of the Aedox will go in the second car. Before we leave, our shackles are secured to bolts in the floor and blindfolds are placed over our eyes. I feel the car sway as the two Aedox climb in and we begin to move. There aren't any windows or protective covers for the openings so we're exposed to the elements, the cold air stinging our faces as we travel.

The journey seems never-ending. I can tell we're passing smelting factories, rubber mills, and sewage plants by the smells that invade my nose. They're at times overpowering, causing my head to hurt and my nostrils to burn. We swing through a loop, manageable only because we're practically sideways, then straighten out again. We eventually slow, but we don't stop. Clanking noises echo over our heads as the carriage jerks violently up and down. The ride becomes smoother once the noises stop. The air around us is a little warmer and I smell pleasant aromas of balsam and cedar. The car stops, our blindfolds are removed, and our shackles detached from our wrists. The room we're in is vast and well-lit, with carriages lining the wall off to the side. Many have fancy scroll-marks along their doors, which is the mark of the headmaster.

"This way," one of the Aedox says to us, pointing towards a stone archway with a staircase behind it.

We follow them, my heart pounding heavily in my chest. I glance at Brink and spot sweat covering his brow, and his hair is wet at the base of his neck. We come into a large entryway where clunky chandeliers dangle precariously from the ceiling, and are led across the hall to a study paneled in dark wood, heavy maroon-colored carpeting that's pushed up to the baseboards, and a stone fireplace in the far wall. The room is filled with copious amounts of ratty furniture that must've been glamorous in its time.

"Wait outside," a tall man in cotton pants and a bulky, dark-red robe says. His back is to us as he watches a large screen above the fireplace.

It's not the *Litarian Battles* playing, but rather a news program. I guess it's the kind of thing only viewable by those in the government.

Once the doors are closed he turns around, a glass tumbler in his hand which is filled with a dark liquid. He takes small steps forward, sizing us up as he goes. It's been a while since I saw the headmaster, and he hasn't aged well. His thick gray mane has thinned, his once-fit and muscular frame is now frail, and his skin feels rough when he touches my face. I try to pull away, but he grabs me around the throat.

"What trouble you've been, Max," Edom says, practically spitting.

"I haven't done anything," I protest. "What the hell is wrong with everyone?"

He removes his hand and slaps me hard across the face. "Don't you dare talk to me like that. I could have the Aedox remove you to be tortured if I so desired." He steps back, almost tripping over his own feet. "I do have a reason for bringing you two here," he says, gesturing for us to have a seat on one of the couches while he sits across from us and places his glass on the closest table. "You've been selected to participate in the *Litarian Battles*."

"What?" I practically shout.

"Really?" Brink asks, cheering up slightly.

"You'll be transported there tomorrow morning after my staff gets you two properly scrubbed and presentable."

"You can't be serious!" I say. "They already drew the two from the Outer Limits a couple of days ago. Why would they do it again?"

"Since the government has implemented a change to the game, they need more participants."

"You mean those who are disposable," Brink adds.

"You aren't the only ones from the Outer Limits who are going," Edom responds, picking up his drink. "Some of those in the second-level housing will be joining you."

"But I'm not of age," I say. "I'm only nineteen, and you need to be at least twenty to participate."

"It doesn't matter, Max. You were selected, so you don't have a choice." Edom presses a button on the table and the Aedox return. Brink and I are practically yanked out of our seats. We're almost out the door when Edom stops them. "It's best if you don't act out," he says. "The government has made it clear that anyone who purposefully undermines any segment of the *Litarian Battles* will be formally executed on live television."

The door closes as Brink and I are escorted up two different flights of stairs located on either side of the entryway. Three Aedox take me up to the first landing, down a lavish hall, and to a room on the left. I'm shoved inside and the door locked behind me. It's too thick to break, unlike the doors at the orphanage, so I give up before even trying. I go over to the four-poster bed that sits in the middle of the room and collapse. I'm uncomfortable in such lavish surroundings, but as I look closer at the furnishings I notice that the glamour is actually decaying. Everything's old, chipped, faded, and ragged; almost like the carriages when they come to the grove for repair.

I close my eyes as I try to figure out what to do, but a sharp noise causes me to bolt upright. Three women around the age of sixty enter from a secondary door on the right and escort me into a large bathroom, complete with a sunken tub. For the next hour they scrub me until I'm almost raw. I shy away from their grasp, but they're surprisingly quick and strong. As soon as I'm dry they dress me in satin pajamas, have me brush my teeth, and send me off to bed. The mattress is lumpy, but it's still better than the one at the orphanage.

I pull the thick bedspread as far over my head as possible, trying to hide from the world. I wish I knew why I was chosen. I know the government monitors us daily, but why pick me? Nothing will get done at the orphanage now, which means the Aedox will be raiding the building frequently and torturing those inside until work resumes.

Okay, that last part I don't feel so bad about. Maybe it'll do them good since they're nothing but lazy asses anyway.

My door unlocks in what seems like minutes later, but from the light creeping in around the heavy curtains I can see it's morning. The three women pull me from bed, brush my hair, and clean the crap that was missed under my nails. One woman hands me an outfit and tells me an

Aedox will be up shortly to escort me down to the dining room. They leave and lock the door behind them. Undergarments are concealed under the hanger carrying the clothes, so I put those on first followed by brown leather pants, a black tank top, a brown leather jacket, black socks, and knee-high brown leather boots. A mirror hangs by the door, so I glance at myself and am struck by my high cheekbones and plump lips. I'd never really looked at myself like this before since there aren't any mirrors in the orphanage. They say that would lead to vanity.

The door opens a few minutes later and I'm taken from my room, down the stairs, and to a room across the hall from the study. In the center is a long table, five seats on each side with one at the head. I take the only unoccupied chair next to Brink, with Edom seated at the head of the table. We're served scrambled eggs, bacon, fruit, and orange juice. It tastes just like the food at the orphanage, so I guess having luxuries only goes so far. We eat in silence, all probably too nervous or scared to speak. Once the meal has been consumed Edom calls for our attention.

"You'll be leaving for Tarsus in a half-hour," he says, leaning forward in his chair. "Two Aedox per carriage along with two of you. The journey to Tarsus will take approximately three hours, as you'll need to pass through the Dead Zone to get there."

"What? You can't be serious!" a young man off to my left shouts. "Those carriages won't protect us from the radiation. We'll be dead before we even get there."

"The Aedox have specialized cars they use when moving through the Dead Zone, so you'll be well-protected," Edom replies.

"What's this all about anyway?" a young woman on my right asks.

"Tarsus is becoming overcrowded, so the government has decided to build a new collective next to it. To prevent clashes outside the ruling party it was decreed that whomever wins this event will be awarded the new city. The winner will be reporting directly to Leader Fallon, but in order for the contestants to be narrowed down they must first show their willingness to truly fight. Normally the young men and women who volunteer for the *Litarian Battles* are doing it for fun, or to prove they're better than their compatriots. Many of the winners receive luxurious living quarters, wealth, and freedom in Icarian."

"They already have all those things, so why would they need to compete for it?" Brink asks.

"You have to understand the type of culture that's fed to the people in Tarsus. It's hard to explain since everyone here has had a much different upbringing. The rules for the event are that no one under 50,000 points may participate. The contestants will have eight weeks to get to that amount, or higher."

"And they need us for this?" someone at the far end asks.

"Yes, to slaughter," the young man from earlier replies.

"Garrett, everyone here will be given the same opportunity as those who've already been participating for months or even years. But yes, the damage and kill points for you will be a lot higher, giving them the advantage."

Everyone begins to shout in protest, but I retreat into my own thoughts.

Kill points? People actually die in this game? Why didn't I pay closer attention? I'm probably the only one in this room who's never watched more than a few minutes of it, which means I'm going in at a severe disadvantage.

I think I'm going to be sick.

"Enough!" Edom shouts. "The government has made its choice and there isn't anything you can do to change these circumstances. You either follow through with the commitment made of you or be executed." He gets up and storms out of the room.

"I wonder how they decided who from the Outer Limits was going," Brink says to me, leaning in so I'm the only one who can hear him.

I look around the table. I don't recognize any of the others. Of the three women and seven men, only Brink and I are from the orphanage. Which means the others have been living with their parents in the shanties at the base of the hill the orphanage sits on top of. Second-level housing is for singles, so when or if you pledge your commitment to someone else you're moved to the shanties.

"That's a good question," I finally respond.

The Aedox come for us a few minutes later. We're gathered in pairs, doled out to two Aedox, and leave out the front door. Twenty carriages wait for us, but they're ones I've never seen before. Thick lead plating makes up the body, heavy paned glass covers all openings, and there are wheels underneath which the normal carriages don't have. Brink and I are escorted to the first car, and before I get in I notice a thin iron gate sitting between two stone columns next to the large mansion we just exited. Men and women in tattered clothes, with dirty faces and mournful eyes gather on the other side, watching us. I can't help but stare at them, mesmerized by their sudden appearance. An Aedox pushes me forward and away from them. The doors for the carriage swing up and out, then lock back into place once we're seated. When the Aedox take the front their doors close, and hissing sounds escape from the joints and connectors holding the vehicle together. We roll forward, turn left at the end of the paved road, and start our journey east.

We leave smokestacks and poverty in the distance as we make our way into a small forest. It's the first actual nature I've seen in my entire life. Plants don't survive in the harsh environment of the Outer Limits, and if they do it's always brown. These plants, however, look well-tended. Their thick leaves scrape along the top and sides of the carriage. The foliage is vast and variant in the types of vegetation present. I look through the glass covering our heads but can't see the sky above the canopy as moisture drips down the windows.

We slow down as we approach a guard post. In front of us is a large dome, reaching as high as I can see. The Aedox opens his window, reaches out to a keypad to type in a code, then closes the window and double-checks the seals around the vehicle using a diagnostic panel in front of him. A concealed entrance in the dome opens and we move forward, with it quickly closing behind us. Each carriage has to stop at the post and punch in their own code before the gates will open, so the process to move all twenty into the holding area becomes tedious. Once everyone is in another door opens, allowing us access into the Dead Zone.

I always thought the stories of this area were created to scare us, so I had no idea that it actually existed. No one knows exactly who bombed this location, or even when the dome was placed on top of it to prevent the radiation from seeping into Tarsus and the Outer Limits. The only thing ever told was there was a great war many years ago, perhaps more than a century past. The country was sent into a dark period after the war, which led to the loss of all our historical records. The Dead Zone is said to be so heavily polluted with radiation from the nuclear fallout after the bombs fell that it had to be capped with a glass dome rising at least three miles high.

I'm in awe of the destruction.

Homes blown into splinters, while other structures have melted or are burned beyond recognition. The land is so covered in debris that the only clean space is where the carriages are traveling. It's almost like time stopped here, perfectly preserving the moment that millions of lives came to a grisly end. I'm sure having the dome is helping in that preservation, since fresh air can't get in and deteriorate the materials. We turn a corner and pass an old-style crane holding the façade of a home, the rest of the house is gone.

Brink nudges me in the side and points above our heads. A small spider-like apparatus hovers overhead, then flies off. Two more enter our field of vision, then move away. I look off and see several more of the devices close to the ground far off in the distance.

"What are those things?" Brink asks as one comes awfully close to the carriage.

"Drones," the Aedox in front of me responds. "We have to closely monitor the Dead Zone for any violators who may be trying to hide in here."

"People can actually get into this place?" I ask.

"Unfortunately, yes. We usually don't find them until they've succumbed to the radiation poisoning. At which point we just leave the body where it fell, since there's no reason to collect them if they were dumb enough to enter in the first place."

An hour later, the Aedox tell us we're halfway through. My ass has gone numb from sitting on the metal bench so I try to adjust my position, but it's no use. My body is starting to ache everywhere. I actually find myself leaning on Brink's shoulder for support, so he puts his arm around me and pulls me closer. He doesn't try anything, which still bothers me since this isn't his true nature.

I wish I knew what caused the change, but maybe I'm asking for an answer I don't want to know.

My eyes hurt from the sun's rays that are filtering in through the dome; I've never seen so much sunlight before, since the air in the Outer Limits is extremely polluted. I adjust my head to where I'm back to looking out the windshield. A building in the distance catches my eye, mainly because it's the only one still standing. It's constructed out of metal and purple tinted windows, and is intact. It stands fifty stories high and is in the shape of a squared soda bottle with a pointed roof. Just below the roofline is a sign in large looming letters, also perfectly intact. The word Pentras hangs solidly against the structure. We pass the building along our right and I see the sign is on this side as well as the back.

"What is that?" I ask, pointing to the structure.

"A building, Max," the Aedox in front of me responds, laughing a little.

"Thanks, smartass, but why isn't it damaged? Everything around it has been obliterated, yet it stands perfectly unscathed."

"Ever think that maybe it was built *after* the bombings?" the other Aedox asks.

I hadn't thought of that. I just assumed that once the fallout occurred the dome was placed immediately. Would they have let the Dead Zone be re-inhabited just after a nuclear war? Is that why the new community is being called Pentras? I want to ask more questions, but I know that would be pushing it. I'm surprised the Aedox actually answered the ones we did ask, since that's not like them.

Am I being paranoid, or is everyone acting out of character lately? Brink has stopped harassing me, Vernon gave away my hiding spot, and now the Aedox are allowing us to speak freely. Is something else going on that I'm unaware of? And why was Tilda arrested? She didn't break any laws. Where is she?

The final hour of getting through the Dead Zone seems to be taking forever. I understand that we can't move fast like we do in the Outer Limits, but this is ridiculous. When we do get closer to the other side I can see that the glass dome is no longer clear, but cloudy, obscuring anything that might be visible on the other side.

The carriages slow as we approach a set of airlocks, and just like before we all have to enter the first set before the next set of doors will open. When we're all secured inside the holding area, the carriages are bombarded by water mixed with some kind of chemical tinted a light-blue. The next set of doors open, we enter through another set of airlocks, and after the door closes we're hit again with another liquid. We go through this routine two more times before finally exiting the dome and connecting to a cable.

Tarsus starts right where the dome ends. Tall metal structures glow brightly with colorful flashing signs adhered at different levels. It's early afternoon, but Tarsus is lit up like it's night. I'm surprised we didn't see these lights when we were in the airlocks, but the glass was so coated we couldn't see anything through it. Our pace picks up, but we're still not going nearly as fast as we were in the Outer Limits. People rush past, dodging into alleyways and open storefronts. Items of various shapes, sizes, and colors hang from store windows, tantalizing shoppers to come in and buy. Everything is bright, flashy, big, and extravagant. It's a far cry from the Outer Limits, and it makes me uncomfortable.

We come to an intersection, turn right, and stop a few blocks in front of a tall, wide, and heavily-plated building. Lights hidden under each floor's ledge change color simultaneously, illuminating an otherwise dull structure. Our carriage switches cables and we swing around to the side of the building, rest on the pavement, and are lowered about three stories before linking up to another set of cables and moving forward. The lift heads back to the surface as we move deeper, and then we finally stop outside a set of steel doors. The carriage doors disengage and rise. I have to slide across the seat in order to exit since my door is blocked by a concrete wall. The driver from our car enters a code by the doors which causes them to swing open smoothly, introducing us to an empty room with a lone light hanging in the center.

The ten of us are ordered inside and the doors close behind us, with the Aedox still on the other side. We drift towards the light, making sure to stay close together. Within moments of us hitting the center, monitors drop from the ceiling and encircle us. Bright colors dance across their screens as they come on.

"Contestants, welcome to the *Litarian Battles*," a hidden male voice echoes through the chamber. "In a few moments, you each will be directed to the door on your left." A spotlight turns on, illuminating the single door that we didn't know existed. "From there you'll be escorted to the main floor, where your position in the game will be determined. Once that's been decided, you'll take a seat in the row assigned to your position until everyone has been through the designation process." The display changes to a name in large print. "Brink Ford, please step towards the door."

Four

It's only been twenty minutes since we started and there are four of us left. Garrett is called next. He's a few inches taller than Brink, with chestnut-colored hair that barely covers his ears. He disappears behind the door while the rest of us grow anxious. I can't take the waiting; it's wrecking my nerves. A few minutes pass before the light above the door turns on and the next name is displayed.

"Max Sutton, please step towards the door."

I swallow the lump in my throat and step forward. The door slides open at my approach, and as I step across the threshold I'm immediately blinded by light. The door closes behind me and a pair of hands presses against my back, propelling me forward onto what seems to be a platform. I'm made to stand in the center of a metal disc that takes up the entire floor and then rises. The hole in the ceiling spins open the closer I get. Applause reverberates over my head, then around me. The spotlights above me pull back, allowing my vision to adjust.

I'm standing in the same center the announcer did the other night. Circling me are four tiers of contestants, all dressed in absurd clothes in bright, colorful patterns. In front of me stands a digital display, but the screen is currently blank. I glance around the room, trying to find Brink, but he's buried in the sea of audacious tones. I feel someone behind me and turn to see the host, a bright white smile plastered across his face.

"Max," the man says, pushing the microphone above his head towards me. "Congratulations on being selected for this bold undertaking. You must be so excited to be here and away from the Outer Limits."

I can't tell if that's a question or just a simple comment, so I humbly smile.

"It's now your designation time. In front of you is an indicator, which will assist in placing you into the right position for the *Litarian Battles*." Those around me clap, cheering slightly. "Just stand still, look directly at the screen in front of you, and we'll have your placement in seconds."

The host steps off the metal disc and the digital readout begins to spin rapidly. It's taking longer than a few seconds, bordering on what feels like minutes before the display finally stops. *Looper* flashes across the screen. Those in the top row scream with joy and begin chanting my name.

"Wonderful, Max. You're the first Looper chosen today." The rows move back, revealing a staircase on my left. "Join your group by taking a seat in the Looper row, and once the remaining contestants' designations have been determined we'll move on to the next phase."

As I climb I spot Lil sitting in the first row marked *Nius*. Her clothes are tight-fitting with a top cropped just above her stomach, and her hair is now purple with glitter plastered into it. Brink is in the next row marked *Rapid*, and Garrett is in the row labeled *Dead Mark*. I have to step over a couple of feet before getting to an empty seat in my row. The dark-red upholstery is soft with thick padding and a backrest that comes all the way to the top of my head, so I'm able to lean back comfortably. A blank monitor is secured in the headrest of the person in front of me while down in the center of the arena displays hang from the ceiling just outside the spotlights, allowing us to see the full extent of the metal disc as it brings up the next person.

The platform the young woman is standing on, the one I stood on, has the same intricate scrolls across its surface as the headmaster's carriages do. The design almost looks like a laurel, a type of wreath. The disc is black with gold markings. When the host steps off the device an outer ring moves clockwise. I never even felt it move when I was standing there. It slows as the digital display shows what the position is. It's Nius, so the young woman takes a seat next to Lil. The last participant is designated Dead Mark, and after he takes his seat a tile slides over the disc, covering it, and the host retakes center position.

"Now that everyone has been placed, the next step is for the beginners to be taken to the Progression Room for scoring. Please stay in your seats and you'll be lowered to an awaiting transport. Everyone else get ready for the selection to determine who you'll be fighting today."

The others erupt in excitement, and their arms flail above their heads while safety straps come out from the base of the headrest to cross my chest and secure my thighs. My seat slides back a foot, then slowly descends. The air in the shaft I'm entering is much cooler than the room I'm exiting, and I can't see everyone else because a wall is in front of me. I come to a stop, spin around, and in front of me stands a dark-skinned older woman. Her tightly curled black hair has several strands of silver woven into them. The red pantsuit she's wearing makes her look like a stick and she's standing under a lone light with a carriage behind her.

"Hello, Max," she says, assisting me out of my seat. "I'm Matron Kaniz and I'm in charge of the Looper unit here in Thrace Tower. Before we get you settled into your quarters, you'll need to spend some time in our Progression Room."

She clicks a button on a small device in her hand and the side door of the carriage swings up. She gestures for me to slide into the front row while she gets in next to me behind the wheel. The ride is pleasantly short and we come to a stop in front of an elevator, climb aboard, and ascend. We're the only ones on the floor when we exit. The walls are covered in shiny metal, just like the exterior, with colorful lights hanging from the ceiling and sconces on the walls. Between the fixtures, monitors display people dancing, partying to music that blares out from hidden speakers. Displays that aren't playing these scenes show colorful mosaics ebbing and flowing in rhythm with the music.

Matron Kaniz gestures for me to follow her down the corridor on our left. We pass a large room on our right, which the matron tells me is one of two bedrooms on the floor. At the end of the current hallway is an emergency exit, a bright red sign glowing above the door. We turn right after passing the bedroom, then immediately left into a smaller room. Screens cover the four walls, each showing a different type of weapon. In the center of the room is a tablet atop a narrow, glass pedestal.

"In here you'll select the weapon you'll be using in the game," she says, stopping next to the tablet and gesturing for me to step in front of it. "The weapon you select is uniquely yours. It can never be used by anyone else, so even if you were to lose possession of it in battle your opponent won't be able to use it against you. Also, each position has a specific type of weapon, so no two will ever be the same. For a Looper, your weapon will be a blade." The screens around me change to various kinds of blades differing in length, metal, and style. "Place one of your palms on the screen and you'll be given a small selection of blades to choose from."

I hesitate to touch the smooth device since I wonder if the scars on my hands are going to inhibit the screen's ability to select a proper weapon. I press my palm against the glass, stretching my fingers out as far as possible. Green lights scan my print and a few moments later the displays on my left change to show nine different types of blades. I'm drawn to the one in the center: a heavy knife with a short handle and forward-curving blade. It has a dark-blue aura around it, almost as if it's glowing.

"That one," I say, pointing to the screen.

Matron Kaniz smiles. "Nice choice." She comes up next to me, taps the side of the screen, and pulls up the full schematics for the weapon. "It's called a Kopis. The blade is thick steel with a polished wooden handle. Unless, of course, you want a different design."

"I can customize it?" I ask, enjoying this process a little too much.

What's wrong with me? I shouldn't be acting this excited in regard to creating a weapon for death.

"Of course. It's your weapon, Max; we'll make it however you like."

She pulls up a design menu and I spend the next ten minutes selecting the metal and color of the blade, as well as some intricate markings I want embedded. I choose a light-colored steel, the exterior sides of the blade are to be etched with smaller versions of the weapon, and an ivory handle in the shape of an elephant. The matron seems pleased with my design and sends it to be created.

My stomach sinks at the thought of what I've just done. This isn't right, none of this is.

"Next, you'll need to select your shield," she says as we step to the other side of the room where another nine monitors display various types of shields. "Shield selection can be tricky since they don't defend against all weapons. Each one is a great defender in its own right, but only towards one type of weapon, so you'll want to choose carefully."

I wander from screen to screen, each displaying a different type of shield and what weapon they're able to protect me against. Apparently the weapons the other positions use are arrows, a Deer Horn knife (which I have no idea about), and explosives. Unfortunately the monitors don't tell me which position has which weapon. This is a much harder decision to make, and the longer I take the more impatient Matron Kaniz becomes. I finally settle on a shield style called *Ancile*. It's elongated with what looks like two half-moons encompassing the sides.

"Perfect. Just wait here one moment." She steps through a door in the side wall and returns several minutes later, holding the door open and gesturing for me to follow her.

The walls in the next room are white, spotless, and covered with medical instruments. In the center of the bright room is a lounge raised waist-high, a surgical table beside to it. A man in a blue gown, hands covered in gloves and a mask over his face, signals for me to have a seat. My heart races, my palms sweat, and I try to back out of the room, but the door I stepped through is now closed and locked. Matron Kaniz stands next to me, grabs my arm tightly, and plunges a syringe into my neck. I collapse instantly though I'm still conscious. Nurses I didn't see earlier pick me up and carry me to the lounge, strapping me down. My arms are extended away from my body onto extensions that are pulled out from the chair. My wrists are secured, palms up, as machines are rolled out from hidden cabinets. The doctor examines my hands and notices the scars.

"How did you get these?" he asks, his tone alarming.

"I…I don't know." I barely get out before they place a breathing device over my face.

"Breathe deeply," one of the nurses says.

I can't breathe, and it shows. My body tightens as I begin to panic, so I'm injected again. The lights grow dim, my breathing slows, and the world is gone.

I don't need to open my eyes to know I'm no longer in the sterile room; too many voices are bouncing around the walls. A soft blanket covers me, but I toss it off when I see where I am. I'm on the bottom of a three-tiered bunk bed. The room I'm in is filled with them, except for two corners at opposite ends. Those look to be bathrooms from what I can tell as the doors swing back and forth with people running in and out of them. I set my feet on the floor, noticing my whole body is shaking. I place my hands on my knees to keep them still and that's when I see it. Covering my left wrist is a black wristband, the size of a shirt cuff, with a digital display all around the device. It shows my position and my points, which read 1,000. The display changes to my name scrolling across the screen and alternates colors as it moves. I try to slide it off, but it's imbedded in my skin. Shock sets in as my imagination floods with what's been done to me.

"Don't look so freaked out," a young woman says, standing in the doorway to the main hallway. "We all have one." She raises her left arm, showing me an identical band. She enters, grabs something from one of the beds, and sits next to me. "I'm Addie," she says, holding out her hand.

I shake it, but I'm still too stunned to speak.

"It's okay, Max, we've all been through it. The Progression Room is torture. I actually think the matrons enjoy it when we're in there," she says, smiling. "So, let's see what you've got." She takes my arm, taps on the band, and pulls up a menu which displays my personalized weapon and shield. "Not bad for a beginner." She stands, takes the item she picked up, and pulls her shoulder-length light-blond hair adorned with purple streaks behind her head, tying it up. "Come on, it's almost dinnertime."

She pulls me to my feet and we exit into the chaos. Laughter, screams of joy, and lively conversation penetrate my ears long before we get to the source. A couple of young men and women run past, playfully chasing each other. Gone are the crazy hair styles and outlandish clothes. Everyone is dressed in either tank tops or short-sleeved shirts, along with jeans, leggings, or sweatpants. There are a couple of people with extremely short haircuts, dark-blue or maroon-colored hair, and odd styles, but nothing like what you see on the selection floor.

At the end of the hall are couches arranged around several televisions attached to the walls, where windows would normally be. Behind the one set is another in the same formation. Opposite the seating area is a dark, wood bar with stools and black-walled refrigerators with glass doors. Addie takes me behind the bar and shows me where everything is kept, from utensils to plates and cups. She says the kitchen staff will be up shortly with the dinner carts, but she raids one of the refrigerators for an apple anyway. I take a seat on one of the couches, with Addie sitting next to me. The screens each show a different show or video. Some are set to music, others to variety shows that people are laughing at when someone does something outrageous. Only one of the eight shows the *Litarian Battles*, but it doesn't look to be a live feed. I ask Addie about it since the image currently displayed shows her opponent being selected.

"The game is mainly played during the day, but to fill up the time the government runs the battles continuously all day long, until the next morning when selections begin again," Addie replies, then taking a big bite of her apple. She devours it in a matter of minutes and tosses the core into a waste bin under the screen in front of us. "So," she begins, pulling her legs up underneath her, "what do you think?"

I look at her puzzled. "Of what?"

"Being chosen to participate. It's not every day that contestants are plucked from the Outer Limits, especially so many of them at one time."

My response is simply a blank stare. I have no idea what to say, or even articulate how I feel since I'm unsure about all of this. My fingers move over my wristband, feeling its sleekness and wondering what the purpose of it is and why they had to embed it in my flesh.

She sees me fidgeting with the device and places her hand on top of mine. "You'll get used to it eventually," she says. "It does take a little bit, but soon you won't even know it's there."

"What's it for?"

"You're kidding, right?" she asks, completely astonished by my question. "You've watched the show before, haven't you?"

I shake my head.

She purses her lips and cocks her head to the side. "Huh, I thought everyone in the Outer Limits watched it. Well, Rem will explain it all to you tomorrow during training."

"Who's Rem?"

"She's the lead trainer for the Looper unit and I'm her assistant. It'll be fun," Addie says, smiling then getting up as the scent of food wafts into the room.

I turn and see a staff member in the same regulation uniform worn by those at the orphanage – dark-blue pants with a white dress shirt and black coat – pushing a large cart loaded down with food. The man stops, places the trays along the bar, and leaves. It's a frenzy to get a plate of fried chicken, freshly baked rolls, corn, and brownies. I get in line with everyone else, but there isn't much left by the time I'm filling my plate. Addie gestures for me to follow her back to the couch we'd been on and we use the coffee table in front of us to rest our plates on. She gets a couple of water bottles from the fridge, but before she can sit down she's scooped up from behind by a young man and flung over his shoulder.

"Frey," she says, squealing, "put me down."

He smiles, complies, and sets her back on her feet. He then jumps onto the couch next to me, taking her seat. "Hi, Max."

"Hi," I respond nervously.

"I'm Frey, unit troublemaker," he says, laughing, then sticks out his hand and bumps me to shake it.

I comply and am surprised at how gentle his grip is compared to how bulky his body is. I thought he would've crushed my bones without even trying. His smile is slightly crooked, and his auburn hair brushes the top of his shoulders. He's several inches taller than Brink, almost Garrett's height.

Brink. How could I have forgotten about him? Is his unit just as crazy as mine? Is he glad to be here? I wonder if the only time I'll see him is during battle.

"Leave her alone," Addie says, pulling Frey off the couch so she can sit down and finish her meal. "Go bug someone else."

"Fine, crabby, but I'll be back." He winks and leaves.

She rolls her eyes, hands me a bottle, and picks up her plate. We finish our dinner, tossing the remnants into the trash before setting the dishes into one of the sinks behind the bar, and reclaim our spots on the couch. We spend the next several hours just watching music videos. I ask Addie if every day is like this. She's replies yes, and no.

"It depends on what happened during the game. If no one died, then it's a good day like today."

"How often does someone get killed during battles?"

She scrunches up her face and looks up at the ceiling, obviously trying to think about the answer. "At least every couple of weeks. Unfortunately, there'll be more deaths occurring with the upcoming event." Her body language changes from joy to discomfort and she pulls her knees up to her chest as she lies sideways on the couch.

An hour later Addie retreats to the women's bedroom to sleep. Everyone else slowly starts making their way to one of the two bedrooms the later into the night it gets. I stay up, partly because of anxiety but also to be alone. I focus my attention on the screen playing one of the battles that was supposedly recorded earlier, according to Addie. The battlefield is constructed out of concrete rubble, collapsed metal structures, and a lot of debris. I can't tell if the landscape is real or something the government cooked up. At the top right-hand corner of the display is a digital clock counting backwards. I'm not sure what time it started on, but there's an hour and twenty-seven minutes left. In the upper left-hand corner are the names of the two players battling and their points.

A young man with a quiver slung over his shoulder and an arrow ready in his bow is slinking around the rubble, looking for his opponent. I can barely catch a glimpse of the other person since they're moving too fast. The man with the bow winces as a gash appears along his ribcage. The points next to the name Lok decrease by ten, while the ones next to the name Drake increase by ten, which causes me to wonder if it's the same Drake from the Outer Limits.

Lok is struck again, this time in the arm holding his bow. His points decrease by another ten, bringing his total down to 5,070. He steps on top of the rubble he'd been hiding behind, looks intensely off into the distance, and fires his arrow. Drake is struck in the chest. He drops to the ground as his points descend. The minutes slowly pass before Drake touches a spot on his wristband, which ends the battle and Lok is declared the winner. He's awarded 100 points for the strike on Drake, but since he'd already taken a loss of twenty, he only gains eighty.

The rubble, debris and metal structures disappear, leaving a large open space. The walls and floor are covered in gray tiles with light-blue illumination acting as mortar. Drake disappears, the battle clock resets to two hours, and the final points are tallied. I look at my wristband, making sure to pay close attention to the 1,000 points that flash in my face. My eyes find their way back to the screen and I stare at Drake's points, which now show as totaling 230.

If we start out with 1,000, what happens if we hit zero?

Five

I stay up most of the night, trying to get caught up on how the game works. No one appears to be seriously injured by their opponents, so I wonder if the outfit they all wear provides some kind of protection. Many use shields that are generated by their wristband, but as Matron Kaniz said they don't protect against everything. All the matches I watch end with someone surrendering. Drake, from what I've seen so far, has the least number of points. I still can't figure out where the actual positions of the players come into play. Maybe that's what Rem will explain to me. I finally go to bed just after two in the morning, according to a small clock on my wristband.

I don't bother changing my clothes and get under my blankets, burying myself. I feel like I've been given a death sentence. There isn't any escaping this, bargaining my way out, or hoping for some sort of miracle. I wish I knew why I was chosen. How was it determined who would be sent? Were the names selected at random, or purposefully? I wonder if there's a way to get out of this. Could I just leave through the emergency door? Where would it take me? Does the wristband have a tracking device?

The lights automatically come on just before six, but I keep my head covered while everyone else makes their way to the bathrooms or out to the common room. Addie pokes her head under my blanket, our noses almost bumping. She drags me from the comfort of my mattress and into one of the bathrooms. She grabs a change of clothes from one of the cupboards, hangs it outside a shower stall, shoves me inside, and orders me to wash. I don't argue, but I do try to avoid getting the wristband wet for fear it'll electrocute me.

Once I'm clean and dressed, we go to the common room to eat breakfast. There's enough food this morning to get second helpings, which I do. Just after nine, everyone begins lining up in front of the elevator except Addie, who nudges me to follow her. We pass through the common room and towards the side of the floor where the Progression Room is located. I fear she's taking me back there, especially since Matron Kaniz is standing in the hallway waiting for us.

"Hello, Max," she says, her hands behind her back. "Addie, Rem is waiting for you in the training room. I'll bring Max along shortly."

Addie returns the way we came and enters a room on her left before she reaches the common room. Matron Kaniz gestures towards a door next to her, so I open it and a room the size of a walk-in closet sits just beyond. Secured against the walls are labels flashing the names of everyone on our floor. Behind the labels are empty sheaths, except for one. I recognize the handle sticking out of the leather case and my name bounces underneath the weapon. I have to step far into the room to retrieve it since it's almost all the way to the back. The Kopis practically sings in my hand when I touch it. I feel like it's always been a part of me, an old friend I'm finally reunited with.

"The weapons can only be used in the training room and the battle floor," Matron Kaniz says. "If you attempt to use it outside of these areas, the weapon becomes non-operational and is immediately returned to the storage room you're in now. This will be the one and only time you can carry your weapon out of this room. All other times your weapon will be brought to you."

"I thought I was the only one who could handle my weapon. How can you bring it to me if no one else can touch it?"

"There are ways to transport items without physical contact," she replies as she steps out of the room, then locks the door behind me and escorts me to the door Addie disappeared behind. "Rem and Addie should be ready for you." Matron Kaniz leaves by making her way towards the common room.

I don't see a doorknob, so I push on the wall where the entrance is supposed to be and the wall slides open. The interior of the training room looks just like the battle floor: gray tiles one foot in length and width, illuminated from behind and underneath by a light-blue glow that flows between the slats. The room is far larger than I imagined. Addie is standing off to the side with another young woman whose red hair is short along one side, and buzzed almost to the scalp on the other.

"Max, this is Rem," Addie says, introducing me to the young woman. "Put your weapon in the holder over there." Addie points to a small rack on the wall to my left.

"Won't I be needing it?"

"Not at the moment," Rem says.

I place the Kopis on the rack and follow the two of them to the center of the room.

"Before you can be placed into the game, you must learn how to use your new ability," Rem says, pacing in front of me.

"New ability? What do you mean by that?" I ask.

"I told you she'd have no idea what you're talking about. She's never watched," Addie says, crossing her arms over her chest.

Rem's lips curl up, but not quite in a smile. "Then this should be fun," she says before disappearing right before my eyes. "A Looper," she begins, her voice echoing through the chamber even though I can't see her, "moves through both space and time." She pops back in front of me. "It's so we can avoid our enemies and use the element of surprise."

"How'd you do that?" I ask, my mouth hanging open.

She picks up my left hand and taps on the wristband. "This is what gives you the power," Rem responds. "It can only be used in the training room or the battle floor, so you won't have this ability outside of these areas."

"That's why it's adhered to my skin," I state.

"Kind of," Addie says. "It's internally wired into your nervous system. It's also used to transmit your whereabouts in the battle to the Keepers."

"Who are they?" I ask.

"They create the battle plans for the day, are in charge of giving us our weapons when we get to the floor, and determine the points awarded for each hit. Though I'm sure the points will be increasing tremendously as soon as the new candidates are all trained," Rem says.

"Why train us at all?" I say, walking backwards as the air around the three of us has become too intense. "We're only here to make your advancement into the event easier, so what's the point of any of this?"

Rem crosses her arms over her chest, puffing it out. A scowl causes lines to form around her lips, making her look old. "My intention is to have the best unit in this complex, and that even means you, Max. I want the best Loopers to advance to the event, no one else, and in order for that to happen I need the best. And to become the best you have to train. I don't care that you're from the Outer Limits. As of this moment you're a Looper. You're one of mine, and I'll do everything I can to make sure you last. Understand?"

I nod.

"Good." Rem unfolds her arms and her scowl is replaced with a smile. "Now, take my hand and we'll begin."

She stretches out her right arm, and this is the first time I notice all the scarring she has on both limbs. That much torture had to have come from the Aedox, but I never would've thought Tarsus would abuse its own citizens. What kind of discipline did Rem need to warrant such torment? Or did she earn them during battle?

I hesitate, then slowly reach out and take her hand. Everything flashes around me and I feel the air in my lungs being sucked out as if I'm flying through a void. I can see the training room, and Addie standing in the center, but I can't touch anything. It's like I'm floating and falling at the same time. I begin to panic as my body disconnects from time.

"Breathe, Max," Rem says from somewhere nearby. I can still feel her hand in mine, but I can't see her. "Concentrate on where you want to go. You can pick a point in time or one in space."

"I don't follow," I almost scream.

"You can either project yourself to an alternate point in the room, or you can jump to the future, but only by a few minutes. Or you can do both. Let me show you." She lets go of me and I fall to the floor, hitting the tiles hard with my stomach. When I sit up, Rem is now on the other side of the room. "You're going to need to work on your landing," she says, laughing. "Addie, why don't you take her this time?"

I don't even get a chance to get on my feet when Addie takes my hand and we vanish. The same sensation comes over me and I have to continually tell myself to breathe. I see Rem walking across the floor and heading in the direction we'd been.

"Think about what you want to do," Addie says. "Picture where you want to go and you'll arrive."

I concentrate on the far corner where Rem was. Addie and I are swept over there, the floor materializing beneath us. Our feet make contact and the room stops spinning. We're solid again.

"Not bad," Rem says. "It'll take some time for you to get the hang of it."

We spend the next four hours practicing. They each take a turn with me, but I have to direct where we're going. I've only been able to do the aerial projection, where I can move us from one location to another, but I haven't figured out the time one. At least not yet. We break for a late lunch, and since everyone is still down on the selection floor we raid the refrigerators for food. The monitors show the same images they did yesterday, except one is now showing a live feed of the battle floor where two people are fighting.

The points for one keep going down to almost below the 1,000 threshold. I turn and look at Addie and Rem, but neither is paying attention to the screen since they're both watching a music video, the volume of which is too loud for my ears. I glance back at the fight and notice the young man's points drop close to 800.

"How many points do you both have?" I ask just as the young man declares defeat.

Addie is the first to respond after a quick glimpse towards her wrist. "8,950."

"12,400," Rem says without even looking at her wristband. "And they expect us to get up to 50,000 in eight weeks. They'll have to increase the number of battles per day, or the number of players per sequence."

"How many are there now?" I ask, tossing my trash into the receptacle.

"The Keepers only allow five battles per day since they max out at two hours each, and there are only two participants in each sequence."

"So not everyone gets to fight in one day," I say.

"Yup, which sucks because you can get bored really easily," Addie says, standing up. She gets something from the fridge, then sits back down. "I wish they would let us go out just for a few hours into the city."

"Did they used to?"

Rem lets out a slight snort. "A long time ago," she says. "The problem back then was the wristbands couldn't be tracked outside of Thrace Tower, so people would start disappearing. No one knows if they just simply returned to their parents, or if something else happened to them. So, they widened the spectrum on the newer wristbands they started using." Rem holds up hers, shaking it. "Now it doesn't matter where you are, they can find you."

"But why stop the outings? I'd think since they now have a better way to keep an eye on everyone it would be easier to let them out and explore."

"We thought so, too," Addie says, pulling her legs up underneath her. "But then people started missing their battle times."

"So?"

Rem and Addie look at each other, obviously annoyed by all my questions. "If you miss your scheduled time the Keepers automatically transport you to the battlefield, knock your points down to fifty, and hope that your death will be a lesson to others," Addie replies.

"Or, if you happen to survive, they punish you anyway. Making sure to display your subordination to everyone," Rem adds, holding up her arms.

"So, no more excursions," Addie says. "The lessons didn't exactly take."

"Ladies," Matron Kaniz utters as she stands behind us in the main hallway. "I think you've had a long enough break."

Rem rolls her eyes as she stands, and Addie and I have to muffle our laughs. The rest of the day is spent with me trying to move on my own. It takes some getting used to and I almost make myself sick a few times, but it gets easier the more I do it. I still haven't figured out the time piece of it, but Rem says I'll get there. We finish just after seven and it's now I notice that my weapon is no longer on the rack, so I ask Addie.

She tells me the Keepers would've moved it back to the storage room by now.

I'm not comfortable with the idea that these Keepers can move anything from one location to another. What if they decide to send us all to the battlefield at once? Do they monitor us even outside the game or the training room? Rem said they were able to, but is that still the case now that we're all confined to the tower?

Everyone is much more subdued when they get off the elevator tonight. No screaming with excitement or laughter like yesterday. Frey plops down on the couch next to me, not looking well, while others either go into the bedrooms or just collapse on any open space in the common room.

"What happened?" Addie asks, moving to the edge of her seat.

"Jax and Hannah… both of them… gone."

"How?" Rem asks, her voice clearly alarmed. "They were two of the highest pointed players in our unit."

"Lok somehow managed to damage Hannah's wristband, preventing her from looping, using her shield, or ending the battle."

"That's not possible," Addie says, practically crying. "These are indestructible. Why didn't she use her weapon?"

"She did, Addie, but he's a Dead Mark. Without her ability it wouldn't matter. She was dead the moment he broke the band."

"And the Keepers didn't stop it?" Rem asks.

"Of course not," Frey almost shouts. "They awarded him double points for doing it."

"What about Jax?" I ask, trying to become part of the conversation. I didn't know either of these people, but if I can learn what happened to them maybe I can prevent it from happening to me.

"He was being stupid and got too cocky. He was up against a Nius, the newer one from the Outer Limits," Frey replies.

Lil.

"She placed explosives in a couple of locations, but only arming them to go off if movement was detected, or something like that. Jax thought he could loop his way around the battle floor, teasing her and trying to get her to mess up. Dumbass stepped close to a mine and blew himself up. He wasn't paying attention to where she put them and only aerial projected instead of time looped."

"His shield didn't help?" I ask, trying not to sound stupid.

"The one he had was to defend against Dead Marks, not Nius. The Keepers could've saved him if they'd called the game, but they let him bleed to death."

"I guess Addie and I won't be competing for a while if they'll be recruiting replacements that we'll have to train," Rem says, leaning back on the couch.

"There won't be any replacements," Matron Kaniz says, entering the room. "With the event approaching the Keepers want to make sure the points continue to rise, so that means no more volunteers. Max and her friends from the Outer Limits are the last group being brought into the game."

"What did they say about Hannah's wristband? How could that have possibly been destroyed?" Frey asks.

"Lok intentionally targeted it with his arrow. Since he's a Dead Mark, once he's made up his mind where he's shooting the arrow will always obey him. It's a tactic no one has thought of before or even considered," Matron Kaniz says, sitting opposite us with a very concerned look on her face. "The battles are supposed to be for fun, or at least they used to be. But now… the Keepers seem to have let go of all rules pertaining to fair play."

Addie looks at all of us, pausing a few seconds between faces. "What do you want us to do?" she asks.

"Make them pay," Matron Kaniz replies before leaving, and heads down the hallway towards the Progression Room.

The four of us spend the next hour just sitting in the common room with no one saying a word. Dinner is brought up a little later and we eat what we can, but no one in the unit seems hungry. Rem leaves sometime later but quickly returns, a little out of breath.

"Frey, Matron Kaniz has given me permission to turn Max's training over to you. Addie and I will be rejoining the others tomorrow."

"Why?" Addie asks, before Frey can.

"You and I are the two highest-ranking members in the unit. Our damage against the others will be heftier, so we're going to make sure Nius and Dead Mark pay tomorrow."

"Sweet," Addie says, jumping off the couch.

"Why do I get stuck training?" Frey asks, protesting.

"You can use the practice," Rem smirks.

"Real funny, Rem. Just you wait. I'm sure you won't be laughing long when it's Looper against Looper for the top prize."

She sticks her tongue out at him in response and leaves, Addie close behind. Frey gets up, shuts off the television that was showing the battles for the day, and sits down next to me.

"What did you learn today?" he asks, annoyance heavy in his voice.

"How to do an aerial projection."

"Well, that's a start," he grumbles as he shifts his position and pulls his leg up in front of him so he's sitting sideways on the couch. "I've heard that you've never watched the show before coming here. Do you have any questions about it?"

I'm going to sound so stupid with what I'm about to ask.

"What does each position do, other than Looper?"

His eyes roll into the back of his head as he expels a deep sigh. "Unbelievable," he mutters. "Okay, well the other three positions are called Dead Mark, Rapid, and Nius. A Dead Mark hits their target every time. Rapid moves quickly, almost blindingly fast. And a Nius is smart, problem-solving. All are deadly when their skills are mastered, but that takes years and no one has been here long enough to do that. Normally, once someone has reached the point level of 35,000 they're retired to Icarian. To hit the mastery level, you need 50,000."

"Which you have to do in eight weeks," I say.

"Yes, which means things are about to get worse and you'll need to catch on quickly." He begins to look tired. "Meet me in the training room at seven tomorrow morning."

As he's walking away I notice a small, black dragon on the back of his right shoulder. It looks familiar, but I don't know why. I've never seen that mark on anyone before yet it feels reassuring, almost comforting. I shake my head, trying to rid myself of the sensation, then head to bed.

Six

The door to the training room is wide open and Frey is inside, looking anxious. As soon as I step through the door it closes behind me and the lights dim. The air is so cold I can see my breath. The room changes to the grove, its snow-covered grass crunching under my hesitant steps. Tilda is talking to Vernon by the gate, but I can't hear what they're saying because the wind is blowing too hard. Brink is standing next to me, two circular knives with deep curves in each hand. I take his arm and loop us out of the grove, finding ourselves in the foyer of the headmaster's mansion.

"Did you bring us here?" Brink asks, shaking me loose.

"Yes."

"Why?"

"I don't know," I reply.

He doesn't like my answer and swings his knives in my direction, cutting my arm. I reach for my Kopis, but I can't find it. I try to loop out of the foyer and that's when I notice the wristband has been damaged. I try my best to defend myself, but Brink has me outmatched. Blood pours from my wounds as he stands over me, grinning as I die.

My clothes and sheets are soaked with sweat. Everyone is still asleep so I slip into the bathroom, grab a quick shower, change my clothes, and discard the dirty ones along with my sheets into the laundry bin in the corner. I make sure to close the door slowly behind me then go to the common room, which is empty. I try the training room door, hoping it's unlocked, which it is. The lights turn on the moment I step inside and the door closes. I look at the rack, but it's empty. The time on my wristband says it's four in the morning. I probably should go back to bed to try to get more sleep, but I want to get as good as I possibly can before the Keepers decide to throw me into the game. I work on my aerial projection, looping through the room from one end to the other, but it's the time portion that still eludes me. If I can just think about getting ahead of time, think of where I want to be in the next few minutes, perhaps that'll work. I try it a couple of times, but wind up with only a headache. I sit against the wall, lean my head back, and hope I can get this completely figured out. At some point I fall asleep because when I open my eyes Frey is staring down at me, bewilderment on his face.

"A little too eager this morning?" he asks, kicking at the soles of my feet.

"No, just couldn't sleep. Thought I'd get an early start."

"What have you been able to practice so far?"

I tell him about the aerial projection, but that I can't figure out the time loop. "Can you really only go forward?"

"I've never known anyone to go backward, and I'm not sure I'd recommend it if you did figure it out." He slaps my knee, ordering me up and goes towards the rack, which now holds two weapons. Frey visually looks mine over since he can't physically pick it up. "A Kopis, nice." He holds his knife towards me. It's a simple small curved blade with a black handle. "It's not much, but it's easy to conceal when approaching my opponent. More of a surprise for them."

He spends the next several hours showing me how to swing the blade around and the proper method for holding it, especially when looping. It's difficult to do, but Frey assures me it gets easier and that our uniforms have a built-in sheath for us to house our weapons when we're not carrying them. We break for lunch, then the rest of the afternoon is dedicated to using my shield. To get it to expand from the wristband it's a simple flick of the wrist in a sharp, downward jab. The shield is larger than I thought it was going to be, bright blue, and hums. It adds a little weight to my arm when it's functioning, but nothing I can't handle. To get it to retract, I pull my fingers into a small ball and release them quickly. Frey's shield is called a *Buckler* – a full, round shield that is good against explosives. It's green in color, thick in the center, and spiked around the edges.

"What made you decide to volunteer for this?" I ask while we're putting our weapons back on the rack.

"Probably the same reason you did – to have a better life."

"I didn't volunteer for this," I say, spinning him around to face me. "None of us did."

He's clearly puzzled by my outburst. "That's not what we were told," he says as he presses a panel next to the door to open it, exposing an empty hallway.

"What did they tell you, Frey?" I ask, following him down to the men's bedroom.

He stops and blocks me from entering the room with him. "That Outer Limits scum is competing for the chance to govern their own utopia," he says, seething. "That Headmaster Edom is orchestrating a takeover and he needs those most loyal to him to be sent to the *Litarian Battles* in hopes of succeeding." He pushes me away, practically shoving me to the floor. "Watch your back, Max; you have no friends here."

He slams the door behind him. I retreat to my room, burying myself under my blankets. Addie and Rem enter a little over an hour later with big smiles on their faces. I'm in no mood to be around anyone, but there isn't any place for me to go and hide. Addie practically drags me from bed, covers and all, down the hall to watch the replays of the day's battles. Both she and Rem were awarded 1,000 points each.

"The points would've been much higher if the cowards hadn't claimed defeat," Addie says, sitting down.

I sit across from her, hoping my change in demeanor isn't too apparent. Rem asks how my training went and I lie, saying it went great. Dinner arrives a few minutes later but I don't have much of an appetite, so I only grab one sandwich from the large tray, eat it quickly, and excuse myself just as Frey walks in. I avoid his stare as I make my way back to the bedroom, tucking myself into one of the bathroom stalls.

Did Frey believe what he was telling me about why the players from the Outer Limits were sent here? Do they all believe the same way he does? And how were the ten of us really chosen? I doubt Lil was taken to the headmaster's mansion when she was selected, so why were we? I wish I could talk to her and Brink, to see what's going on in the other units.

"Max?" My name rings out from the doorway. It's Addie, but I ignore her at first. "Max, Matron Kaniz needs everyone in the common room," she insists.

I roll my eyes, open the stall door, and we head to the common room where everyone is crammed on the couches, so Addie and I stand against the far wall. All the monitors are off and the music has been turned down significantly.

"The Keepers have decided the new recruits have had enough time in training, so beginning tomorrow they'll be participating like everyone else," Matron Kaniz says, standing in front of the bar. "The five battles tomorrow will be among the ten from the Outer Limits. You all will still need to report to the selection floor like usual."

"How can all ten of them battle each other? Some were placed in the same units," Rem asks.

"I'm not sure what the plan is. I can only convey what I've been told. Max," the matron says, looking through the crowd, finally locating me. "I need you to come with me to get your uniform ready for tomorrow."

She dismisses everyone else, and the monitors are turned back on and the music starts to blare. I meet up with the matron just outside the training room and she escorts me down the hall, past the Progression Room and into the room where I chose my weapon and shield. On the monitors this time are six styles of uniform; all but one is very revealing. The other outfits have either a crop top, are sleeveless, or very short shorts with thigh-high boots, so I select the one with the most coverage: a pair of black capri pants, along with knee-high boots with leather laces, a long-sleeved collared jacket that's fitted around the waist, and a black tank top to wear underneath.

Matron Kaniz tries to talk me out of my selection, telling me that though the uniform will offer me a lot of protection, it'll be very cumbersome to have on when looping… especially the jacket. She advises that the other designs have the same amount of protection and are easier to move in, but I tell her I've made my decision. She escorts me from the room and tells me the uniform will be ready in the morning.

I hesitate in trying to decide where I want to go now, so I head towards the training room. I'm the only one inside when the door closes behind me, but I catch a flash off to my left. My weapon has been placed in the rack, so I pick it up and practice using it along with my shield. I'm getting quite good at aerial projection, but doubt I'll ever figure out the time one. After a couple of hours, I place my weapon back on the rack and head off to bed. Since no one in the unit except for me is battling tomorrow, everyone is wide awake. I change clothes, get into bed, and hope tomorrow never comes.

Sleep eludes me. I'm both anxious and scared. What if I wind up getting paired against Brink? I don't particularly like him, but would I be able to hurt him? Or any of them? I toss off the covers and go to the common room. It's empty, which I'm thankful for, so I plop down in front of a video and drown out my thoughts with the music piping from the walls. The song and the scenes make no sense to me and I'd turn it off if I knew how.

"Hey," Addie says, entering the room. "Can't sleep?"

I nod.

She sits by me, pulling her knees up under her. "You'll do fine. Just remember to use your ability and your weapon, and that everyone tomorrow is at the same level as you."

I slump down in my seat, resting the soles of my feet on the table in front of me. "Can I ask you something?"

"Sure," Addie says, curling into a ball.

"Frey said something to me and I'm not sure what to make of it." I pause, trying to gather a complete thought before continuing. "He said that everyone here was told that the Outer Limits is trying to gain control of the new utopia being created, and that I'm only here to make sure that happens."

"Yeah, we were told something like that."

"Well, it's not true. I never volunteered for this. I was arrested by the Aedox and forced to come here. We were warned that if we try to act out in any way, we'll be executed on live television."

"Huh," is the only response I get.

"Is that all you can say?"

"Max, I don't know what to tell you. No one really believes much of what the government tells us, except for a few like Frey. He's from the upper-class of Tarsus and has had the world handed to him, so he'll buy anything he's told. I, on the other hand, am from the working class, so I don't believe anything I'm told."

"And I thought all of Tarsus was upper-class."

"Wow, Max, you really are sheltered in the Outer Limits," she says with a slight chuckle. She stands, and as she stretches I notice the top of a dragon's head sticking out just above her left hipbone. It looks just like the one Frey has. "You should try to get some sleep. Tomorrow isn't going to be any fun for you." She turns and goes back to the bedroom.

I wonder what the dragon is for. Some kind of emblem for being a Looper maybe?

I stay on the couch, where I fall asleep, and wake up surprised to find a blanket tucked around me. I take it back to my room, toss it into the laundry bin, and step into the shower. Breakfast has been brought up when I return to the common room, but I eat very little since my stomach is full of knots. Just before nine, we line up in front of the elevator. I try to linger towards the back of the group, hoping to go unnoticed.

We descend to the elevator corridor and have to walk the distance to the shafts instead of taking a transport like I did a few days before. A couple of feet from the shafts the group turns left, and we proceed into a large dressing room, which is divided into two sections. I follow the women and go right; the men are on the left. Row upon row of tops, pants, jackets, sweaters, and wigs are stacked several floors high behind a plate-glass window and moving by conveyor belt. In front of the window are several terminals, which are currently occupied. It takes ten minutes before I'm able to get to one.

From the display I choose the outfit and hair I'll be wearing on the selection floor. The choices are all atrocious, skimpy, and colorful. I settle on a light-blue sweater, yellow leggings, and a white wig with blue sparkles. The racks above my head move as a crane selects my garments and drops them down a chute that empties next to the terminal. I take my items, find an empty changing room, step inside, and try to put on the tight clothes.

"Max, you in here?" Addie calls from the other side of the curtain.

"Yes. I'll be out in a moment." I discard my other clothes into a bin in the back wall and step out. "What's the point of these stupid outfits?" I ask as Addie is adjusting my leggings.

"It's a way to get the younger kids amped up about joining. They look at the clothes and colors and are made to believe it's always this way. It's not until anyone is actually in Thrace Tower that they realize the truth, but by then it's too late. You're here until you either point high enough to go to Icarian or die."

She hooks her arm around mine and we follow everyone else towards the shafts. Lights flood the dark space, illuminating the many seats that circle a lone dark wall. Addie points to a shaft with my name and tells me to sit down. She disappears around the corner, probably going to her seat. The chair is the same one I sat in the other day. Once I'm seated, straps cover my chest and down to my thighs before my chair swings around, so I'm facing the wall and begins to ascend. I look through the glass enclosure and notice everyone else is moving skyward as well.

We come up through the floor to thunderous applause and rise above the other rows. Our seats are locked into place and the straps removed. Displays descend from the ceiling in the center just as the host takes his position. He waves to an invisible crowd as shouts and applause grow louder from the speakers next to our heads.

"Thank you," the man says, his white teeth almost blinding from the spotlight that illuminates his face. "Children, this is so exciting. Today we will have our newest recruits battle for the first time. Those who survive will move on to regular game play with the rest of our contenders." This time those around me clap and shout with joy, but I don't join in their reverie. "The Keepers have already selected who'll be battling against each other, so watch the monitors in front of you for the line-up."

My stomach tightens and I have an overwhelming urge to fling myself down the shaft underneath my seat. Names spin by on the display in front of me. The first name that stops is Garret's, followed by a woman named Uli from the Rapid unit. Their seats descend, then rise empty a few minutes later. The next sequence of names appears: Brink and Tog, a player from the Dead Mark unit. They also disappear below the risers.

Four down, six to go. At least I won't be going up against Brink.

Two more names erupt on the screen. Then my name flashes along with my opponent's, a man named Pan from the Rapid unit. My seat lowers and stops in the elevator corridor, where Matron Kaniz is waiting for me. She gestures for me to follow her around to the other side of the shafts, through a heavy metal door, and down a small hallway till it ends. The wall in front of us slides open, revealing a large common room full of couches, monitors, a couple of refrigerators, and several doors lining the far back wall as well as the other contestants.

"See those cubicles?" Matron Kaniz asks, pointing to an area off to my right. "Locate the one labeled Looper and your uniform will be waiting for you. Wait in here until your battle time is announced." She closes the door, sealing me inside.

Everyone in the room looks confused, so I'm glad I'm not the only one. I go to the stall labeled Looper, close the curtain, and find my uniform neatly folded on a bench. I quickly change, wanting to be rid myself of the itchy sweater and horrid wig. The capri pants and tank top are more comfortable, and the leather boots stop just above my knees, so my legs are completely covered. The jacket is a little stiff, so perhaps Matron Kaniz was correct and it'll make looping difficult if I wear it, but I put it on anyway. I find a hair tie in the pocket of my coat, so I put my hair into a ponytail, then exit the room to join the others.

I'm the only women who isn't showing her off midriff. The men have the same type of uniform as the women, except they have long pants, work-style boots, and long, short, or sleeveless shirts. I sit next to Brink, and surprisingly he doesn't say anything. It's almost like he's shut himself off from the world. I nudge him, but he doesn't react.

"Ladies and gentlemen," a young olive-skinned woman says as the entrance from the hallway closes behind her. "I'm Matron Violet from the Rapid unit, and in just a few minutes you'll be called to begin your battle sequences. Behind you are four doors, each one leading to a different section of the battle floor. Your name will appear above the door you're to go through, and at the end of the hall is where your weapon will be waiting. Make sure to secure it to your uniform before you enter, since you won't be allowed to come back and retrieve it if you forget. Your battle will begin the moment you step onto the floor and, as Hammond stated earlier, only one person from each sequence will be permitted to continue. Normally you're given two hours to complete your battle or declare defeat, but that won't happen in this case. The Keepers are determined to see if any of you are competent enough to compete in the upcoming event, so this is a do-or-die challenge. Good luck."

She leaves through another door just as the monitors turn on and the signs above two of the doors flicker to life, displaying the names Garrett and Uli. They approach the doors cautiously, but pass over the thresholds quickly when the doors open. On the screens, we see them making their way down the hallways. Brink grabs my hand, squeezing it tightly. I wasn't sure if he'd realized I was even there.

"This isn't what I expected the game to be like," he says, his eyes focused on the screens. "Why does anyone volunteer for this? Life in Tarsus can't be any worse than the Outer Limits, so why put yourself through this cruelty? They never showed anyone actually dying during the battles, so those of us who watched always thought they simply sent the losers either back to their home or someplace else. I don't want to die, Max."

"At least you have some inkling as to what you're going into," I say as I lean against him, not sure which of us needs the support more.

Garrett and Uli hit the battle floor. At first they try to avoid each other, crossing the floor at great distances apart. Uli stops, bends down, and fiddles with something, but we can't see what because the rubble she's behind blocks our view. Garrett climbs atop a metal structure, bow and arrow at the ready. He jumps from one obstacle to another, keeping his eyes on Uli. She finally stands and begins to backtrack towards the door she entered through. Garrett aims his arrow at Uli, firing, but her shield is designed to deflect it. The arrow disintegrates when it makes contact. She presses a button on her wristband, detonating explosives she hid a few feet from where Garrett stands.

He's thrown backwards, hitting a concrete column, and falls to the ground. He has a gash in his lower leg, and another across his cheek. He's stunned and winded, but otherwise all right. Uli removes a small device from a pack on her back, twists the top, and throws it in Garrett's direction. He rolls away just before it lands and explodes. I notice that the upper left corner of the screen isn't showing the points being awarded to Uli and taken from Garrett, so I wonder if they aren't doing that because all points will automatically go to the surviving competitor.

Uli removes another device, arms it, and hurls it towards Garrett. He's faster this time and shoots an arrow at the explosive while it's in the air, destroying it. He reloads his bow and fires several shots rapidly, but Uli opens her shield, protecting herself. Garrett pauses, looks skyward, and fires his arrow. It strikes a shattered window pane from a severely damaged building, causing the glass to rain on Uli. She's hit by multiple shards, several piercing her skin. Garrett climbs and tries to get a better visual on Uli as she crawls on the ground because of her wounds. He aims his arrow at the pack on her back and fires.

The explosion is bright and shakes the whole building. When the dust clears, there's nothing left of Uli except blood-spattered concrete. The rubble and structures vanish, leaving Garrett alone in the large room. He's declared the winner and is directed to a door on the opposite side of the room.

"What the hell was that?" I almost shout, surprised that the realistic structures used to create the battle environment are fake.

"Tarsus is far more advanced in their technology than the Outer Limits will ever be," someone responds. "This is simply their playtime."

This makes me feel even less confident in my ability to survive the round. If they're this advanced, what else could be out there that isn't real? Could everything be an illusion?

"Make me a promise," Brink says, grabbing my arm and turning me towards him. "Win. You have to make it to the event. Do whatever it takes to get there." He kisses me hard on the lips as his name flashes above the door behind us. "Promise me."

Shocked by his actions, but worried for his safety, I reassure him. "I promise."

He gets up and disappears quickly behind the door. I hide myself in the Looper clothing stall, so I can avoid watching Brink's battle. My head begins to pound, and my stomach tightens as more time passes. He's annoyed me to no end, been morally disgusting most of the time, but I can't picture him not being around. I curl up in a ball in the corner and cry.

Seven

"Max, where are you?" My name echoes through the small chamber. "It's almost time."

I come out of my hiding spot and find Pan standing a few feet away. I hesitate about asking how Brink did, because if he died it would weigh heavily on my mind and it's a burden I can't afford to have at the moment. I pass Pan, take a seat, and watch the rest of the battle between the pair that was selected before us. The competitors are evenly matched, causing very little damage to each other.

"They're both Nius," Pan says, sitting down next to me. "So, this could go on for some time."

I ignore him and try to scoot further down the couch.

"Crazy, isn't it?" he says, following me. "Just the other day I was working in the smelting plant and now I'm here."

"I wouldn't be too excited about it," I say, still trying to distance myself. "One of us is going to die shortly."

Pan stops, leans forward, and begins wringing his hands. "Yes, and it's an unfortunate necessity."

"None of this is necessary," I grumble.

"For some of us, Max, it is."

I look over at him to see sorrow heavy on his face.

Our names are called as the signs above two of the doors begin flashing brightly. Pan gets up and is through his door before I've even left my seat. I stand and approach my door cautiously. It slides open when I'm in front of it and closes quietly behind me. The corridor is narrow, poorly lit, and stuffy. My Kopis is waiting for me at the end, so I take the sheath off the wall and strap it around my waist as another door opens, revealing the battle floor. I step forward, my boots crunching small bits of debris when I enter. The room is bright, as if the sun were shining through the ceiling, and warm air filters in the deeper I go.

I hear noise behind me, so I activate my shield and remove the Kopis from its sheath. Pain radiates down my back and I can feel blood trickling from a wound Pan must've inflicted. He's a Rapid, so he'll be able to move quickly. I close my shield and disappear, hovering above the battle floor, trying to decide where to land. I choose a tall structure and plant my feet on the rusty metal. Pan darts below, trying to find me. It would be smart to just wait him out up here, but that would only work if we were being timed for the two hours.

I start to loop again, but am abruptly stopped when my jacket catches on a metal piling jutting out next to me. I'm dangling from the structure and the coat is the only thing preventing me from falling. I must've let out a shout when I was jerked out of the loop because Pan is rapidly ascending the building. The only way I can get out of this is to remove my jacket, but the Kopis is too large to slide through the tight-fitting garment, and I can't sheathe it since I can't reach my waist. I wiggle as best I can, trying to free the jacket from the piling, but I wind up dropping my weapon.

"You're mine now," Pan says, a few feet below me.

He reaches up, swiping at me with his weapon, which is a Deer Horn knife. The same one I dreamt about Brink carrying. I kick at him, trying to fend off his blows. The boots protect my feet, and his reach isn't long enough to get to the rest of me. He moves quickly, climbing higher to get above my position. I unbutton the jacket, slip my arms out, and fall, but I loop before hitting the ground and project myself behind a pile of rubble on the far side of the room. I land hard, knocking the wind out of my lungs.

Pan isn't far behind, leaving a trail of dust as he moves. I loop back to where my weapon is, pick it up and loop again, this time hovering in the now-familiar void for as long as possible. I'm not sure how long I can hold it, or even if I'm supposed to be able to, but I'll keep it up for as long as possible. Pan has stopped in the center of the battle floor, so I project myself next to him, my Kopis held firmly in front of me. He doesn't see me until it's too late. The blade plunges into his abdomen, but he's able to push me off. He's bleeding, but the uniform is holding him together, keeping him alive.

He swings at me, but I activate my shield in time. I take my blade and fight back, cutting him severely. He drops his knives and I kill him by thrusting my weapon into his chest. A moment later his body vanishes, as does the rubble and concrete around me.

What kind of place is this? Where did Pan go? What other tricks do the Keepers have up their sleeves?

A voice booms over my head to exit through the door on the other side of the room. Once the door closes behind me, I lean my head against the wall and begin to shake. My body goes almost into a seizure with the reality of what I've just done, and I collapse to my knees.

How could I have just killed someone? Do the wristbands contribute to this type of behavior? I don't think I can continue to do this.

Lights flash over my head, so I hang my sheath on the hook and proceed down the corridor. At the end is another common room, this time with the victors, but I don't see Brink. Matron Kaniz congratulates me, hands me a healing gel for my injury, and gestures me to a changing room, where the clothes I had on this morning – not the audacious ones, thankfully – are waiting. I change, apply the gel to the cut along my back, and return to the common room.

"I told you about the jacket," Matron Kaniz says as I sit down beside her and Garrett.

"I wasn't expecting it to get caught on anything," I answer. "But I guess I'll need a new one."

"You keep what you have. We just won't replace the jacket." She stands and leaves the room.

Unlike the other common rooms, the monitors in here aren't playing the show, so we won't know the winner of the next battle until they walk through the door. Garrett gets up and brings me a glass of water from a bar along the far wall. I'm still too afraid to ask about Brink. I only want to know if he's alive, but since he's not here I'm assuming he didn't make it. Yet his opponent isn't in the room either.

I swallow the last of the water before asking Garrett. "Where's Brink?"

"He was hurt pretty badly when he exited the floor, so he's been taken to the medical office. He'll be back soon."

I let out my breath, not realizing I'd been holding it. I go to refill my glass and sit back down.

"Are you and he a couple?" Garrett asks.

I practically spit out my water but instead it goes down into my lungs, making me cough. "No. Why would you ask that?"

"I hear you two were pretty close at the orphanage and that he kissed you before he went onto the floor."

"He was my roommate, nothing more."

"That's good," Garrett replies.

Out of the corner of my eye I catch him smiling. He's attractive, but as this is a winner-take-all situation, I'm going to try to avoid getting into any kind of relationship. What would be the point?

I lean back, resting my head against the top part of the couch, and close my eyes. This battle will have been my easiest, as I'm sure the next one will be against a more experienced player. I'm on the verge of falling asleep when my arm gets bumped. It's Garrett and he's pointing to my hands.

"Where'd you get those?" he asks, leaning sideways so he's fully facing me.

"Aren't you talkative."

"What's wrong with that? There's no telling how long we'll be in this room and I can't stand the music videos they play on the displays, so conversation is the only alternative."

"True." I take a deep breath and tell him about the raid at the orphanage and how I woke up with my hands butchered.

"Aedox don't usually return people they take," he says. "I wonder what their motive was in regard to you."

"I have a feeling that these scars are the reason I was selected to be sent here."

"You don't remember any of what happened? The only thing you noticed were the scars on your hands?" he asks.

I hadn't thought about looking elsewhere on my body, since I was too stunned by what happened to my hands. So, how do I do that now? I can't ask Addie or Rem to examine me, since that would be awkward. Brink would be extremely thrilled with the task, but he'd be more distracted in satisfying his own needs than helping me.

"I guess I was too much in shock to notice anything else," I finally respond after too long a silence.

"You might want to. I'm not sure who you trust in your unit, but make sure if you have someone assist that it's someone who won't notify the matrons."

"Why do you say that?" I ask.

"They really haven't told you much in your unit, have they? Mine are all too willing to share information."

"What have you found out?"

"The real reason we're here in Tarsus."

I almost laugh but am able to stifle it into a chuckle. "You mean that Headmaster Edom is trying to infiltrate the *Litarian Battles*, so he can take over the new utopia?"

Garrett looks wounded at my rebuke. "I take it you don't believe the rumor."

"Since you've never met the man until probably just the other day, let me enlighten you. He doesn't have a solid bone in his body, he's too much of a weakling to cook up such a scheme, and when we were at the mansion I noticed he's aged quite badly since I saw him last. It's almost like he's been tortured like the rest of us."

"How do you know I've never met Edom? He's in charge of the whole Outer Limits, not just the orphanage."

"Just a feeling," I say with a smile.

He laughs, which brightens his face. A door off to our left opens and Brink hobbles in. Matron Violet escorts him to the couch across from me, then leaves. Brink has a newly healed scar above his eyebrow, a puncture wound in his arm, and scrapes all over his legs.

"You look like hell," I say to him.

"Thanks, Maxy," he replies.

"You know I hate it when you call me that."

"Yeah, I know," he says, winking.

"Looks like you're back to your old self, and I was starting to enjoy the new and improved you."

"What can I say? I missed the old me." He stands, plops down beside me, and proceeds to stroke my arm. "I wish I could've seen you kick ass."

I pull my arm away, almost knocking myself into Garrett. "I hate you. For once I was actually missing you, but I must've been out of my mind."

"Come on, Maxy, you know you want me." He squeezes my knee before moving his hand up my thigh.

"Don't touch her," Garrett says, knocking Brink away from me. "It's obvious she wants nothing to do with you, so leave her alone."

Brink leans in towards Garrett. "What's it to you, Garrett? She's been mine since she came of age. She was promised to me, and I'll be damned if I'm going to let some miller prevent me from having her."

"Watch your mouth, boy," Garrett says, seething. "It won't take much for me to end you."

"With what, tough guy? Our weapons don't work outside the battle floor and I highly doubt the matrons will let us have it out right now."

For his next response, Garrett slams his fist into Brink's face and I hear his nose break. I have to plaster myself against the couch to get out of the line of fire as Brink grabs Garrett and they fall to the floor. Fists fly, along with blood. Matron Violet flies through the door moments later, breaking up the fight. She escorts both of them out of the room, and from the sound of it she's taking them to the medical office for treatment.

The final winner enters the room an hour later, that battle being the longest of the day. Brink and Garrett return shortly after, both properly mended. We're escorted from the room to waiting transports, each taking us over to another set of elevators that'll take us back to the main building, so we can return to our units. I'm thankful I'm the only one in my elevator, so I don't have to deal with any questions about the fight Brink started. I exit into the corridor, walk the several feet to the next elevator, and ascend to my floor.

The hallway is crammed with a cheering crowd as I step off and I'm patted on the back, hugged, and congratulated by all. I don't feel much like a winner, so once I'm through the gambit I go to the bathroom for a long, hot shower. My brain hurts from jumping through an emotional range of fear, sadness, anger, and disappointment. Here I thought Brink was being a decent person, only to have it thrown in my face.

What did he mean I was promised to him? It has to be all in his head, but something about the way he said it made it sound like a fact.

I look down at my hands, trying my hardest once again to recall the events of that night, but nothing comes to mind. I must've been drugged really well in order not to recall anything. I do a quick scan of my body, at least what I can see of it, but I only find the same scars that have been there for years. I shake my head, clean, dry off, and dress. Addie is waiting for me in the doorway when I exit.

"That was awesome," she says, escorting me down the hall towards the common room. "I wasn't sure if you knew you could loop in mid-air, but you did it."

I smile in response.

There's a line for the food when we enter but I'm allowed to cut in front of everyone, which I find odd yet gratifying. Frey even starts being nice to me again, bringing me a bottle of water and sitting on the couch next to me, practically on my lap. All anyone can talk about are the battles, though I would prefer not to think about them since there are more to come, but everyone is too excited, so I try to join in.

Around midnight people start wandering off to bed. Frey, Addie, Rem, and I are the only ones still up. Twenty minutes later it's just Frey and me, and the room becomes cramped and stuffy. I want to excuse myself, but something is preventing me from moving. Frey is staring intently at me, almost like he's transfixed.

"What's the matter with you?" I ask, trying to break the tension.

"Nothing," he says, then smiles. "I'm just impressed, that's all. Didn't know you had it in you to kill someone so easily."

"Seriously, what the hell is wrong with everyone? It wasn't easy and I didn't like it, but it's better than me being dead."

"It gets easier the longer you've been at it," Frey says.

"I don't want it to be easier. This isn't how life is supposed to be. Why does everyone from Tarsus think this is fun? Your life can't be so bad here that you're willing to risk it on the chance you'll go live in Icarian."

Frey scowls at my last remark. "Do you want to make a bet?"

"What?"

"Spend a few hours in Tarsus, especially the area I'm from. You might change your mind," he says.

"We're not permitted to leave Thrace Tower, so that'll never happen."

"What if I could arrange it? A small outing, just you and me. Would you go?"

"No." I get up and start towards the hall when Frey calls me back.

"Think about it, Max. You'll change your mind in a few days."

I stomp away, but only make it halfway down the wall when Matron Kaniz appears and signals for me to follow her. We enter the Progression Room, but this time there isn't any medical staff, so I doubt I'm being maimed any further tonight. She has me sit on a chair in the corner of the room while she slides a stool over to sit down.

"Tell me about the fight," she says.

"There isn't much to tell. Brink was being an ass, so Garrett decked him."

"It's more than that, Max. Something had to have triggered such a violent response from Garrett."

"He was defending me, that's all. Brink wouldn't leave me alone, so Garrett stepped in to stop him."

"How well do you know Garrett?"

"I only met him a few days ago, so I don't know anything about him. What's with all the questions? Is he in trouble?"

She doesn't respond right away, but simply taps her index finger against her lips. "We've been notified by the Keepers that some of the players from the Outer Limits may cause some issues with the upcoming event, and we're just trying to figure out if he's one of them."

"What kinds of issues?"

"Nothing that should concern you. I'm sure you aren't someone I need to be worried about, right?"

I nod.

"Good. Now get some sleep, as tomorrow will be a busy day."

I leave and then go to bed after brushing my teeth, but I can't stop thinking about what Matron Kaniz said. We were all warned by Edom that if we caused any trouble we'd be executed on live television. Why would the Keepers think we're here to cause problems? Is what Frey and Garrett said true? Does everyone in Tarsus think the ten – now five – of us were sent here to take over Pentras when it's completed? Is that another reason we were the only ones set to battle today? To eliminate the possibility of traitors? But aren't the Keepers the ones who make the final selections about who gets to participate? I'll need to ask either Rem or Addie in the morning.

Eight

"Hold still," a female voice whispers behind me.

I can't turn my head to see who it is since my neck is in a brace, which is secured to a metal operating table that's cold under my bare skin. The bright lights overhead prevent my vision from acclimating to the environment. Something is injected into the biceps of both my arms. It doesn't hurt, but within seconds I can't feel either of them. I catch glimpses of movement around me, but nothing will come into focus. A mask is placed over my face and I'm instructed to breathe deeply. I doze off and on for hours it seems, only managing to catch snippets of conversation.

"Will this work?" someone asks.

"Yes, I'm sure of it."

"What if someone finds out what we've done, and—"

"Don't even think it. We have our orders, so we won't get into any sort of trouble."

"Yes, but—"

"You want to stop the realignment, don't you?"

"Of course, but why her?"

"She's the one they've been looking for, and if we make the first alteration to this impending war we'll benefit in the end. This is for our protection, Cil. The leader gave us our orders and we're following them. End of discussion."

My head hurts when I wake, and I can't tell if what I experienced was a dream or if I'm starting to remember what happened to me that night. I shake my mind free of the conversation and meet everyone in the common room for breakfast. I eat with Addie, Rem, and Frey; the topic this morning is the possible match-ups for today. Will the Keepers have the highest-ranked players battle against the five survivors from yesterday? I hope not, as I don't want to go down my second day. We dress and stand in front of the elevator just before nine. It's the same routine as yesterday and I even pick the same outfit to dress in. Within minutes of reaching the selection floor Hammond smiles, waving at us. Those around me cheer and scream, but I don't join in.

"Good morning, children," he says in his happy manner. "I hope you're all ready for today's action. For the next four days we will have our standard five battles. After that we'll be taking a brief break while the battle floor and points are reconfigured. The Keepers have decided to move the end of the event forward, meaning you will now only have three weeks to make 50,000."

Grumbling takes over the cheers, along with some shouts in anger. I glance at Frey, who is five seats to my right. He has a big grin on his face; he catches me staring and points at me, mouthing something I can't understand.

"Now, children, I know you expected more time, but circumstances have changed and Pentras will be ready sooner than expected." Cheers erupt behind my headrest, but I know they're just audio effects. "The Keepers have made their choices for today, so watch the screens in front of you for the selections."

Lok is pitted against Drake again. Garrett and Brink are also selected, but not to battle each other. I don't recognize the other names, and none of them are from Looper. Their chairs descend while the rest of us stay put. When the first battle begins an hour later, Addie seat-hops over to an empty chair next to me. I have a hard time looking at her because of the cotton candy-colored hair loaded with glitter, her turquoise sweater, and blue hip-hugger pants.

"So, Frey told me he's going to take you into the city," she says, before completely sitting down.

"There's no way I'm leaving the tower."

"Come on, Max, it'll be fun. Rumor going around is that the break will be for a couple of days and the Keepers may be letting us venture out. Aren't you curious about what Tarsus looks like? It has to be better than the Outer Limits."

I've never really wanted to see Tarsus, let alone leave the Outer Limits, so having the break sounds unnecessary to me. I'm more interested in what changes they're going to be making to the battle floor, as well as to the point system.

"I suppose," I say, lying. We both stare at the monitors secured in the headrests of the seats in front of us as the first duo takes the floor. My mind suddenly clicks with the question I wanted to ask her. "Addie, how are the contestants chosen? I don't mean for the battles, but to be participants."

She's silent for a few minutes. "Well, for those of us from Tarsus, we enter a draft when we're twenty," she responds. "It's optional, but everyone here wants to prove themselves better than everyone else, so a majority of the young adults enters. We can get selected immediately or a year or two later. It depends on the leader."

"He makes the decisions, not the Keepers?"
"Yes."

So, if their leader makes the choices perhaps Headmaster Edom did the same. Would that mean what Frey was saying is true? Were we sent here to manipulate the outcome of the event?

The battles last two hours each, with no one dying. Drake manages to only lose 100 points, but I think he won't last much longer. I'm completely bored sitting and doing nothing. We're brought lunch about halfway through the day and are allowed bathroom breaks, but I'd rather be on the battle floor than the selection floor. Garrett and Brink are both victorious, adding 400 and 500 points, respectively. The rest of us head back to the elevator, and by the time we're in the unit everyone is exhausted. We eat a quiet dinner and I go to bed before anyone else.

The next morning arrives quickly. I choose the same outfit when it comes time and I'm selected to battle third. My chair descends and I follow the same routine I did the previous time. Matron Kaniz is in the common room but is too busy in conversation with the matron from Dead Mark to notice me. I step into the changing room, put on my battle outfit, and sit on one of the couches facing the doorways to the floor. My opponent is a woman from the Nius unit. She has the same number of points that I do, but since this is only my second time in the game, I'll still be outmatched.

Frey sits down next to me, as he's supposed to battle a young man from Dead Mark before me. He seems perfectly relaxed, almost a little too at ease in these surroundings.

"So," he begins, placing his arm across the back of the couch behind my head, "I've arranged our little excursion with Matron Kaniz."

"You did *what?*" I practically shout.

"The Keepers are letting us leave the tower for a couple of days while they get things ready. There's a handful of us going home, so I've fixed it so you'll be staying with me."

"I told you, Frey, I'm not interested."

"Matron Kaniz has already made the necessary arrangements, so you really don't have a choice."

I roll my eyes, irritated with the fact that I don't have any say in the matter. I'm sick and tired of decisions being made for me. What good could come of me going into Tarsus? So I can see how much better off they are than those of us in the Outer Limits? So they can flaunt their wealth and abundance in my face? I wonder if I can find a way to get out of going.

Frey's name is called, so he pats my thigh before standing then goes through the door on the right. I spend the next several minutes trying to figure out what I can do to get out of this. Frey's battle sequence begins and is over in a matter of seconds, his sword practically cutting his opponent in half. The man from Dead Mark never had a chance to put up any type of defense. Frey is automatically awarded 10,000 points, which puts him in the lead for our unit.

The door on the far left lights up and my name appears above the frame. The woman from Nius almost trips me as we pass each other. She glares at me as I enter the hallway. I strap my weapon around my waist and proceed to the battle floor. The first thing I do is loop to the far side of the room, over where the exit doors should be. I can't see my opponent, so I'm hoping I can wait out the two hours just by looping around the floor. I hide behind some boulders, waiting for time to pass.

A high-pitched screech pierces the silence. I poke my head out just as a metal plank sails across the room in my direction. I dive and roll out of the way just before it shatters the boulder I'd been hiding behind. Two more planks fall from the sky, and all aimed perfectly at me. I can't think quick enough to loop, so I simply run. Once out of range I loop, but I don't land anywhere. The woman from Nius is setting up her next launch and the explosives she's using aren't a type I've seen before. They're small and adhere to the metal planks, causing them to rocket into the air. I'm in the process of changing directions when I'm hit in the shoulder. I'm knocked out of looping and slammed into the floor. My left shoulder is ripped open, blood pouring from it. Since my top is sleeveless, I have nothing keeping the wound together. I take my right hand and scroll through my bracelet. Another plank hits me in the knee and I scream as my leg is savagely disfigured; blood, muscle, and bone shards fly in all directions. I hit the surrender icon and the battle automatically stops. The rubble-filled landscape disappears and the woman from Nius exits the floor.

I feel myself being pulled, ripped from my body. I try to fight it, fearing I'm going to die, but I'm too weak. A moment later the hard metal floor is replaced by a soft mattress and nurses swarm around me. I want to see what they're doing, but all I can tell is that they're shredding my uniform, removing it as quickly as possible. Pressure is applied to the wound in my shoulder, and a device placed over my knee. I feel bones being pushed together, then fused. I scream from the pain, begging for it to stop before I'm given something to make me sleep. When I wake sometime later, Matron Kaniz is standing next to my bed with a concerned look on her face.

"You'll be mended within the next couple of days," she says, setting down a tablet she'd been holding. "You were lucky the plank didn't completely sever your leg. The doctors and nurses were able to reattach everything, so you'll regain full functionality."

"Will this prevent me from going with Frey?" I ask, hoping the answer will be yes.

"You'll be released from the medical office the morning you're to leave," she answers with a smile.

I slam my head back into my pillow.

Matron Kaniz turns to leave, then stops in the doorway. "You're down to 500 points, so depending on how the Keepers reconfigure the game you may be one of the first players eliminated when you return."

After she leaves I let out a large scream. It calms me down some, but my head begins to pound. I look at my battered body, noticing that the mending device is still on my knee. My left shoulder is already healed, with a new scar to add to my collection. No one from my unit visits, so the only people I see are the nurses who bring me meals and check on my knee every couple of hours. There's a monitor secured to the corner of the room, running the games that I'm missing. No one has died since Frey's battle, and Garrett and Brink haven't been selected to participate.

I'm released early in the morning a few days later, the mending brace removed from my knee. Matron Kaniz escorts me up to our floor and packs a bag for me while I eat breakfast. Rem is nowhere to be found when everyone starts pouring into the common room. Addie tells me she was able to go home last night, which I find odd since the Keepers weren't supposed to allow any of us to leave until this morning. After eating I take a shower and am met by Addie, waiting just outside my stall with some clothes. They look like the ones I wore when I first arrived, only cleaner.

"You're going to love Tarsus. Especially the area Frey is from," she says as I slip my undergarments on.

"Are you going home?"

"Yes, so maybe I'll get to see you." She gives me a hug and skips out of the room.

Matron Kaniz and Frey are both waiting for me in the common room, bags in hand. I begrudgingly take the duffle from Matron Kaniz and it's heavier than I expected, which causes me to wince from residual pain in my shoulder.

"The carriage will be arriving in about ten minutes," she says as Frey moves to stand beside me. "It'll take you directly to Frey's home, where you'll both be picked up in five days."

"Five days?" I shout. "I thought it was only going to be a couple of days, like two or three."

"Five days, Max. That's what the Keepers are allowing, nothing less," she responds, her tone stern, almost forceful.

She gestures for us to head towards the elevator; at the moment it's only the two of us leaving, but I see other bags sitting along the hallway. Frey is almost giddy as we descend, but I'm dreading this entire outing. A transport is waiting for us when we exit, but it's not the one that'll take us to his home. This one swings us around the basement of the building and drops us off where the main carriages enter. Garrett is standing along the wall, a bag at his feet. Brink is further down the way. They both catch my eye but Garrett walks over to me first, which makes Brink frown then kick his bag like a child having a tantrum.

"So, you got roped into this, too?" Garrett asks, stopping less than a foot away.

"Unfortunately. Who are you going with?"

"Lok, believe it or not. He offered, so I thought why not."

"At least you had a choice in the matter."

"Wait, you didn't? They're making you go?"

I nod.

He steps closer and bends down so he can talk into my ear. "Be careful. I don't know what they've got planned if you're being forced to go. I'll try and figure out if I can find you. Where will you be?"

"Frey's house," I whisper. "But I don't know where that is."

He squeezes my arm. "Stay safe."

He walks away just as Frey approaches, signaling that our carriage has arrived. Frey takes the duffle from my hands and places it next to his in the front seat. The two of us climb into the back; the door swings into place and locks. We do a quick U-turn and enter into a busy morning.

Our carriage slips in line with the others as they whisk by before changing over to other cables when they approach their drop-off points. Frey scoots closer, almost bumping into me. He drapes his arm along the back of the seat, practically tickling my shoulder with his fingers. The electric signs cascading down each building are bright and flashy even though the sun is out. I wonder if they leave them on all the time. We head south, swinging around skyscrapers before turning left.

Tarsus is larger than I anticipated, so a half-hour later we finally emerge from the main part of the city and out into a calmer, more sporadic setting. Small trees line the streets that branch off into subdivisions with large, ornate houses. It's another thirty minutes before we slow, change cables, and move down a stone path. The house we're heading towards is a single-story with lots of windows, gray wood trim, and covering several lots. The carriage comes to a stop just outside a portico covering the beginning of a walkway that leads up to the front door. Frey takes our bags and we make our way to the door as the carriage leaves. The air smells sweet and the ground is made up of sand more than dirt, but the vegetation grows perfectly.

"This is a far cry from the Outer Limits," I say, taking in all the color from the various plants and flowers.

"I told you so."

Frey opens the door and gestures for me to go before him. He closes it once we're inside, leaving our bags by the door. Tall windows line the back wall of the common room, showing waves crashing against the beach at the back of the property. The only water I've ever seen in my life comes out of a faucet or rains down from the sky. I have to step down into the common room as I try to move closer to the windows, fascinated by the waves beyond. I can feel Frey standing behind me; he places his hands on my biceps, gently stroking them.

"Nice, isn't it?" he asks.

"Yes. Why would you want to leave a place like this?"

"Because Frey is never happy unless he's in charge," a man answers, entering from a dining room on our right. The man's face is long with doe eyes, brown wispy hair graying at the temples, and a stunning smile. Frey resembles him, but only slightly. "I didn't know we were going to have company," the man says.

"Sorry, Dad, the Keepers didn't allow us to contact anyone about our retreat. I didn't think you and Mom would mind having us."

The man smiles, but I can tell he's not pleased with the surprise. "Are you going to introduce me to your friend?"

"Max, this is my father, Avery."

"Is Max short for something?" Avery asks, extending his hand to shake mine.

"No," I lie.

I'm not a fan of my full name, so I only go by Max and refuse to tell anyone what it is. Tilda and Vernon were the only ones to ever know, and I find myself growing sad at the thought of Tilda gone and angry with Vernon for ratting me out to the Aedox. I try not to show my feelings to Avery or Frey since I'm sure they'll ask questions that I don't want to answer.

"Frey, you can have her stay in your sister's room. Your mother and I will be going out this evening, so you're on your own for dinner."

Frey takes our bags and nods for me to follow. Avery stays in the common room, watching us as we leave. I glance back before entering the hallway leading towards what I assume are the bedrooms and see that Avery is gone. We pass several empty rooms before stopping outside one on the right, its door partially open. Frey pushes the door open with my bag and I follow him into the large room. The walls are covered in rice paper decorated with intricately scrolled designs. The bed sits against the back wall, stretching out into the center of the room. A desk sits on one side of the room and a tall dresser against the other. Frey sets my bag down at the foot of the bed.

"You can store your clothes in the dresser or the closet since both are empty. You have a private bath through that door," he says, pointing to the sliding door on the right.

"Won't your sister be home?"

"She's not here anymore," he says, frowning.

"Oh," is all I reply.

"Get settled in and I'll be back in about an hour." He shuts the door when he leaves.

I scout the room, looking for what, I don't know. There doesn't seem to be any personal belongings of his sister anywhere in the room, so I check the bathroom but I only find towels, soap, shampoo, a toothbrush, and toothpaste. There's a sunken bathtub in the far corner next to a shower stall. I go back into the bedroom and put my clothes away, not paying much attention to what Matron Kaniz packed for me since I didn't arrive at Thrace Tower with any clothing of my own. I tuck the bag into the closet, then sit on the edge of the bed. The only décor in the room, other than the rice paper, are two dragon statues on each of the side tables next to the bed. Both are small, green, and cemented to the furniture. They remind me of the dragon tattoo that Frey has, and I wonder if they're connected.

I get up and stand in front of the lone window in the room. The waves move in rhythm with some unknown force, crashing quietly against the sand. The backyard is covered in tall grasses that look stiff and unyielding. I don't hear Avery enter the room and I only know he's there from his reflection in the glass. Tension in the room increases and I feel more uncomfortable the longer he stares at me. I wish he would say something, but instead he takes a step closer. Seconds drag by like minutes. He cocks his head to the side then scans my body, which makes me even more uncomfortable.

"You look just like her," he says, coming closer.

I'm frozen to my spot, too afraid to move. "Who?"

"Your mother."

Nine

"How do you know my mother?" I ask, trembling.

"I knew both your parents," he says, still coming closer.

"That's not possible. You're lying."

I can feel his breath on the back of my neck even though my hair is covering it. He takes his hand and brushes the hair onto my shoulder. I shudder at the touch, revolted by it. I shove him off and try to escape around him, but he has me blocked.

"What do you remember?" he asks.

My brain stops and is void of all thought. I can't find my words.

He places his hands on my shoulders. "You must not remember, Max. Try to forget everything from your past, as it'll only harm you. Frey may try to coax your memory, but don't let him inside your head. Your life depends upon it."

He leaves just as quietly as he entered.

I'm still standing by the window when Frey returns. He's puzzled by my demeanor, but I tell him I'm just not used to such luxury. He wants me to go with him on a walk through his neighborhood but I decline, stating I have a headache. He's upset at first, but quickly recovers, telling me to get some rest. He tells me he'll come and get me for lunch, and closes the door while I sit on the bed. I take off my shoes and socks, tucking them under the bed frame, slide under the covers, and close my eyes.

It doesn't take me long to fall asleep, but I fall right into a nightmare. I relive the battle against the woman from Nius, only this time the metal plank slices me in half and I bleed to death. Avery's words echo in my head as I float above my body, which the Keepers are leaving on the floor as the next battle begins. I'm suddenly back in the orphanage in my old room, with Brink asleep in the next bed. I push back the covers and place my bare feet on the cold floor. I can actually feel the cold penetrate my skin, causing it to prickle. I open the bedroom door, walk the couple of feet towards the stairs, but stop before going down.

Aedox flood the foyer, followed by a tall woman in green with long red hair. The staff move out of her way, almost as if they're trying to hide from her. She has a sense of power about her, almost defiant. Headmaster Edom is dragged in behind her and his body shakes between the hands of his guards. He's released, but doesn't move from his spot.

"Has it been done?" the woman asks Edom.

"Yes. She was returned tonight," he replies. "I've been told the alterations were successful."

She chuckles. "We'll see about that." The woman turns to face him. "Make sure she's selected, as I need her in the *Litarian Battles*. Understand?"

"Yes," Edom responds.

"You know what will happen to you if she's not, don't you?"

Edom cowers before the woman. He's acting as if he's being tormented, yet no one is touching him. "She'll be sent to Tarsus, I promise."

"And none of the staff will say anything, correct?" the woman says, addressing everyone.

Heads nod in agreement, except one. Out of the corner of my eye, just below me, stands Tilda, a quizzical expression on her face.

"Good. You all know what the punishment is for treason, so there shouldn't be any issue."

The woman leaves, Edom following closely behind. The Aedox secure the building, question the staff to make sure they understand their orders, and then leave. Tilda hid in the closet under the staircase, slipping in without being noticed, so the Aedox never questioned her. As soon as the foyer is empty, Tilda steps out and hastens to the kitchen. I'm about to follow her when I feel myself being roused from sleep. Frey is sitting next to me on the bed, gently rocking me so I'll wake up.

"You all right?" he asks, perching next to me.

"Just a nightmare," I reply as I pull myself up into a sitting position but stay under the covers.

"Lunch is ready if you're hungry."

I am, so we exit the bedroom and have to pass through both the common room and dining room to get to the kitchen. Avery is nowhere to be found, which makes me feel a bit more relaxed. On the counter sit two bowls of an orange-colored soup topped with crumbled crackers. Frey pulls out the stool closest to the fridge and gestures for me to have a seat. I'm hesitant but oblige. The soup is hot and smooth, and much better than anything served in the orphanage. We eat in silence, but I catch Frey watching me every so often.

What is up with him? Why is he watching me? It's creepy.

I help him clean up the dishes when we're done. He escorts me from the kitchen and out the back door. The sand is cool against my bare feet and the air is a lot warmer here than in the Outer Limits, which puzzles me. It's wintertime back there, yet here it feels like spring. How can there be that much of a climate difference between the two areas? We follow a path through the tall grass, down a small slope, and out onto the beach. I'm nervous about approaching the water, but Frey takes my hand and coaxes me along.

We stand just at the edge, letting the waves wash over our feet. The water has a slight chill to it, but I don't let it bother me. I grip the sand between my toes over and over again and I'm actually relaxing with each passing minute.

"What's on the other side of the water?" I ask.

"Icarian."

"Can't you just sail over to it if you wanted to? I mean, if it's just on the other side there has to be an easier way of getting there than through the game."

"It's not that simple," Frey says as he quickly steps back, removing himself from the water as if it suddenly became acidic. "Icarian only appears when you've been selected to live there. If you travel by water, you'll never find it."

"Then how do you know it's real? Have you ever actually seen it? Has anyone come back from there?"

"You think it doesn't?" he asks, his tone turning harsh. "My father gets daily reports from the leader about Icarian. He's one of the people tasked with sending the winners over there. How could he have a job if it didn't exist?"

I let the moment pass, but still wonder if Icarian is real regardless of what Frey says.

Clouds begin to swiftly move in from the east, followed by thunder and lightning. We take cover in the house but not before the sky opens up. I'm soaked through, my feet leaving puddles in the doorway into the kitchen. Frey strips down to his underwear, tells me to stay put, and heads towards the bedrooms. A few minutes later he returns, wearing a robe and carrying a towel in one hand and a second robe for me in the other. I use the towel to wrap up my hair and then I begin to undress. Frey shies away but I'm used to having to change in front of men, so it really doesn't bother me. I do catch him looking, a concerned expression creasing his face.

"What happened to you?" he asks, noticing my damaged body.

"Oh, the scars? Aedox aren't known to be kind when it comes to doling out punishments."

"What could you have possibly done to warrant such abuse?"

"It's a long story."

"I've got time," he says, gesturing towards the common room.

He picks up our wet clothes, tosses them into a laundry room, heats up a kettle for tea, and turns on the fireplace next to a television along the far wall. He hands me a blanket, then fetches our drinks when the kettle whistles. I've never told anyone about my indiscretions, and no one in the Outer Limits ever asks because we all have them. I don't think there's a body in all of the Outer Limits that hasn't been marked by the Aedox. I tuck the blanket around me just as Frey returns, handing me a cup. I take small sips, enjoying the soothing cinnamon flavor. He sits down next to me, but not too close, which makes me happy.

"It took me several years to realize that I wasn't in control of my life," I say. "When I was thirteen I tried to sneak out of the orphanage. You see, no one is allowed to leave until you reach the age of twenty-one and are moved to second-level housing or die." I take another sip of tea and notice Frey's cup hasn't been touched and is turning cold in his hands. "An Aedox was patrolling the outer wall and caught me. I was blindfolded, bound, and taken to a detention center. For two days the Aedox put metal restraints around my ankles, making sure they were tight, so they would rub my skin when I walked around the center's courtyard for hours. Let's just say, I didn't learn my lesson."

I sigh and lean back further into the couch, my body almost going limp with relief. "A year later I started a fight with one of the other residents. Again, I was blindfolded, bound, and taken to the detention center, but this time I was strapped to a gurney and inflicted with knife wounds up and down my body. This punishment lasted a week. When the Aedox saw the wounds were healing, they'd open them up again."

"That's horrible. Why would they do that?"

"I'd used a knife to attack the girl, so it was my punishment to be tortured with the same weapon I used on her."

"Why did you attack her with a knife?"

"She called me a whore because I was rooming with several boys. It wasn't my choice where I slept. That's where the staff placed me. She wouldn't stop mocking me, so I went after her with a steak knife."

"Is everyone in the Outer Limits as violent as you are?"

"You should talk," I say. "Tarsus has made a game out of killing, so you're no different than us."

"I wouldn't go that far," he says, placing his untouched drink on the coffee table in front of us.

I try to do the same, but find myself drinking the rest of the concoction instead. My head is starting to feel light, almost as if it'll detach from my shoulders and float away. I look over at Frey, noticing he has a funny look on his face. He's smiling and his eyes are dancing with flames in their irises.

"What's wrong with you?" I ask, almost slurring my words.

"Nothing," he replies as he moves closer, pulling part of the blanket over himself. "What else did you do?"

I'm having a hard time focusing on what I was talking about. I try to respond, but I'm too distracted by Frey getting closer. His leg bumps into mine, then moves on top of it. He removes the towel from my head, causing my damp hair to fall.

"What are you doing?" I ask, but my voice sounds disconnected from my body.

"Nothing. I just thought you'd be more comfortable with that off your head. Besides, you shouldn't hide such beautiful hair – even if it is wet." He runs his fingers through a couple of strands, letting them fall gently over my shoulder. "Why don't you tell me more about the Outer Limits? It had to have been hell living there."

"It had its moments. Once I learned that my life wasn't my own, I adjusted. The punishments stopped and the Aedox left me alone."

He takes one of my hands and turns it palm up. "How did you get these?" he asks, stroking my fingers.

I try to pull away, but I'm too relaxed to move. It's almost like my body is out of my control. "The Aedox did this to me just before I was selected for the game," I say without even thinking. "But I don't know how or why."

Frey takes my hand, brings it to his lips, and kisses it. He leans over, touching my cheek before kissing me on the lips. I fall back onto the couch with Frey following and lying on top of me. He throws the blanket to the floor, unfastens my robe, and begins kissing every scar he sees. I find myself enjoying his touch, his closeness. His hands search, finding areas I didn't know needed tending. I know this is wrong but I'm allowing it to happen, at least I think so.

Heat builds between us and I don't want it to stop. Part of me is hoping that Brink finds out that I slept with someone. I want him to feel rage at my actions and I want the thought of me having sex with Frey to anger him, taking him to a breaking point. This thought drives me onward, heightening the pleasure. Frey kisses me hard on the lips, then pulls the blanket from the floor to cover our naked bodies. He holds me tight against his chest as he runs his fingers up and down my spine. My euphoric feeling turns into tiredness and I find myself dozing off. When I wake, I'm wrapped in the blanket on top of my bed.

Did what I think just happened, happen? I would never succumb so easily like that, so could I have been drugged? But why would Frey do that?

The storm outside has diminished to a slight drizzle as I get up and head into the bathroom for a quick shower. It takes me over thirty minutes to clean the sand from my toes and legs. After I'm dry, I pull on black cotton lounge pants, a gray sweatshirt, and a pair of socks since my feet are unbelievably cold. I find Frey sitting in the common room, watching a music video and dressed in almost the same attire as me, but his sweatshirt is dark-blue.

"Did you drug me?" I ask when I enter.

"What? What kind of question is that, Max?" he responds, clearly irritated by the suggestion.

"I'm just making sure that I was acting of my own free will and not being manipulated, which is something everyone in Tarsus is good at."

"I would never force anyone to do something they didn't want to."

I don't know if I fully believe him or not, so I let the air settle before I speak again. "How can you watch that stuff?" I ask, pointing to the display and trying to diffuse the tension now in the room.

"You don't have this in the Outer Limits? It's entertainment. It takes real talent to put something like this together."

"The only programming ever on for us is the *Litarian Battles*," I answer. "It's on all… the… time."

"Huh," is his only response.

I try to watch the mess on the display, but it's starting to hurt my head. I get up, head towards the kitchen, and open the fridge and cabinets looking for something to snack on, but nothing looks appealing. I locate glasses in the upper cabinet next to the fridge; as I reach up to get one Frey wraps his arms around my waist, pulling me into him. I didn't even hear him approach.

"Will you stop?" I say.

He lets go, allowing me to take the glass I'd been reaching for. I fill it with water and go back to the common room, but Frey stays in the kitchen. He returns a few minutes later with crackers and cheese. We munch on them while looking for something else to watch. I clean up the plate while Frey goes towards the bedrooms, emerging a few minutes later with shoes on and a pair in his hands for me.

"It stopped raining, so let's head outside," he says, handing me the shoes.

I glance out the window and see that night has set in. "Why now? It's dark, so we won't really be able to see anything."

"Trust me, Max; there's something I want to show you." He extends his hand out to me after I've secured the shoes on my feet.

I take it and he escorts me to the front door. Lights illuminate the damp pathway to the entrance and down to the main road. We follow it, turning right at the end of the drive. Each house along the road has some kind of light shining at the end of their driveway and all the way to the entrance. People are milling about inside their homes. We can't see much, but it's enough to know that no one here thinks about privacy or curtains. We continue north for about twenty minutes, coming upon a large complex – only it's not a complex, but a house. One so large it makes Frey's look like a shack.

We turn up the path and are still some distance from the entrance when I hear music thumping through the open windows. Frey takes my hand as we step onto the porch and he rings the bell. The door appears to open automatically, and we step forward into a foyer containing marble statues, pure white tile floors, and a staircase ascending three stories. Frey pulls me to the left and we follow the music down an elaborately decorated hallway to a large common room on the right. We have to descend two steps before we can completely enter the room. The carpet is so lush I almost sink into it. The walls are paneled in maple with various displays hanging all around, each one playing a different music video.

There are only a handful of people mingling about, but one stands out to me immediately. I don't need to see his face to know that Brink is standing in the corner, pouring drinks from the bar. I try to slip behind Frey, but he nudges me forward and introduces me to the owner of the house. Or at least, the son of the owner.

"Troy, this is Max," Frey says.

We shake hands, but I instantly dislike the man. He's taller than Frey, but only by an inch. His blond hair is cut short, but still long enough that it brushes the tops of his ears. He's extremely muscular, almost causing his shirt to rip. A dragon's tail peeks out from under the sleeve of his right arm. He sneers when he smiles, but I can't tell if it's just natural or if there's something more behind it.

"So, you're Max," he says, still holding my hand. "Brink has told me a lot about you."

Great, I wonder what sordid tale he wove. He probably made it sound like we were an item in the Outer Limits. Like I was one of his conquests, though I think he's still a virgin. I wish Frey hadn't brought me here.

"Oh," is what I reply.

Troy looks down at my other hand, noticing I'm gripping onto Frey. He frowns slightly, but recovers. "So, Frey, is Max yours now? My, how quickly we change beds," Troy says more to me than Frey.

I'm on the verge of punching Troy when Frey pulls me away, escorting me out of the room and down the hall. We enter what Frey calls a trophy room, but all I see are dead carcasses of animals long extinct. Sitting in the middle of the menagerie is a bow and arrow with a plaque underneath. I let go of Frey and try to get closer to the weapon so I can read what's written.

Owner: Jack Larsen – highest pointed participant in the history of the Litarian Battles.

"Who's Jack Larsen?" I ask after Frey's made his way over to me.

"He's Troy's older brother and the only one in history to have reached 50,000 points. The Keepers let his family keep the weapon he used before sending him off to live in Icarian."

I instinctively begin to reach for it but Frey grabs my arm, halting my progress.

"Same rules apply here as they do in the game. Only Jack can handle it. Watch." Frey tries to grab a hold of the bow but his hand falls right through it, almost like the weapon is only an image and not a solid object.

"Hey, Frey," Troy calls from the doorway. "Stop dicking around with Jack's shit. I've got something you'll want to see."

Frey follows Troy and they disappear.

I look back over at the bow, then down at my hands, and begin to wonder.

Was I damaged for a reason? Matron Kaniz told me that only the weapon's owner can use it and no one else.

I hesitate, but I know the longer I stay the more Frey will wonder where I am. I reach out, my hand hovering above the bow, and slowly let it fall. My skin makes contact, the smooth steel cold against my flesh. My palm wraps around the weapon and I pick it up. I don't hold it for long and quickly put it back in its place. I should be startled by the discovery, but a voice in the back of my mind is telling me not to be. That I knew it would happen. But what did they do to my body to allow me such an ability? And better yet, why?

Ten

Frey and Troy aren't in the common room when I return, so I try to escape before Brink sees me, but I'm not fast enough. He sidles up next to me, wraps his arm around my waist, and pulls me up against him. The smell of alcohol on his breath is heavy and his eyes are a bit droopy. Everyone else in the room ignores us, which I'm fine with. Brink practically drags me over to an empty couch, pulling me down on top of him.

"How I've missed you," he says, groping my ass.

I push myself up and try to get off him, but he has a tight grip on my arm, so I wind up on the floor with him now on top of me.

"Brink, you're drunk," I say, working on maneuvering myself out from under him.

"Just a little bit," he answers.

His hand begins making its way up my shirt, so I push him away, but he seems to have gained strength since the last time I had to fight him off.

"Get the fuck off of me!" I shout.

"Now, is that anyway to talk to your future mate?"

He begins to kiss my neck, almost sucking on it. No one in the room is helping me, which is concerning.

Are the people in Tarsus so morally corrupt that they'll let anything happen? Is something like this a normal occurrence for them? Where do they draw the line on what people can and can't do to each other?

Brink is in the process of unbuttoning his pants when Frey lifts him up by the collar, then throws him across the room. Brink crashes into the wall, putting a massive dent in it. He gets to his feet, wipes the blood from his nose, and charges Frey. I swing my legs out, knocking Brink on his ass. Frey is punching him mercilessly, to the point where Troy has to step in before Frey kills him.

"The Keepers won't be happy if you kill him outside the battles," Troy says. "Wait until he gets selected."

Frey uncurls his fists, helps me to my feet, and we leave. The walk home is quiet and awkward. I'm glad Brink got his ass kicked because he deserved it, but now I feel as if Frey is taking it out on me with his silence. I'm not sure why I care so much, but being stuck with Frey for the next several days will only get worse if he stays quiet.

When we're back at his house he escorts me to my bedroom door, kisses me, and heads down the hallway, disappearing around the corner. I go inside, get ready for bed, and slip under the covers. Falling asleep is easy, but I can't stay asleep. Perhaps it's because I'm in a strange place. My mind is working on overdrive, trying to figure out the reason for my mutilation and what would happen to me if the Keepers find out. And it's that last thought that drives my eyes open. Or is it the murmuring of voices in the hallway just outside my door?

"I'm telling you the truth, Nan," Avery says, my door slowly opening and letting in a little light from the hallway.

I quickly close my eyes and pretend I'm sleeping, but I strain my hearing to make sure I don't miss anything.

"Leader Fallon would never have allowed her to return to Tarsus," a light, wispy female voice responds.

"Well, she did."

"Can you find out why?"

"Doubtful. She's been pretty tight-lipped lately and hardly comes out of her compound now, which is odd."

I can tell they step deeper into the room, almost so close that I can feel their breath on my face.

"Max does look a lot like her mother," Nan says. "Do you think she's just as dangerous?"

"I don't know, but that's what I'm planning on finding out during their stay here."

The door closes and I'm alone. I automatically try to think back to my early childhood, but all I can remember is being at the orphanage.

Am I really from Tarsus? How did I wind up in the Outer Limits? And where are my parents? Are they still alive? What else don't I know?

I begin to realize that my whole life seems to have been nothing but a lie. Everything that I am isn't real. I start panicking as anxiety expands to all areas of my body and I begin to shake. I'm about to get out of bed and splash some water on my face, but my body won't move. I'm cemented to the mattress, but how? A green light catches my eye and I'm only able to move my head. A beam is emerging from the dragon statue on the nightstand, heading right towards me. I look the other way and see the same light coming out of the other statue.

The beams penetrate my temples and my mind is no longer under my control. I close my eyes, but all I see is destruction and bloodshed. Groups of Aedox are attacking the workers in the Outer Limits, gunning them down as they try to flee. Explosions level several units of the second-level housing while people run from the rubble. Some survivors are on fire; their screams fill my ears and it's almost like they're right next to me. I feel myself suffocating as I breathe in the polluted air. I'm seeing all this as if I'm participating in it, but I can't control any of my actions. I know it's not real, as it just doesn't feel real. A bright flash blinds me and when it dissipates I'm in Tarsus, standing amongst the shoppers who line the streets.

The ground shakes, knocking us all off our feet. Drones fly over our heads, dropping small devices to the ground that explode when they make contact with the stone pavement. Moans of the injured fill my head, but I still can't move to help. The displays that dangle from every building change from their dazzling lights to a lone face, and it's one I've seen recently.

"You all brought this upon yourselves," the woman says, her long red hair piled high atop her head. "There will be no peace until our society can be reformed, built up from the ashes of your lives."

More bombs drop, killing everyone around me, yet I remain uninjured.

"Give in to us, and you shall be spared," the woman says.

She vanishes and is replaced by a bright green laurel, a wreath made of small branches, with a silver infinity sign in the center. I continue to stare at the symbol while the world around me burns. A unit of Aedox marches up the road, shooting anyone still alive. They get close to me and I hold my breath, hoping I'm invisible. Instead of being shot I'm hit in the side of the head with the butt from one of their guns, and everything goes black.

My eyes flash open and I have to blink a couple of times to bring them into focus. Sunlight floats into my room, telling me it's morning. I try to move my arms, but I can't. My body feels like dead weight. I can move my head, noticing that the green beams are gone, but I'm panicking from not being able to move the rest of me.

Frey enters my room a few moments later, and when he sees the look on my face he's next to me in less than a second.

"I can't move," I whisper since my breathing is out of control.

"Did you have any nightmares?" he asks.

"Yes."

"Then you more than likely have sleep paralysis. It happens to me all the time. I'll get you some tea since it'll help." He leaves before I can tell him what happened.

I've had plenty of nightmares before and have never woken up like this. I try to focus on getting my breathing under control and it's taking a lot of effort. Frey returns with a hot cup, places his hand behind my head and pushes me up slightly so he can bring the cup to my lips. I take small sips since it's very hot. The cinnamon tastes particularly strong this morning, but I do begin to feel better. The heat travels the length of my body and limbs, waking them up. After several minutes I'm able to move. Frey sets the cup on the nightstand and sits next to me on the bed.

"What did you see?" he asks, voice calm.

I'm about to blurt out the details of the dream, but stop myself. Something is telling me to lie and not divulge anything. But why?

"I was just dreaming about Brink attacking me again."

He looks to be contemplating my answer, then he kisses my cheek and leaves. I head into the bathroom, strip down, and take a long hot shower. My nerves are frayed. What did I see? Who put that in my mind and why? I'll make it a point to not sleep on that bed again. Once I'm dry and dressed I head into the kitchen where a tall, thin woman with sandy-colored hair is leaning over the sink, rinsing out a bowl.

"You must be Max," she says, only glancing at me briefly.

"Yes," I say, not sure I want to move further into the room.

"I'm Nan, Frey's mom. Are you hungry? Frey made breakfast before he left."

"He's not here?"

"He had an errand to run, but he should be back soon."

I take a plate sitting on the counter across from her and place some eggs, bacon, and toast onto it. Nan pours me a glass of orange juice as I sit on the stool. I try to eat quickly so I'm not around Nan any longer than I have to be, because I'm still disturbed by the conversation she and Avery had in my room last night. She finishes the dishes, puts them away, and sits on the stool next to me.

"Frey told me you're from the Outer Limits," she says with a tone of disdain. "How did you wind up in the *Litarian Battles*?"

I swallow the food I have in my mouth and drink some juice before responding, giving me time to come up with a reasonable answer. "I'm not sure. According to Headmaster Edom, the Keepers wanted us to participate. But I don't know how they drew the names."

Her eyes bore into me and I get the feeling she's trying to read my mind, or at least my mannerisms. "You lived in the orphanage?"

Is that a question or a statement? I can't tell.

"Yes. Since I was three."

She seems to mull the answer over, thinking it through before speaking. "I've often wondered what it'd be like living in the Outer Limits. Leader Fallon usually sends Tarsus rule-breakers or miscreants to live there. I wonder how a nice girl like you got placed into such a horrid environment."

"What are you implying?" I ask, my temper rising. I keep my eyes focused on my plate, which is almost empty, as I don't want to see what kind of expression Nan has on her face.

"Your parents, Max. Do you remember them?"

"My parents are dead," I snap.

"Oh? How did they die?"

"In an industrial accident at a smelting plant in the Outer Limits," I reply as I place my fork down. I'm in the process of getting up when Nan places her hand on my arm, preventing me from doing so.

"You might want to rethink that, Max. At least, do a little research at the Archive. I'm sure Frey can get you in."

She gets up, takes my plate, and washes it. I'm halfway through the common room when I change direction and run outside to the beach. The sand is cold and damp, but I don't care. I head south, walking along the shoreline, trying to distance myself from everything.

So, I *am* from Tarsus. What did my parents do to cause our expulsion? Where did we live in this massive society? Will I ever remember anything from my youth? Is three years old an appropriate age to begin having memories? Why is Nan giving me clues to my past? Avery was adamant that I not remember, so why is Nan pointing me where to go?

I keep walking as my name washes over me from a voice muffled against the crashing waves, but as it gets closer I recognize it. Garrett steps in front of me, stopping my forward momentum and surprising me by his sudden appearance here out by the shore.

"Hey, Max. You all right?" he asks.

"No, I'm not. All I want to do is go back to the Outer Limits and forget about this whole thing. I don't want to be in the *Litarian Battles*," I ramble. "Why were we sent here?" I begin to cry since I feel very emotional.

Garrett pulls me into his chest, wrapping his arms around me. "Tell me what happened," he says.

I spill it all: Brink, the nightmares, Frey's parents, and even my ability to handle another player's weapon. I'm not sure why I tell him, it just seems like the right thing to do. Everything comes out until I feel hollow inside.

"Come with me," he says, taking my hand and directing me up a partially buried wooden staircase.

We climb up a small sand dune and cross over a few yards until we reach a road, where we go several blocks before Garrett turns left. The house we're approaching is identical to Frey's, but Lok is standing in the doorway holding it open for us. The interior of the home is almost the same as Frey's, a slightly different pattern on the rice paper covering the walls. Garrett has me sit on one of the couches while Lok bolts the door.

"How did you know where I was?" I ask Garrett as Lok joins us on the couch.

"Your wristband," Lok answers. "There's a tracker in it. We just needed to find your frequency to locate you. It's another way the Keepers can monitor us, especially if we're out of the tower."

"Lok's father is the head of communications for Tarsus, so he's got a room down the hall filled with equipment," Garrett says.

I don't know if that comforts me or elevates my concerns, especially in regard to privacy. There seems to be heavier monitoring of Tarsus citizens than those in the Outer Limits, which seems odd.

"Does Frey know you're here?" Lok asks.

I shake my head. "He isn't home, and I don't know where he is."

Lok looks at Garrett, gets up, and then disappears down the hall.

Garrett makes sure that Lok is out of earshot before speaking. "Don't let Lok or anyone else know that you can pick up the other players' weapons," Garrett says quietly. "They'll make you a target, and the Keepers and matrons will ensure you die on the battle floor or while you sleep. You're a threat to them… all of them. I'm not sure why the modifications were done to you, but you can bet it wasn't by someone who has your best interests in mind, or even your survival."

Lok returns a few minutes later with a concerned look on his face. "I can't locate him," he says irately.

"What?" I ask before Garrett can.

"I have his frequency, but he's not showing up anywhere in Tarsus."

"That's not possible," Garrett says.

"I know. It just doesn't make any sense," Lok says.

Silence falls between us. I look around the room and notice that the television isn't on. Lok follows my gaze, a laugh forming in his throat.

"I bet Frey has those music videos playing all the time, doesn't he?" Lok asks.

"Unfortunately. I don't see the need to watch such stupid behavior or even listen to that kind of noise."

"Those videos didn't used to be that outrageous," Lok says. "It wasn't until about a year or so ago the media outlet changed them. They're trying to aim more for the younger kids now, but some people our age have caught on to the budding trend."

Garrett goes to the kitchen and returns a few minutes later with some hot tea and small sandwiches. He hands me a cup but when I begin to sip it, anticipating the warm cinnamon flavor, I'm met with a smoky tang instead.

"What kind of tea is this?" I ask.

"Tarsus Delight," Garrett replies. "It takes some getting used to, but it's good."

"I wonder what kind of tea Frey has been giving me," I say without thinking.

They both stop mid-drink, their cups hovering just below their lips and with uneasy looks on their faces.

"What?" I ask, putting my cup down.

Garrett is the first to respond. "Does it taste like cinnamon?"

"Yes, why?"

"Don't drink that stuff again," Lok says, almost shouting. "It contains a mind- and body- altering drug. Leader Fallon outlawed it a few years ago, but not all supplies were confiscated. If he gives it to you again dump it or do something that'll prevent you from drinking it."

I feel sick to my stomach as my head begins to pound, and all I want to do is curl up in a ball and hide from the world. Garrett scoots closer to me, pulling my head onto his shoulder as Lok takes the cup from me and places a blanket on my lap. I put my feet up onto the couch and wrap myself further into the blanket. Garrett hands me a sandwich, which I take and slowly eat.

"Lok, do you know where the Archive is?" I ask as I start to feel a little better.

"Yes, why?"

"Is it easy to get in to?"

"Why would you want to go there?" he asks, stunned. "I mean, it's open to the public, but it doesn't contain any information on anyone from the Outer Limits."

"Okay, but can you show me how to get there?"

"Max, what's this about?" Garrett asks.

"I'm looking for someone," is all I say.

"Well, that's cryptic," Lok responds. He stands and signals for me to follow him. "Come on, I can program the map into your wristband."

We go down the hall and enter a room on the right. Lok has me sit on a stool next to an elaborate array of electronic equipment, tools, and computers. He pulls up a complete schematic of Tarsus, the Dead Zone, and the Outer Limits, then moves the files over to another screen that has the data from my wristband listed in great detail. The device on my wrist begins to glow blue as the images download. It only takes a few minutes for the information to transfer.

Lok takes my arm, touches the screen on the bracelet and scrolls through the items until he locates the maps, each one nicely labeled. He taps the one for Tarsus and an image projects from the screen, levitating a few inches above my arm. I'm able to swing the image around, zoom in and out, and tap my finger onto a structure, at which time it displays the description of the building, entrance locations, and the active population of those inside.

"This is awesome," I say to Lok. "Why did you put all three on here?"

He smiles. "You never know when it may come in handy."

I smile back then deactivate the map just as the doorbell rings. Lok turns to another bank of monitors to see who's at the door. It's Frey.

Shit.

Lok tells me to take deep breaths then shouts down to Garrett, telling him to take his time answering the door.

"Just remember what we told you. You can always come here if you need to," Lok says, giving me a hug and escorting me to the front door.

Garrett opens it when I'm next to him. Frey at first has an expression of complete hatred and anger on his face, but it softens a bit when he sees me. No one invites him inside, and Frey doesn't step past the welcome mat under his feet.

"I was wondering where you disappeared to," he says, trying to sound concerned.

"I went for a walk and got lost. These two found me. We've just been having lunch," I lie. I'm not surprised it comes quickly to me since I've been telling them for most of my life.

"Well, come on, let's get back to my house," he says, then steps aside so I can exit.

I thank Lok and Garrett, then follow Frey down the path to the main road. He takes my hand, pulls me against his side, and begins kissing my neck while we walk. I don't want him to think anything has changed between us, so I play along.

Both his parents are gone when we enter the house, however Brink is sitting on the couch in the common room. His face is slightly swollen, and he has a bad cut above both of his eyes. I stiffen and stop, as I'm shaken by the intrusion. I'm also surprised Frey let Brink into the house since he almost killed him last night. Troy walks in from the kitchen, munching on some food before plopping down beside Brink on the couch. Frey places his hand against my lower back and gently pushes me forward. I take a seat in a chair under the bay window while Frey sits beside Troy.

"I told you she was at his house," Troy says almost with a laugh.

"Shut up," Frey snaps. His cheeks flush red with anger and he balls his hands into fists.

"What are they doing here?" I ask Frey, my tone a bit rough.

"We need Troy if we're going to get into the Archive," Frey responds.

"Why would we go there?" I ask.

"My mother suggested it. She says there's something I should look up, but to make sure I bring you."

"The Archive is open to the public, so why would we need them?" I say, gesturing to the others, anger in my voice.

"The public isn't allowed in the section where we need to go," Troy says, smiling devilishly.

An uneasiness settles over me. I do want to go, but under my terms, not theirs. What could possibly be so restricted that we need Brink and Troy to come with us? I do have the map, so if I need to escape the Archive I can.

"When do we leave?" I ask, my anger replaced with confidence.

"Now," Troy replies.

Eleven

A carriage is waiting for us when Frey opens the door. Brink gets into the front with the driver while I'm sandwiched between Frey and Troy. The doors slide shut and we're whisked away down the path and towards the city. It takes almost an hour to get to the Archive. The building is a tall, thin, metal and glass structure with a massive plaza encircling it, making it look like it's on an island. We're dropped off at the south end of the plaza since there isn't a closer area to the building. There are very few people outside at this hour and Frey comments that they're all inside the surrounding structures working.

He takes my hand as the group of us cross the slate-covered area and into the main floor of the Archive. I look up and can see the high point of the building, a tip that juts out from the roof. Walkways crisscross from one level to another, almost reaching the top floor which is at least several hundred feet high. I grow dizzier the longer I stare, so I refocus my eyes on the front desk of the lobby where a man in orange stands talking to Troy. He hands Troy something; they shake hands and part.

"It's going to be a few minutes before we can go up, so let's head over to the café across the plaza," Troy says when he returns.

I recall what Lok said about Frey spiking my tea with cinnamon, so I wonder if it'll still happen even if we're out in public. We exit and head over to a small one-story building with an open patio. Frey and I take a table while Troy and Brink get our drinks. Frey pulls my chair next to his, places his arm around my shoulders, and begins nuzzling my neck. I try not to show how uncomfortable I am with the affection now that I know how he got me to sleep with him. He pulls my face towards his, our lips touch, and I actually feel myself melting. Heat rises between us and I pull him closer.

This can't be right. Why am I feeling this way? Do I actually like Frey? I'm not fighting this… in fact, I'm enjoying it.

We release each other just as Troy and Brink return. They hand us each a cup filled with a light brown liquid. I take a small sip, checking for the cinnamon, and silently sigh when I don't taste any. The only flavor that jumps out at me is jasmine, which I find refreshing. We chat about what we might expect when we return to Thrace Tower. Troy thinks the Keepers will place more of us into the battles, so instead of two contestants there'll be at least four. Frey laughs at that suggestion since his opinion is that the points will be increased, especially if you kill someone.

Brink doesn't join in the conversation since he's too focused on me, anger clearly visible in his eyes. I spend the time glancing around the plaza and looking at the various people dressed in outrageous clothes as they walk by. I thought we dressed oddly for the selection floor, but these people make our outfits look positively tame.

An alarm goes off on Troy's bracelet, so we finish our tea and return to the Archive. We follow Troy toward the center of the building then over to a bank of elevators along the side wall. We step into the one in the middle, Troy punches in the code he was given by the front desk onto the keypad, and we rocket skyward. We're moving so fast I feel like I'm being shoved into the floor. Several seconds later we slowly come to a gentle stop. The walkway surrounding the top floor is covered in blue carpeting and lined with waist-high steel rails. None of the walkways crisscross to a lower level like those in the rest of the building, and I don't dare look down since I'll only make myself sick like I did looking up. We're the only ones on this floor, which makes me extremely uneasy.

Troy leads us towards the front of the building, which has sectional seating with two monitors hanging against the far wall. Frey guides me to a chair in the middle of the group and tells me to sit down. I do what he says without protesting or even second-guessing the command. He instructs me to lean back so the footrest will extend out from the chair, which it does, and then to relax and take deep breaths. I follow everything he tells me to do, which gravely concerns me.

What was in the tea that's making me obey his every command? Fuck! What are they going to do to me and how do I stop it? How I wish Garrett and Lok were here.

I want to panic, but my body won't let me. Whatever my tea was spiked with has taken complete control over my actions, and I'm terrified since I'm now at their mercy. Frey kisses me hard on the lips, backs up, and presses a button on the end table across from me. Blue lights shoot down from the ceiling, encircling me, placing me in an electronic cage.

"What the hell is this?" I protest, finally finding my words as I try to move. My body is stuck to the chair like it was to the mattress last night.

"Max, this is a memory scanner. It'll only take a few minutes, then it'll begin broadcasting the images from your mind onto this screen," Troy says, pointing to the monitor behind him. "It won't hurt, and you might even thank us for it."

"Doubtful," I say, my teeth clenched in anger.

Out of the corner of my eye I catch Brink smiling. He seems to be enjoying my discomfort, as he probably thinks I deserve this for being with Frey and not him.

Wait till we're back in the *Litarian Battles*, then they won't be laughing.

The screen on the right comes to life with my memories, but no sound. It displays my visit with Lok and Garrett, my nightmare, and my lovemaking with Frey. Troy pats Frey on the back, obviously congratulating him on his conquest, but Brink is seething. His face is red with rage, and his hands are balled up into fists. He's going to try to make Frey and me pay for our supposed betrayal of him, I just know it, since it's the kind of thing Brink would do. If not today it'll happen when we return to Thrace Tower, so I'll have to be on my guard.

I hold my breath, waiting to see if it'll display what happened the night the Aedox came for me, but it doesn't. I become younger and younger with each passing minute as my entire life winds down before my eyes. The screen on the left turns on several minutes later, displaying its own set of pictures, but I don't recognize any of them.

"What's that?" I ask, but I can't gesture to anything since I'm stuck to the chair.

"It's checking your memories against anything in the Archive's files," Frey replies. "Such as faces and locations."

"Why? Why would you want to do that?" I ask nervously.

"To find out who you are," Troy responds.

What? I know who I am: Maximiana Sutton, an orphan from the Outer Limits.

I'm nobody special.

Several pictures appear on the monitor to the left as the one on the right turns off, but the blue beams around me don't retract. The images are of a man with a strong jawline, piercing blue eyes, and short black hair. The second is of a woman with long black hair, high cheekbones, and thick eyelashes. The final is of a very young child who resembles the woman quite a bit. I recognize the child as me because Tilda always kept photos of us from when we first arrived at the orphanage, but how and why is it in the Archive's files? Troy steps forward and taps on the man's face, which causes the other two pictures to slide to the left as his enlarges. The name Liam Thomas appears underneath the image as a menu flashes next to it, showing additional files. Troy selects one and a news story begins to play.

"Good evening, Tarsus," Hammond says. His face is a lot younger than it is now, but still covered with that ridiculous mustache. He's standing in front of a large paned window, which overlooks the skyscrapers and bright neon signs of downtown Tarsus. He has to be at least several stories high since the tops of most of the buildings behind him are at the same level. "Leader Fallon has dispatched a unit of Aedox to the northern section of Tarsus, as there are rumors going around of a possible uprising among some of our more elite citizens." The window behind Hammond changes to an overview of a very well-manicured landscape with immense houses sporadically positioned around fountains and pools, but no signs of any carriages along the paths.

Does having a carriage line connected to your dwelling actually signify that you aren't as prominent as those without one? I don't remember seeing a cable running along the path in front of Troy's house, or any of the houses in his neighborhood now that I think about it.

"Minor uprisings aren't new to us since they happen quite frequently in the Outer Limits," Hammond says, almost with a laugh. "What is concerning about this one is the couple implicated in such a scheme. Yes, children, I'm speaking about our loving and kind-hearted former leader, Liam Thomas."

"What does this have to do with anything?" I ask, irritated.

"You don't recognize them?" Frey asks.

"Why would I?" I ask, my voice rising. "Nothing like this has ever been transmitted into the Outer Limits since we're only permitted to watch the *Litarian Battles*."

"Max, these images are from your memory," Troy says. "The Archive simply matched up the data from your mind to their files, as well as showing related content to what was located in your head."

That can't be. None of this can be true. This has to be a trick.

Troy paused the video after my outburst, so he touches the screen again to continue the video.

"Liam and his wife Clio have been outspoken opponents of the newly appointed leader. Especially since Mr. Thomas wasn't allowed to serve the normal timeframe for his term in office, which is twenty years. In fact, he was only our leader for a total of four years, which is an unprecedented short amount of time. Leader Fallon has never explained why she was chosen to replace Mr. Thomas, nor has she commented on any of his statements against her. So for now, children, we will sit back and watch the fun."

The video stops, and the files reappear on the screen. Troy looks them over and selects another one. Hammond appears on the screen again, standing in the same spot as in the previous message.

"Severe actions were taken today against the Thomas family," Hammond starts, looking a little frazzled. "Leader Fallon had no choice but to seize Liam and Clio Thomas this afternoon, placing them under arrest. Not much detail is known as to why they were taken into custody, only that they've been moved to a secure location. The whereabouts of their daughter, Mera, have not been disclosed."

"You honestly think I'm these people's daughter?" I ask with a slight chuckle. "Wow, the three of you are nuts."

Troy stops the video and walks up to me, but he can't get close enough with the beams. "You really don't get it, Max," he says furiously. "Do you not understand your role in regard to the future of Tarsus? Your parents were formidable opponents to Leader Fallon and you can help us take back the city from Fallon's rule, liberate the Outer Limits, and allow anyone to go to Icarian, not just those who pass her torture ritual."

"You're making this all up," I protest. "My parents died in an industrial accident. I've been in the Outer Limits my whole life. I'm not their daughter." Fear grips me as the possibility of all of this being true sinks in.

Frey presses the button on the end table, which allows the beams to ascend. He pulls me to my feet, and I'm surprised I can now move. With his hand on my back he gently guides me to the monitor, then switches the images so the child is the main focus. I know it's me because I recognize the outfit. It's the one I was wearing when I was sent to live at the orphanage, since Tilda kept that as well. But I still don't want to believe any of it's true. I stare into the eyes of my younger self, trying my hardest to recall what happened.

I begin to pull away, but Troy is blocking my path. He touches Liam's picture and chooses another video. I don't know how much more I can take, but I'm pinned to the spot.

"Good evening, Tarsus. Traitors have been located among us," Hammond says. "Leader Fallon has made it her priority to rid Tarsus and the Outer Limits of them by making an example of the two most dangerous people we've ever encountered. Liam and Clio Thomas were executed today, according to Leader Fallon, and their bodies have been destroyed. Their daughter has vanished, but many people are speculating that Mera was killed along with her parents, while others believe she's been tucked away somewhere, never to be seen again. Nevertheless, peace has finally settled over Tarsus and its territories once again."

Frey stops the video. "Are you still not convinced you're their daughter?" he asks.

I hesitate in answering, which is a bad move, and he sees right through me. The doubt that's formed in my mind of who I really am shines like a beacon. I don't want to believe what I just heard, but parts of it ring true. I look down at my hands and remember the dream I had about Leader Fallon ensuring I was sent into the *Litarian Battles*. Or was it even a dream? Did she do this to me? Why? Was killing my parents not enough that she felt she had to mangle me as well? But why send me to live in the Outer Limits? Why not kill me when she murdered my parents? She would've known I could be a possible threat when I got older, so why spare me at all?

I don't say a word to any of them on the ride home, as I'm too lost in my own thoughts. Once we're back at Frey's house I tell him I need some time by myself to think things over, which he doesn't give me an argument about. My head is pounding and I want to hide under the covers, but because of last night I don't dare. So instead I take one of the pillows and a blanket and pull them down onto the floor with me. I curl up in a ball and try to sort out the feelings that are currently running rampant around my mind, with the main one being confusion. Why would my parents want to cause an uprising? So, my father only led for a short time. Big deal. It wasn't the end of the world and it obviously didn't affect their home life.

None of this makes any sense.

I feel myself starting to drift off to sleep, so I try to fight it since I'm not really tired, but I'm failing. My wristband begins to glow green as the room begins to vanish, and it's at this moment I realize I'm looping. I'm being pulled from my current location to another one, but how and why?

The warm air is replaced by cold, almost to the point where I can see my breath. I can't tell the size of the room I'm in due to the extreme darkness. I'm puzzled by how I got here since it's definitely the same method used to move me from the battle floor to the medical office. I thought the Keepers couldn't transport anyone who was outside Thrace Tower, so how did they send me here? But what if they aren't the ones who did it? I get to my feet slowly, waiting for someone to attack, but I'm not sure why. The sudden flash of light above my head causes me to jump and I'm momentarily blinded. My eyes eventually adjust, but the light doesn't move.

"Maximiana Sutton," a female voice echoes through the chamber. "You've been brought here at the request of Leader Fallon."

I squint my eyes and scan the room, looking for where the voice could possibly be coming from. "Why? Who are you?" I ask.

"We're the Patrician, the rulers of your world."

"I thought Leader Fallon was in charge."

"She's in charge of the city. We're in charge of her."

I let silence settle between us, so my brain can quickly think of questions to ask. "Why am I here?"

"Leader Fallon will tell you," the woman replies coldly.

The light above me vanishes as another one turns on across the room, illuminating a tall woman with long red hair. Her dark green pantsuit causes her hair to glow like a fire that's just been started. Individual lights begin to pop on as she makes her way towards me. I can't decide if I should be terrified, angry, or relieved.

"Hello, Max," she says when she's only a few feet away.

"How did you bring me here?"

"The Keepers aren't the only ones who can teleport people," she answers with a smile. "We've been able to prevent them from taking anyone outside of Thrace Tower for a little over a year now, but it won't be long until they figure out how to override our protocols and re-establish their connection to the outside. They've been trying unsuccessfully for months, but with some changes that have occurred at Thrace Tower recently they're almost close to succeeding."

"What kind of changes, and what does it have to do with me?"

She ignores my question. "Have you heard of the Dracken?"

I shake my head.

"Have you noticed anyone with a dragon tattoo?"

I hesitate in answering because I'm not sure why she wants the information, so do I tell the truth or lie? What'll happen to me if I just don't answer?

"Max, I need to know," she says, becoming insistent. "You're my only set of eyes in Thrace Tower, and I can't trust anyone else."

"What makes you think you can trust me?" I say with anger.

"You owe me, Max, you just haven't realized it yet."

"I don't owe you anything!" I shout. "You killed my parents and stuck me in the Outer Limits. Did you do this to me, too?" I show her my hands, shoving them as close to her face as possible.

"I know you've been to the Archive, which is why I had you brought here, but you only saw what they wanted you to see and not the whole truth. There's more going on here than you could possibly know."

"What if I *have* seen people with a dragon tattoo? What does it matter to you so much?"

"Because it means they belong to a group called the Dracken, which is an anti-Patrician group set on causing a realignment of our world. The Keepers are the ones orchestrating this rebellion and we believe they're using the *Litarian Battles* to initiate new members into their growing army."

"And what about the event? What could be the purpose behind it?"

"It's a means to select their new ruler and begin a war with the Patrician."

"So, there is no Pentras," I state.

"Yes… and no."

"What does that mean?"

An alarm sounds behind me, which causes Leader Fallon to rush towards me and grab my arms. "Max, don't trust the matrons or any of the Dracken. I'll try to contact you again, but you have to go back now." She lets go, steps back, and is about to leave when she stops mid-step. "I didn't kill your parents, but now I wish I had."

She disappears into the now-darkened room as I feel myself being pulled, thrust backwards. I try not to hold my breath as I loop. My feet touch cold tile and I'm in the bathroom off the bedroom.

"Max, where are you?" Frey calls from somewhere in the house.

The Patrician must've been monitoring the house, so when Frey began looking for me they sounded the alarm.

"Max, are you hiding from me?" Frey asks with a slight giggle.

I quickly step over to the toilet and flush, so he thinks I was using the facilities. When I exit into the bedroom, Frey is entering the room. "Can't a girl use the bathroom in peace?" I ask, chiding him.

"There you are. I was wondering if you're hungry."

I nod and follow him into the kitchen. His parents have apparently left for the evening, so we eat in the common room with the monitor off. I'm thankful for the silence, as my head is too cramped with everything that's happened today to tolerate any extra noise. I don't eat much and take my plate back to the kitchen, where I stand in front of the sink and look out the window at the night sky.

"What's the matter?" Frey asks, putting his arms around my shoulders and leaning his firm body against mine.

"With everything that's happened today, I just can't process it all."

"I know what'll relax you," he says playfully.

It's only a matter of minutes before we're both naked in his bed. The heat rising from his skin eases the tension in my muscles and his touch feels comforting and natural. I rest my head against his chest and listen to the air moving in and out of his lungs. I want to ask him about the tattoo but feel this may not be the right time, so instead I ask him something else.

"Why did you take me to the Archive?"

"I wanted you to know who you really are, since it's been kept from you for so long. I felt you had a right to know," he replies, stroking my spine with his hand, and I begin to drift off. "I need you, Max. We all do."

Twelve

He's gone when I wake. I put my clothes on, head down to my room, and take a long hot shower. When I emerge wrapped only in a towel Avery is there, and his presence is unsettling. I head right to the dresser and rummage through the drawers as quickly as possible, since I don't relish the thought of being in the same room as him with only a towel covering my body.

"You know, don't you?" he asks as I rush from drawer to drawer, pulling out clothes.

"I don't know what you mean," I reply, feigning ignorance.

I turn around, but he has my path blocked. He takes a giant step forward, which causes me to fall back into the dresser, and his hands are almost touching my towel. "Who you are, Max," he says anxiously. "And what really happened to your parents. I told you not to remember, to bury it, but you didn't listen and now we're all going to pay for it."

He pulls out a knife from his waistband, grabs my wrist, and swings my arm behind my back. He shoves me to the floor, straddles my back, and is about to plunge the weapon into me when a shot rings out. Avery falls off me while I scramble away as fast as I can, trying to get some distance between us. Nan steps further into the room and shoots Avery again. She then turns to me, aiming the gun at my head.

"Where's Frey?" she asks, her voice not wavering.

"I…I don't know," I squeak out.

"Get dressed and meet me in the common room."

I sprint into the bathroom, lock the door, and start to cry. I don't know why I'm sobbing; perhaps it's the thought that my life almost ended that's causing the hysterics. I've never been afraid of death, since you face it so often in the Outer Limits, especially at the hands of the Aedox. So why does this feel different? I tap the wristband and scroll through the options, looking for the map of Tarsus. There has to be a way I can escape from the city and get back to the Outer Limits where I can hide, but the only connection between the two areas is the Dead Zone, which is too toxic to venture into without a specialized Aedox vehicle. I decide to splash cold water on my face, dress, and meet Nan in the common room like she instructed.

"Please, sit," she says, gesturing to the couch. The gun no longer in her hand.

I take a seat, but as far from her as possible.

"Frey can't know any of this," she says, pacing in front of me. "I'll get rid of the body, but you have to promise me you won't tell Frey what happened."

All I can do is stare at her, still trying to process everything.

"Promise me," she says louder.

I nod.

She inhales deeply and lets it out slowly. "All right, now that we have that settled there's something we need to discuss," she says. She sits in the chair by the window, trying to calm herself down even more. "When you get back to Thrace Tower you need to do everything you can to get to the event."

I'm shocked by her request, since she thought I could be as dangerous as my mother.

"Even if that means killing your friends," she adds. "Including my son."

"Why?" I ask, trying to sound like I'm in control of my voice, which I'm not.

"Our survival depends on it."

"Why!" I shout as I stand. "What the hell is going on that everyone is saying they need me? I'm just an orphan from the Outer Limits. I'm nothing special."

"Yes, Max, you are. If only I could explain it to you, but we're running out of time." She looks down at her watch, which displays something other than time that I can't quite make out. "Just trust me, please, Max."

I don't have time to respond before Frey walks through the front door. Nan quickly conceals her agitation with a smile. She gets up and gives Frey a hug before heading back towards the bedrooms. He steps down into the common room and places his hand on my shoulder, his other hand turning my face towards his.

"You all right?" he asks, a concerned expression on his face. This one looks genuine.

"Is there another place we can stay for the next two days?"

"Yes, but why? What happened?"

I'm trying to think of a lie, but one isn't coming fast enough.

"Max, you're shaking." Frey pulls me into his chest and I wrap my arms around him, holding on tightly.

"I don't feel safe here," I say.

He kisses my forehead, releases me, and goes into the kitchen. I sit down on the couch, trying to think of a better story to tell when he returns, which isn't for quite some time. When he does come back he tells me to go pack. I hesitate in proceeding down the hallway, knowing what lies on the other side of the bedroom door, but when I open it the room is empty. I grab the duffle, stuff both my clean and dirty clothes into it, then go down to Frey's room. I make sure to close the bedroom door since I don't want Frey noticing the large bloodstain next to the bed that still remains.

"Where are we going?" I ask, hoping he doesn't say Troy's place.

"Addie's house; she's excited to see you."

I let out my breath, not realizing I'd been holding it. When we exit the house I'm surprised there isn't a carriage waiting for us, so I ask Frey about it.

"I don't want it recorded," he replies, which causes me to give him a quizzical look.

"Every pick up the carriages make is automatically recorded. Don't they do that in the Outer Limits?"

Since I only repair them I never noticed if they recorded anything, but I don't remember seeing any such devices in the carriages, so I doubt it. Why would Leader Fallon want to know where every carriage in Tarsus has been, unless it's the Patrician that want to know. But why? Frey takes my hand and we walk casually down the street. It's midmorning, so most of the houses are empty. We have to cross several blocks, almost as if we're going to Lok's house, but pass that street and turn right. It's another ten minutes before we get to Addie's neighborhood. She has the door wide open before we're even near the path to her house. She runs out and throws her arms around me, hugging me tightly.

"I'm so glad you came," she says, releasing me. "Come on in, I've got everything situated."

Addie's house is much smaller than Frey's and not as well maintained. The walls are plastered in soft blue wallpaper, scuffed hardwood covers most of the floor and the common room is small, as is the kitchen. We follow her down the hall towards the bedrooms. Addie says I can bunk with her and Frey can stay in the spare room. Her parents' room is across the hall next to the lone bathroom. I set my bag at the foot of her bed; I'm not sure how the two of us are going to fit on such a small mattress, but I don't comment and smile instead.

"I know this place isn't as nice as Frey's, but it's home," she says, plopping down on the bed. "So, what do you want to do for the next two days?"

I hadn't really thought about it since I just wanted to get away from Nan. In reality, I'd like to do nothing.

"What do you recommend?" I ask, sitting next to her.

"Well, there's the Arcade that opens later this evening. It's so much fun," Addie replies with enthusiasm.

"What is?" Frey asks, entering the room. He'd gone to the spare room to put his things away.

"Going to the Arcade," Addie says.

"I haven't done that in years, so why not."

We retreat to the common room and spend most of the day watching music videos and munching on food. I don't pay the display much attention, unlike Frey and Addie. There are certain videos they can't keep their eyes off of, it's almost like they're in a trance. Those are the ones that hurt my head the most – mainly because the scenes move too fast for my mind to process. I excuse myself and go back to Addie's room to lie down and rest. The end tables next to her bed both have the same dragon statues as Frey's sister's room, which disturbs me.

How am I going to sleep in Addie's bed? What if her statues have the same effect on me that the others did?

I forgo the nap and sit on the floor under the lone window in her room instead. I close my eyes and concentrate on what's transpired over the last several days. I need to sort it all out, so I start making a checklist in my head.

My parents are alive. So, where are they? My father was once the leader of Tarsus, but only for a short time. Why was he removed? What did Leader Fallon do with them if she didn't kill them like everyone believes she did? Why was I placed in the orphanage and not with my parents?

Leader Fallon is somehow responsible for the damage done to my hands, I just know it. She's modified me, given me the ability to handle any competitor's weapon, both inside the game and out. But why? She says I owe her, but for what? Should I even trust anything she says? She lies easily to her people, so why not to me?

The Patrician: who, or what, are they? How do they control society through Leader Fallon? What's their purpose? Why did they loop me into their headquarters, or wherever that was?

The Dracken. I know Frey and Addie belong to this group since they both have a dragon tattoo. Leader Fallon says they're trying to conduct a realignment, but how and why?

Who do I trust? Frey's drugged me, yet I do really like him and feel safe around him. Brink has reverted to his atrocious behavior, and it's escalating. What he tried to do to me at Troy's house he never would've done at the orphanage. Why the sudden change in him? And why did he tell Garrett I was promised to him? Who made that promise to him? Garrett, with Lok's help, found me wandering down the beach. They told me about the cinnamon and what it does. Lok even programmed the maps on my bracelet. I feel like I can trust them, at least, but who knows if they have some ulterior motive that I don't know about yet.

My mind races with so much information it gets to a point where I feel like it'll explode. I cradle my head between my knees and cover my ears with my hands as I will myself back to the Outer Limits, trying to push my body through both space and time. My eyes catch a green glow emitting from my bracelet, and when I raise my head I hit it on something hard. Looking up I notice I'm no longer in Addie's room, but under my workbench in the grove.

I've looped again? This can't be possible… I have to be imagining it.

Cold air whips around me, causing my skin to breakout into bumps. I see a small bolt lying a few inches away, so I reach for it, grabbing it in my hands. The metal is hard, rough, and feels real. I close my eyes and think of Addie's room, the softness of the carpet and the warmth of the surroundings. When I reopen my eyes, I'm sitting under the window just like before, but when I open my hand the bolt is still cradled in my palm. I begin panicking to the point of almost being unable to breathe.

What the hell did they do to me? How can I loop outside of the game without help from the Patrician? Garrett was right, they did more to me than just mutilate my hands. But why?

I throw the bolt under the bed, stand, and brush small pieces of debris from my pants before returning to the common room. I stop briefly in the bathroom to quickly wash my face and hands. I look at myself hard in the mirror, trying to comprehend this new ability and its possible purpose.

"Max, you in there?" Addie calls, knocking on the bathroom door.

"Yes. I'll be out in a minute," I reply as I dry myself off, then adjust my hair into a ponytail using two bands I locate under the sink before stepping into the hallway.

"It's time to go," Frey says, turning off the monitor.

Addie wraps her arm around mine and escorts me outside, Frey following. The air is slightly chilled, but not enough to make me cold. We have to walk to the Arcade since Addie can't afford to call a carriage, and it works out well for Frey since he doesn't want anyone to know we're now at Addie's.

The walk is long and tiring. We reach the outskirts of the city then head south for a couple of blocks, having to stop because our path is blocked by people milling about in the street. As I look carefully I notice they're actually in line, waiting to enter a three-story structure. Music is pumping out of wide openings on each floor where windows should be. The doors along the street and neighboring alley are being pushed open to allow the crowd inside. Bright lights flash, illuminating the night in neon green, pink, and yellow. There isn't any external signage for the Arcade, as it's all inside.

Each wall is plastered with either a screen playing a music video or an ad in annoying, audacious colors. The first level is covered in game modules. They line the walls and create aisles throughout the main floor. Where there are openings, scantily-clad women stand giving out thin tubes of liquid, their cotton-candy-style hair sweeping down their bare backs. What little clothes they do have on remind me of the outfits we have to wear when going to the selection floor. Young men and women are almost jumping over each other to get at the tubes, which sit cradled in carriers around the women's necks.

Frey points towards a staircase over in the far wall, so Addie nudges people out of our way as we head towards it. It leads us to second floor that isn't as crowded. Couches fill in the center of the room surrounding a bar. Dartboards, pool tables, and beanbag games take up the rest of the space. Frey has us grab a spot near one of the openings, then disappears into the growing crowd. Addie points to the people below in the street, many already drunk and stumbling about. She laughs at their expense, as do I, which is out of character for me. Being in Tarsus is having an effect on me that I'm not happy about.

Frey returns a few minutes later, his arms laden down with drinks. He sits next to me, pulls my legs onto his lap, and hands me a tumbler filled with a pink liquid. Addie gives us a long look, winks, and takes her glass. The drink is refreshing, light, and fruity. I finish it in a matter of seconds. Frey hands me his and leaves to get more. Addie's name is called from across the room and she sets her drink down on the floor to wave.

"I'll be right back," she says, standing, then crosses the room and disappears into a wave of new people.

The music emanating from the top floor grows louder as I stare out into the night, watching the crowds in the street dancing to the rhythm of the music.

"Anyone sitting here?" Troy asks, catching me off guard.

He hands me a drink and I notice it's the same one Frey went to get for me. I set down my now-empty glass and take the one from Troy's hand. My eyes frantically scan the faces of all the patrons, trying to find Frey, but I can't see him.

Troy sits where Addie was and leers at me. His hand is cupped around a small shot glass filled with a creamy green liquid.

"Frey said you wanted that," Troy says, gesturing to the tumbler in my hand.

"Do you know where he went?" I ask loudly, trying to be heard over the noise.

"He's still in line, getting himself another drink."

Somehow I feel that's a lie.

Troy nudges my arm, eyeing the drink. I take a small sip, waiting to taste something unpleasant, but it's the same concoction I already had. I still decide to nurse this one and not chug it like the other two, in case there's something wrong with it. I've only taken a couple of sips when I start to feel light-headed. I know I need to get away from Troy, so I ask him where the bathrooms are. He points to an alcove behind the stairs leading up to the third floor. I excuse myself, taking my drink with me, but I set it down on the first table I come across.

I glance behind me and see Troy is no longer in his seat. I almost have to elbow my way through the mass of people to get to the alcove. The air in the Arcade is quickly becoming hot and stuffy, which is making me dizzy. I make it to the bathroom and lock myself in. I splash cold water on my face and neck to help cool myself. Someone starts pounding on the door, yelling to be let in. I open it and step past the forming line of women. Standing in the opening of the alcove I scan the room, but can't see Addie or Frey, so I move up to the third level.

The floor is lit by brightly-colored squares that change color in rhythm with the music. Lights hang from the ceiling in a variety of styles; some look like cylinders while others resemble teardrops. The dancefloor is covered in revelers so I keep to the walls, sliding my way around the room. I stop when I'm halfway, as the crowd is just too thick to pass. I'm about to head back when a hand presses against my back, stopping my motion.

"Where's Frey?" Brink asks, his voice thick with rage. His mouth is right against my ear, so his hot breath begins to heat up my already-warm body. He pushes me against the wall and his hand starts to slide up the back of my shirt. I try to shove him off but his legs are pinned against mine, preventing me from turning. He leans his body as far into me as he can. "You know, it really doesn't matter since you're mine anyway. You can fuck him until I kill him in the game, then you won't have any option but to uphold your parents' promise."

I go rigid as my heart stops.

"What did you say?" I ask, turning my head so I can see him out of the corner of my eye.

"You heard me," he whispers into my ear, pressing himself harder into my back. "When this realignment is over you're mine – heart, body, and soul." Brink begins to nuzzle my neck, but I'm too stunned to resist. "You're my reward for bringing an end to Leader Fallon." His hands wander my body, pushing and pulling at my clothing. Then he stops and is gone.

I turn around, but he's vanished into the crowd. I race towards the stairs, almost knocking down a couple of people in the process. I don't stop running until I'm in the alley. The cool air feels refreshing. I try to calm myself down while I lean my head against the brick of the building, letting the cold, rough surface burrow into my forehead. My cheeks are wet with tears that I didn't know existed.

This can't be real. It isn't true. Would my parents really make such an offer? Why? Do they hate Leader Fallon so much that they'd sell their own daughter to make sure her rule ended?

I feel sick to my stomach and clutch my midsection as I bend over, trying not to throw up. My head pounds with the fast beating of my heart and I shake as sobs come up instead of bile.

"Max?" My name echoes through the racket.

I pull myself together as quickly as I can before I'm caught and questioned about my appearance. I wipe my cheeks dry with my hands before responding. "I'm in the alley."

Addie and Frey lean out of the opening on the second floor where we'd been sitting, concerned looks on their faces.

"I just needed some air," I say to them, then signal I'll be right up.

I take several deep breaths before heading back inside. Frey has another drink ready for me when I get to the seats and I take it before sitting down. I don't see Troy or Brink among the patrons, so I relax. But only a little.

As the night wears on I try my hand at a game of darts against Addie, but she's more skilled than me and hits close to the bullseye every time. I'm happy if my dart even makes it onto the board and not stuck in the wall behind it. We eventually make our way down to the first floor and Frey has me play some of the game modules. I find them quite fun, almost addicting, and he has to drag me away from them when it's time to leave.

The walk home is much faster, and Addie's parents are in the kitchen when we return. They make us some snacks then head out for the night. A short time later, Addie and I go to bed. I change in the bathroom and brush my teeth. Addie is sound asleep when I return to her room. I drop my dirty clothes onto my bag and hesitate about crawling under the covers with her. Just as I'd suspected, a pair of green beams exit from the dragon statues and penetrate her temples. Her relaxed body goes rigid and I can tell she's in the midst of a nightmare, so I back out of the room and go towards the one Frey is in. When I open the door, Frey is snoring slightly. I close the door and cross the threshold, but stop when I see the dragon statues on the end tables. Their green beams emerge and strike Frey in the temples. He tries to fight them, but eventually succumbs.

What's the purpose of these? Is this a way for the Patrician to control their citizens? But wait, the nightmare they gave me was against Leader Fallon, so is it Dracken-related? That can't be right. Frey has their dragon symbol, but I don't remember seeing these statues in his room.

He twitches every couple of minutes, his face grimacing at whatever images are being projected into his mind. I search the room, trying to look for something that I can use to stop the beams. I locate two handheld mirrors in one of the dresser drawers, but I need something to secure them into place. I remove the bands from my hair and stretch them around the statues and the mirrors. When I have the first one secured, Frey's body starts to relax a little. As soon as I place the other one Frey's eyes flash open, sweat running down his face and arms. He looks at me, frightened at first, but then smiles.

"What happened?" he asks, rubbing his temples.

I show him the statues. He leans on his elbows to examine the dragons and his hand automatically goes to the tattoo on the back of his right shoulder. He seems puzzled and slightly frightened.

"Where's Addie?" he asks.

"She's sleeping, but –"

"She's like I was, isn't she?"

I nod.

He throws off the covers and runs out of the room, with me following closely behind. We look through her drawers and closet, trying to find something to block the beams, but we come up empty. Frey grabs her legs and starts to pull her away. She screams, possibly from pain, but we don't know for sure. She kicks at him, flailing around. He lets go and she slides back onto her pillows, her eyes never opening. I sit next to her on the bed and try waking her. I shake her gently, then a little rougher, but she won't wake up. Addie is back in the midst of a nightmare; she starts to cry, and no matter what we do she won't stop.

"Let's leave her," Frey says.

We go back to the spare room, take the pillows and blankets off the bed, and lie down on the floor. Frey pulls me in tight against him, kisses me, and falls asleep. But all I do is stare at the closed door of the room and wonder what the hell is going on.

Thirteen

Neither of us says anything to Addie about the beams. Before she wakes up, Frey removes the mirrors and gives the bands back to me. I slip into Addie's room and pretend I just got up from her bed as she wakes. She appears groggy, but otherwise fine. A storm moved in overnight, so we're stuck in the house for our last day. None of us is in the mood to watch anything on the television, so we just basically sit around doing nothing. The silence is killing me, so I decide to ask a question that's been bugging me for a while.

"How do you time loop?" I ask.

"Rem didn't tell you?" Frey asks.

"Nope," Addie responds. "She wants Max to figure it out on her own."

"She only told me to think of a point in time where I want to be, but that really doesn't help," I say.

"You kind of have to predict what your opponent is going to do next, then either project yourself into that spot or away from it," Frey says. "If you guess correctly, you'll have no issues and will be ahead. If you guess wrong, anything can happen."

"What does that mean?" I ask.

"Think of it this way," he says. "Say you're up against a Nius. They love to hide their explosives everywhere, so if you can predict where that person is going to place them throughout the battle you can lay a trap for them. You can wait in one of the locations and let time catch up, and the Nius won't know you're there until it's too late."

"I think I get it," I say. "Is it possible to go back in time?"

"You asked me that before," he says.

"What do you mean?" Addie asks.

"Well," I begin, "if you loop forward and set a trap can you loop back to your original point in time, so your opponent hasn't realized you've looped?"

Addie and Frey look at each other, puzzled.

"You'd have to be precise in your looping backwards," Addie says. "Otherwise who knows what could happen, so I wouldn't recommend it."

We spend the next couple of hours talking about the game and who we think will make it to the event. I don't know half the names Frey and Addie mention, so I just listen and learn what I can in case I meet any of them on the floor. We're about to make lunch when our wristbands display an emergency message.

"Players, carriages will arrive for you in the next two hours to bring you back to Thrace Tower," a woman's voice chimes. "We apologize for the inconvenience, but all players must return today."

Frey nudges my arm and we go to grab our bags before stepping out into the rain and heading back to his house, since that's where the Keepers think we are. Addie gives us an umbrella before we leave, so we have some protection from the elements. Frey holds it above our heads and takes my hand.

"Those statues," I begin when we're far enough away from Addie's house, "they're in your sister's room also."

"I know."

"Did you know what they did?"

He hesitates in answering, which causes my stomach to fall. "Yes and no."

"What does that mean?" I practically shout, jerking my hand out of his.

"They're used to control those who otherwise can't be. I used to have them, but stopped causing trouble, so they were removed from my room. My sister never did… which is why she's not here anymore." His voice wavers a little when mentioning her, but there's also an undertone of resentment or hatred mixed in. "But they've changed. They're not showing the same messages they used to." He stops walking and lets the umbrella fall to his side. "I saw you in my dreams," he says, looking down at me. "Leader Fallon was torturing you, burning you alive, and I couldn't stop her."

I step in front of him and lift my hand to his cheek. "It was only a nightmare. None of it was real," I say, trying to reassure him.

"But why would they project such an image into my head? They're supposed to be supporting a stable society, but nightmares like that could send anyone over the edge. It seemed so real. I could smell your skin burning."

"Who, Frey? Who's operating them?"

"The Patrician," he says.

"Come on, we need to get going," I say, trying to pull him forward and out of whatever thought has him trapped.

He lifts the umbrella, but we're already soaked. Nan isn't around when we walk in, which I find relieving. Frey grabs a couple of towels from the laundry room to dry ourselves off. We have an hour until the carriage arrives, so Frey disappears down the hall towards the bedrooms while I quickly strip down to my underwear and toss my wet clothes into the dryer. I go to his room, but he's not there. His sister's room is empty, and the bloodstain has been removed. I check her bathroom; Frey is standing there, shirt off, looking at his dragon tattoo in the mirror.

"She was right when she told me to get this," he says, his eyes never leaving his reflection.

"Your sister?"

He looks over at me. "How did you know?"

"Lucky guess," I say, lying… sort of.

I really don't know how I knew she was the one, but it just seems to fit. If his sister was starting to align herself with the Dracken, which it seems like she might have been if she experienced the same nightmare I did, then it would stand to reason she would recruit her younger brother. But where is she and what happened to her?

He puts his shirt back on, gives me a hug, and we go to the common room to wait. Our carriage arrives right on time. The driver takes our bags and places them in the space behind the back seat. Frey and I nervously stare out the windows as we head towards the city. We don't talk but I get the feeling it's by his choice, not mine. Our carriage queues up with the others outside of Thrace Tower and it takes ten minutes before we're finally able to get into the holding area. Matron Kaniz is waiting for us in the elevator corridor, a troubled look covering her face. She tells us to set our bags next to her and she'll join us upstairs after everyone else has arrived.

The elevator to the Looper unit is barely full. When we reach our floor Rem and Addie are already in the common room, but the monitors are all off. Rem gives me a hug and playfully punches Frey in the arm as her way of saying hello. We join them on the couch as others arrive, but they head mainly to the bedrooms; only a few wander into the common room.

"What do you think happened?" Rem asks.

"I heard someone was killed," a guy with cropped red hair says from his seat in the corner of the room.

"Don't be so dramatic," Addie says. "It's probably nothing. The Keepers just want to make sure we all return on time." But she doesn't sound convinced.

An hour passes before Matron Kaniz arrives, but our bags aren't with her. She calls for everyone to gather in the common room. As soon as everyone is situated she clears her throat, tightens the bun at the back of her head, and clasps her fingers together in front of her.

"As many of you know from our recent history, there's a slight rift between the ruling party and those who oppose it," Matron Kaniz says as she fidgets, putting her hands behind her. "The *Litarian Battles* were meant to bridge that gap and bring us together as a society. However, this is turning out not to be the case." She tucks her hand in her pants pocket and removes a small device, which she points towards the monitors. They all turn on, showing the same newsfeed.

"Citizens of Tarsus," Hammond begins, the city brilliantly laid out behind him. "A Dracken leader has been murdered."

Only a handful of people in the room react. Many just take it in like it's an everyday event, which for me it almost is.

"Now, as you know, the Dracken are a group of people who are anti-Patrician. I don't know how all of you feel about the proposed realignment the Dracken are rallying for, but everyone needs to pay attention to what's happening to our society. Murder isn't the way to further any agenda," Hammond practically shouts to the camera. "We're a civilized people, and actions like this will only throw our world into chaos."

I have to hide the chuckle that's building inside. Such a contradiction to how these people value life. People are killed in the *Litarian Battles* and it doesn't faze them. They allow other atrocities to occur, such as Brink almost raping me in front of a room full of people, and they permit the horrid treatment of the people in the Outer Limits by the Aedox. Yet someone of authority gets killed and now everyone needs to take notice.

Leaders are replaceable, just like everyone else.

"The body of Avery Canton washed ashore this morning in the southern section of Tarsus," Hammond says.

The image changes to show Avery lying face down in the sand, several bullet holes in his back. Frey grips my arm, almost cutting off the circulation. He looks to be on the verge of crying, but not from sadness. Joy maybe? Relief? But why? Addie moves next to Frey and takes his other arm to comfort him.

"It's still not clear who killed Mr. Canton, but at this moment his wife Nan is a suspect and her whereabouts are unknown at this time. The Aedox are scouting all sections of Tarsus looking for her, and we will let you know when there are further developments."

Matron Kaniz turns the monitors off and asks Frey to go to the Progression Room. I begin to follow him at his request, but Matron Kaniz stops me and orders me back to my seat. He kisses me and leaves. I take my seat with Addie huddling next to me.

"That's the reason you've all been brought back early," Matron Kaniz says. "Your bags are currently being searched by the Aedox and each unit will be assigned two Aedox, each with a six-hour rotation. This is for everyone's safety. Tomorrow, Hammond will distribute a broadcast that'll advise you of the new rules and procedures for the *Litarian Battles*. For now, everyone relax and try to get back to your normal routines. Dinner will be delivered momentarily." Matron Kaniz heads towards the Progression Room while everyone stares at each other.

The monitors begin to display the typical music videos as everyone slowly goes back to their business. Rem joins us, and we sit in silence since we can't really talk with all the noise and other conversations going around. Rem stands and signals for us to follow her into the training room. She opens the door and we slip in before anyone notices. The lights turn on automatically and we each take a spot on the floor against one of the walls.

"What do you think?" Rem asks.

"About what?" Addie responds. "It's obvious the Dracken are getting close to achieving their goal, so the Patrician are panicking."

"I don't think that's it," Rem says, folding her arms over her chest.

"It has to be!" Addie shouts. "What else could it be?"

"Does anyone know who the Patrician are?" I ask.

"Well, Leader Fallon obviously," Addie comments in a snide tone.

"I mean besides her," I say.

"What do you mean, Max? She's the only one," Rem says, looking confused by my remark.

I bit my tongue, not saying anything further while Addie and Rem spend the next several minutes arguing. I know Addie is a member of the Dracken because of her tattoo, but where does Rem stand? Better yet, where do I? Do I even really care? None of this affects me since I don't live in Tarsus, so why should I let it bother me? It does, though, and I have a feeling my parents are involved in it somehow. I wish I could talk to them and find out what they were thinking making that deal with Brink… if it's true. Leader Fallon said she didn't kill them, so where'd she put them? And is there some way I can get a message to them?

Rem and Addie are close to brawling with each other when we smell dinner, so they decide to put their fight on hold for another time. Frey isn't with the crowd that's gathered by the bar when we emerge. The meal tonight consists of thinly sliced roast beef, green beans, and mashed potatoes. I take a small helping since I'm not really that hungry, and sit down on the couch that lines the far wall. From my angle I spot two Aedox now standing by the elevator, their weapons held firmly in their hands. Addie sits next to me, but Rem leaves to eat elsewhere.

I go back for seconds, but Matron Kaniz stops me. She takes my plate, sets it down, and escorts me to the Progression Room without saying a word to me the entire time. Frey is sitting on a stool in the corner, being tended to by a nurse for an injury I can't quite see. I'm directed to take a seat in the same chair I was forced into upon my arrival, and the minute I do my arms and legs are secured by straps along with a collar around my throat.

"What the hell is this?" I yell.

"Max, since you were with Frey we need to scan your memory to see if you saw anything related to Avery's death," Matron Kaniz says as a doctor adheres electrodes to my forehead and temples.

I know they're going to see Nan shoot Avery, so I try to think of a way to manipulate my memory, possibly replace the images with something else, but I can't think fast enough. In a matter of seconds, the incident is running on a monitor to my left. Frey watches as his father attacks me, pulls out a knife, and then Nan fires. Frey turns to me, a look of shock on his face.

"Why didn't you tell me?" he asks through tears. "You knew he was dead and you didn't say anything to me."

"I was scared, Frey," I respond, trembling. "He almost killed me. I told you I didn't feel safe there."

"Yes, but you didn't say why," he says. He stands and crosses the room, stopping next to me. "What else haven't you told me?"

The doctor is in the process of removing the electrodes from my head when Frey stops him.

"Leave us," he orders everyone in the room.

I'm surprised to see them all comply, even Matron Kaniz. Frey steps to the door, locks it and switches off the lights, the only light in the room is being projected from the display, which is paused on Avery's execution, but that too gets turned off. The temperature in the room soars and I begin to sweat. Frey paces around me, slowly, almost tauntingly.

"Why?" Frey asks from somewhere behind me, but I can't tell where he is exactly. I only know it's not too close to me.

"Why what?"

"Why would a Dracken leader try to kill the daughter of another Dracken leader?" he asks, sounding closer this time. "He must have thought you were a threat, but why? What did he know about you that I don't?"

"I have no idea what you're talking about," I say in a panic. I struggle with the restraints, trying to free myself.

"I thought getting you into bed might win me your trust and honesty, but I guess I was wrong."

"You had to drug me for that!" I shout. "How pathetic!"

Pain radiates up my legs. I try to scream, but Frey shoves a bite plate into my mouth. The agony from his torture almost brings me to the breaking point before stopping. I spit the device out and swear at him.

"You fucker!" I scream.

The pain immediately returns, followed by a burning sensation. I let out a scream, hoping to alert someone in the common room to my distress, but no one comes.

"The room's soundproof, Max," Frey says into my ear. "I can spend hours in here with you, doing all sorts of things and no one will know."

I need to loop. Time loop preferably, but I'm in so much pain that I can't get my mind to focus. I try to concentrate on a spot in the room, but I'm so unfamiliar with the layout I fear I'll wind up inside the wall, or worse.

"I know you're one of them," I spit out, frustration replacing my anger. "Addie is, too."

"So?" he says nonchalantly. "There are a lot of us, and if I guess right, after the contestants of the event have been determined, there'll be many more."

"And your goal is, what? To take over Tarsus?"

"Not just Tarsus, but everything," he says. "There'll no longer be an Outer Limits, and no one will be rewarded for being loyal to the Patrician by being sent to Icarian."

"I thought only battle winners went there."

"They do, but they're all Patrician favorites. Manipulated somehow, giving them the advantage over the rest of us."

I curl my fingers into a ball, realizing this is probably why I was maimed. So, do they do this to everyone they want to win? How have they managed to get away with it and not get caught by the Keepers? Garrett was right, I'm a threat now… to all of them. If I demonstrate that I'm another Patrician favorite I'll be placed higher on the Keepers' kill list, regardless of who my parents were. Maybe my points will even be knocked down to where I can't recover and I'll be killed in the game.

I need to manipulate the situation, get Frey to believe I'm on his side until I can figure things out. This whole realignment can't just be a battle over governmental power; there has to be more to it. I take a couple of deep breaths to get my temper and anxiety down. Frey is standing next to me, so close that I feel his breath on my cheek.

"What do you need me to do?" I ask, sounding calmer and more in control.

I sense him smiling. "Do what I tell you, no questions asked. Don't hide anything from me. I need your full trust and honesty. Can you do that?"

"Yes," I answer without hesitation.

He's on top of me, pressing his heavy body against mine. "Good."

He kisses me hard on the lips and I return the gesture, determined to show my allegiance. He lowers the chair until it's almost supine. He doesn't remove my restraints, but does loosen my clothes. I feel him… all of him, and I hate myself for letting Frey inside, but I need him to trust me. Time passes slowly, but he does eventually free me.

"Matron Kaniz will be coming for you in a few hours," he says, getting dressed and removing my restraints so I can put my clothes back into place. He helps me from the chair and pulls me against him. "You'll be branded with the Dracken mark and I suggest you get it here," he says, tapping the top of my chest. "That way, I can see it on you at all times." He kisses the spot, then opens the door and leaves.

I linger in the room, afraid to step outside and get bombarded with questions from Addie or Rem. The light from the hallway allows me to see the damage Frey inflicted on my legs. Gouges, not deep but severe, line both my calves.

Seems Frey's familiarized himself with Aedox torture methods.

The blood that had seeped out of the wounds is now mixed with a gel that acts as a rapid healing solution, which is what causes the burning sensation. The Aedox use it to quickly heal our injuries so they can be reopened for maximum scarring.

The common room and hallways are empty when I finally emerge. I look at the time on my wristband, which shows it's just after midnight. I hustle across the way, change into something to sleep in, wash the gel from my legs as my wounds have healed, brush my teeth, and get into bed. But I don't fall asleep, since I know I'll be woken up in a little while to be maimed again.

Fourteen

I must have dozed off since I didn't even hear her come in, because when I open my eyes Matron Kaniz is standing next to my bed, her face too close to mine. We quietly exit the room, heading towards the hallway that'll take us to the elevator. But instead of turning left we go right and exit through the emergency door. No alarms go off as we go down four flights of stairs. The lighting in the stairwell is minimal, so I have to watch my footing as we descend. Once at the bottom, we turn right and proceed down an even darker hallway. Voices emanate from behind the only door I can see. Matron Kaniz opens it and practically shoves me inside. She closes the door and joins the other matrons by a metal door that's currently closed. I'm the only one from the Looper unit, so I take a seat far from the others. A woman I recognize as belonging to Nius gets up from her seat and sits next to me.

"You're Max, right?" she asks cheerfully.

"Yes," I reply, trying to stifle a yawn.

"I thought so. You're from the Outer Limits like Lil."

I nod.

"So… where are you getting it?"

I look at her, puzzled, not quite grasping her meaning.

"Your tattoo," she says, since I haven't responded.

"Oh, I don't know. Why?"

"Placement is everything, Max. The position of your tattoo determines where you rank among the Dracken," she replies. "Anything above your diaphragm means you're important, a top-ranked official. Place it on your abdomen and you're classified as a second-tier soldier. Anything lower than that means you're simply a lackey, someone to boss around."

"I didn't know that."

She cocks her head, sizing me up and down. "Strange that the person who recruited you didn't tell you about it," she replies. "They're supposed to direct you where you're to have it placed."

"He did, I just didn't know the location was pre-determined."

"Frey talked to you, didn't he?"

I nod.

"He's one of the top officials, just below the actual leaders," she says. "So, where's your spot?"

I tap the top of my left breast.

Her jaw drops open, then she squeals with excitement. "That means you're his," she says, beaming. "And no one else can have you. It also means you're high ranked like he is. I'm so jealous." She stands and goes back to where she'd been sitting.

Now I understand why he selected that area. A good portion of the dragon will be visible under all my shirts, including my battle outfit. It's like he's marking me as a target if I go up against anyone who's opposed to the Dracken. What'll happen to those I fight who are lower-ranking than me? Will they try to kill me faster, or avoid me?

The metal door opens and a man from Rapid is beckoned forward. I can't see who or what's in the room since the door is only partially opened. Hours pass before I'm finally called. Matron Kaniz places her hand on my back as I walk towards the door. The room is white and sterile, just like the Progression Room. Harsh lighting floods the small space, hurting my eyes. In the center is a leather-covered table next to a stool, and small workbench covered in black ink and transparency paper. A small, thin woman is bent over another table in the corner, busily designing my dragon, or so I assume. Her blond hair is cut short and her outfit looks too baggy for her frame.

"Lie here," Matron Kaniz says to me, gesturing to the table.

I slide on and lie down. The light is too bright at this angle, so I have to cover my eyes with my hand. Matron Kaniz advises the woman that I'm ready, then leaves. I begin to sweat from the heat being generated by the lights, but I also feel chilled.

"Please remove your shirt," the woman says, not even turning around.

I do as she says, grateful I left my bra on or I'd be completely exposed.

The woman gets up from her seat, goes over to a storage unit with several drawers, and rummages through a couple of them until she locates the needles she's going to use. She sits down on the stool next to me, slips gloves onto her hands, and prepares her instruments.

"I'm going to need you to put your arm down," she says, still not looking at me.

I place my arm against my side, but in such a way that I'm gripping the side of the table. She rubs lotion over the spot she's going to place the tattoo, right where Frey wants it. The transparency paper is placed on top of the lotion and patted down so the temporary ink will stick to my skin. She takes her tools, hunches over me, and begins to work. The pain is minimal at first, but increases when she goes over one spot multiple times. I grit my teeth and close my eyes, wishing for the whole thing to be over.

"I'm almost done," she says some time later.

She takes a cloth, wipes off the extra ink, and applies the rapid-healing gel. She hands me a mirror so I can take a look.

The dragon is bigger than I was expecting, covering almost the entire top portion of my breast and moving up toward my neck. The dragon's head is sharp, angling downward, and showing in profile. Its mouth is wide open, its tongue and teeth exposed. The body twists into a couple of loops as its scales project out like barbed wire. The wings are tall, stretching from the top of my breast to my collarbone. My heart sinks at the sight of it.

What did I do? What am I doing? How could I have agreed to this? Then I remind myself I didn't have much choice.

"It's going to be tender for a while," the woman says. She leans over to take the mirror from me, and that's when I finally see her. Recognition flashes on both our faces, but she's the first to speak. "Headmaster

Edom isn't going to like this," Cil, the woman who helped mutilate my hands, says.

"Why?" I ask, thrusting my hands into her face. "Why did you do this to me?"

"Not here, Max. Not now."

"Yes, now. I'm tired of being lied to. I want to know the truth. Who are you and why was this done to me?"

She hushes me with a wave of her hands and then busies herself with cleaning up. Matron Kaniz pokes her head in to see what the fuss is about.

"I just need to do a couple of touch-ups," Cil says. "It'll only be a few more minutes."

Matron Kaniz smiles and closes the door.

"You're going to get me killed," Cil says angrily. "They think I'm on their side. If you give me away, I'll kill you myself."

"Explain," I say, my teeth clenched in aggravation.

"Leader Fallon wanted to make sure that when Headmaster Edom submitted the names to the Keepers of those being drawn from the Outer Limits, you would be one of them. The Patrician instructed us to alter your body to ensure you made it to the final event."

"But why me? Why not someone else?"

"What better person to use than a Dracken leader's daughter? Your parents had no idea where you were, but Leader Fallon did because she placed you in the orphanage. She thought it would be fitting for the Dracken to be defeated by one of their own, but you're here getting marked." Her expression changes to one of concern.

"It's not by choice," I croak.

"You always have a choice, Max. You can choose who'll win this realignment. Both sides are betting on you, they just don't know it."

"Where do you fit in?"

"Wherever I'm needed, but my real loyalties are with the Patrician. They're trying to keep civilization together, while the Dracken want to rip it apart and start over."

"Would that be such a bad thing?"

"For someone like you, no. Your kind will survive, but not mine. I grew up in the second-level housing in the Outer Limits, so I'll have no future if the Dracken win. All those workers will be killed, obliterated like the Dead Zone."

I want to ask her more questions but Matron Kaniz enters, ending our conversation. I put my shirt back on before I'm escorted up to the unit and settle into bed as quietly as possible. I get very little sleep, dreading having to explain the tattoo to Addie and Rem in the morning.

How far am I willing to take this before I actually pick a side? Frey uses control and deception to get what he wants, yet that's what Leader Fallon and the Patrician have done as well. Why am I a pawn in their game? Will I make that much of a difference to either side? What if I choose to die in the *Litarian Battles* and not continue with their plan? They'd have to find someone else, but would they even allow that to happen? I'm sure I'm being monitored continually by both sides, at all times.

I give up on trying to figure things out and finally fall asleep. Frey is sitting on my bed when I wake. Men normally aren't permitted in the women's quarters, and vice versa, so I'm guessing Matron Kaniz gave him permission this one time. His fingers gently caress the outline of the image. The touch is comforting, warm, and full of desire. I take his hand off my chest and hold it.

"It looks nice," he says, leaning closer to me. He kisses me on the lips, then curls up in bed with me.

I'm hoping the room is empty, otherwise this is really going to be awkward. He holds me in his arms, nuzzling my neck. My stomach rumbles since I'm starving, so Frey pushes the covers off and we head to the common room for breakfast. We're the last ones to get food, and find a seat where we can to eat. Addie bounces over to me, almost knocking the bowl of cereal out of my hands when she plops down. I sit hunched over, trying my best to hide the tattoo, but Addie catches sight of the wings.

"Oh my God, you got one!" she shouts, alerting the whole room. "That's awesome. Can I see it?"

I pull down the collar of my shirt to show her.

"Rem is going to be so pissed when she sees it. Don't be surprised if she scolds you. She gave me crap, but I got over it." Addie wraps her arm around mine, making eating almost impossible.

"When is Hammond making the announcement?" Frey asks.

"In about an hour," Addie replies. "Matron Kaniz has already left to make arrangements for the changes. Apparently she knows what they are, but won't tell any of us."

My mind floods with possibilities, which causes me to lose my appetite, so I toss my food into the garbage and go take a shower. All but one of the stalls is occupied, so I grab it before someone else can. My skin is sensitive this morning, and not just around the tattoo. I have to wash slowly and gently, then dry in the same manner before I can put on clean clothes and return to the common room. Addie and Rem are arguing again, which makes me wonder what changed between the two of them that they're fighting so much. Rem glares at me and starts yelling.

"Traitor!" she screams, charging at me, her finger pointed in my direction. "How could you? I didn't train you to become one of them!"

"Stop it, Rem," Frey says, coming up behind me.

"No, she has to know."

"She does," Frey says.

"Probably only what you want her to know, and not the whole truth."

Frey grabs Rem by the arm and drags her down the hallway. She's wincing from the pain of his grip. I follow them, but Addie stays behind.

"You have no idea what kind of havoc you're going to cause if you keep this up," Frey says through gritted teeth. "Max is a Dracken now, just like her parents."

Rem looks confused by the last remark, but it takes her only a few minutes before she puts the pieces together. "The conspirators? That's not possible," she says, her mouth falling open. "The girl was killed with her parents."

Frey shakes his head. "You were led to believe that. We all were."

"How did you find out?"

"Troy. He had Max's roommate from the Outer Limits staying with him during the break. Apparently, Brink felt that bragging about his endowment would put him in high standing with Troy."

"Endowment?" Rem asks.

Frey leans in and whispers to her. I don't need to hear it to know what he's saying. This makes me wonder how many other people Brink has told about my parents' promise to him. Was I the last one to find out? How could mentioning something like that possibly benefit Brink in any way? Maybe he's hoping it'll make him a Dracken leader, or at least a top official. If I'm up against him in the game, he's not coming out alive.

"It doesn't matter," Rem blurts out. "You're all dead to me now." She walks up to me, our faces close together. "If we're in the same battle, don't plan on surviving."

She storms away just as Matron Kaniz steps off the elevator with two Aedox. They look to be the replacements for the ones currently stationed next to the elevator, but they continue down the hallway towards the common room. Frey and I follow, squeezing into the crowd that's steadily forming.

"Hammond will make the announcement shortly," Matron Kaniz says once everyone is accounted for.

"What's with the Aedox?" a girl in the front asks.

"They're for your protection," Matron Kaniz responds.

This makes the room fall silent. That isn't the answer I was expecting. Why would we need protecting? And from whom?

The monitors flicker on at the same time, showing Hammond standing in the center of the selection floor. His suit today is somber, not as wild as the ones he normally wears. He looks nervous and uncomfortable, but smiles through it.

"Hello, children – I hope you all enjoyed your break," he says, then pauses for imagined applause or cheers. "The Keepers have been hard at work, determining the next phase leading up to the event. As you can guess this wasn't easy, and with circumstances changing almost daily additional alterations are continually being made." He clears his throat, adjusts his tie, and strokes his mustache before continuing. "This new phase of the *Litarian Battles* is being broken up into three rounds. Now, not everyone will be in the first round, as many of our higher ranking players will automatically start in round three."

I catch Rem smiling in her little corner of the room. Frey squeezes me against him. He has the highest points in the unit, so he's guaranteed to start in the third round.

"So, not to get ahead of ourselves, we'll just discuss the first round," Hammond says, adjusting his tie again. He looks to be sweating more than usual under the hot lights. "All contestants who have 500 points or fewer before the break will meet on the selection floor shortly. Of the 125 players we have, the Keepers have determined that eleven of you meet this criterion. The wristbands of those selected will begin to glow blue momentarily and you'll be escorted by your matrons to the selection floor. There, the rules of the first round will be explained. Good luck to you all."

The monitors turn off and I bury my wristband under my arm. I only had 500 points left after my last battle, so I know it's glowing. Everyone cranes their necks, looking around the room to see who it may be. I see two people close to the bar whose wristbands are blue. I pretend to not be paying attention, but I catch Matron Kaniz's stern look in my direction. I linger back, hoping to disappear as everyone else disperses from the room.

"Max," Matron Kaniz calls. "Let's go."

Frey won't release me. I don't think he realized I had so few points. I feel his heart rate skyrocket in his chest, but I'm not sure if it's out of anger, fear, or excitement. I turn, kiss him on the lips, and force his fingers from my waist.

"Win," he whispers.

I nod and make my way over to the others, who are standing next to the Aedox. No one speaks as we take the elevator down and bypass the dressing area. We're secured into our seats before they spin, and we rise into darkness before breaching the selection floor. Hammond is still standing in his spot, but the screens in the seats in front of us and around his head are off. No computer-generated audience cheers radiating in our ears this time. I quickly scan the room, looking for familiar faces, but only find one. Drake is cowering on the Rapid level of the auditorium. Of the eleven players chosen there are three Loopers, four Nius, three Rapids, and one Dead Mark.

"Welcome, contestants," Hammond says, outstretching his arms as if to embrace us. "In order to get to the second round you must reach 10,000 points. For that to be accomplished, only one of you will come out of this round alive. The battle floor has been modified to accommodate these new conditions, and the winner will be reunited with his or her unit before advancing to the second round. Alliances won't be tolerated. If you team up with someone from your unit, your kill rate will become higher and your shield automatically deactivated. This sequence won't end until we have a winner. All units will be watching you in their common rooms, so do them proud."

We descend, heading back into the darkness.

The Keepers are getting desperate, but why? Are they with the Dracken? If so, why place their own people into these battles? Why not advance us to the third round automatically?

I'm so involved in my own thoughts that an Aedox has to nudge me from my seat after I reach the bottom. We make our way to the holding area, where our outfits wait for us in the designated stalls. When we're all dressed, we sit and wait. Hammond never told us how long we would have until we're thrown onto the floor so the eleven of us nervously pace the room, trying to avoid each other.

The signs above the four doors light up with our unit name. Once we're all in position, the doors slide open and everyone enters. Our weapons are waiting for us at the end of the hall, but the door to the battle floor remains closed. The three of us belt our sheaths around our waists and anxiously wait.

Fifteen

"Players," a voice booms over our heads, but it's not Hammond, so perhaps it's one of the Keepers. "Once the doors open you each will be swept to a different area of the battle floor. If you look down at your wristbands, you'll see the total count of those currently alive in this round. When someone is killed, a chime will go off and the number will update on your wristband. Good luck to you all."

The door opens, exposing us to a blinding light which causes the three of us to hesitate before stepping forward. I go first and immediately loop, landing at the base of a tall metal structure with blown-out windows. The concrete below my feet is cracked and burnt with small grasses trying desperately to grow through. In front of the building is a plaza containing a fallen statue of a woman with a gold crown atop her head. She's holding a long spear in one hand and a shield in the other. She had to have stood at least a hundred feet tall if not more when she was originally built. Below her feet is an empty pool covered in what once must have been blue tile, each one engraved with a green laurel surrounding a silver infinity symbol. Beyond the pool is a road with a few rusted vehicles sporadically spaced.

This battle floor looks and feels far different than the others. The textures are grittier and the air thicker, which makes me wonder where they've placed us… or what they've moved onto the battle floor. Could they have teleported the Dead Zone to the tower? Is that even possible?

The sky is slightly overcast, but I hear the distant rumbling of an approaching storm. I climb several narrow steps, cross a large patio, and enter the building into what once must've been a lobby. In the center of the open space are three elevators, all rusted and collapsed; their cables drape over the enclosure and across a couple of broken wooden tables outside a defunct café. The ceiling of the thirty-story structure consists of broken glass panels that allow anything from the outside in, which explains the birds that are fluttering about. The lobby's interior is grimy, covered in either mold or moss, but I can't tell which. The air is heavily scented with decay.

I meander around the ground floor, taking in as much as I can. Monitors that once clung to the walls lay smashed on the ground. I try every doorknob I come across, but they're all locked except one marked as the emergency exit. I open the door and step into a stairwell where one of the walls that supports part of the stairs has crumbled away, revealing the plaza outside. I need a good vantage point to locate the other players, so I decide to head up. When I come upon a gap too large to step over I loop to the next safe landing. I could probably loop all the way to the top of the building, but I actually want to look at how everything is laid out.

The entrance to the twentieth floor is the first unlocked door I come across, so I step onto the floor which is covered in broken computers, demolished desks, and partitioned walls that have been burned. I step carefully toward a wide hole in the far wall, my boots crunching the glass that still sits in the window frame as my toes dangle over the edge. A desolate landscape lies before me. Skyscrapers reduced to only a few stories, highways either cracked or completely destroyed and covered in vehicles in various stages of disintegration, and a building a great distance away that looks to be completely intact. It reminds me of the one I saw when we were making our way to Tarsus.

Am I actually in the Dead Zone and not on the battle floor? That's not possible. No one can survive in the Dead Zone's atmosphere, so this has to be a trick of the Keepers.

I shake my head to clear the thought, when an explosion a few blocks away catches my attention. A chime rings on my wristband and the tally of players reduces by two. I tap the tiny screen and it shows that a Nius and a Rapid have been killed. My gaze moves back to the building in the far distance and a new plan forms in my mind. I decide to forgo the battle and make my way to the structure. If I'm lucky, the rest will just kill each other off. I go back the way I came, exit the building and follow the crumbling asphalt, making sure to keep my Kopis at the ready and my shield up as I make my way around the wreckage.

My progress is slow since I have to keep an eye out for the other players, although I'm guessing they'll get to me before I notice them. I can't tell how much time has passed, since the clock on my wristband is currently off. Apparently, the Keepers don't want us to know how long we're going to be trapped in here. The rumbling I heard in the distance earlier is closer now, so I glance back towards the direction I came from and see rain pelting the building I'd been in. Lightning strikes the top of it and radiates down the outside of the structure. If I'd stayed there, I'd have been electrocuted. Weather was never a factor in the previous battles, so I wonder what other changes the Keepers have made to the battle floor environment.

The road I'm on turns into an on-ramp to the highway above, but before I can continue my path is blocked by a Looper and Dead Mark fighting. I crouch behind the remnants of a burnt vehicle to wait it out. The person from my unit tries to loop, but I notice her wristband is broken. She begins to run away but doesn't get far when the Dead Mark shoots her in the back, his arrow piercing her heart. The rain begins to pour down on us as he makes his way over to her body, checking to make sure she's dead. Normally the body would disappear after death, but the girl stays in her spot. I keep my eyes on the Dead Mark as he turns and starts to head up the ramp. The vehicle I'm hiding next to disappears, causing me to fall on my face. I must've made a noise since the Dead Mark turns in my direction. I turn off my shield and loop just as he readies his bow, landing on the ramp several yards behind him. He aims at me and fires but I loop again, moving a few feet away. His arrow misses, which causes him to scowl.

He runs up the ramp to get a closer shot, when the ground begins to shake. Between several holes in the ramp I catch a glimpse of a Nius prowling around. Another small quake jostles us, knocking the Dead Mark and me to the ground. Perhaps the explosives this Nius has isn't strong enough to bring down the structure, so he's doing it piece by piece. The Dead Mark gets back to his feet, aims his arrow at me, and fires. I loop towards the top of the ramp as another explosion goes off, this time leveling the ramp. Both the Dead Mark and Nius are crushed by the chunks of concrete and rebar. I don't bother to look to see if they're dead, as my wristband confirms it.

Seven of us remain.

I'm half-tempted to open up the map of the Dead Zone that Lok downloaded, but since Hammond said our units will be watching I don't want to give away the fact that I have it. Also, I'm not sure this is even the real Dead Zone.

The rain soaks through my clothes as I continue down the highway, causing me to shiver as the temperature also begins to drop. The highway stops when sections of a bridge used to cross old railroad tracks several stories below are missing. I loop myself across one section at a time, but after I make it to the other side and begin to step forward I'm abruptly stopped. My body hits an invisible barrier, so I try to loop around it, but even my abilities are non-existent on this side of the bridge.

"Having issues?" Drake shouts from his side of the bridge.

"I could just stay here," I say. "You can't cross those gaps and no one can get behind me, so I'm actually in a pretty safe spot."

"You know the Keepers won't let you just stand there and watch the rest of us die. They'll loop you somewhere that isn't safe."

I know he has a point, but I try not to let it get to me. I walk to the edge of my section of the bridge, then look down. A jump from this height would kill me, so I'm hoping I've stepped far enough away from the barrier to loop. I give it a try and focus on the section of bridge in front of me. My feet slip on small particles of debris mixed with water as I land, causing me to fall. I try to grab on to the concrete or one of the several pieces of rebar jutting out of the bridge, but they're too slippery. I loop again as I fall, and project myself behind Drake. It's a risky move, but one he shouldn't be anticipating.

I'm wrong.

His weapon slices my arm as I land, and I quickly put up my shield to deflect his other blows. I swing at him with my Kopis, but his shield looks to be designed to fend off my weapon. The temperature continues to drop, the rain begins turning to snow, and the puddles around us turn to ice. The sudden decline in weather is having an effect on both of us, and our movements become sluggish. Pain radiates from my side as another wound opens, fresh blood trickling down, but it's not from Drake. The Rapid who sliced me is now attacking Drake, so I close my shield and loop further down the highway and away from the melee.

The snow starts to stick, covering everything in a pure white blanket. Blood drips from my wounds leaving a trail, so it won't take long for the others to find me. My wristband chimes as the count drops to five with a Rapid being killed, but it doesn't tell me if it's Drake or the other one. Since it was close to nightfall when we were brought to the selection floor, I'm surprised it's still light in the world around me. However, with the Keepers in control of the environment, I doubt darkness will ever come if they don't want it to.

I follow the road past the on-ramp and towards smaller buildings that look to have once been homes. Many have been blown off their foundations while others have collapsed roofs or are just burnt-out shells. I need to find a place to hide so I can check my injuries and wind up choosing a partially collapsed house, its yellow shutters the only truly distinguishable feature left on the exterior. I enter where the kitchen must've been and collapse to the floor. The slash mark on my arm has already ceased bleeding, but the wound in my side won't stop. I scramble across the tile, so I can get to the cabinets and I rummage through the ones I can reach, trying to look for anything that'll help stem the flow of blood.

I finally find a greasy towel shoved behind some rusted pots, so I place the rough fabric against the wound and involuntarily scream from the pain. If my blood doesn't lead everyone to my location, that scream definitely will. The towel is soaked in seconds, so I scoop some of the snow and pack it between my shirt and gash, hoping the cold will slow down the blood loss. I lean against the counter as I try to stand. My legs feel weak and my head is pounding from the effort.

Metal hits the floor next to me.

"Shit," I say, diving for whatever cover I can find.

The explosion is deafening. My outfit protects my legs from getting burned, but I can still feel the heat. Another disc sails into the structure, landing closer to the common room just opposite me. I move further into the house and enter one of the bedrooms. The building moans in reaction to the detonation and begins to shift further off its foundation. I quietly step through a hole in the back wall of the room as another disc goes off, this time igniting the dry pressboard that makes up much of the interior. I slink around the side and peer around the corner, finding two Nius are taking turns lobbing their arsenal into the house.

Why haven't the Keepers stopped them? Hammond said if we buddied up our kill rate would increase, and our shields would be turned off.

So, let's see if that's true.

I pull out my Kopis since it had been sheathed, and loop behind them. My blade slices through one of the Nius before he can react. He drops dead as his partner works on generating her shield, but just as Hammond said it's been deactivated. She turns to run, but my blade cuts through her before she's an inch away.

Three left. Two Loopers, including me, and one Rapid.

I loop, projecting myself as far from the house as possible. Through the haze that occurs in the void I experience while in transition, I notice the other Looper hovering in mid-air by the statue I was near earlier. I land in my chosen location then loop again, heading for where I started. The Looper is still hovering in the same spot, perhaps not sure of where to land. I select a different location to set down and choose an area alongside the building instead of in front. I call up my shield and approach the plaza with caution.

Drake is sitting against the small wall that encircles the pool below the statue's feet, staring up into the sky. I follow his gaze, and from my vantage point I notice the Looper has been spliced between realities. Portions of his body are displayed in the air like puzzle pieces, only grotesque and distorted.

"I wonder how he managed to do that," Drake says, now standing beside me. "That's a gruesome way to die."

I try to step away, but Drake places his hand on my back and pushes me forward. As he does this his weapon carves a deep incision into my arm. I bring up my Kopis and slam it against his shield.

"You know, Max, we're evenly matched," he says nastily. "My shield protects me against your weapon and yours against mine."

"I can loop away from here, but you can't," I counter.

"I don't think you'll do that since something tells me the Keepers have moved the barrier to this plaza."

I look at him quizzically.

Drake drops his shield so he can pick up a piece of concrete, which he hurls towards the street, but it hits an invisible barrier and falls to the ground.

That must be how the Looper got caught. They must've been moving the barrier while he was looping. I'm surprised that didn't happen to me since I was further away than he was, so I wonder why it didn't.

I step away from Drake, keeping my eyes on him, and I don't stop until my legs hit the barrier around the pool. My Kopis remains extended in front of me. Drake doesn't put his shield up, but he also stays out of reach.

"You know what Brink told me before I left the unit?" Drake asks, mocking me. "He said for me to make sure you survive, which means he wants me to die since only one of us is leaving here." He paces between me and the steps up to the building. "Can you believe the gall of that asshole?"

"It's only because he cares for me," I say. "If you can beat me then you deserve to win."

He's suddenly next to me, one hand wrapped around my throat while his other one pins my arm to my side, preventing me from brandishing my weapon. "Aren't you confident, Max," Drake mutters in my ear. "But what are you going to do now? You can't loop away from me since you'll be spliced like your friend." He nods towards the other Looper, but my gaze is focused on the pair of birds flying in and out of the lobby door.

"How about we go for a ride," I say, taking my free hand and grabbing his wrist.

I loop us inside the building, and when we land I shove Drake off me since he's disoriented from the experience. He skids across the floor, only stopping when he hits the elevators. I loop again, this time landing right at his feet and stabbing him in the shoulder with the Kopis. He screams from the pain and sweeps my legs out from under me. My Kopis is still in his shoulder when I lose my grip, but since it can only be touched by me, the minute my flesh is no longer making contact it vanishes.

Drake notices I'm now weaponless, so he slashes at me with his knives, cutting deeply into my arms. As he's about to pull them out when I grab them with my hands and loop. Drake is stunned by my move. I let go of the weapons while still in the void and they disappear.

"How?" he screams from below when I land in front of him.

I grab him by the collar and loop again, this time projecting us high above the lobby floor. I'm not sure if the Keepers or our units can see and hear what's going on inside the void Drake and I are currently in, but I speak my mind anyway.

"Look, I don't want to be here anymore than you do," I say through clenched teeth. "But I've been maimed, drugged, and almost killed outside of Thrace Tower one too many times to *not* want to see what this all means. I'm making it all the way to the final event and no one, not you or anyone else, is going to stop me."

I let him go. He leaves the void and spirals to the floor below. I stay in my position as he cracks open when his body hits the half-wall encasing the lifts. I project myself outside and next to the statue. The building vanishes as does the other props around me, and I'm back on the battle floor where I collapse from the loss of blood.

"Congratulations, Max!" a female voice calls out. "We will now transport you to the medical office for evaluation."

The room spins as I close my eyes and wait to be teleported.

Sixteen

When I open my eyes, Matron Kaniz is standing at the foot of my bed with a large smile on her face. Obviously, she's pleased with my victory, but I'm not. I murdered Drake. Dropped him out of the void so he would hit the floor. As his death plays over and over in my head part of me regrets it, but not all of me, which means I'm turning into one of them. I'm starting to think everyone else's life means nothing and can be easily eradicated.

"That was quite a showdown you had with Drake," Matron Kaniz says, slowly walking up alongside my bed. "I didn't think you had it in you to kill that way. Matron Violet wasn't too thrilled with how Drake died. I think she'll order the other Rapids to target you regardless of who else is on the floor."

"What else is new," I mumble.

"You'll be released tomorrow and sent back to the unit. The second round will begin in a couple of days, which will allow you to get some much-needed rest."

"What's the format for the second round?"

She smiles, pressing her lips tightly together. "You know I can't tell you that," she replies before stepping towards the door and then stopping. "How did you strip Drake of his weapons? It appeared as if you touched them."

"They were stuck in my arms," I lie. "He must not have had a good grip on them when I looped."

She seems to buy my answer and leaves. I lift my arms to look at the heavy bandages they're encased in… great, more scars to add to the collection. I plop my head back down on the pillow and close my eyes. My stunt with the Deer Horn knives was a risky move, so I'll need to be more careful if I try it again. Who knows what the Keepers will do if they realize the Patrician have modified me.

I don't get much rest, since the nurses come in every couple of hours to change my bandages. I'm only able to catch glimpses of the injuries, and they look as bad as they feel. The one along my side is giving the nurses the most trouble; it doesn't want to heal on its own, so they wind up stitching it closed. I'm not sure why they didn't do that to begin with; the doctors in the Outer Limits would've done that first. At least, that's what they did when the Aedox were done with us. I'm pumped full of medication before I leave and the nurses hand me a clean pair of clothes. I'm almost done dressing when my door opens, but it's not Matron Kaniz. It's Matron Ancilla from the Dead Mark unit.

"Hello, Max," she says from the doorway. "Matron Kaniz has been called away to see the Keepers, so I'll be escorting you to the elevator back to your unit."

Matron Ancilla is an inch taller than me, with blond hair so white that it bleaches out her already extremely pale complexion. She looks a little nervous to be down here, but covers it up when she sees that I've noticed. I put my shoes on, comb my hair with my fingers, and join her in the hallway. We walk the length of the corridor then exit out the door that'll take us down another long hallway to the elevators. The area is poorly lit, with only sporadic patches of light cascading down through grates along the ceiling. The air is cool and the hallway feels more like a large chamber by the way our footsteps echo around us.

"Max," Matron Ancilla says, grabbing my arm and pulling me to a stop. "Be careful that you don't show the Keepers your ability to grasp the other players' weapons."

My mouth falls open, but I can't speak.

"The Patrician are counting on you getting to round three of the event without incident. What you did with Drake was too risky. Another trick like that and they'll catch on."

"What makes the Patrician think I'm going to help them?" I ask, irritated by everyone's assumptions. "They mutilated my hands for their own purposes. There's no reason for me to support them."

"What did you do?" she asks, her voice rising in alarm.

I pull down the left side of my shirt, showing her the dragon.

"You joined the Dracken?" she asks, stunned. "But why?"

"I have my own reasons," I reply, then continue heading in the direction for the elevators.

She has to hurry to catch up to me. "Does this have anything to do with your parents?" she asks. "If so, Max, then you don't know the truth. You don't know what we're up against."

"Then tell me!" I shout, stopping so abruptly she almost runs into me.

"I can't."

"Then don't trust me," I say angrily.

I'm tired of being kept in the dark by everyone. I've made up my mind that I'm not fighting for anyone but myself. I'm not going to be a puppet for either side, and I won't protect anyone but myself. Getting to the third round is my only goal now. I have a feeling a lot will be revealed during that time since everyone is alluding to my need to be there.

I step out the door, cross over to the elevator, and head up to my unit. Frey and Addie are waiting for me when I step off, both rushing up to hug me. I wince at their touch, my injuries still tender. We go into the common room where those sitting around and watching music videos applaud as I enter. The three of us take an empty spot in the back by the training room; they start bombarding me with questions before I even get a chance to sit down.

"So," Addie begins, "tell us about it."

"There isn't much to tell other than what you saw on television," I respond.

"I've never seen a battle floor like that before," Addie continues. "Where do you think it was?"

"The Dead Zone," Frey answers.

Addie and I look at him, surprised.

"That's not possible. The Dead Zone isn't habitable," Addie says, brushing off his answer.

"If it wasn't the real Dead Zone then it was staged to look like it," I say.

"You've seen it?" Addie asks, a smile forming on her face. "What's it like?"

"You have to travel through it from the Outer Limits in order to reach Tarsus," I reply, trying to calm myself since my anxiety has risen considerably. I'm not sure why, but having to talk about the Dead Zone is causing me to panic. "There's nothing but devastated buildings, broken highways, and rusted-out vehicles. Everything has either been blown to dust, burned, or melted. I'd hate to see what a person would look like under such conditions."

"I'm sure no one was there when the place was obliterated," she says. "I mean, why murder millions of people?"

"Do you even know who used to live there?" Frey asks, his temper rising. "The Patrician did, and the Dead Zone was nuked *by* the Patrician… they slaughtered their own people to start society over again. They felt it was becoming too chaotic, that they were losing control. That's why the Outer Limits and Tarsus were created… to separate those who follow orders from the ones who won't."

"Where'd you hear that shit from?" Rem asks, joining us.

I'm surprised she's sitting anywhere near us, let alone talking to us. I wonder if she's still mad that I've got the Dracken mark or if her anger is finally waning.

"It's not shit," Frey says heatedly.

I move next to him, placing my body against his to see if it'll calm him down. I can feel his heart racing against my shoulder, but it speeds up instead of slowing down.

"My sister did research on the Dead Zone," he says, becoming emotional. "She discovered the truth and they killed her for it."

"Who killed her?" Addie asks.

"The Patrician," he replies, trying to hold back tears. "Aedox came during the night and dragged her from her bed. My parents were helpless in stopping them, so that's why I'm here… to win so I can put an end to the Patrician's reign. We need this realignment so our society can go on and not wind up as another Dead Zone."

He abruptly stands, storming away and disappearing into the men's bedroom.

"He's full of crap," Rem says. "He's always making shit up to get everyone on his side. Frey has to always be in control of everyone and everything." Rem stands and places her hand on my shoulder. "Watch out who you align yourself with, Max. You may have the Dracken mark, but if your heart isn't in it you'll quickly become their enemy." She steps away and sits on another couch, joining a new group's conversation.

I retreat to the training room, leaving Addie by herself. I lock the door behind me, go to the center of the room, and sit. I need to get my thoughts straight and this is the quietest place on the floor. I pull my knees up to my chest, hang my head, and take a couple of deep breaths as I close my eyes.

What do I do and what do I know? My father was once the leader of Tarsus, but he was removed. My parents started a rebellion against the Patrician, which led to them being taken from Tarsus and sent… where? Leader Fallon convinced everyone my parents are dead then proceeded to hide me, but why? Who are the Dracken, really? Were my parents involved with them in some fashion? Who are the Patrician and where do they come from? Are they people like us, or something else? Was what Frey said about the Dead Zone correct? Did the Patrician murder the people who lived there?

My head begins to hurt from all the questions. More slam against my skull and I let out a scream to deafen them. Someone tries the handle of the door, but when they discover it's locked they start banging on it. It's Addie, who shouts to me asking if I'm all right. I tell her I'm fine, but she continues to pound on the door. I stand, think of a quiet place to go, and loop.

The carpeting under my shoes is gritty, like it hasn't been cleaned in a while. One of the chandeliers sways from an invisible breeze. Headmaster Edom is having a conversation with someone in his study. Since everyone else I need to talk to isn't accessible, he's my only option. I'm just hoping the Keepers can't track me way out here, that their devices can't get past the Dead Zone and into the Outer Limits. I step quietly towards the half-open door and recognize the voice of the woman he's arguing with as belonging to Cil.

"This isn't going to work," Cil says.

"It has to, it just has to," Edom responds, and it sounds like he's pacing.

"She's a Dracken now. She's chosen her side, and it's not the one you and the Patrician want her on."

"Maybe she's just trying to fit in, Cil. Max has always had issues finding her place in society. Perhaps she thinks this could be what she's supposed to do. We just need to remind her of the true reason she's there."

"And what if she starts asking questions? Do you want her finding out the truth about her parents?" Cil asks, her voice cracking. "Fallon will kill you if she discovers what you've done."

"I had to!" he shouts as the pacing stops. "They left me no choice."

"What about Tilda? She wasn't a threat to you, and she was the only person who actually gave a damn about Max."

"Again, I had no choice."

"That seems to be your excuse for everything," Cil says loudly. Springs squeak and footsteps approach the door I'm near. "Don't be surprised when this all comes crashing down on you. It'll either be the Patrician, the Dracken, Fallon, or perhaps Max herself who'll be your executioner. I just hope you put in a good word for the rest of us before you die."

I press against the wall as the door opens and it almost smacks me in the face. Cil storms out the front door and into a night filled with rain. I push the door away, step around it, and walk into the study.

"Why?" I ask. Edom is sitting on the couch with his back to me.

He jumps upon hearing my voice and drops his drink, the glass shattering on the floor. "Max, how…how did you get here?" he stutters.

"Answer my question," I say louder, stepping closer to him.

"You don't understand what's at stake, Max," Edom says, standing. His bathrobe hangs open over gray pajamas that look like they've been worn for days.

"Then explain it."

He moves around to the back of the couch, then leans against it. "Leader Fallon and the Patrician need you to stop this realignment the Dracken are trying to cause," he says nervously.

"That part I got," I say, anger dripping from my tongue as I show him my hands.

"So, you know what you can do now."

"It was more than just my hands, wasn't it? Especially since I'm able to loop away from Tarsus and all the way into the Outer Limits. The position of Looper was selected for me on purpose, so is Hammond one of yours as well? I know Vern is since he gave me away to the Aedox, and Matron Ancilla because she noticed my trick with the Deer Horn knives in the first round and didn't tell anyone."

"No, Hammond isn't on anyone's side. He only cares about what's going to benefit him, so he's waiting to see who has the upper hand before deciding where his loyalties will be," Edom says as he leans his head back, then shoves his hands into the pockets of his robe and swings the garment around his frail frame. "Our way of life is dependent upon the Patrician. If the Dracken start a war, we'll all die."

I cross my arms over my chest and place my weight on one leg. "Explain."

"Can I pour myself a drink first?" he asks, gesturing towards a bar behind the desk I'm beside.

I nod and move out of the way as he crosses the floor. He pours himself a drink, gulps the contents, then pours another.

"We aren't the first to live here, but we may be the last."

"That's cryptic."

Anger creases his face and he slams the glass down on the top of the desk. "The Patrician are very particular about what kind of society they want. Any signs of a rebellion and they'll do anything to stop it, including killing millions of their own people."

"That's how the Dead Zone was created?" I honestly thought Frey was making that part up.

He nods, picks up the glass, and refills it. "The Outer Limits and Tarsus only exist because of the destruction done to the people who lived in the Dead Zone. Only, back then, it was called Pentras."

"What a minute… the winner of the event gets to govern Pentras. Are you saying they're reopening the Dead Zone?"

He sighs. "I don't know what the Keepers are doing, honestly. It may be their way of reigniting the past."

"And the Patrician are trying to prevent this by using me?"

"Yes."

"But why?"

"So they don't have to nuke another one of their civilizations," he says. He begins to sway the more he drinks. He sets the glass down and goes to sit on the couch. The roar from the blaze in the fireplace is causing the temperature in the room to soar to an uncomfortable level, but Edom seems to be enjoying it. I can't see his face, but his posture is showing he's relaxed.

"What about my parents?"

"They're dead. And if your next question is who killed them, well, you're looking at him."

"Why?" I ask, trying to sound angry.

"For our safety, Max," he replies. "I thought if the creators of the Dracken were dead then whole group would cease to exist, but I was wrong. You joining them only solidifies their existence." He turns to face me, laying his arm over the back of the couch. "If only you would see the danger you've put everyone in."

"It looks to me like society did it to itself."

"You may have a death wish, but I sure don't," he says before turning his back to me.

My hand balls into a fist, but it doesn't close around air. I feel the texture of the handle for my Kopis nestled against my skin. The Keepers must know I'm here and they've given me a task. I move around the couch and place myself between Edom and the fireplace.

"What about Tilda? Where did you take her?"

He sees the weapon and his eyes widen. "She's with your parents," he stutters.

I thrust the blade into his stomach. "Cil was correct… I *am* your executioner." I twist the blade to drive it in deeper.

He gurgles as blood escapes his lips. I pull out the Kopis and Edom falls to the side. I hear the front door open followed by heavy footsteps. I know it's the Aedox, so I loop back to the training room where Matron Kaniz is waiting for me when I arrive. She points towards the shelf, so I place my Kopis on it. In seconds it's gone, probably back in the weapons room or being cleaned.

"Did you learn anything useful?" Matron Kaniz asks while opening the door.

"Only that everyone who ever cared about me is dead."

"How does that make you feel?"

"Angry. The Patrician need to pay for what they've done and may do."

When we leave the room, there are only a few people still up. I go into the bedroom, take a quick shower mainly to wash the blood from my hand and cleanse my wounds, dress, and get under the covers. Sleep comes quickly.

Seventeen

The glass of our apartment window is warm from the sun. I'm amazed by the colors captured in the light that's shining on the carpeting beneath my feet. I curl my toes in it, savoring the softness. The plaza below is full of people scurrying about, their arms loaded down with packages, or dining in the outdoor café by the lobby of our building. I've always loved being able to see Pentras Tower from our home. It stands tall and majestic, but I'm not permitted to go inside. No children are allowed into the structure, which is odd to me.

My mother has been out all morning, getting provisions for the festival. Patrician Day has always been my favorite holiday. It's the one time a year that everyone is allowed out, especially children. It's not often we're permitted to leave our dwellings. If we have to travel with our parents or see a doctor, we can leave, but otherwise we must stay inside. I learn my daily lessons, like all children, from the monitor that hangs in our common room. Just like my parents did. I prefer it actually, as I'm not a fan of being around strangers. My father tells me when I come of age that I'll be going to a special academy to learn my trade and meet my mate. That's three years away, so I try to enjoy my time with my parents as much as I can.

"Sadie, come here," Father calls to me.

I leave my spot by the window and join him in the kitchen. He wants help baking the traditional breads and dishes for Patrician Day. Normally my mother handles this task, but this year my father volunteered to do it. He has his hands elbow-deep in dough when I enter the tiny space. I laugh at him, then proceed to help extricate him from the prison.

"Thanks," he says, wiping his hands on his apron. "I don't know how your mom does this every year."

"How many people are coming tonight?" I ask, rolling up my sleeves and placing an apron over my head, then tying it around my waist.

"Let me think. Probably at least twenty," he replies.

"That's double than previous years. Is there a reason?"

He grunts while trying to lift a roasting pan out from under the counter. He sets it down next to the stove, plugs it in, and begins filling the pan with various vegetables and cuts of meat before finally answering.

"Yes, but you know I can't tell you." He smiles, tosses me an onion, and has me start cutting.

My mother returns around seven that night, an hour after she was due home. All our guests have already arrived and I've been busy entertaining them while my father finishes getting the dishes ready. She apologies to everyone for her lateness, rushes to the back bedroom, and quickly changes.

My father hands me a plate and tells me to eat in my room. I don't argue, but I'm confused as to why I'm being exiled. Usually I'm permitted to stay and share the festivities with the adults, but not this year. I've always been the only child in the group my parents meet with. None have children my age. My parents had me late in life, so even though I'm only thirteen my parents are considered elders at the age of fifty-seven. I'm their only child, though sometimes I think they wish they had more.

I kiss my mother as she joins the group, then take my plate and close my bedroom door. I turn on the monitor hanging on the back wall, climb into my bed, and eat while watching the global coverage of Patrician Day. Large banquets are happening all over, and all to give thanks to our creators. My parents aren't big on government celebrations, but Patrician Day is one they always honor. I asked my father once about the Patrician, but he said to ask my mother. She told me to ask my father, so I stopped asking.

As soon as I'm done eating I put my plate on my desk, go into the bathroom to wash my face, and get ready for bed. Fireworks explode outside my window when I return, so I turn off my lights to enjoy their colors. Of course, they're also showing on the monitor, but at a five-second delay. I don't normally go to bed this early, but it's been such a hectic day that I'm exhausted. I crawl under the covers and fall asleep to the booms of celebration.

I don't feel well when I wake. It's been several years since the last time we had a happy event in our household. Today is the day my father goes on trial for the murder of my mother. I'd only been at the academy for a few months when I was called down to the headmaster's office and informed about the incident. At least that's what he called it. My father was found covered in my mother's blood, a knife in his hands. He says it was an accident, but the Aedox detained him anyway for prosecution.

I dress in my academy uniform – a white, short-sleeved, collared shirt, blue vest with matching pants, and heavy black shoes. I leave my hair down in its curls, just like my father likes. I don't care for the outfit, but I'm forced to wear it every day by the matrons regardless of where I go. I stand at the base of Pentras Tower, home to the academy, and wait in the cold air. The carriage pulls up and I climb inside next to an Aedox. I'm not permitted to sit in the actual courtroom during the proceedings, so I'll be staying in the family room down the hall to watch the event over the display.

I don't know what to believe is the truth. My father and mother loved each other deeply. I just can't accept that he would kill her. She was brutally assaulted. Butchered, really. The Aedox received an anonymous tip about the incident and that's how they found my father. I wasn't allowed to speak with him after the arrest, so this is the first time I'm being allowed near him since that day.

The carriage stops, and the Aedox escorts me up the steps into the squat building and down to the family room. I'm the only one in the room and the door is locked behind me. The monitor takes up almost the entire wall. I sit on the couch as the display flickers to life, showing a shallow man too thin for his clothes. I hardly recognize my father, but I know it's him. He sits alone in a cage in the center of the room as a magistrate sits high above him, propped up like on a pedestal.

"Mr. Faulkner," the magistrate begins, adjusting his robes, "you've been brought here to answer for the death of your wife. The Patrician

have already made their ruling as to your fate, so this is simply a final hearing."

I knew justice in Pentras was quick, but not that fast. How can the Patrician decide the verdict without having all the evidence? Are they going to question anyone as to my father's character and the love he had for his wife? Doesn't that mean anything?

"Mr. Faulkner, it's with great regret that your sentence is death for the murder of your wife," the magistrate says solemnly.

The courtroom gasps and I scream, tears running down my face. I fall to the floor and place my hand on the monitor, trying to touch my father to let him know I'm there.

"Do you have anything to say before your sentence is carried out?"

"Yes," he replies in a raspy voice. "I'd like to see my daughter."

The magistrate thinks it over before finally agreeing. The courtroom is cleared of all spectators to give us privacy. A pair of Aedox escorts me from the family room, down the hall, and through a secret door by the stairs leading to the second floor. The magistrate is the only one in the room when I enter, and the Aedox stay by the door. I approach my father with caution. I know he won't hurt me, but I can't tolerate seeing him in this state. He stands and grips the bars in front of him when I'm only a few feet away. I run towards him, taking his hand, and leaning my head against the hard metal that surrounds him.

"Sadie, I need you to listen to me," he says, his voice shaking horribly. "Don't believe anything you hear, or what anyone tells you. It's all lies. Leave the academy, get as far from here as possible. My death is just the beginning of many."

"Dad, you're talking crazy," I mumble through sobs.

"Your mother loved you. I love you. She didn't die by my hand. You have to believe me. Her death cannot be in vain."

"Stop, please," I beg.

He places his hand on the back of my head, pulling me closer, but it only drives the bars into my skin. "This is your only warning, Sadie. I'll be dead in a few minutes and then you'll have no one."

I yank my head free. His eyes are full of terror as I step back, not quite understanding his ramblings. The floor beneath the cage opens and he begins to descend, but his eyes don't leave me, not even as he dies below my feet. His screams fill my ears and the floor closes, cutting off his agony mid-scream. The Aedox escort me back to the academy where I lock myself in my room, not ever wanting to come out.

The sirens have been going for hours, but when I look outside I only see clear skies. It's been weeks since the last raid, but everyone is still on edge. I hide with my mate and our two children in the basement of an old office building. A tiny window is our only link to the outside world. It's the four of us, along with five other families, trying to hide from the marauders who have infiltrated Pentras. They began insinuating themselves into our community a few years ago, but no one noticed. I didn't do what my father asked of me. I didn't leave the academy like he wanted. I stayed, eventually met my mate and had a family, but that was so long ago it feels like another lifetime has passed since then.

My son curls up in my mate's lap, our daughter in mine. We left our home almost a month ago, leaving everything we owned behind. We had to, or we'd be dead like the others. We've heard the marauders talking about realigning society, but that's only when they get close enough to the building to be overheard. Talk of a possible realignment has been going on since before my mother died, but I really didn't pay attention to it. Now I wish I had.

"How much longer?" an older woman asks, her husband dead beside her.

"Just a few more minutes," my mate says. "They'll be gone soon."

The sirens stop but I hold my breath, waiting for them to sing out again. An hour passes, and silence still reigns. We emerge from our cover, the older woman bidding her husband a farewell before joining us on our climb to the surface. Nothing in the lobby or café has been disturbed, which means our building wasn't targeted. The power has been off for a few days, so we have to take the stairs up instead of the elevators. Our family is staying on the twentieth floor and the kids decided to make forts out of the old cubicles. Each tries to make theirs bigger than the other.

"What do you think?" my mate asks. He sits down on a broken couch in one of the former break rooms.

"I don't think we'll have much longer."

"What about the kids?"

I walk towards the window and stare at the overcast sky. Pentras Tower looms in the distance, almost like it's calling me home. "What if we can get back to the academy? We'd be safe there. It's a fortress."

"I'm sure it's been locked down," he replies. "Probably when the first wave hit, but if you want to try for it let's go."

We tell the kids we're going on a journey, which causes them excitement. They're so young they won't know what's coming when it happens. When we're down in the lobby my mate is the first to step out, making sure everything is clear, then waves us out. We each pick up one of the children and begin running for the highway down the street. We have to slow down a few blocks later, too exhausted to keep up the hurried pace. Others join us along the way, emerging from their hiding spaces even though they don't know where we're headed. Many who have gathered talk about the realignment and what it could mean if it's successful.

"Why would you want it to be successful?" my son asks a man next to us.

"So that my grandchildren can have a future."

"Wouldn't they have one already since they're alive?"

The man smiles. "That's a good point, young man. What part of Pentras did your family come from?"

"Waverly," my son responds, happy to provide the answer.

"Ah, you lived in the same area as my daughter did. Were you happy there?"

"Yes."

"That's good. You should always be happy where you live."

"But I'm not happy anymore."

"Why not?" I ask.

He changes his focus from the man to me. "We had to leave because people didn't like us anymore. And I miss my friends."

I squeeze his hand, which makes him smile.

We're a block from Pentras Tower when a bright flash behind us ignites the air. I turn to see a mushroom cloud rise to the heavens. People begin to scream and run. We grab the kids up into our arms and race towards the academy. The air is already getting hard to breathe, not from the heat but from the radiation that I know is following us. Another bomb goes off, this one to the north.

Pentras is in our sights though its doors are closed, the purple glass obscuring our view from whatever or whomever may be inside. Our kids are screaming as another bomb detonates to the south. We climb up the steps, but the doors are locked. Only a few of those who had joined us make it to the building. The glass barely rocks when we bang on it. I know there are people inside, there have to be, so why aren't they letting us in?

"Look," my daughter says, pointing to someone approaching the door.

The man stops a few feet away, hands crossed over his chest. He smiles as another bomb detonates, this one closer... it's the one that'll kill us. We scream to be let in, to be saved, but he just stands there watching as the world outside dies. The blast cloud finally hits us, knocking us down. My children die instantly and my mate a few seconds later. As I take my last breath I stare at the man, memorizing his face so I can haunt him in the afterlife, but all I can see are the dragon tattoos up and down his arms. A marauder has captured Pentras Tower.

Not a marauder, but something I haven't seen in a long time. A brief memory falls into place. One day I caught my mother hiding a marking on her shoulder from my father. This was just before I left for the academy. It was that of a dragon. I asked her about it and she made me promise never to tell my father that she was joining a force to bring down the Patrician. A force called the Dracken.

Eighteen

A scream catches in my throat and I bolt up so fast in bed that I almost hit my head on the springs of the bunk above me. My clothes and sheets are soaked in sweat, and my heart races. I strip my bed, toss the sheets into the laundry bin, add my clothes to it, and jump into the shower. I scrub my body until I'm raw, trying to erase the images of incinerated bodies from my mind. In the dream I felt like I was Sadie. That everything happening to her was happening to me. I could even feel the heat from the bombs as they fell.

After drying off, I dress and go to the common room. Matron Kaniz is sitting on the couch with Frey, but their conversation abruptly stops when I enter the room. Frey rushes to my side, puts his arm around my waist, and has me sit on a couch.

"Max, are you all right?" Matron Kaniz asks, sounding alarmed.

"It was only a dream," I say, more to myself than to them.

"What happened?" Frey asks, his arm still around me as we sit together.

I give them an abridged version of the nightmare. Keeping much of the gory details out of it, especially how the children looked when they died.

"Shit," Matron Kaniz says, standing. She walks to the elevator and descends, leaving us without any reason as to why. She returns a few minutes later with Cil beside her.

"What is *she* doing here?" I ask, jumping up from my seat, pointing at Cil.

"She's going to take a look at your wristband. It may have been compromised."

"How do you mean?" Frey asks.

"The nightmare Max experienced was Patrician-generated," Matron Kaniz replies. "They've managed to highjack her mind, probably through the wristband since they can't get into Thrace Tower any other way."

"But why?" Frey asks.

Matron Kaniz turns her attention towards me, speaking to me more than Frey. "To make her one of theirs. To show her what can happen if a realignment was to happen."

"I'll need the Progression Room in order to take a look at the device," Cil says.

We go to the room, but Cil and I are the only ones permitted inside. Matron Kaniz needs to alert the Keepers as to what's occurred and Frey will only cause problems. I take my seat on the chair while Cil gathers supplies from the cabinets.

"You're not going to fix my wristband," I say, sneering at her. "You're with them. You want me to be on the Patrician side."

"So what if I do? Did you not learn anything from the message?"

"Only that the Patrician are monsters who are happy to murder innocent people – even children – to stop only a few."

"They did what they had to do to protect society, Max. We're just trying to prevent a repeat of the past."

"I should rat you out."

Cil sits on the stool, slides over to me, and yanks my left arm towards her. "What good would that do? You think you're valuable to the Patrician? They'll kill you before you completely turn on them. Leader Fallon will make sure of that."

"I'm not afraid."

She stops working and looks up at me. "This isn't about fear, Max. This is about living. No one wants to die, but some deaths are necessary. Don't make your death one of the necessary ones." She focuses her attention back on the wristband.

The tools she's using are small and delicate. She manages to project the bracelet's inventory onto the monitor behind her, then sweeps through several layers of data before finding the embedded program. It's tied into the maps that Lok downloaded. Cil works for several minutes, trying to sever the connection. She's successful but I also lose the maps, which upsets me.

"Next time don't let someone make modifications to your wristband without you knowing exactly what they're loading onto it," she says in a condescending tone. "Stay still for a few more minutes while I run a diagnostic on the data to make sure there isn't anything else creeping around in there."

Ten minutes pass before she finally lets me leave. Nothing else is located, so Cil heads down the elevator while I join Frey in the common room. Breakfast was brought up while I was in the Progression Room, so I grab a plate of eggs, bacon, and fruit, then take a seat next to Frey. He hands me a water bottle just as the monitors flash an image of a green laurel with a silver infinity sign in the center, followed by a high-pitched siren. Hammond's face replaces the image just as the alarm stops, and he looks almost giddy.

"Hello, citizens of Tarsus," Hammond says, placing his hands behind his back.

I stop eating and hold my breath, waiting for the death of Headmaster Edom to be announced, but I'm wrong.

"Leader Fallon has declared a state of emergency due to increasing threats from Dracken leaders," Hammond announces. "Aedox will now begin patrolling areas of Tarsus randomly and arresting anyone with a Dracken symbol. Thrace Tower has also been placed on a temporary lockdown until Leader Fallon can ensure the safety of those inside." The monitors go black as people begin to discuss in subdued voices what this could mean.

"Do you think they'll raid the building?" one girl asks.

"If they do, what'll happen to those of us with the tattoo?" someone else responds, his voice cracking with nervousness.

Matron Kaniz enters the room and everyone falls silent. "I need everyone to remain calm," she says, making a calming gesture. "The Keepers know full well about Leader Fallon's plans and have taken every precaution to prevent anyone from entering Thrace Tower. The *Litarian Battles* is set to continue in two hours, beginning with Hammond's announcement as to the format for the second round." She leaves, but everyone is still on the verge of panicking.

I take my empty plate, place it on the counter, and go to the bedroom. I slide under the covers, pulling them over my head, and try to take a nap since I'm still extremely tired. I get very little sleep, especially with everyone talking loudly about Hammond's broadcast. I could just loop out of the room, but now with additional security perhaps I'm limited in where I can go. Addie calls from the doorway that it's almost time. Frey and Rem are arguing when Addie and I enter the common room, but they stop upon seeing us. Frey takes my hand and guides me to the back couch while Rem moves towards the front. Addie sits next to us as Matron Kaniz steps forward and stands next to the monitor closest to the far wall.

"The Keepers want to keep the *Litarian Battles* moving, so those who'll be moving to the second round will be removed immediately from the room and taken to the selection floor," she says. "There's been a slight change in how this is all going to go since there'll be thirty-two participants in this round. I'll show you the names of those moving to the second round, and Hammond will meet you all once you're seated."

Matron Kaniz touches one of the monitors, turning it on. The names and units of the players are listed in four columns. Eight players from each unit. I don't have to look to know my name is up there. Addie screams when she sees her name, but it's not from joy. I guess she thought she was pointed high enough to make it all the way to the third round.

Four Aedox enter the room and Matron Kaniz motions for us to join them. Frey squeezes my hand before letting me go. I take Addie's arm to help her walk down the hallway and into the elevator. Tears are streaming down her face as we descend. She's the only one of the eight of us crying. She may talk a big game, but when it comes down to it she's as terrified as the rest of us. When we reach our floor, we bypass the carousel of clothes and go right for the chairs that'll take us to the selection floor. Addie forgoes her usual seat for one next to mine. When we reach the top, Hammond isn't anywhere in sight. Looking at the other players, I notice Garrett and Brink have both been selected. As the lights dim Addie reaches for my arm, grasping it tightly. The displays in the center of the room come on, showing Hammond dressed in the same suit from the earlier broadcast. This time, though, he's not giddy. His face is creased, quite deeply.

"Welcome, children," he says, his voice somber. "For round two you'll be placed into teams of four, one person from each unit. Your teams have been assigned a color, which has already been added to your uniforms. This will help the Keepers know where each unit is on the battle floor at all times. Only an intact team will advance. If anyone from your team is killed or deemed irretrievable, the remaining members of the team will be immediately terminated. Good luck."

Our chairs begin their descent. Addie lets go of me, but her face is full of terror. Hammond failed to mention how many teams are allowed to win, or even how long the round is going to take. I wonder how the Keepers are going to dispose of incomplete teams. However they do it, it won't be painless. And I'm sure our units will be watching like the last time.

When we've reached the bottom, Addie practically drapes herself over me as we make our way to the common room. All the matrons are there when we enter, calling us over to various parts of the room. Matron Kaniz has a worried expression on her face which surprises me as she's usually so confident.

"Now, as you have no doubt realized, none of you will be on the same team," Matron Kaniz says once we've assembled. "I'm not sure what type of landscape the Keepers have selected, but don't trust anyone. Not even members of your unit. Once you hit that floor, you're each other's enemy."

"How many teams are permitted to win?" a young man next to me asks.

"I don't know," Matron Kaniz answers awkwardly. "Your uniforms are waiting for you in the designated changing rooms. Your unit will be watching, so do them proud." She smiles, but you can tell it's forced, then leaves.

As we're queuing up to get in to change, the other matrons leave. Brink sidles up close to me until we're practically hip to hip. I roll my eyes and try to ignore him. Addie strikes up a conversation with Garrett, which bothers me. I'm not sure why it does, but something about her body language towards him makes me mad. The line moves quickly, and when it's my turn I take longer than I should. I remove my uniform from its storage and notice two green stripes have been added around the torso.

As I change I try to avoid the mirror as much as possible. I don't want to be reminded of what my body has already been through.

Once I'm dressed I join the others in the common room, paying particular attention to the colors everyone has been designated. My stomach drops when I see that Brink's uniform also has green stripes. Garrett is busy talking to a young woman wearing a uniform with red stripes when he sees me, and he excuses himself to come talk to me.

"At least I have one friend on my team," he says to me, showing off the green stripes around the edges of his short sleeves.

"I don't know if I'd go so far to say we're friends."

"What's the matter with you?"

"Nothing," I say. "I just want to get this over with."

I start to walk away from him, but he grabs my arm and halts my progress.

"Talk to me," he says quietly.

"I'm not who you think I am."

He pushes the hair off my shoulder, revealing a portion of the dragon tattoo. "Is it because of that?" he asks, pointing to it.

"It's more than that."

"Then tell me, Max."

I take a deep sigh. It's not that I don't trust Garrett, I do. In fact, I trust him more than Frey. I just don't know how much to tell him.

"How much do you know about what happened in the Dead Zone?"

"That's an odd question," he responds, taken aback. He seems to ponder the inquiry before responding after a few minutes of silence. "Not much. Just that it's been like that for a long time. Nothing can live there because it's so toxic."

"What about Pentras Tower?"

"You mean the purplish building that isn't damaged?"

I nod.

"Only that it's out of place in all that destruction. Why?"

Chimes sound over our heads and everyone begins to assemble into their teams.

"Never mind. Just forget I asked."

Brink and a Nius player by the name of Van join us. The monitors spring to life, Hammond's face plastered in the center.

"In just a few moments the first set of teams will enter the assigned tunnels," he says. "Since there are eight teams there'll be a delay of five minutes between each set. Your team color will appear on the screen above your assigned door. See you all on the other side."

The first four teams are called. Addie is a part of the team with gold stripes, which is among the initial groups entering the battle floor. The doors open, and they slowly go into the tunnels. As the doors close the monitors turn back on, showing each group heading to the entrance for the battle floor. The screens change to music videos when the teams get close to exiting, obstructing our view of what the world in there might look like. The display above each door changes to a clock counting down the five minutes until the rest of us go. I sit on one of the couches, my eyes glued to the timers, my heart racing and sweat running down my face and back.

"Why did you ask me about the Dead Zone?" Garrett asks, sitting next to me. "Do you think that's where they're sending us?"

"No," I reply. "Something tells me this round is going to be a lot more dangerous."

"In what way?"

"If I had the answer, Garrett, I would tell you," I practically snap.

Four minutes to go.

"Do you still have the maps on your wristband?" he asks.

"No, and please do thank Lok for me when you see him again. It was so much fun having the Patrician broadcast a nightmare into my mind while I was sleeping."

"What are you talking about? How could that be possible?"

I tell him about the hidden program and what the Patrician had me experience.

Two minutes to go.

"Did you join the Dracken before or after that?" he asks.

"What does that have to do with anything!" I shout. "Does it really matter? The Patrician murdered millions of innocent people, their own people I might add, and for what? Just because they couldn't handle a few radicals doesn't mean they should've annihilated a whole civilization."

"Then the Patrician showed you the wrong information, Max," he says rather calmly. "They should've displayed what the Dracken did to bring that kind of destruction on."

"I don't believe this." I stand since I can't tolerate sitting next to him any longer. "You actually think this is all okay? If we weren't on the same team, I would kill you the second we hit the battle floor."

He stands, folding his thick arms across his chest. "The feeling is mutual," he says angrily.

One minute to go.

"Will you two stop having a lover's quarrel and get ready?" Van yells at us.

I step past Garrett and cross over to Van, Brink joining us a few seconds later, but Garrett doesn't move from his spot. When the timer reaches zero, the displays show the remaining team colors, and the doors open. The four us enter, Van leading and Garrett at the rear. Our weapons are stationed in the center of the tunnel instead of at the end, which immediately raises a red flag for me. We all find this odd and extremely unsettling. I notice that Van's weapons are all in a sack that he slings over his shoulder, so I give him a quizzical look.

"Detonators," he says as he opens the bag and removes one of the devices. It's the size of an apple, round, metallic, and with lights along the top and around the button. "They're easier to manage than the other types of explosives."

Garrett places his Dead Mark bow around his arm, flipping it towards his back next to his quiver loaded with black-shafted arrows. Brink places his Deer Horn knives into a pouch secured to the side of his pants. My

Kopis and sheath hang ready on my hip as we begin heading towards the door.

When we're only a few feet away the lights in the tunnel go out, throwing us into complete darkness. A woman's scream pierces the quiet; we can't tell where the sound is coming from as it appears to be all around us. The tunnel shakes then violently jerks to the right. We hit the floor for protection more than from the movement. Metal grinding against metal takes the place of the woman's shrieks and my feet begin to slip as the tunnel tilts forward. There isn't anything to grab on to in order to prevent our falling, so I remove my Kopis and drive it into the wall. Garrett and Van slide towards an opening where the door is supposed to be and fall through. Brink grabs my waist as he slips past, pulling me and my weapon, along with him. The wall disappears and the two of us fall into darkness.

Nineteen

My lungs fill with water when I hit the bottom. The others kick and splash around me as I continue to sink. I feel someone grab my collar and pull me up, dragging me onto a muddy bank. I forcefully cough up the water, my head pounding with every inhalation. Garrett lets me go before collapsing to the ground while Brink and Van each rest against a tree on either side of me.

"What… the hell… was that?" Brink asks, trying to catch his breath.

I pull myself up onto my knees, still coughing. Van pats me on the back trying to help free the rest of the water from my body. I plop down next to him, lean my head back, and stare up into a star-filled night sky.

"Where are we?" Van asks, pushing his soaked blond tresses back from his eyes. He's tall like Garrett, but thinner.

"This definitely *isn't* the Dead Zone," I comment.

"Do we just sit here until morning, if there is a morning, or do we try to figure out where we need to go?" Garrett asks.

"I say we stay here," Brink says. "If the other teams are around they'll be just as disoriented as we are."

"Except for the four who have a five-minute head start," I add.

"Well, since we can't see anything I say we wait until at least daylight begins to show," Van says. "No need to head out, only to be killed seconds later because of some kind of trap we couldn't see."

He has a point, so we all agree not to move until first light. I hate waiting unprepared, so I go rooting around the water for my Kopis which I dropped during the fall. I'm lucky enough to find it a few minutes later, buried in the mud an inch below the surface. I clean it off in the water before retaking my seat next to Van.

"Max," Brink says, tapping his foot against mine. "Is it true? Are you a Dracken?"

"Yes, she is," Garrett answers for me.

"Let me see it," Brink says, grinning.

"Fuck off, Brink," I say. I lean my head back and close my eyes, still exhausted.

"Van, where do you stand?" I hear Brink ask.

"Does it matter?" Van responds.

"Yes, it does," Garrett replies.

I open my eyes and watch Van's expression change from contemplative to serene.

"I stand with no one but myself," he says cordially. "I mean, in the end only one person is going to walk away from the final event. It'll be up to that person to decide which side wins this realignment."

I can see an argument forming in Garrett's head, but he bites his lip to keep his mouth closed. I shut my eyes again and feel myself drift off.

"Max." I hear my name echoing around me. "Max."

When I open my eyes, I notice it's still dark and the others have fallen asleep.

"Max."

This time my name washes over the water, stopping at the banks as light glows in the distance. I stand, hold my weapon by my side, and head to the bank. The light sways slightly as if being carried, then stops. My eyes have to adjust in order to make out the figure on the other side. The woman is my height with long black hair that's streaked with gray. Her face bears a resemblance to mine, but that can't be possible.

"Hello, Max," the woman says, holding the light up by her shoulder so I can get a better look.

"Mom?"

She nods.

"This isn't possible," I mumble.

"You've grown quite a bit since the last time I saw you," she says sadly.

I close my eyes, count to five and open them again, but the woman is still there.

"It's so good to see you," she says.

"You're not real."

"Why would you say something like that?"

"My mother's dead."

"As you can see, I'm not," she says, sweeping her arms out to the side, which takes the light off her face for a brief moment, concealing it in darkness.

"My mother would've called me by my real name and not the one Leader Fallon gave me."

She hesitates in answering. "Why can't you believe that it's me?"

I glare at her. "Cross the water," I instruct.

The woman vanishes and I'm thrust into darkness, confused by the encounter. What are the Keepers trying to test? Why show me my mother, a woman I don't remember? An Aedox would've been much more preferable. I step back and bump into someone. As I turn around my nightmare comes true. An Aedox grabs me by the throat and begins choking me. I can't call out, as my windpipe is closed off. I try to raise my Kopis but my arms are stuck to my sides, bound by an invisible rope.

This isn't real. None of this is real.

My vision begins to darken and my hearing fades. I'm on the verge of passing out when an arrow pierces the Aedox's heart; I drop to the ground when he vanishes. Garrett is beside me checking my throat, which is red and a little swollen. He wakes Brink and Van, having them do a quick sweep of the area around us, but the only things here are bushes, trees, and mud.

"What happened?" Brink asks, kneeling next to me since I'm still having trouble getting air into my lungs.

"An Aedox, but how did he get in here?" Garrett asks.

"Illusions," I whisper, which is followed by a coughing fit.

"That Aedox looked plenty real to me, Max. He almost killed you," Garrett says.

I crawl back over to my spot under the tree and lie down. My head is pounding and my eyes won't focus as another scream rips through the night. Garrett readies his bow, swinging it around to follow the motion of the sound. It finally stops, but Garrett doesn't put his weapon down.

"What are the Keepers up to?" Van asks.

Brink removes his knives and throws one in the direction of Garrett, nicking his arm. Garrett starts yelling at Brink until the Deer Horn Knife hits its intended target. Van trudges through the water, grabs the person who's fallen into the murk, and drags her back with him.

Brink's aim was exceptionally good: the knife is embedded deep into the girl's chest. Her face is covered in mud, so I inch forward and roll her over after Van lets her go. She looks to be a player from the team with navy-blue stripes, but I'm not sure. I begin to wipe the mud from her face, but when I'm halfway done Van shoves me to the ground, picks up the girl in his arms, and begins to yell.

"What the fuck did you do, Brink?" he screams.

"I saw movement and knew I had to protect the group," Brink responds, perplexed by Van's behavior.

"She's not the enemy… none of them are," Van cries. He presses the woman's face to his shoulder.

"Who is she, Van?" Garrett asks.

"My sister."

"That's not possible," Garrett says. He walks over to Van and sits down next to him. "Siblings aren't allowed to be in the game at the same time."

"She wasn't in the game. She's been living in Icarian for the last year," he says through his sobs. "How did she get here?"

I expect her body to vanish like the other two, but it doesn't. As Van continues to cradle her I spot a mark on her wrist just above her wristband, but it looks too dark to be mud. I bend down and wipe away the area, revealing a laurel with an infinity sign in the center.

"Look," I say, lifting her limp arm so everyone can see the mark.

"What's that?" Brink asks.

I wait for someone to answer, but they all remain silent. "It's the Patrician symbol," I tell them.

"She must've gotten it when she moved to Icarian," Van says.

After several minutes of coaxing Van, Garrett and Brink take the body and place it several yards away, hiding it under a bush since we don't know what else to do with it at the moment. Brink discreetly removes his knife from her chest while Van isn't looking. They return a few minutes later, but sit some distance away from Van. I choose to sit next to him so he's not alone.

"How did she get here?" he quietly repeats to himself.

"When was the last time you saw her?" I ask.

"The day she packed up and was sent to Icarian."

"They don't send you right from the tower?" I ask, confused.

He shakes his head. "The winner is given a chance to say goodbye to his or her family and take a few belongings to Icarian," he replies.

"How does someone get to Icarian?" Brink asks.

Van and I stare at him.

"I don't mean by way of the *Litarian Battles*, but by what kind of transportation is provided. Where is Icarian located in conjunction to Tarsus?"

"No one knows," Van says, wiping his eyes. "A carriage did come to pick her up, but she let it slip that the carriage was only the first leg of the journey. I don't think she knew of the other ways."

We fall silent while Van tries to refocus on where we are. I feel as if we're to stay in perpetual darkness for this entire round, which will make seeing the other teams difficult. The only light is that of the moon, which has now joined us. I feel myself dozing off again, when the sky to my right ignites from a vast explosion. We all stand as a second round goes off, this one followed by shouts as tree branches break from an approaching stampede. Van removes a detonator from his pack while the rest of us hold our weapons in front of us.

An arrow strikes Garrett in the shoulder. He tries to fire back but is hit again, this time in the lower arm. I move in front of him to protect him from another attack while Brink tends to his injuries. He rips off the bottom of his shirt and wraps it around Garrett's wounds after removing the arrows. Van activates the detonator, throws it, and we duck seconds before it goes off. The explosion doesn't appear to have harmed anyone, it simply propels them forward at a much faster rate. A group of four contestants jumps out at us and I'm tackled to the ground by the only woman in the group. She slashes her weapon at me, but I manage to counter with mine.

"Come on, Max, die with dignity," the woman says.

I put my feet into her stomach and shove her off. She lands at Brink's feet, but he's too busy fighting off his attacker to be of any help. I step backwards going towards the water, and yell at the others to follow. If the group is an illusion they won't come into the water. The four of us stop when the water is up to our thighs, leaving the other group on the bank. The fire in the night illuminates their clothing, revealing player uniforms with green stripes, but not their faces.

"Who are you?" I shout.

"We're you, Max," the woman answers. She sounds like me, yet doesn't. "We're all of you."

Their faces finally come into focus and gasps escape us. The woman is me, including the tattoo. I look between our team and the other one, but it's hard to tell who's who. I can only tell Brink and Garrett apart from their counterparts because of the ripped shirt and bandages.

Why would the Keepers do this to us? What's the point of fighting ourselves?

"They're not real," Van says, trembling beside me.

"Aren't we?" Van's twin says, then they all step into the water.

Garrett fires an arrow at his twin, but it sails through him. Brink charges his twin, but the Deer Horn knife is also useless and he has to quickly retreat to his spot.

"If we can't hurt them with our weapons –" Garrett begins.

"– how do we kill them?" I say, finishing his thought.

"Also, how did Garrett get hit with the arrows if he's the one shooting them?" Brink asks, pointing to Garrett's twin.

I have a feeling I know how, but revealing it could cause problems for me.

"Everyone take a different opponent – someone not you – and don't let them touch your weapons," I say.

After switching our positions, we advance. I take on Brink's twin, Van attacks Garrett's, Brink attacks Van's, and Garrett attacks mine. Since my shield is designed to repel the Deer Horn Knife, taking on Brink's doppelganger is the obvious choice. I manage to push him back onto the bank before he produces his shield, which is made to defend against the Kopis. I loop behind him and ram my blade into his back. He lets out a scream and vanishes, or so I think. Within seconds, two more have taken the one's place.

"Don't kill them," I yell, but Van doesn't hear me and kills Garrett's twin, which is instantly replaced by two new ones.

"Shit," Van says as he battles both new opponents.

Van doesn't have a conventional weapon like the three of us, so he has to use whatever he can get his hands on, which isn't much. He winds up taking an arrow to the side, so I go to protect him from the four players now advancing on us.

"What kind of weapon does your shield protect you from?" I ask Garrett.

"Explosives," he says between grunts of exertion.

If Brink's works to protect him against a Kopis and Garrett's to protect against an explosion, what would happen if Van threw an explosive at Brink's twin and I slashed Garrett's?

I grab Van by the hand and loop him out of the water and into one of the trees.

"Stay here, and when I give you a signal throw one of your bombs at Brink."

"Wait, you want me to do what?"

"Toss the bomb at Brink. The *real* Brink, I'll take care of the rest."

I loop back to the water and try to locate Brink amongst the others. I find him trying to prevent Van's twin from releasing an explosive that looks to be armed.

God, I hope I get this right. Nothing like trying something new in the heat of the moment.

I charge at Brink's clones, grab them by the arms and loop, but forward in time. I land us where I think Brink and Van's clone will be, and in a matter of seconds they come into focus just as the real Van sees us appear. Brink kills Van's clone just as I nod. The real Van launches his explosive and I take the real Brink by the hand and loop just before the explosives hits. The explosion is massive and kills the Brink clones. I hold my breath while I set us down on the bank. Brink's clones don't reappear, however Van's have now doubled. Garrett's clones begin to attack the two of us, so I yell at Van to stay in the tree since he doesn't have any combat weapons like the rest of us. He doesn't argue.

Garrett's clones are as strong as the original, so Brink and I struggle to stay on our feet. As we fight along the shore, the ground becomes muddier and more slippery. One of the clones grabs me by the throat and hurls me into the water, holding me under. I struggle as water and mud fill my lungs, so I swing around and ram my Kopis through the clone's torso. He falls into the water and disappears. I cough as I reach the surface, noticing the clone doesn't regenerate.

So, they can only be killed by a weapon they don't have a shield for or are carrying.

The two clones of Van have split off, one going after Garrett and the other after Brink. I choose to help Brink since Garrett's shield can defend against Van's weapon.

"Van!" I shout up to him. "What does your shield protect you from?"

"Arrows!"

I slash Van's clone across the back just as he's arming a bomb. He tosses the device at Brink's feet just before he falls to the ground. I can't get to Brink, so I yell. He sees the device and runs, making it a good distance away before the device explodes. I stab Van's clone in the chest and he disappears before I go after the last Van clone, who's not daring to arm his weapon since he knows Garrett's shield will protect him from them. What he *is* doing is wrestling Garrett to the ground so my twin can kill him. My Kopis slams into my twin's just as she's about to come down on Garrett.

"You do know this is useless, Max," my clone says to me. "You're all going to die just like the others."

Brink shrieks as Garrett's clone fires an arrow into his back. He falls to the ground and lies motionless.

"One down, three to go," my clone says, smiling.

"I know something about all of you," I say mockingly.

"And what's that?"

Garrett's clone moves over to our group, his arrow ready to fly at me.

"You can hold each other's weapons."

My clone smiles. "I knew you were smart, Max."

I grab her free arm and swing her around so she's now between Garrett's clone and myself. "But there's something you don't know about me."

"And what's that, Maxy?" she asks.

"So can I."

I shove her in the direction of Garrett's clone, reach for the real Garrett's weapon, which is at his feet, and fire an arrow as quickly as I can into my clone. I then fire another one towards Garrett's clone to distract him, drop the bow and arrow, and drive my Kopis into Van's remaining clone. I then slice up Garrett's clone.

I sheathe my weapon and run over to Brink to remove the arrow. Luckily it missed his spine, but I don't know what else it may have damaged internally. Van drops from the tree as Garrett gets to his feet. I apply pressure to Brink's wound while Van gives me a piece of his uniform to help stem the bleeding.

"How the hell did you do that?" Van asks.

"Not now," I say.

"Do you think that was it? That it's over?" Garrett asks.

"I don't know, but if I don't get this bleeding under control we're all dead," I say.

It takes all of use to tend to Brink's wound and we finally get the bleeding stopped, which helps bring Brink back around.

"What happened?" he asks, his face half covered in mud.

"Nothing," I answer. "You just got nicked by an arrow. You'll be fine." I take his knives from his hands and secure them in their pouch.

He narrows his eyes at me. "Liar."

An alarm pierces the darkness. It's so harsh that we have to cover our ears to make sure they don't rupture. We look around to see where it could possibly be coming from, but there isn't one general direction since it's pulsating all around us. The trees, mud, and water begin to flicker as if losing power, then finally vanish, and the four of us find ourselves on the gray tiles of the battle floor. The building shakes and dust falls from the ceiling. After another rumble the walls begin to crack.

"Do you think this is the next part?" Brink shouts to be heard over the noise.

Something tells me no.

The alarm finally shuts off as the lights begin to fade. The entrance to the battle floor bursts open, Matron Kaniz flying in our direction, blood and ash covering much of her left side as a group of Aedox pursues her.

Twenty

"Max, get them out of here!" she screams.

"Where are the others?!" I shout back.

"Don't worry about that. Take your group someplace safe," she says, pointing to everyone around me.

Matron Kaniz is struck with a bullet from behind, killing her instantly.

I take Garrett and Van by the hand while Brink takes Van's other hand, and I loop us out of Thrace Tower. The landing is rough since I project us to a location I've never actually been in before. It's a gamble, but I hope it's the right choice.

"Where are we?" Garrett asks, letting go of my hand. He cautiously steps towards a pair of thick glass doors tinted purple.

"Pentras Tower," I respond, quickly scanning the room.

"You brought us to the Dead Zone?" Brink practically screams at me, but stops when his body seizes with pain. He takes several deep breaths before continuing. "You were supposed to take us someplace safe, not kill us."

"We'll be fine as long as we stay inside," I reply. "Van, go see if you can find something to help Brink's wound."

Van sets his bag on the floor and heads off down the corridor at the back of the lobby.

Dust should be thick over all the furnishings but there isn't any trace of it, which disturbs me. Garrett helps Brink to his feet and sets him down on one of the couches that circles the large lobby. Along the back wall on either side of the corridor are monitors displaying four distinctive maps, which detail the Dead Zone, Tarsus, the Outer Limits, and someplace else.

Icarian maybe?

Van returns a few minutes later with a medical kit. He sits down next to Brink, cleans his wound, and begins sewing him up.

"Where did you find that?" Garrett asks.

"There's a room full of medical supplies down there and to the left," Van says, pointing down the corridor he just came from. "I was about to give up searching when I found it."

Garrett walks around the lobby, which is painted a light-blue, and filled with flourishing plants and a functioning waterfall that stretches up to the third floor, antiques, and two main desks by the monitors.

"What is this place?" he asks from the other side of the room.

"Your sanctuary," a voice booms over our heads from hidden speakers. "Max, you've done well. It was very smart of you to bring them here."

"Who are you?" I ask, unsheathing my weapon for protection.

"We're the Keepers," a number of voices respond.

"What's happened?" Brink asks, grunting slightly from the pain.

"War has begun. We weren't able to start the realignment in time," the group replies.

"Where are the others?" I ask, still holding my weapon.

"We're able to track only those who survived Thrace Tower," they answer. "We've moved them to other safe locations throughout the Dead Zone, but not all made it out alive."

"The Dead Zone isn't safe!" Garrett says loudly. "It's full of toxins from when you bombed the hell out of it."

"Untrue!" the voices cry out as just one again. "We've spent many years cleaning the air and the ground. The Patrician bombed the people when they began to revolt, and we stood by helplessly as millions perished."

"Lies, all lies," Garrett says.

"Don't provoke us, Garrett. Remember you're still connected to Thrace Tower, and we can return you there at our discretion."

He looks down at his wristband and remains quiet.

"How do we stop this?" I ask.

"Find the others and bring them back to Pentras Tower," the multiple voices respond. "But be careful of the drones. They're controlled by the Patrician, and if they catch you, they'll kill you."

"Why can't you just loop the others here like you did when you moved them from Thrace Tower?" Van asks.

"Better yet," I begin, "why not bring them here to begin with?"

"We had to act fast, as many of our children were dying. We felt it was better to spread them out, so the Patrician can't locate all of you at once."

"That still doesn't answer Van's question," Garrett says.

"Pentras Tower can only be accessed by a modified Looper. Since Max was altered by the Patrician she can loop in and out of the structure whenever she wishes, as well as anyone connected to her. We, however, can't physically penetrate the building's safety protocols. We can gain access to the video and audio portion, but even that is minimal."

"Huh, you *are* liars," Garrett says, almost laughing. "You can't send me back to Thrace Tower any more than you can transport yourselves into this building."

I glare at him and he quiets down.

"So, it wasn't a coincidence that you placed me in that unit," I say. "You knew what the Patrician had done to me before I even got there."

"Yes, but we didn't know to what extent your alterations had gone until you took Garrett's weapon."

"Who told you?" I ask.

"Tilda," they reply with sadness. "It unfortunately led to her death."

"And Vernon?" I ask. "He told the Aedox where I was hiding, so he's with the Patrician, isn't he?"

"Yes."

"What was the final event going to really be about?" Van asks, packing up the medical kit.

"We needed a leader for our army, as we knew war was imminent, and we wanted someone in place before the realignment started.

However, we were too slow. Pentras isn't a new utopia, but a new beginning."

The speakers cut out, leaving nothing but silence around us.

I need to think. Who could've made it out? The Keepers would've tried to save everyone, but the Patrician would've only saved those loyal to them. So, who do I look for first, and do I even bother trying to retrieve a Patrician loyalist since they're more than likely the ones responsible for the violence in Thrace Tower?

I sheathe my weapon, notice a door with the word 'Stairwell' stenciled across it and go through the door, then up two stairs at a time. I don't know where I'm going, I just know I need to get higher in the building to get some perspective.

"Max, wait," Garrett calls.

But I don't stop until I reach the twentieth floor, where I have to catch my breath. I don't want to loop inside the building since I've never seen any of the floors and don't know their layout. I knew the lobby from the nightmare, so that's the only reason I got us in here safely.

"Where are you going?" Garrett asks when he catches up.

"The top floor, since it's the only way to see if we can locate the others."

"You're not serious," he says as he takes in deep breaths. "They're more than likely dead; killed by whatever is outside these walls."

"I don't believe that," I say, and begin climbing again with Garrett at my heels.

"You're going to get yourself killed, Max. Then everything the Patrician did to you will have been for nothing."

I stop and turn around. "Don't you dare defend their actions," I say angrily. "They mutilated me."

"And the Keepers are using it to their benefit," he counters. "All right, how about we don't trust either of them – at least until we can figure things out?"

"We may all be dead by then."

I start climbing again and don't stop until we reach the fiftieth floor. The heavy metal door is jammed, and it takes both of us to force it open. The air is stale, but everything is dust-free. The entire top floor is a large open space with couches, tables, televisions that aren't currently functioning, and lots of windows that stretch from floor to ceiling. Off to the right of the stairwell is a large kitchen including stoves, ovens, and refrigerators. Two massive pantries line the wall by the stairwell door.

Lightning flashes in the distance as a storm rolls in, but I'm not sure how this is possible since the Dead Zone is completely encapsulated. We go over to the far wall and watch the light show, but we don't hear any thunder. The building is so protected from the outside that not even sound will penetrate.

Why build a structure like this? Unless you knew you were going to need it. So, was the bombing of the original city of Pentras really premeditated murder? Were the Dracken at that time trying to prevent it? Why would the Patrician build a society, only to destroy it later? Is that why the Dracken are forming again? To stop a second wave of merciless destruction?

"Max, you all right?" Garret asks, taking my elbow.

I hadn't realized I was swaying. He takes me over to a nearby couch and helps me sit down, then goes over to one of the refrigerators and opens it. We're both surprised that it's still functioning. Inside are perfectly preserved fruits, vegetables, meats, and drinks, and they all look to have been recently stocked. Garret takes a bottle of water and gives it to me, then gets one for himself before sitting next to me.

"Who do you think is out there?" he asks, taking a sip.

"I'm not sure," I reply. "But we have to go find them."

Lightning flashes brightly, and rain pelts the windows.

"What do you think this building was used for?" Garrett asks after several minutes of silence.

"It was an academy of some sort, or at least that's what the Patrician showed me."

"Do you believe the last part? That the Dracken were the ones safely secured in the building?"

"No," I say as a finish my water.

Flames shoot up into the sky from several miles away and a couple of drones that I hadn't noticed fly in that direction. Garrett and I go up to the windows to get a better look, but with the rain coming down in torrents it's almost impossible to see. Another explosion ignites the same area, then the rain falls harder, followed by another explosion. I get so close to the glass that my face is almost pressed against it. The rain is now coming down in sheets. Several more balls of fire light up the sky, all still from the same location. As the flames flicker down, the rain tapers off and stops.

"We need to talk to Van," I say, dropping my empty bottle and heading back to the stairwell.

Going down is a lot easier than going up, but it's not something I want to do continuously. When we reach the lobby we find Van and Brink lying on separate couches, their eyes closed, snoring.

"Hey," I say to Van, tapping him on the shoulder.

He jolts awake, looks confused for a few seconds, and then focuses his eyes on me.

"For Nius, what types of options were you given for explosives?" I ask.

"Um, let me think," he says as he rubs the sleep from his eyes. "The bombs, grenades, land mines, and propellants shot from a small pistol. There are a few others, but I can't remember what they were called."

"Could any of them have been ignited by water?"

He scrunches up his face before replying. "Yeah, a magnesium bomb," he says. "They're small, maybe the size of your palm. Not many people picked them since you need water to set them off, but a few did."

"Who, exactly?"

"What are you getting at, Max?" Garrett asks, but I wave him off so Van can answer.

"Only one person comes to mind. Lil," he says. "I think she came from the Outer Limits like you. She always made sure she had a full bottle of water or two before hitting the selection floor."

"The explosions we saw," Garrett says, starting to put some of the pieces together. "That's why the Patrician made it rain, so they could flush her out and whoever she's with. They have to know exactly what types of weapons we have and how we use them."

"Was she a Dracken?" Brink asks, waking up.

"Yes, she was," Van replies.

"So, what do we do?" Brink asks, searching from one face to another.

"Get to the others before the Patrician do," I respond.

"But we don't know the layout of the Dead Zone, or where they all could be hiding," Van says.

"Max has a map," Garrett blurts out.

I turn to look at him. "Not anymore, remember?" I say heatedly. "I told you that when Lok downloaded the maps onto my wristband he added an extra program, allowing the Patrician to hack my mind and implant that nightmare. When Matron Kaniz had the program removed, the maps went with it."

Garrett's mouth tightens up, and he begins to shift his weight from one foot to the other. He looks both antsy and uncomfortable, but I'm not sure why.

I step closer to him, my hand resting on the handle of my Kopis. "Did you know that he was going to do that?" I ask.

Sweat breaks out on his forehead. "Not exactly."

"Then what, exactly?" Brink asks.

"I didn't know what the program would do," Garrett blurts out. "I thought it would just help turn Max against the Dracken."

"I should kill you," I say, gritting my teeth.

"Then why don't you?" Garrett asks, challenging me.

"Because we need as many people as possible to make sure this realignment happens," I respond.

"I thought we weren't going to take sides, Max," Garrett angrily responds.

"I'm not taking anyone's side… at the moment," I snap as I walk over to the double doors. I begin to wonder where everyone could be. "So, who's going with me?" I ask, keeping my back to all of them.

"I'll go," Brink says.

"No," I say, turning towards him. "You're injured."

"I'll go," Van says, standing and slinging his bag over his shoulder.

I look over at Garrett, but I don't want him to come with us. I think he senses it since he removes his bow and quiver from his shoulder, handing them to me.

"You'll need these," he says.

I take them without hesitation and secure them across my shoulder. Van grabs my hand and I loop us out of the building, landing under an overpass a few blocks away. I want to keep low and hidden so the drones don't spot us, so we keep to the side of the road as we move further away from the tower. I wish I knew how to locate the others, so I decide to start where the explosions erupted. I take Van's hand and loop us mile by mile along the road until we come upon the burning remains of structures… and players.

There isn't much left of Lil, but I can tell it was her. I don't recognize anyone else amidst the wreckage, but Van does.

"They're mainly from Nius," he says, moving from one body to another. "But I don't see everyone, so maybe they didn't all get sent at the same time."

I check for any useable explosives, but they've all been detonated. I loop us a mile to the southeast and onto the plaza from round one. Everything looks just like it did on the battle floor, right down to the Patrician symbol on the tiles of the pool.

"Who do you think she was?" Van asks, pointing to the fallen statute.

"She was a very powerful god," someone says behind me.

I pull out an arrow and secure it to Garrett's bow, turning around to get a better look at the intruder. It's Rem, but I still don't lower my weapon.

"How do you know that?" I ask, narrowing my eyes.

"We learned about the various rulers of this world in the academy," she says. "Not all were great, but those who made their mark were rewarded. Just like I will be when this is all over." Rem removes her weapon from its sheath. "What do you plan on doing with that, Max? Shooting me?"

"You know I can."

Rem starts to pace around us, slowly, so I match her steps with mine.

"Where's the rest of the unit?" I ask.

"Around," she answers, tossing her sword between her hands.

"The Patrician moved you from Thrace Tower, not the Keepers," I state.

"What makes you think that?" Van asks.

"Because they knew I would come here," I answer. "The markings in the pool are the Patrician symbol. Your sister had the same marking, Van, and I'm sure Rem does as well. This is also where I won the first round, so why wouldn't I return to someplace I'm familiar with?"

"You are perceptive, Max," Rem says with a crooked smile. "The Patrician were wise in selecting you." She rolls up her long sleeve, exposing her bicep. The Patrician symbol is large and colorful against her pale skin. "But what makes you think the Keepers didn't send me here? After all, they set up the *Litarian Battles*."

"They didn't, because they already knew where I would go first," I say. "It's where Brink and Garrett are now." I glance at Van, hoping he'll keep his mouth shut about the exact location in case the Patrician are watching and listening, which I'm sure they are.

He removes a bomb from his bag and caresses the button that arms it. "What do you want to do, Max?" he asks, glaring at Rem.

"Tell me about the statue," I say to Rem.

"She was a warrior," she replies. "A true Patrician leader when there was more to this world than just the city of Pentras. She was sacrificed for the greater good."

"What was here before?" I ask.

"Many things, but all too dangerous to survive," she responds. Her eyes narrow and I can see bloodlust in them. "Kind of like you, Max. Just because you can hold another person's weapon doesn't mean it'll work the same for you. A Dead Mark is always accurate, but you're a Looper." She bends forward slightly, into a charging position. "I doubt you have control of all abilities."

She charges at me as I let the arrow fly. She's gravely mistaken about my abilities. The arrow hits its mark, the center of her heart. She falls dead at my feet, which causes me to step back a bit. Seconds later, several drones swoop in and begin firing at us. Van tosses his weapon towards one and it adheres to the metal and explodes, bringing the drone down. I take his hand and loop us inside a nearby building. It's not the smartest move, as I'm sure the Patrician have eyes everywhere, but it gets us momentarily out of the way.

If they can see and hear everything, why didn't they come for us in Pentras Tower? Obviously, they would've seen us via the security cameras that line many of the walls. Are the Keepers not the only ones unable to penetrate the building? Why wouldn't the Patrician be able to access their own structure?

I continue to loop us until we're on the top floor, but we're not alone when we get there. Standing by the broken windows is Addie and her group from round two. Scattered around the floor are two of the other groups from the last battle. She runs up to me and throws her arms around my neck. Several members of her team are injured, so I take them first and then head back for everyone else. It takes several trips to loop the group towards Pentras Tower. Once we're safely inside, Garrett and Van hit the medical closet located earlier to get supplies.

"Is this part of the round?" Addie asks as I tend to a cut above her eye.

"No, it's not," I answer.

"What happened?" a Dead Mark asks while Van bandages her leg.

I give them an account of what's occurred so far. Some believe me, but not all. Not that I care who doesn't believe me at this point, since I have more important things to think about.

"I need to find the others before the Patrician do," I state.

"What makes you think the Patrician are the bad guys?" a Nius asks.

"I don't, but seeing as how they're killing us off out there," I say, pointing towards the doors, "I definitely don't trust them."

"It's going to be dark soon, Max," Garrett says from behind me. "I don't think you should go out anymore today."

I turn towards him, tears in my eyes. "I can't just leave them."

He touches my arm, brushing it gently. "I know who you're worried about and I'm not sure why you are, considering some of the things he's done to you, but Frey can take care of himself."

I brush his hand off and turn my attention back to Addie. The cut barely missed her eye and I bandage what I can.

"I explored the building, if you're interested," Garrett says in a hostile manner. "The elevators work, so we don't need to take the stairs."

I don't respond, but move on to assist Van with another injured person.

"Don't you want to hear what I found?" Garrett asks, becoming persistent.

I glare at him. I know he's right about Frey, but his comment still pisses me off. Frey has manipulated me and used me for his own purposes, but I can't shake the feelings I have for him. Maybe I'll eventually be able to rid myself of them, but not at this moment.

"Tell me," I say, sitting on the floor while Van moves the man to sit on the couch next to Brink.

"Floors two through four are offices with lots of computers, monitors, and not much else. Floors five through eight are sealed. The elevator doors won't open at all, and neither will the ones along the stairwell, so there's no telling what's inside."

I'll have to see if I can loop inside later to find out.

"Floors nine through thirteen seem to be some kind of research facility, but nothing like I've ever seen before. Floors fourteen to seventeen are medical, with several operating rooms, labs, and examination rooms. Floors eighteen to twenty-eight are nothing but classrooms. Floors twenty-nine to forty-nine are individual living quarters with communal baths. And, as you already know, the top floor is a dining hall."

I rub my forehead, a headache beginning to form. "Let's get everyone into a room and settled so we can start fresh tomorrow," I say.

The elevators are located down the corridor between the front desks. We take the injured up first, then everyone else joins. We all stay on the forty-ninth floor and I pick a room closest to the elevators, with Garrett and Brink across the hall. The room is small with the bed pushed up against the lone window. Next to the door a dresser sits, full of clothes, but nothing like I've seen before. They aren't the academy uniforms I saw Sadie wear, nor does the room look the same as the one from my nightmare.

I remove a pair of cotton pants, underwear, and a shirt, then head down to the communal bathroom. Towels line the walls, all looking freshly laundered, so I take one and hang it on a hook outside the middle stall. As the water runs, I can hear others coming in to shower as well. The bar of soap sitting in a caddie around the showerhead smells like lavender, and I have to scrub hard to remove the mud and grime from my skin. My hair is caked, but there isn't any shampoo, so I lather up my hands with the bar soap and use that.

Addie is standing at one of the sinks when I emerge. She's wearing an outfit similar to mine, but hers is red where mine is gray. The material is soft and loose, but I actually prefer the tightness of my battle uniform. Those who are hungry make their way up to the next floor, but I'm too tired so I lock my door, drop my dirty clothes in the corner, get under the covers, and fall asleep immediately.

Twenty-One

I don't sleep well, so after a couple of hours of fighting off monsters in my nightmares I get out of bed and head upstairs. Van is sitting on a couch that's been moved close to one of the windows. He hasn't changed his clothes since round two, so he's in desperate need of a shower.

"Couldn't sleep?" he asks as I sit.

"I see you haven't even tried."

He lets a laugh slip along with a small smile. "Yeah. I guess I should get cleaned up."

We let silence settle between us, but something that Rem said is bugging me. "Rem mentioned going to an academy. I didn't know they had that in Tarsus."

"Only if you're wealthy," Van responds.

"I take it you didn't go."

"It's one of the reasons my sister and I wanted to be a part of the *Litarian Battles*," he says with a tinge of pain at the mention of his sister. "We wanted to improve our position in society, so we thought getting to Icarian would do that."

"So, someone like Lok, Frey, or Troy would've gone to the academy," I state.

"Yes, especially Troy. His family is one of the highest-ranking families in Tarsus, and his father is very close to Leader Fallon. He was also one of the people who got Leader Thomas replaced all those years ago."

I try to hide my reaction to my father's name since I'm not sure how much of the truth about my identity has spread throughout Thrace Tower. I'm sure some of it has, though. "Why did he get replaced?"

"It was so long ago and I was only five, but I think because he was supporting a new regime that was rising to challenge the Patrician."

"You mean the Dracken."

He nods. "Yes, but I think Troy's father was playing both sides."

"Why do you say that?"

"Troy is a top-ranked Dracken official just like his father. The man wanted to be the one to replace Leader Thomas, but after much mud-flinging against Leader Thomas it backfired on him, and Leader Fallon was sent in as the replacement."

"How do you know Troy is top-ranked? You sure seem to know a lot about the Dracken for not being one of them."

He laughs. "Let's just say I was almost recruited, but changed my mind at the last minute."

"Is there anyone here who would've gone to the academy?"

"I'm not sure. Why are you so hung up on it?"

"Rem knew who the statue was of, and I want to know how. What are they teaching at the academy and nowhere else, and why?"

"You think it has something to do with the realignment?"

"Possibly."

Van gets up, pats me on the shoulder, and heads down to his room. I sit and stare out the window, wondering where Troy and Lok are… in addition to Frey. They both pose a threat to me: Lok for being a Patrician sympathizer, and Troy, especially if he's anything like his father. Troy knows who I am, so he may try to eliminate me if he believes I'll outrank him when this is all over with.

What am I thinking? I'm acting like the realignment has already happened. What if it all fails? What will happen to us then?

"Hey," Garrett's voice echoes behind me. "You look drained," he says, sitting next to me.

"Just stressed."

"You're a terrible liar, Max. Out with it."

"Yeah, like I trust *you.*"

"Hey, you still have my weapon, and it's not like I've asked for it back."

"Then go with me. Prove I can trust you."

"Fine, what time do you want to go?"

"How about in an hour?"

"You want to go out in the dark?" he asks, sounding a little frightened. "I thought you were going to wait until daylight."

"The sun should be rising in two hours, so an hour of darkness isn't going to hurt anything."

He stares at me as if surprised, but I can see the idea is actually pleasing to him. "You know why I'll do this, other than to gain your trust back?"

"Because you secretly have a death wish."

He laughs, stops, and takes my hand, so I return the hold. He moves closer, pulls me towards him, and kisses me hard on the lips. A fire lights up my insides and I crave more, but I only permit the kiss. I can tell he wants to go further as well, but now isn't the time. He releases me and tells me to meet him in the lobby with his weapon in an hour. We head down the elevator separately. I'm not going out in the flimsy outfit I currently have on, so I spend much of the next hour rummaging through the dresser drawers, trying to come up with something more substantial.

In the bottom drawer, under several blankets I locate a pair of black leggings with a matching top. The leggings are tight, but slide on easily. The material is soft, yet I notice small metallic threads woven into the fabric. The top is form-fitting with short sleeves and has a collar that goes around my throat and almost up to my chin. When both pieces are on, they blend seamlessly into one. I find a pair of socks and boots under the bed, noticing the material of the socks is the same as the leggings and top, but the boots are made of something I'm not familiar with. They fit like they were made just for me. I run my fingers through my hair trying to work out the knots. Under the dirty clothes are the weapons, so I put my sheath around my waist. I'm frozen in my spot by what happens next.

The outfit blends around the belt holding the sheath and changes the material to match it, along with altering the sheath, but my weapon doesn't change. The effect is quite stunning… and disturbing. I don't put Garrett's items over my shoulder, for fear they'll change like mine. I exit the room and take the elevator down, making sure to pay close attention when the elevator moves past floors eight through five. There's only a second's hesitation between the floors, so maybe it'll be enough for me to loop in there.

Garrett is standing by the doors when I arrive, wearing his uniform from when we escaped Thrace Tower. His eyes move up and down my frame as I get closer. I hand him his weapon, which he quickly places over his shoulder.

"Where did you find that?" he asks, touching the outfit.

"At the bottom of my dresser."

"It looks really good on you."

I feel myself blushing, then I take his hand and loop us to a destroyed building across the street. In a half-hour we're practically on the other side of the city, at the barrier between it and the Outer Limits. I wonder what's happening there, since they're probably under attack like Thrace Tower was. I haven't even stopped to wonder whether the rest of Tarsus was overtaken, or if it was just the tower.

The sun is slow to rise this morning, so we're not able to begin searching right away. Garrett scouts several yards in front of me, mainly looking for the drones since none have made an appearance lately. I wish they would show because then I could follow them to the others. A faint green light catches my eye; my wristband is glowing and I feel myself looping.

"Garrett!" I shout.

He charges towards me and is able to grab my hand just as I disappear. The two of us are pulled through the void and land in the same dark corridor I was in before, when I met Leader Fallon. Garrett readies his weapon and I unsheathe my Kopis as a single light turns on above us.

"Hello, Max," a female voice echoes through the emptiness. "We've been looking for you."

"Well, you found me," I say obnoxiously.

"We know you've been sent to the Dead Zone, but where are you hiding?"

So, they can't penetrate Pentras Tower. My modifications weren't just so I can handle the other players' weapons, but so I can access the tower. But why? What's in that building that the Patrician want so badly?

"I haven't been hiding. Perhaps the tracker in my wristband is faulty."

"Perhaps," the woman replies, but she doesn't sound convinced.

"What do you want?" Garrett asks after a few minutes of silence.

"Are you still loyal to us, Garrett? You haven't betrayed us like Max has?"

"She hasn't betrayed you!" he shouts. "She's infiltrated the Dracken and gained their trust. Isn't that what you wanted?"

"Then why isn't she with them now?" the woman asks, anger heavy in her tone.

"You raided Thrace Tower before she could get to the final round. Now they're all scattered throughout the Dead Zone and Tarsus," Garrett responds.

"We had no choice," another voice chimes in, this one male. "The Keepers discovered Max's ability. She was foolish to have demonstrated it."

"I was forced to!" I scream. "You needed me to win, so I did what I had to in order to survive."

"Nevertheless, we had to accelerate our actions and activate our army before they were ready."

Garrett and I look at each other, bewilderment on our faces.

"What army? You have the Aedox, so why would you need an army?" I ask.

"To destroy the Dracken, of course," Leader Fallon says, emerging from the darkness.

"I should kill you," I threaten, bringing my weapon close to her neck.

"Edom had no right to do what he did to your parents," she says. "The punishment you inflicted on him was just."

"Then why keep his death quiet?" I ask, not backing down. "You'll announce the murder of a Dracken leader, but not one of your own? Why?"

"Preservation," she responds. "If the Dracken followers believe they're being targeted, maybe they'll change their strategy."

"But broadcasting the death of a Patrician leader would show your weakness," Garrett says, sidling up to me, his arrow now aimed at Leader Fallon's heart.

"That's *your* interpretation," she replies.

An uneasiness settles between us and several awkward minutes pass before the silence is finally broken.

"Max, we still need you," the female voice says.

"Why? You have an army now, so what do you need me for?"

I know the answer, but I just want them to admit it.

"We need you to get into Pentras Tower," Leader Fallon says. "Our army can only do so much, and they can't access the Dead Zone at this time. Every moment counts, and we're wasting time as it is. The Keepers have proven to be a vigorous opponent and are growing stronger by the minute. We can't afford to lose this realignment, so you need to get into Pentras Tower and stop this war."

"What's in the tower that's so important?" Garrett asks.

"The truth about the Dead Zone," Leader Fallon says. "Once everyone learns what the Dracken and the Keepers have done, they'll be destroyed."

"They're responsible for the destruction in the Dead Zone?" Garrett asks, sounding dumbfounded. "They dropped the bombs that vaporized millions of people?"

"Yes," the female voice answers. "Max has seen it for herself in her vision. It's imperative that you gain control of Pentras Tower, as we need to end this senseless slaughter."

I can tell by the expression on Garrett's face that he believes them. There probably is some truth in what the Patrician are saying, but I'm not sure how much.

"Then I need something from you," I say, lowering my weapon.

"What is it?" the male voice answers.

"Control over the drones," I say. "There are other players from Thrace Tower scattered across the Dead Zone, and they'll be useful accessing the tower."

"We will locate these people for you and transmit their locations to your wristband, but drone control stays with us," the man says.

"Fine," Garrett says before I can respond, which angers me.

The Patrician send us back to the spot by the dome wall, but the sun still hasn't risen. Time must not exist when you're with the Patrician, but how is that possible? Who are the Patrician, or *what* are they? They've always kept their surroundings in darkness when they've looped me, and I wonder why that is.

"Do you want to go back to the tower now that we won't need to blindly hunt for the others?" Garrett asks.

I sit on the ground.

"I take that as a no."

"They know the Dead Zone isn't toxic anymore, yet they make everyone believe that it is."

Garrett sits next to me. "So?"

"Why lie about it? What's so valuable in the Dead Zone that they're keeping everyone isolated from it?"

"You're over-thinking this, Max."

"You don't find this strange?" I ask. "The Keepers clean up the toxicity of this place so that it can be re-inhabited, but the Patrician tell everyone it'll kill you. Why? What are the Patrician after that they're lying to their own people to keep them out of this area?"

"Tell me about your nightmare again."

The sun finally rises as I recount the entire event, making sure to not leave out any detail no matter how small.

"The Patrician called it a vision, so it's obvious they're the ones who projected it into your mind," Garrett says. "The part before you wake up bothers me, though."

"Yeah," I say with a snort. "How could the Dracken have been in Pentras Tower then and not be able to get into it now?"

"There aren't any suggestions of anyone having been in that building for ages, except for the sterile environment and fresh food. If the Dracken had been in the tower, where are they now? Why not let the Keepers in if they're on the same side?"

"I need to get onto those sealed floors."

My wristband chimes and a map pops up, showing a group huddled along the southern rim of the dome. I tap the image and it minimizes into an icon on the tiny display. I don't move right away because I want to think a few things over, but I only wind up giving myself a headache. We stand. I take Garrett's hand, and loop us across the city, heading south. After an hour, we stop so I can recheck the map. It's showing that we're still a good hour away from the group. I hadn't realized how large the city is.

The more we move south the fewer structures we come across, and the land has started to reclaim the urban area. Tall grass and trees cover much of the surroundings. My next loop lands us next to a river, its muddy banks covered in footprints.

Our footprints.

"Garrett," I say, letting go of him.

"I know," he says in shock. "This looks like the battle floor for round two, right down to the impressions in the mud."

I pull up the map, and the red dot indicates that the group is on an island across the river. The area is a lot easier to make out now that we have light. I step into the water but Garrett grabs me, trying to pull me back on shore. I shove him off and start to make my way across. The water only goes up to my thighs, like it did on the battle floor, and I climb up onto the ridge of the island, unsheathe my weapon, and begin trudging my way forward.

Smoke billows like a cloud in front of me, but on the other side of the glass. The drone that located the group still hovers in the sky off to my left. It shines a beam that penetrates the glass and illuminates the players on the other side. I run down to that position so I can get a better look.

Frey is leaning against the glass. He's covered in soot and barely breathing. There are others from our unit around him. Some lay burned and are either dying or already dead. I pound on the glass, but it's useless since it's too thick for him to hear me. I try looping but I can't, which bothers me. I stare up at the drone and it's almost like it's looking back at me. The Patrician know he's a Dracken, so they won't let me rescue him. So, not only do they have the ability to modify my body, but they can also control when I use my abilities.

I look back through the dome. The world on the other side is filled with fire. Buildings burn beyond control and it reminds me of the devastation from my nightmare, only this is live. I can't let them die, so I move along the edge until I come to the river. I can't tell if the water is able to flow under the dome or not. I take off my belt, drop it to the ground, and jump in. It's much deeper on this side, allowing me to dive further below, but I find that the glass does penetrate the river's floor.

Dammit.

I kick at the dome, mainly out of frustration since there isn't any way to break it, but my foot goes right through the glass. I quickly pull it out since I'm severely startled by the event. I swim to the surface to get some air and the suit begins to change. The material stretches down my arms and over my hands, creating gloves, then creeps up my face, covering my head. I feel as if I'm being suffocated, yet I can easily breathe and see through the material. I dive back down and swim through the glass.

Rising to the surface, I grab hold of a tree root and pull myself out of the water. The sleeves and gloves retract, as do the mask and hood. I run over to Frey, take him by the collar, and drag him through the mud to the water. I wrap my arms and legs around him as we dive, hoping the uniform knows what my intention is. It wraps the both of us up so we can pass through the barrier. I get him onto the island and go back for those

I can, but I'm only able to get two more since the fire has spread to the city's rim and sucked all the oxygen from the air.

Garrett is standing over Frey when I surface with the last one. I get out of the water and I'm instantly dry. The uniform returns to its normal state as I begin checking their injuries. Frey is starting to come around as another drone flies over our heads.

"What happened?" he wheezes.

I lean into him, placing my mouth almost against his ear. "Now isn't the time to ask questions," I whisper. "Keep your mouth shut until I can get us someplace safe."

He looks at me puzzled as I secure my weapon, take hold of the two who are still unconscious, with Frey and Garrett holding on to my waist, and begin to loop us to the tower. It takes several hours before we're back since I made sure to make my loops quickly, so the drones weren't able to follow.

Van is in the lobby with several others when we arrive. They take the two Loopers from me, placing them on the couches to tend to their wounds. Frey is fully awake now, so Garrett and I escort him to the lift and up to the forty-ninth floor. Garrett shows him to the communal showers while I secure an empty room for him and the two other Loopers.

I stand in the hallway and wait for Garrett and Frey to return. Frey is wrapped in several towels and freshly scrubbed. I open the door to his room and the three of us step inside. Garrett closes the door while I take a seat on the bed.

"I don't get to dress alone?" Frey asks, winking at me.

"I just want to make sure you're all right," I respond.

"And him?" Frey asks, pointing to Garrett.

"I'm with her," Garrett answers, pointing to me.

"Well, isn't that cozy," Frey says, a hint of contempt in his voice.

He drops his towels, exposing himself. Garrett turns away, but I don't.

"How did you wind up outside the dome?" I ask.

"I'm not really sure," Frey answers, digging through the drawers and removing a few items of clothing. "We were sent to the Dead Zone by the Keepers when the Aedox invaded, but then half of us were looped beyond the dome."

"You mean those who joined the Dracken," I state.

He shakes his head.

"Was the place on fire when you got there?" I ask.

"No. The buildings were old and falling apart. The structures looked ancient, actually. Like they were from another time period."

"How did they start burning?" Garrett asks, turning back around now that Frey is dressed.

"Firebombs rained from the sky," Frey answers. "We couldn't tell where they were coming from because they fell everywhere, trapping some of the unit between collapsed structures. A few were able to loop out, but then we wound up being blocked by the dome. I hadn't realized we were outside of it until you came and got us." Frey walks over to me, wraps his arms around my shoulders, and pulls me into his chest. "Do you have any food? I'm starving."

Twenty-Two

Garrett glares at Frey while he eats, his eyes full of disdain. Brink and Van join us a short time later. The other two I rescued are being treated for second-degree burns and smoke inhalation on one of the medical floors. There are several groups of us on the top floor, but Frey is the only one eating. I should eat since I haven't had anything all day, but I have no appetite.

"What happened in Thrace Tower?" Brink asks.

"We were all in the common room, watching round two. Each screen was dedicated to a different team, so we were constantly bouncing from one display to another," Frey responds. "However, the moment Max touched Garrett's bow all hell broke loose. The two Aedox who were stationed on our floor opened fire on anyone with a dragon tattoo. Matron Kaniz activated an alarm under the bar and our wristbands began to glow. Then our weapons appeared in our hands. We fought back as much as we could, but the shields weren't designed to block bullets." He takes a gulp of water, washing down the rest of his meal. "We began being looped out of the building; I knew it was the Keepers moving us to safety."

"But the two with you aren't Dracken," Brink says.

"The Keepers looped everyone," Frey says. "I think because those two were in a group consisting mainly of Dracken members, the Patrician must not have known they weren't actually a part of us and teleported them outside the dome with the rest."

"Wait a minute," Garrett says, almost knocking the bottle of water from Frey's hand. "Are you saying the Keepers were saving all the players, even if they weren't Dracken, and that the Patrician moved you out of the Dead Zone?"

"That's exactly what I'm saying," Frey says, setting the bottle down.

"How do you know?" Garrett asks.

"Because it's what both sides would do, Garrett," Frey says, sounding annoyed. "You've been so hung up on believing everything the Patrician have fed you that you think they're incapable of that kind of cruelty. Lok has made you think the Keepers are the enemy, but he's wrong."

"Where is Lok?" I ask.

"No idea," Frey replies. "The Keepers scattered us, so the Dead Mark unit could be anywhere."

Dead Mark and Rapid are the only units we haven't come across yet, so where could they be?

"How many do you think are out there?" Brink asks.

"Not many," I reply.

"Who have you found?" Frey asks.

"Addie's group, the blue and red groups from round two, you, and the other two Loopers."

"That's not a lot," Frey says.

"No, it's not. And since the Patrician have an army, we're greatly outnumbered," Garrett adds.

"What do you mean they have an army? How is that possible?" Frey asks.

"Maybe they recruited people like the Dracken did," Brink says.

I think back to round two, particularly to Van's sister. She had the Patrician mark on her wrist, so was she part of the army? How *did* she get onto the battle floor? Did the Keepers transport her from Icarian so that Van could see what his sister had become? But that would only work if the army was made up of the winners who were sent to Icarian. Didn't someone tell me that all previous winners had been Patrician favorites who somehow modified the game and won?

I get up from the table and head toward one of the elevators. Garrett rushes up behind me and I catch Frey glaring at the two of us before the elevator door closes and we descend.

"What's on your mind?" Garrett asks when we pass the thirtieth floor.

"Where are the Patrician getting their so-called army?"

I hit the emergency stop button when we get to the sixth floor and we come to such a jarring stop that we almost fall off our feet. I take my Kopis and try to pry the doors open, but they won't budge.

"Don't do it," Garrett says. "You could wind up looping into something."

"I have to try."

I go into the void and think about what the other side of the door could possibly look like, then project myself there. The room is filled with light cascading through the large windows that line the walls. The tiles on the floor resemble those from the battle floor, right down to the blue light outlining each. The entire space is empty with the exception of four narrow white pedestals positioned in the center of the room. I cautiously walk up to one and notice thin displays sitting atop the pedestals. I tap the screen of one and it comes to life, displaying a menu of options. I carefully review them before choosing the one marked 'Cities'.

Large panels slowly descend over the windows, throwing the room into darkness. A few seconds later each panel shows what look to be ancient cities, many destroyed beyond repair. I have to carefully walk around the room so I can view them all. At least twenty cities lay in waste before me. Among the destruction I can make out pieces of buildings, homes, statues, and roadways. When I get close to one panel the image flies over the area, and I feel like I'm actually soaring above it. Three panels behind me show the Outer Limits, Tarsus, and another location I've never seen before. The Outer Limits is burning, and I catch glimpses of people scrambling to safety as buildings collapse. Tears pour down my face when I recognize the orphanage, or at least its outer shell. It's the only truly recognizable piece of the structure. I put my hand to my mouth as Aedox parade up and down the ash-covered streets, shooting anyone they find.

The flashy signs that hang from Tarsus' buildings still glitter in the waning daylight. It looks like Thrace Tower was the only building affected by the raid, but there's an Aedox stationed at every intersection around the building. Citizens pass them without a second look. Life appears to be normal in Tarsus; nothing burning, everyone freely walking on the streets, carriages swinging around corners full of passengers, and no signs of a war.

The third city I don't recognize, but it's full of young people all wearing player-style uniforms. I squint my eyes and notice they all have a laurel tattoo on the side of their wrists.

"Where is this?" I ask myself.

Icarian flashes across the screen and I'm startled by the response.

"The Patrician army?" I ask, wondering how much information I'll be given by whoever, or whatever, is responding.

Yes appears.

"Former battle winners?"

Yes.

"How?"

Go to the seventh floor.

I hesitate, but comply with the request. I loop back into the elevator, take off the emergency stop, and bring us up one floor. Garrett doesn't ask any questions when I reapply the brakes before I loop again, and I'm immediately stuck between the outer door of the elevator and a security gate. Red lights spin overhead, but I don't hear an alarm. The room is poorly lit with only light from the monitors that hang down from the ceiling every three feet giving off any kind of brightness.

I touch the handle of the gate, but it won't turn. The suit begins to glow a soft yellow, which radiates out towards the metal. The door swings open and the red lights shut off, but no additional lights turn on. I step into the room, the gate closes behind me, and I feel the temperature drop ever so slightly. Square metal pillars break up the open space and between each are steel-plated walls that come up waist-high, creating openings into another workspace. I walk around the center to glance at each monitor, each showing a different view of the exterior of the building. Computer banks hum in the corners of the vast room; large windows line the far wall, but the tint of the glass is darker than the rest of the building, which I find odd.

I go into the center of the room, mesmerized by the number of workstations that are still running with no one manning them. I bump into a wide table in the middle of the area; it's glass shiny but with a blue fluid racing from side to side under the surface. I place my hand on the tabletop and an image automatically appears, hovering just inches above the surface. It's not a picture, but a list of my personal details.

```
Name: Mera Thomas, aka Maximiana Sutton
Creators: Liam and Clio Thomas
Place of creation: Tarsus
Place of residence: Outer Limits
Directive: Save us
```

I remove my hand and the image vanishes. A shiver runs down my spine and enters my core. I step back, bumping into one of the workstations.

"Max," a voice says behind me.

I turn and see the face of Sadie in the monitor attached to the workstation.

"You're not real," I say, more to myself than to her.

"We're quite real," she responds.

"Who are you?"

"We thought this type of communication might be easier for you, so we took the form of a face from your memory."

"It's from a nightmare, and one I would like to forget."

The image changes to my mother, but I still don't know what to make of any of this.

"How do you know me?"

"You were selected by the Patrician for a task. One that will change all of humanity, and not just in this world but in all others. Because of this, we've been monitoring you closely."

"You're the Keepers."

"No, we're not," she replies calmly.

"Then who are you?"

"We're the Dracken."

"That's not possible. The Keepers and the Dracken are the same."

"No, Max, we're not," she says. "The Dracken are the original inhabitants of this world, where as the Keepers aren't… and neither are the Patrician."

"I…I don't understand."

"All will be explained if you go to the fifth floor."

"It's sealed, just like this floor."

"Yes, but with the suit and your modifications you can easily access that level."

"Why should I believe you?"

"Your very existence depends upon it. We can't afford to lose this world, or the tower."

"And if I refuse?"

The lights turn on, flooding the room and throwing odd shadows in every corner. I begin retreating to the elevators as the monitors hanging from the ceilings show images from within the tower. Frey is sitting at the table where I left him, but he's only with Van. Garrett paces in the elevator. Addie is patrolling the lobby, but keeping her distance from the door. Brink is in one of the classrooms, going through cabinets.

"If you don't, you leave us no choice," the voice changes to a low hum, but I can still understand it. "All will die, even those you care for. Their deaths will be painful, but necessary. Don't be afraid, Max. You're one of us now."

I slam myself into the security gate. My fingers hastily search for the handle behind me, finally locating it. I pull the door open and begin to loop back into the lift, but I get stuck in the void.

"We'll help you, but in turn you must help us."

"Let me go!" I scream.

"You're one of us now, Max."

My face hits the floor of the elevator hard, cracking my nose. Garrett grabs my arm, helping me to my feet. I slam my fist into the console in anger and we start to ascend to the fourteenth floor. Blood is pouring from my nose, yet the suit isn't stained. Garrett directs me to one of the exam rooms and takes care of my injury.

"What happened?" he asks, applying a healing ointment to the bridge of my nose. It mends in a matter of seconds and the blood stops.

"I want to get out of here."

"And go where, Max? Pentras Tower is the safest place in the Dead Zone."

"We're not the only ones in here."

"You're not making any sense," he says as he helps me down from the examination table. "Let's get you upstairs. You haven't eaten all day." He takes my arm and guides me back to the elevators.

"I'm not hungry," I say, protesting. "Please, I just need to get out of here for a while."

The elevator door opens and a Dead Mark and a Rapid, both from the second round, are waiting inside. Garrett instructs them to take me to the top floor and make sure I eat. The door closes without Garrett getting on board. When we reach the top floor, I sit down at the table I'd been at earlier. Frey has left and I'm almost force-fed by Van. I finally succumb to Van's threats of sitting on me and eat. When I've satisfied him, I'm allowed to go back to my room.

As soon as my door is shut and locked, I strip the suit off and throw it into the corner with the other dirty clothes. I put on the outfit I had on the night before, turn off my light, and get into bed. It's not even completely dark yet, but I feel like if I don't shut down now I'll regret my actions.

I doze off and on. The light outside has completely faded when I wake several hours later. As I open my eyes, I hold my breath since I know I'm not alone in my room.

"You were never subtle in your lurking," I say to Brink.

He emerges from the corner off to my right. I try to move but discover I can't, and I catch him smiling out of the corner of my eye as he comes closer.

"Paralyzers are wonderful things," he says, sitting on the edge of my bed. He taps the device that currently rests on my abdomen.

"Why?" I ask, choking back my fear.

"You betrayed me, Max. I thought I could forgive you after your affair with Frey, but now you're with Garrett? A Patrician sympathizer?"

"What the hell are you talking about?"

"We all saw you leave together, and no one could find either of you in the building for quite some time. It's like you two didn't want to be found."

"You're crazy. Get this thing off me."

"Frey thinks it, too," Brink says, lying next to me.

"Nothing happened. We were in the center elevator."

"Yes, but it was stopped next to a sealed floor, and the elevator didn't move for almost thirty minutes."

"This is unbelievable. I would shake my head if I could since this is all utter nonsense."

"Then what were you doing?"

"Nothing. I wanted to see if I could loop into the sealed floors, that's all."

"And did you?" His tone changes to one of intrigue.

I'm about to answer, but stop just as the words are forming in my mouth. "You're not Brink."

"Why would you say something like that, Maxy?"

"This isn't real."

Brink begins caressing my arm, then nudges his legs against mine. "Yes, Max, it is."

"How did you get in my room if the door is locked? You're not a Looper, and no one's abilities work outside of Thrace Tower except for mine."

He stops.

"You're the Patrician and I'm waking up now."

Brink and the paralyzer vanish, but I still can't move.

Sleep paralysis.

"Frey!" I shout as loud as I can.

I'm finally able to sit up. Sweat drips down my forehead and my heart races as someone pounds on my door. I fall out of bed and have to crawl over to unlock the door. Frey and Garrett burst in, weapons drawn. Frey sheaths his blade, picks me up, and we head upstairs. He sits me down on one of the couches far from the windows. Garrett joins us a few minutes later, having checked the entire floor for any intruders.

"Destroy this," I say, shaking my wristband. "They're in my head."

"Who is, Max?" Frey asks.

"The Patrician. They know we're in Pentras Tower. I thought I could hide it from them, but they know."

"What happened?" Garrett asks.

"They wanted to know if I'd managed to get onto one of the sealed floors." I bring my hands close to my face. "They want something in this building and have never been able to access it until me. That's why I was maimed. They did it so I could get them what they've been searching for."

"How do you know?" Frey asks, sitting next to me.

"I just do," I say, panicking.

Garrett sits by my feet. "We can't deactivate your wristband, Max. We'll never be able to move in and out of the tower or the Dead Zone."

Tears run down my cheeks. "I don't want this… any of this. Why are the Patrician targeting me and no one else? I could just loop away and never come back, then where would they be?"

"You're just tired," Frey says. "You need to get some sleep. We can talk more about it in the morning."

My wristband chimes, which is odd. A display appears, showing someone on the roof of the tower. The Nius who was in Addie's group rushes from the elevator.

"You need to come. Hurry," she says, out of breath.

We follow her towards an exit at the far end of the room that leads to the roof. The night air is chilly and the wind strong, so the four of us have to hold on to the guardrail along the roofline to keep from being blown off. The Nius points to a lone figure standing at the corner of the roof. We cautiously step over to the person facing us.

"Don't!" Addie shouts.

We all stop.

"How did you get up here?" Frey asks.

"I don't know," Addie answers, terrified. "I was in the lobby but fell asleep on the couch, and when I woke up I was on the roof." Her voice trembles, as does her body.

I step closer. Frey grabs at my shirt, trying to stop me, but I swat at him. "Addie, hold on. I'm coming," I say, trying to keep my tone calm.

"They're going to kill me, Max," she says, choking on tears.

"Who is?" I ask, moving one more step closer.

"The Dracken."

I stop.

"I thought they were going to help us… free us from the Patrician, but it was all lies, Max. Your parents lied to everyone!" she screams. "This should be you standing here, not me!"

"You're being manipulated, Addie," I say. "The Patrician got in your head through your wristband. Don't believe anything they're telling you."

"You're wrong, Max. You'll see. You're all wrong."

"Addie!" I shout as she falls backwards off the roof. I try to loop, but I'm being prevented.

"Go get her!" Garrett screams at me.

"They won't let me!"

"Who, Max?" Frey asks.

"The Patrician."

Twenty-Three

Everyone has been instructed to report down to the sixteenth floor of the medical section. The Nius who alerted us about Addie has figured out how to disarm our wristbands; I'm the only one not permitted to do so, as I still have to be able to loop.

I need to be away from everyone, so I sit at a desk in a classroom on the twentieth floor and stare out the window as the sun begins to rise. We'll only be able to hold off the Patrician for so long, but once they figure out the wristbands no longer work they'll send in the army, and we're greatly outnumbered.

"There you are," Frey says, walking in. "I've been looking everywhere for you." He takes a seat next to mine and reaches for my hand, but I pull it away. "It's not your fault."

"I know," I respond, but I continue to stare out the window.

"Our wristbands are defunct now," he says sadly. "We can still use our weapons, but no shields."

I don't respond.

"Come on, Max. I need you to snap out of whatever funk you're in."

"How were you chosen?" I ask after a long silence.

"What do you mean?"

I turn my attention towards him. "For the game and to be a Dracken."

"Troy's father recommended I apply for the battles."

"Why?"

"Because Troy and I are friends. He wanted both of us to go to Icarian so we could get out of Tarsus. Troy's father knew the trouble I had at home, and he thought the game would be a perfect outlet for me to escape."

I turn my head back towards the window. "He lied to you."

The desk legs scrape along the floor as he moves closer to me. "Who did?"

"Troy's father."

"I'm not following you, Max."

"My parents are dead because of him. I spent my life in the Outer Limits because Mr. Larsen wanted to be the leader of Tarsus. The Patrician have been making him promises for years, provided he did what they asked. He set my parents up to be executed, but the Patrician changed their minds when they saw how greedy and ruthless he is. They feared he would try to take them over, so Fallon was sent in to replace my father instead of Mr. Larsen."

"What does that have to do with me?"

I turn my tired eyes to his sorrowful face. Frey looks worn out, beaten, and on the brink of exhaustion. I probably look the same, if not worse.

"Where's your sister?"

"Dead."

"And who killed her?"

"The Patrician. Max, you know all of this. What's the matter with you? Why are you acting so strange?"

"Because my friend just jumped off the tallest building in the Dead Zone and I couldn't save her. Because I'm being manipulated by all sides and it's making me crack. Because I'm trying to figure out the truth and it starts with Troy's father."

I slam my head down on the desk's surface. My arms fall to my sides and I close my eyes.

What's in this building that everyone wants and is willing to destroy cities over? What did my parents know that made them such a threat? Will the right side win when this is all over? But which is the right side? I know it's not the Patrician, but the Dracken are the ones who made Addie fall.

"I need to find Troy and Lok," I say, raising my head.

"Why Lok?"

"He and Troy went to the academy, so they may know something." I turn to him. "You went, too, didn't you?"

"Only for a few years. My father pulled me out when your parents were killed. He thought their deaths had something to do with whatever the Patrician were teaching us at the academy. I'd just turned eight."

"At what age do you start there?"

"Five, but not everyone gets to go."

"I know. Van told me."

"Why do you think Troy and Lok can help you?"

"Because I killed Rem before I asked her any questions."

A look of shock crosses his face. I rest my head on my arms and stare out the windows again. Frey leaves a few minutes later and I let a half-hour go by before I go up to my room and put the suit back on. I belt my sheath around my waist, secure my boots and go look for Garrett, who's down in the lobby.

"I need you to come with me," I say.

"Um, okay. Why?"

"Everyone thinks you're a Patrician sympathizer, and I need the Patrician to believe I've aligned myself with you. So, whenever I leave the tower I need you with me."

"You really think I'm still with the Patrician? After what they did to Addie?"

"It doesn't matter what *I* think. All that matters is what the Patrician think. I need you to go along with me."

"Why not Frey?"

"They know he's a Dracken, so my plan won't work."

"And what is your plan?"

"If I tell you, you won't go along with it."

"Dammit, Max," he says, kicking the couch he's standing in front of. "Fine, when do you want to leave?"

"Now, preferably."

"Are you going to tell anyone that we're leaving?"

"No."

"What if something happens to us? They'll be stuck in this building forever."

"At least they'll be safe."

I step towards the doors and stop, waiting for him to decide whether he's coming with me or not. He hesitates, but it doesn't take him long to join me. I take his hand and loop us out of the building, straight to the plaza where I killed Rem. But her body is no longer there. The minute we land, my wristband goes off with the locations of the other players. I minimize the display to ignore it, then go over to the ledge of the pool and sit down.

"Aren't we going to get the others?" Garrett asks, standing in front of me.

"Not right now."

"So," he begins as he sits next to me, "why are we out here, then?"

I reach up to his face and pull him into me. I kiss him hard, deep, and heavy. His hands pull me in closer, then he pulls me into his lap. I wrap my legs around his waist while he searches for the seam between the top and the leggings. He finds it just as the drones begin to hum overhead. I don't open my eyes, as I want them to think I don't realize they're there. Garrett lowers me to the stone pavers that cover the plaza and now I wonder how far I'll need to take this to convince the Patrician I'm loyal to them, so they'll loop us to where they are.

He's in the process of removing the top, when I feel us being pulled into the void. The floor is cold against my exposed skin and the lone light shines above the two of us as we hastily don our clothing before standing. I can tell Garrett is pissed that he was interrupted. I'm annoyed, too, though also relieved. I know I was tricking Garrett, but at the same time I didn't want it to stop.

"Max," the female voice echoes around us, "have you found your loyalties? Will you do what we have tasked you to do?"

"Yes," I say without hesitation.

Garrett steps behind me and he's so close I can feel his breath. He wraps his arms around my waist and begins nuzzling my neck. "Welcome home, Max," he whispers in my ear.

My heart stops.

Was I just manipulated? Did he really just turn the tables on me? Was it the Patrician who got to Addie, or was it Garrett?

"Has the task been completed, Garrett?" the female voice asks.

"Yes. You can start the transference at any time," he replies.

I push him off, stepping back so I'm only half in the light. "What did you do!" I yell.

"I'm making everything right. Lok told me how to alter the wristbands, so I showed the Nius girl how to do it."

He reaches out to me but I step back further, my head hitting something metal and sharp. I collapse to my knees, reach around, and when my hand is back in front of my face it's covered in blood.

"What is this place?" I ask anyone who'll answer.

"Patrician Nine," Leader Fallon says, coming into focus.

Lights turn on, filling the dark space. We're in a corridor lined in thick dark metal with jagged edges. The portion I bumped into has a window above; a face looms in the room behind it, observing us. The woman in the window disappears, but I can still sense she's there.

"Is that supposed to mean something to me?" I ask, holding my head so the bleeding stops.

"There are ten Patrician ships and you're on number nine," Leader Fallon says, looming closer.

"Ships? As in, what… spaceships?"

"In a manner of speaking, yes," she answers.

"Max, they're trying to protect us," Garrett says, kneeling next to me.

"You're one of them, aren't you?" I say to Garrett. "A Patrician leader, not some miller from the Outer Limits."

"Not exactly." He removes my hand, takes off his shirt, and begins cleaning my wound with it. "My parents were leaders, but I've been in the Outer Limits my whole life. Sent there to keep an eye out for you."

"What?" I ask, my stomach turning into knots. I roll over onto my side, bring my knees to my chest, and begin to rock.

I'm going crazy. This is all nuts. None of this is really happening. What have I gotten myself in to? What have I done?

"Max," Garrett says.

I hear him, but it seems like he's miles away.

"I want to go back," I tell them. "I want to go back to Pentras Tower."

"Shortly, Max," Leader Fallon says. "Once the transference is over, you and Garrett will be returned to complete your task."

I close my eyes trying to keep the tears at bay. I can only imagine what's going on back at the tower. What are they doing to Frey, Van, Brink, and the others? Will they survive whatever is happening to them? Why did I allow this to occur?

I'm moved into a sitting position and my injury is tended to by someone in a medical uniform, or at least I think that's what it is, while Garrett puts his blood-stained shirt back on. A healing ointment is applied, then Garrett helps me to my feet and we move under the light in the middle of the corridor. I feel numb inside as we're sent into the void and placed in front of Pentras Tower. I go through the motions of taking Garrett's hand and looping us into the lobby, but that's all it is… a motion. I can immediately tell that everything inside has changed. That it's just the two us now and the others are gone.

"Where are they?" I ask as Garrett directs me to one of the elevators.

"Someplace you'll never have to go to again," he replies happily.

He pushes the button for the forty-ninth floor and all I do is stare as the doors close and we ascend. My mind has shattered along with my soul. Nothing matters anymore. The Patrician have won, they've beaten me, so I might as well as comply with their wishes, so I can live. At least, I hope I'll still be alive when this is all over.

The door opens. Garrett takes my hand and leads me to his room. I'm his now, the Patrician have made that perfectly clear. He carries me through the door and sets me down on the bed. He's immediately on top of me, removing my sheath and clothes, and I let him finish what we started in the plaza. I should fight, but why? They've won, and I've lost. Time to move on. Garrett falls asleep an hour later, so I grab a long shirt from the dresser, put it on, and go up to the fiftieth floor.

The sunset is actually quite beautiful tonight. Purple and pink hues fill the sky and get darker the further the sun goes down. I step up close to the glass, pressing my palms against the smooth surface, hoping I fall through it.

"I was wondering where you disappeared to," Garrett says, wrapping his arms around me and pulling me tightly against him.

"I wanted to watch the sunset," I mumble. "It's so beautiful up here." I know I'm rambling, but words and thoughts aren't under my control anymore.

He pulls me back to sit on one of the couches. "Why did you need me to go with you?" he asks, nibbling on my neck.

"I wanted to get to Icarian."

"Why would you want to go there?"

"To see the army. I needed to know if it was true."

"If what was true?" he asks as he pushes me down on the couch and lies on top of me, his hands wandering their way up the shirt.

"If the previous winners of the *Litarian Battles* were actually the soldiers. That the laurel symbol is their sign of loyalty, like the dragon tattoo is for the Dracken."

He stops and places a finger against my lips. "None of that matters now. This will all be over soon, and it'll just be the two of us."

"What will be over soon?"

"The end of the Dracken and the Keepers. Now that you're one of us, there's no stopping the inevitable."

You're one of us now, Max.

One of us.

I gently push Garrett back, sliding to the floor.

"Are you all right?" he asks, concern clearly visible on his face.

"I need something to drink."

I get to my feet and walk over to the fridge. It's still stocked full of food, even though there are only two of us now. I remove a bottle of water and drink it where I stand. Garrett approaches me, but slowly, a big smile on his face and longing in his eyes.

Loop, Max. Loop now!

I hear it more than say it in my mind and vanish down to Garrett's room. I quickly put the suit back on, grab my weapon, and loop again since I know he'll be here soon. I'm on the sixth floor and the panels are still down, but the images are gone. I rush up to one of the pedestals, but the display won't turn on no matter how hard I press it.

"You can hear me, right?" I say loudly.

No response.

"You wanted me to go to the fifth floor. Why?"

No response.

"Please, I need your help."

The center elevator dings when it reaches the floor, but the doors won't open. I keep my mouth shut, hoping Garrett will move on, which he does after several minutes of anxious silence. But it won't take him long to come back up.

"You said I was one of you. I am. Please, tell me what you need me to do."

The panels turn on, showing a devastated landscape. It's a Dead Zone, but not this one. The image changes to another city also devastated by war. More scroll across the panels, too many to count.

The fifth floor is where our records are kept, appears on the panels. You must go there without using the elevator.

"How? I can only loop if I know where I'm looping to. It's too dangerous to do it blindly."

You trusted your instincts before, Max. Do it again.

"Do you know where my friends are?"

Yes, which is why you must hurry.

I step back from the pedestal and go almost to the elevator door. I picture what the fifth floor might look like by the elevators and project myself there. The room I enter is much smaller than the other floors. Its walls are white, curved, and the ceiling is folded on top of another ceiling. There aren't any windows, so the outside of this room must be all open space between itself and the structure. Twelve workstations are set in rows of three. Flat, clear, panel screens are attached to a desk-like counter with a chair attached.

I sit at the first station I come to, tap the screen, and scroll through files. I remove my hand at some point and realize I'm not the one scrolling. The other stations descend while mine stays on the floor. A record is selected onscreen and immediately starts to play on the walls around me.

"The Dracken have lived on this world for thousands of years," a voice says as the image shows a budding society. One of true happiness, content, and success. Tall high-tech buildings cover much of the landscape, but there are still plenty of open fields where children can be seen running and playing. "We were a people dedicated to science and technology."

The scenes change, showing other worlds like this one. The lushness of their landscapes is intense. Deep blue oceans, tall forest canopies, and colorful wildlife. I'm transfixed by them; I've seen so much death and decay that I never could've imagined that such elegance existed in nature.

"Almost a hundred years ago a colony known as the Patrician invaded our world. They try to assimilate civilizations, and when they resist the Patrician destroy them, take their knowledge, and move on. It took decades for the Patrician to determine what we had that would benefit them: a material that would allow its wearer to move seamlessly through space, barriers, and detection. It can anticipate the wearer's needs and actions, almost becoming a part of the wearer's body."

I touch the material covering my body and I know they're talking about the suit.

"The Patrician could not penetrate our security forces, so they dropped nuclear weapons on our people in hopes of convincing us to change our minds. They promised that if we turned this piece of technology over to them they would let our people live. But the Keepers knew otherwise, for they are restorers – trying to return annihilated worlds to their original forms. They are a long time enemy of the Patrician and have seen firsthand the promises made and broken by them. With the Keepers' help we've been trying to retake our world, but we've only been able to get so far before the Patrician destroy our progress and we must start once again. Their sole mission is to take everything for themselves. leaving no world unscathed or livable." The images now show the wonderful worlds in ruins. Smoke rises from fires that'll never stop burning. Everything has been laid to waste, including the people.

"But they found a way around your defenses. The Keepers inadvertently showed them by creating the *Litarian Battles* and the Looper unit," I say, standing. "They were trying to help build an army for you, but it backfired."

"Yes," the voice says sadly. "Which is why you were chosen, Max. A young woman the Dracken leaders would remember because of her parents, so she wouldn't pose a threat. An orphan without any ties and who can be easily forgotten in the Outer Limits. You, Max. You became their solution to a complex problem."

"What do I do to stop them?"

"Build our army. There are more uniforms stored elsewhere in the building, but we can't tell you where for fear of your mind manipulation giving away the location."

I know they're right, but it's still going to make this a long and tiring task. "What about the people? My friends? How do I get them here without the Patrician knowing?"

"Your friends are in the Outer Limits, sent to die in the devastation. The suits are easily concealable. If you can get to the Outer Limits, you'll find your army."

"What about Icarian?"

"They'll not invade until you're ready for them."

"Me? But, the Patrician control them."

"And you're now a Patrician leader, Max. Use it to your advantage."

The images stop and the room goes dark. I loop myself back to my room and stash the suit. I put on a basic white shirt and black pants, find my sheath in Garrett's room, which is currently empty, and go back up to the fiftieth floor. Garrett is sitting along the back of the couch, waiting for me, bow in hand and arrow aimed at my chest.

Twenty-Four

"Where have you been?" he asks, clearly agitated.

"Around," I answer, stepping off the elevator.

"I haven't alerted the Patrician to your deception, Max. Not yet anyway."

"What deception? I'm not hiding anything." I take another step towards him, but he holds the bow firm. I don't draw my Kopis for fear it'll only antagonize him further.

"I could shoot you, and find what the Patrician are looking for without you."

"You won't do that. You'll be signing your own death warrant. They need me more than they need you. After all, I'm the one they modified. Not you."

Anger flashes across his face. "Only because it was convenient for them," he says, seething. "If they'd known who you really sided with you'd be dead just like the others."

"Why wouldn't I side with the Patrician, Garrett? The Dracken have done nothing but try to destroy everything the Patrician have created." I'm almost at the couch now, but he's still not lowering his weapon. "Would I have had sex with you if I didn't want to be with you? We can only be together if the Patrician are successful, and isn't that what you want?" I stop just shy of the tip of the arrow piercing my shirt.

His eyes narrow and for a brief instant he almost lets the arrow fly. "Don't ever leave my side again, understand?"

I nod and he lowers the weapon.

As he sets the bow and arrow down on the couch his wristband chimes. An image appears of two people just outside the front doors to the tower. Garrett takes my arm, escorts me back into the elevator, and we head to the lobby. When we're near the doors I loop the two of us outside. Lok and Troy are standing a few steps down from us. Lok and Garrett embrace while Troy gives me the once-over.

"I wasn't sure where you two were sent," Garrett says, releasing Lok.

"It took us a while to get to the tower since there isn't an easy path or complete road," Troy responds, eyes still glued on me. "How'd you get here?" His gaze focuses on Garrett.

"Max," Garrett responds, gesturing towards me. "Her modifications have been more than useful."

They knew? All this time, they knew?

"I'm glad the Patrician chose the right girl," Lok says, winking at me as he adjusts a rucksack slung over his shoulder.

I feel thoroughly disgusted with them, and myself at the center of their betrayal. I know I'm only playing a part at the moment, but just the thought of being stuck in the tower with the three of them sickens me. Still, I have to keep going if I have any chance of success.

They take hold of my hands and I loop us into the building. We take the elevator to the forty-ninth floor, where Garrett shows Lok and Troy to vacant rooms as well as where the communal bathrooms are. They each head to the showers, but Troy is the first one out. He's only wearing boxer shorts as he walks down the hall, mentioning how hungry he is. Garrett has me take him upstairs to get some food while Lok finishes up. I sit across from Troy while he eats a bowl of cereal soaked in milk.

"Where's Frey?" Troy asks after several unsettling minutes of silence.

"I don't know."

"I bet Garrett does," he says as a sneer creases his mouth.

I ignore the ploy since I know he's only trying to antagonize me. I cross my arms and rest them on the table. "So, Troy, where's the rest of your unit?"

He doesn't look up from his food when he responds. "We got separated. I was looking for them when I ran into Lok."

"And what about his unit? Surely he wasn't alone as well?"

He slams his spoon down. "What are you implying, Max?"

"It just seems odd that the two of you didn't have anyone else with you. From those we've encountered, the Keepers looped whole units together out of Thrace Tower. Why would the Dead Mark and Rapid units be treated differently?"

"I don't know," he says, a little more calmly. "I'm sure they're out there somewhere."

I stare at him while he continues to eat. He's hiding something, but I'm not sure what. Maybe he really doesn't know where his unit is. After all, he has a large black and red dragon draped between his shoulder blades, which makes him a Dracken leader. So, perhaps those who are Patrician loyalists were sent to Icarian and Troy was sent here with the Dracken members. But then, how did he meet up with Lok? The Dead Zone is too large to run into someone simply by happenstance. Yet, Garrett was expecting both of them. Maybe they were both directed to come here by the Patrician.

The elevator doors open and Garrett steps out, alone. He gestures towards me, so I get up from my seat and enter the elevator with him. We descend one floor and when the doors open, Lok is standing on the other side wearing tan pants, a black short-sleeved shirt, and both the rucksack and his weapon strapped across his shoulders. On his right bicep is a green laurel with a silver infinity sign in the center. This is the first time I've actually seen the tattoo, as Lok usually had his arms covered. He steps onboard and we descend, stopping at the seventh floor when Garrett hits the emergency button.

"I need you to loop me in there," Lok says.

"What for? Nothing in that room works," I say, protesting.

"All the more reason to get me on the floor," Lok says.

"It's ancient equipment, way before your time."

"Is there an issue, Max?" Garrett asks, crossing his arms over his chest.

"No. No issue," I respond as calmly as possible.

I take Lok by the hand and loop us. I'd left the security gate open when I was on the floor last, so Lok walks right into the room. Everything comes alive at the sound of his steps. He stops and scans the room as the monitors spring to life, showing the outer perimeter of the tower. Lok steps into the center of the room and places the rucksack on top of the plasma display. He begins digging around in the bag, removing various lengths of wire, a handheld display, and wire cutters.

"Want to give me hand?" he says, motioning for me to follow.

"No, not really."

He sets his items down, goes back into the rucksack, and removes a thick, black-handled knife with at least an eighteen-inch serrated blade. I haven't moved from the entryway, standing my ground as he approaches me with the knife positioned in front of him.

He grabs me by the throat and slams me into the elevator door. "Weren't you instructed on what you have to do, Max?"

"What are you going to do, Lok? Slit my throat? That won't do you any good. You'll be trapped in this building and the Patrician can't get in to rescue you. They can barely transmit images into our heads. I know, they've tried."

He squeezes my throat while banging my head again on the elevator door.

"Go ahead, Lok, kill me. I really don't care anymore," I squeak out.

He lets me go and I fall to the floor. My fingers rub the bruises forming around my neck as he goes back to his equipment. I stand and follow him towards one of the banks of computers. He kneels down, removes a panel from the back, and begins examining wires.

"How did you know what was on this floor?" I ask.

"There's a directory in the lobby," he answers after cutting a wire.

He removes the plastic covering from both ends of the wire, turns the hand-held device over, and removes a tiny transmitter from a storage area on the back. He secures the wires to the electrodes on the back of the transmitter, turns on the display, and begins adjusting a small dial until a picture of the exterior portion of the front entrance appears on his screen. I look up at the monitor behind me to see the same image. He works for the next half-hour linking wires together so he can control the security cameras. He places everything, including the knife, back into the rucksack, and I loop us back into the elevator.

"Let's get Troy before we go to the other floor," Garrett says, turning off the emergency button so we can ascend.

Troy is exiting one of the bathrooms when we reach the housing floor. He quickly dresses and we re-enter the elevator, heading down to the twelfth floor. The doors slide open, revealing a wide metal walkway that extends out from the platform we're standing on and towards another platform in the center of the room. The walkway expands from the other side of the center platform towards the opposite wall, then wraps around towards two extensions in the corners of the room. Each pathway is lined with low rails that barely come up to my calves. We walk cautiously down the expanse. I lean my head over to see where the opening goes and it's at least several stories before a floor appears. The entire pathway is lit up by tiny lights embedded in the rails and it's the only light on the floor. I glance down again to the floors below and notice a similar setup.

I'm made to walk in the middle of the group with Garrett gripping my arm. Probably as a way to make sure I don't loop away from them. The center platform barely has enough room for the four of us and the massive workstation that sits in the middle. Lok sits in the lone chair, turns on the display, and begins typing away at the keyboard just underneath. The image on the screen changes every few seconds, almost like it's resetting itself. Lok grumbles at every alteration and after a half-hour he slams his fists onto the counter.

"I thought you could crack this," Garrett says in a hostile tone, still holding onto me.

"The programming isn't like anything I've ever seen before," Lok says, annoyed. "It keeps modifying its configuration. Whenever I get close, it changes and I have to start all over again."

"What are you looking for?" I ask.

"Their research files," he responds as he starts typing again. "I need to locate what they developed, so the Patrician can gain access to it."

I have to bite my lip to keep from smirking.

"You three might as well head back upstairs. This is going to take me a while," Lok says as he rummages through his rucksack which he dropped on the floor earlier.

We go back to the elevator and head to the top floor. The sun is setting, so Garrett makes dinner. Troy takes a plate down to Lok while I clean up the dishes. Garrett wants to retire for the night, but when I tell him I'm not tired it doesn't go over well.

"I need you rested, Max. Who knows how long it'll take Lok to get into their systems, and when he does you have to be ready to go."

"Go where, Garrett?" I ask as he shoves me off the elevator and into the hallway of the forty-ninth floor.

"Home," he says as he takes my hand and pulls me towards his room.

I yank my hand away. "I am home."

"Don't do this, Max," he says, almost pleading. "The Patrician will have no option but to terminate your existence if you violate their directives." He steps up to me, wraps his arms around my waist, and pulls me in close. "You don't want to do that, now, do you?" he asks, sweetness dripping from his tongue.

I think back to what the Dracken said to me. I'm a Patrician leader now, and should use it to my advantage. If I can get Garrett to trust me, I can manipulate him. One way to get his trust is by letting him believe I stand with him and the rest of the Patrician. I'm going to hate myself for what I'm about to do, but I need him to know he can rely on me. I take my hand and run it through his hair, pushing his head slightly backwards.

"You're right, Garrett," I say, aligning my body against his. "That's not what I want."

I kiss him hard on the lips, push him back against his door, and begin to remove his clothes. We're naked before the door is even completely open. I give all the directions and Garrett obeys my every word. It's satisfying, actually, having him practically begging for more. He soon tires and falls asleep. I stay in bed next to him, thinking my options through.

I need to explore the building, and the only safe time to do that is at night. But where do I start? Lok mentioned there's a directory in the lobby, so maybe that's where I should go first. I slip out of bed, put my clothes on, and step into the hallway. If I take the elevator it could alert the others that I'm moving about. I can loop great distances in the open, but I doubt I can do that in a building of this size. I go towards the stairwell, open the door, and gently close it behind me.

I begin looping down every few floors, and it doesn't take me long to reach the bottom. I exit into the lobby and try to find the directory, but I don't see one.

I carefully look at every pillar, display, and countertop, but find nothing. I then scan all the wall hangings, pictures from a very different time in Pentras' history. Still, I come up empty. I plop down on one of the couches, frustrated. While seated I look around the room and finally notice that there are paintings every few feet apart, except in one spot. I get up, walk over to the blank section of wall, and just as I get close my wristband begins to glow yellow and projects an image on the blank wall. A directory sparkles in front of me. Every floor is carefully mapped out and labeled.

How did the Patrician know this was here if they've never been inside the building? Who could possibly be helping them? Does the Dracken have a traitor in their midst?

I try to remember as much detail as I can. The two floors that interest me the most are the eighth and thirteenth. I know the eighth floor is one of the sealed floors, and it's not shown as having an actual label on the directory. The thirteenth floor is part of the research section and is the only floor that doesn't directly connect to floors nine through twelve. I won't be able to access the eighth floor until I can use the elevator, so I'll start with the thirteenth. I take the stairs up and stop just outside the door to the floor, then take a deep breath and loop.

I project myself just on the other side of the door and the lights turn on the moment I step forward, revealing a room crammed full with old work stations, broken displays, and cracked plasma tables. I have to squeeze myself between sharp edges, shattered glass, and metal shards. The door at the other end of the room is slightly ajar, but I'm forced to move some of the junk so I can open the door wide enough to get through.

The room I enter has minimal lighting. The walls and floors are covered in a rough, dark metal that scratches the soles of my bare feet. Hidden blue lights illuminate the outlines of immense workstations, the three elevator doors on my left, and two disk-shaped stands secured to the far side of the room. I carefully step over to one of the stands and realize they're actually virtual imagers, machines that require someone or something to stand in the middle of it while an image is projected down from the upper casing. I'm not sure how I know what these machines are since they've never been used in the Outer Limits, but I do, which frightens me.

A pedestal with a small display is set to one side of the machine, so I touch the surface and it springs to life. I scroll through the inventory of prototypes, finally stopping on the one for the suit. The imager lights up, so I step over the small ridge that encloses the base to get inside the machine. A shield made of pure light rises from the floor, intersects with its other half in the ceiling, and I find myself draped in an image of the suit. I can feel the material as if it's touching my skin. A menu displays in front of me on the wall of light, providing me with the description of the material that makes up the suit: highly compressed polymers that have been radiated to allow the wearer to blend into their environment. Metallic threads woven into the material allow seamless blending with all objects that come into contact with the material.

I tap on the menu and I'm surprised that I can actually touch it. I slide my finger over various schematics about the outfit and stop when I come across a file labeled practical applications. Inside that is what looks like a memo written by one of the researchers and marked with several red bullet points at the top.

```
    This new technology will not only allow our
citizens to explore the worlds around us in complete
safety, but if applied correctly all devices,
machines, and equipment can be synthesized using this
new technology. This will allow our world to
transport seamlessly across the outer rim of space
without any risks.
```

My eyes stop on the last two sentences and I find myself reading it again aloud.

The Patrician don't want the suit itself. They want the technology behind it. If they get their hands on this there's no stopping them from invading other worlds. Those citizens won't know they've been taken over until it's too late.

I scroll through the menu again, trying to locate an inventory list. It takes me several minutes as it's cleverly buried under a file labeled maintenance equipment. I have to read the number a couple of times to make sure I'm seeing it correctly.

`Suits created: one`

I press a red button on the lower portion of the screen and everything retracts. I step onto the floor and turn my attention back to the small display. A green light is flashing in the upper corner, requesting if production should continue. My finger hesitates in pressing accept, but I tap it and the room is flooded by light coming from the back wall by the storage closet. Large machines sealed behind thick glass begin to dance. I'm surprised at the lack of noise being made, but thankful that it won't alert the others to what I'm doing. I go towards the elevators and notice a security panel next to the center lift. It's a biometric reader, so I put my palm onto the flashing panel. The device scans my hand, turns blue, and flashes *lockdown commencing*. The elevator door opens, I step inside, and another biometric reader appears by the floor selections. I repeat the steps, only this time the device tells me the floor is secured and the reader disappears into the wall before I ascend.

I get off on the forty-ninth floor, enter my room, strip down, and crawl under the covers. I fall asleep quickly, feeling somewhat relaxed by the notion that Lok won't find what he's looking for and that none of them can get to the technology without my knowledge.

Twenty-Five

I know Garrett is next to me before I even open my eyes.

"Why didn't you stay?" he asks, pulling me into his arms.

"I was having trouble falling asleep," I say as I roll over, so my face is buried against his chest. "Has Lok managed to break through the system?"

"Not yet, so I sent him to bed about an hour ago." Garrett kisses the top of my head, pulling me closer. "I do have some good news for you, though."

I lift my head so I can see his face. "What?"

"We're going to Icarian today."

"Seriously?" I ask, sitting up. I'm actually excited. "How do you know?"

"Lok has been able to lower some of the building's security defenses, so the Patrician are now able to send a stronger signal into the building, but it's still not enough to get them inside without your assistance," he says, caressing my bare arm. "You just need to get dressed and once we're back at the plaza the Patrician will loop us there."

"Why can't I do it?" I ask, sounding offended, which I am.

"You don't know where it is and neither do I, so they have to be the ones to loop us."

I lean into him and brush my lips against his, then swing my body over his to get out of bed, but he grabs me and wrestles me back under the covers. It takes an hour for us to finally emerge. We shower together, but get dressed separately. I put the suit on under a long-sleeved beige top and my black pants from the day before. I slip on the boots as well as my sheath, securing it around my waist. The suit blends into the colors of my outfit, affirming what the Dracken told me about it being easily concealable.

Garrett knocks on my door as I finish running my fingers through my long hair, trying to work out the knots. He hands me a hairband from my dresser, and I secure my hair behind my head to get it out of my face. We take the elevator down and find Troy lounging on one of the couches, waiting for us. I grumble at the idea of him coming with us, but Garrett tells me he has to go, so I loop us outside and towards the plaza. Troy isn't used to looping rapidly, so he almost gets sick several times, which makes me grin inside. The moment we're next to the fallen statue I remember that I wanted to ask Lok about the academy. I can't believe I totally forgot about that, but with everything that's happened it's not surprising.

We don't stay long in the plaza when the Patrician begin looping us. The void is longer than any I've been in before, and just when I feel as if all the air has escaped my lungs we land on a stone-paved road. Tall grass that lines the road blows gently in the breeze as the sun shines brightly behind us, rising from its slumber. The sky is nothing like anything I've ever seen: it's a translucent purple and not the normal blue in the Outer Limits, the Dead Zone, or even Tarsus. I begin to wonder if Icarian is even a part of the same world.

Troy and Garrett begin walking, but for a few minutes I'm too caught up in the landscape to move. As I go to catch up with them I wonder if my ability works here as well, so I stop and visualize myself several feet in front of Troy and Garrett, close my eyes, and loop. I'm successful, much to their surprise.

"What's with the look?" I ask. "If I can do it in the Dead Zone, why wouldn't I be able to do it here?"

Our wristbands begin to glow red as shouts fill the air. We draw our weapons and begin to retreat when a mob rushes over the ridge at full speed towards us, their weapons drawn, but they immediately stop when the see us.

"Who set off the sensors?" a tall man with thick muscles and scruffy brown hair asks. He's clearly the leader of the group since everyone is now stepping back.

"I must have," I answer. "Why? Is there a problem?"

"No problem, Max," the man says. "We thought perhaps it was the Dracken finally invading."

"How do you know my name?" I ask, my Kopis held firmly in front of me.

"From watching the *Litarian Battles*," the man says. "We know who you all are."

"Well, I should fucking hope so," Troy says, stepping towards the man. He puts his Deer Horn knives away and embraces the leader. "It's been too long, brother."

The leader – introduced as Jack – hugs his brother as the rest of the mob retreats to the city behind them, which sparkles in the rising sun. The buildings remind me of the ones in Tarsus, only not as opulent or as dark. Troy and Jack talk as they walk behind the group. Garrett slowly steps forward as he secures his bow and arrow. I only lower my weapon, opting not to sheathe it just yet. It doesn't take us long to enter the city proper. The buildings are tall and majestic and one striking thing I notice is that there isn't an inch of covering on any of the windows. You can see into every room of each structure, which is very unsettling. Blue ponds with fountains, freshly cut grass, colorful flowers, pristine wood benches, and marble statues like the one in the plaza cover much of the landscape.

"I can see why they call this a utopia," Troy says as we step in to one of the many courtyards.

"You have no idea," Jack says, winking.

He points to a window two stories up in a building by the road we came in on and we can witness a man and a woman deeply in the throes of sex. They're visible to all who can see and they're drawing quite an audience.

"Is that a common sight?" Garrett asks, his eyes not moving away from the display.

"Very much so," Jack responds. "There's no single mating here. It's one of the perks of living in Icarian. You can have whomever you want and no one is permitted to judge or condemn you."

"What if someone gets jealous?" I ask, turning my focus solely onto Jack.

"We have remedies for that," Jack says, smiling.

I shake and grow cold at the thought of what that could possibly be as I sheathe my weapon. I'm hoping we're not here long, as I don't like Lok being left unguarded in Pentras Tower, nor do I want to leave the others in the Outer Limits any longer.

If they're even still alive, I remind myself.

"This way," Jack says, pointing towards a building at the other end of the courtyard. "Your rooms are ready for you."

"We're staying here?" I almost shout in surprise.

"Yes, Max," Jack says, coming to an abrupt halt. "It's part of your directive, or did you forget about that?"

Does everyone know? What the hell? Am I missing something? What do they know that I don't?

Garrett takes my hand and we begin our trek again, heading up a few steps into the building. We're immediately greeted by matrons, just like the ones in Thrace Tower. Only this time they're asking what we need in order to make our stay more pleasurable instead of ordering us around. Jack tells them we'll need breakfast sent up in about an hour and then proceeds to give them our individual room numbers. The look on Garrett's face is priceless, and I have to stifle the laugh that's about to escape my throat since we're in separate rooms.

"Max and I aren't staying together?" Garrett asks, surprised.

"As I said, Garrett, there isn't any single mating here in Icarian," Jack says. "Everyone gets their own quarters. No one is allowed to share accommodations, as that leads to jealousy."

We're not permitted to have anything of value in the Outer Limits since it could lead to vanity. Looks like similar rules apply here in Icarian. So, is this city actually Dracken-designed and not created by the Patrician? Why would the Dracken build such a place if they were focused on science and technology? What have they been keeping from me?

The walls and floors of the building are covered in white marble that's peppered with gold flecks. Sparkling pools filled with koi flow under walkways as matrons hustle about, tending to those who've decided to spend their time lounging in the lobby area. We step down into the center of the structure that houses a single elevator and Jack pushes the call button. We have to wait a few minutes before the doors finally open. Once inside Jack selects several floors, the doors close, and we ascend. The first stop is the fifth floor, so Jack hits the stop button and escorts Garrett from the elevator. When Jack returns, he removes the stop and we climb to the sixth floor. Again, he presses the stop button, but this time he escorts Troy.

This time it takes more than a few minutes for Jack to return and the two of us ascend to the tenth floor, which is the top floor of the building. The doors open and Jack directs me around the shaft for the elevator to an apartment with a biometric reader next to its door. There isn't any type of door handle, so this must be the only way to get into the apartments. Jack instructs me to place my palm on the device. It scans my hand, changes to blue, and the door slides open.

The apartment floor is covered in plush white carpeting. Colorful paintings, like those in the lobby of Pentras Tower, cover the walls that aren't constructed of glass. The room is separated by four columns and a cube in the center. In front of me is a common room with a long, white sectional couch curved in front of a coffee table and a flat screen television attached to the wall between my apartment and the one next door. I walk around, noticing a kitchen and dining room are against the other adjoining wall. The bedroom contains a large bed and a dresser, and around the corner from that is a sunroom with lounge chairs and a side table.

"Better than the orphanage, wouldn't you say?" Jack asks as he stands behind me.

I continue to stare out the windows in the sunroom, mesmerized by the open field behind our building. I feel him step closer, almost to the point that his body is touching mine.

"Yes, it is," I finally reply.

I step around him and go back to the common room.

"If you need anything," Jack says, following me, "simply use the call button in the kitchen and the matrons will bring it to you." He approaches me and places his hands on my arms, caressing them. "If you need me, just enter in my apartment number on the communicator next to the flat screen."

"Thanks, but I think I'll be fine," I say, stepping out of his reach.

He heads back to the front door, turns to me, and smiles. "Remember what I said, Max," he says, grinning. "I can have whomever I want, and that includes you." He pushes a black button on the wall next to the entrance, the door slides open, and he leaves.

"What the hell is wrong with everyone?" I shout once the door is closed, feeling utterly disgusted by Jack's advances.

I'd rather have Brink's horrid behavior over everyone else here in Icarian.

The matron arrives a few minutes later with a breakfast tray, which she sets down on the dining room table, and leaves. I eat only a little of it since I don't fully trust anything here. I finish the eggs and take a bite of the toast. When I taste cinnamon I immediately spit it out then toss the tray into the kitchen sink. I need to get away from everything, so I take the elevator down, exit onto the courtyard, and begin heading away from the apartment buildings down the stone road, but I don't get far when Jack falls in step next to me.

"Stalking me?" I ask, not breaking my stride.

"Just curious as to where you're going."

"Wherever the road takes me," I reply, annoyed.

He steps in front of me, which causes me to stop. "You won't find an escape from here, Max. Not until the Patrician are ready to transport us."

"So, what were you promised if you became a Patrician lackey?" I ask curiously.

"Huh, you think it's only about them?"

"Oh, that's right, you'll play either side just like Troy… and your father."

He punches me in the face and I'm in the process of grabbing my weapon when he swings me to the ground, placing his knee into my back. "You know nothing about my family," he says, seething.

"I know your brother is a Dracken leader, or at least he used to be, and my parents are dead because of your father," I say, squirming under him.

"You're lying. Troy would never side with the Dracken."

"Then ask him why he has a dragon tattoo on his right bicep."

Jack gets up. "I will," he says, anger heavy in his voice.

He grabs me by the back of my shirt, lifts me off the ground, and we head back towards the apartment building with him shoving me forward every few steps. We take the elevator up to the sixth floor and Jack rings a bell outside of an apartment. Troy opens it, smiling when he sees my discomfort, but it doesn't last long when he notices the look on Jack's face. Jack shoves me inside, onto the floor as he closes the door.

"This little whore says you have a dragon tattoo on your arm. Is that true?" Jack asks, stepping so close to Troy that he's forced to back into the cube wall.

"Yes, but only because Dad told me to get it," Troy answers, whimpering.

"Why would he do that? He knows we're loyal to the Patrician."

"It's a safety net, Jack. You were already in Icarian when Dad thought of it," Troy says, sniveling. "He wanted to make sure he had sons on both sides of the playing field."

"Yeah, in case he had to quickly change his allegiance," I say from my vantage point on the floor.

Jack kicks me in the stomach, picks me up by my throat, and starts to squeeze. "Tell me why I shouldn't kill you."

A laugh escapes my lips. "That threat again? It doesn't scare me anymore," I croak. "The Patrician need me to get what they want from Pentras Tower, and I'm the only person capable of accessing the building."

"We'll have what they want soon," Troy says, his confidence returning. "Lok will get it for us since he's working on cracking the security protocols even as we speak."

"Then what?" I ask. "You give it to the Patrician and they let everyone here live, including you? Is that what they taught you at the academy?"

"How do you know about that?" Jack asks, easing his grip slightly.

"People from Tarsus aren't known for keeping secrets," I respond. "The Patrician are parasites. They don't care about you, only what will benefit them. Once they have what they're looking for, your life will be terminated."

Jack squeezes my neck harder, cutting off my oxygen and I begin to black out, but the ring at the door stops my execution. According to the monitor Garrett is standing on the other side of the door, so Troy signals for Jack to release me and I fall to the floor, gasping for air. Jack takes my arm, propels me over to the couch, and forces me to sit down.

"Say anything to Garrett and I'll have Troy gut you both," Jack whispers in my ear.

Troy opens the door just as Garrett rings again.

"Hey, I was wondering if you've seen Max," he says.

Troy steps out of the way to reveal me.

"There you are," Garrett says, stepping into the apartment. "I was wondering if you wanted to take a walk around the city. Maybe Jack could give us a tour."

"I'd be happy to," Jack says, jumping up from his seat, an eager tone in his voice that I know is forced.

I smile, stand, and the group of us leaves. Once we're down in the lobby, Jack takes us out to the courtyard and begins to tell us more about Icarian. I hold tightly to Garrett as we walk, terrified of being left alone with Jack and Troy.

"Icarian is an ancient utopian city created by the Patrician to reward those most loyal to them," Jack says with enthusiasm as we walk through various courtyards. "At first only retired party leaders or high-ranking citizens were sent here, but soon after the *Litarian Battles* were established the winners were gifted with a life of luxury and leisure here as well. Anything we need is provided to us. You'll find no Aedox or formal police of any kind here."

"What if a law is broken? Who doles out the punishment?" Garrett asks.

"The person the Patrician have placed as leader, which at the moment is me," Jack replies. "This position does change, but only after the person has died."

"Law-breaking can't happen too often in a place like this," Troy says.

"Thankfully it doesn't," Jack responds.

"But what if it does? How do you punish the offender?" I ask, trying to stir things up again, which probably isn't the smartest move.

Jack stops, turns around, and looks squarely at me. "We make an example out of them, Max, by displaying them for all to see," Jack says authoritatively. "A good example would be someone like you. If you were a true resident of Icarian and you continued with your smart mouth and defiant manner, I'd string you up by your thumbs in front of the whole city. Then I would strip you down and whip you until you succumbed to your injuries. Now, does that sound like a decent punishment?"

I slink behind Garrett, averting my eyes from Jack who laughs and continues with the tour. I don't speak for the rest of the day or evening. We eat a small dinner in one of the cafés in the lobby of the apartment building. I ask Garrett to stay with me for the night and he's more than happy to oblige, but I want him there mainly for safety. Luckily, he's not into having sex tonight, which I'm overly appreciative of, and he's gone before I wake the following morning.

My bladder calls my attention just as the sun is rising, so I go into the bathroom which is the cube-shaped room in the center of the apartment. Thankfully, it has no windows. The interior of the bathroom is crimson with gold accents. Against the back wall is a sunken tub big enough to fit three people. Clean towels hang between the tub and the toilet, which is next to the vanity. Across from that is a shower stall with a rainspout for a showerhead. I step out into the common room, go to the bedroom and remove a white linen top and matching pants, along with some fresh undergarments.

I refuse to get dressed in a manner where the entire world can see. When I re-enter the bathroom, I make sure to lock that door since it uses a normal door handle. I hang my new clothes on hooks next to the shower stall and place a couple of towels at the base of the tub, since it sits on a raised platform. As the water fills the tub, I rummage under the vanity for bath wash and locate several containers of bath salts. I pick one and pour it into the steaming water before stripping down and easing my way in.

The hot water feels good on my tired body. I hadn't realized how tense I was until now, and I slip down into the water until only my face is above it. I feel everything slipping away: all troubles, all concerns, and all cares. I close my eyes and let my mind drift as I deeply inhale the scent wafting up from the bath salts as they dissolve. The aroma makes me weary, but at first I don't understand why.

Frey enters my mind, and I think about the time I spent with him in Tarsus. I should feel sad about his absence, but I can't think why. I feel as if I'm floating above the world and everything is beneath me.

"That's it, Max, let go," I hear a voice say in my head. "You know you want more… you deserve more. We can give you whatever you want and all we ask for in return is loyalty."

"Loyalty," I whisper.

"That's right, Max. You're a Patrician to the core, a leader everyone will be looking toward when the invasion starts. War is coming, Max, and you've finally chosen the correct side."

I smile automatically at the last comment. The voice leaves me just as the water turns cold. I remove the stopper so the water will drain out and that's when it hits me. The scent of the bath salts… it was cinnamon. Just like the cinnamon in the tea Frey gave me, it relaxed my body, making it easily manipulated. I want to shake myself of the sensation, but I'm suddenly exhausted. I dry off, don my clothes, and am startled when I see a matron setting up breakfast in the kitchen.

"I hope you've found everything to your satisfaction," the woman says. "If you need anything, just call and we'll be happy to supply it." She leaves as quietly as she entered.

I stare at the food, salivating because I'm starving, but also scared to touch it for fear of more mind and body manipulation. My hunger finally wins out, so I sit at the dining table and eat every bit. I put the dishes in the sink, go into the bedroom and collapse on the bed, falling back to sleep since my body is surprisingly drained of all energy.

I dream about Frey. He dies horribly in front of me, burned to death by the fires that ravage the Outer Limits. I don't cry, or even try to help him. I just stand and watch with Garrett smiling beside me. Frey won't stop screaming from the pain so Garrett is forced to shoot him with an arrow, ending his life.

I bolt upright in bed. Not from the dream, but from a noise. Jack walks into the room and sits on the edge of the bed.

"Have a good nap?" he asks, leaning against the headboard.

"How the hell did you get in here?"

"Who do you think programs the biometric readers?" he asks, pride heavy in his voice. "I can get into any apartment I wish. It's one of the benefits of being chosen as a Patrician leader. At least, that's the deal I made with them to become one."

"You're pathetic," I say.

I shove off the covers and am in the process of getting out of bed when Jack grabs my arm, pulling me back down. He presses his massive body on top of mine as his hands wrap around my wrists, pushing them above my head.

"So, Max, how should we play this out? Do you submit, or do I take?"

"Is that another Patrician leader perk, or are you naturally a fucking asshole?"

"Such language, Max."

He kisses me hard, practically ramming his tongue down my throat, but I bite back, splitting his lip. He backhands me across the face and I squirm under him, trying to throw him off, but he's too heavy.

"You wanted to kill me yesterday, but now you want to fuck me? Get off!" I scream.

"Only when we're done."

He leans in closer and I slam my head against his. The world spins and I see stars, but it's enough to daze him also. I slide out from under him and on to the floor, then bolt towards the bathroom, but Jack is only one step behind me. I turn the corner and am reaching for the door handle when Jack's full weight takes me down. My chin hits the wood planked floor, causing me to cut my lower lip. Nausea washes over me as Jack flips me over on to my back. I know I have a concussion since I'm drifting in and out of consciousness, but I know what he's doing. I grab a hold of reality long enough to plant my foot firmly against his crotch, then I take my other leg and knee him in the face. He moans in pain as I move out from under him. I get back to the bedroom and grab the Kopis, which I left slung over a chair at the foot of the bed. Jack gets to his feet and runs after me. I hold the weapon out in front of me and he stops.

"You won't always be armed, Max."

He slowly backs away and then finally leaves. I call for a matron to come and tend to my injuries, then I go check them out for myself in the bathroom mirror.

So much for being a utopia.

I'm sitting on the floor against the wall of the bathroom when the matron from earlier enters. She applies a healing ointment to my lip, an ice pack to the bump that's formed on my forehead, and gives me painkillers. She doesn't ask any questions and says she'll come back in a few hours to check on me, but that I shouldn't go to sleep. She takes my dirty clothes from the bathroom and leaves. I drop my weapon on to the bed since I'd still been holding it, put on clean linen pants and shirt, curl up on the sectional, and turn on the television.

There isn't anything to watch except what looks like security footage from Tarsus. No one is in the streets and the flashy lights are off, making the large city look eerily abandoned. I pick up a remote from the coffee table and scroll through the few channels that are available. Previous episodes of the *Litarian Battles* run in a loop, but none of them look recent, so I guess they're probably from when the show originally started. I shut the screen off, move to the sunroom where I pull one of the lounge chairs closer to the windows, and sit. The sun is high overhead and there are more people in the courtyard today than yesterday.

I wonder how many people actually live here now that Thrace Tower is empty. Would the Patrician have moved any of their loyalists who lived in the city to here as well? Is that why Tarsus looks so empty?

The front door chimes, so I get up and go over to the communicator, which shows Garrett standing on the other side.

"What do you want?" I ask through the device.

"You all right, Max? You don't sound right."

"I'm fine," I lie. "I'm just tired. I guess traveling from the Dead Zone to Icarian took more out of me than I thought possible."

"Why don't I believe you? Max, let me in," he says as he starts pounding on the door.

"Go away."

"No, not until I know you're okay."

"Fine," I say, and push the button to let him in.

The door slides open and Garrett storms into the room. He takes one look at me, picks me up, and sets me down on the couch then closes the door and goes into the kitchen, coming back with a cold drink.

"What happened?" he asks, handing me the glass.

"I don't want to talk about it."

I swallow the contents in one gulp, hand the empty glass back to Garrett, and he goes back to the kitchen to refill it. This time he returns with two tumblers. He hands me one but holds on to the other as he sits beside me.

"Are you going to tell me, or do I have to guess?"

"You just won't give up, will you?"

"Not when it comes to protecting you."

With that last remark he sounds like the Garrett I met back in Thrace Tower, which hurts my heart since I know that wasn't his true self.

"I'll take care of it," is the only response I give.

We sit in silence until the matron returns sometime later with lunch. Somehow she knew Garrett was with me since she brings in two meals. We eat in the dining room but I only pick at my food, not having much of an appetite. Garrett tries to coax me into going outside with him, but I decline, so he kisses me gently then leaves. I go back to the sunroom, but not until I take my Kopis off the bed. I'm not letting go of it and I probably won't sleep either while we're here, since Jack can get into the apartment whenever he wants.

I quickly become bored and restless; sitting idle has never worked out well for me. I go into the bathroom to splash some cold water on my face and notice the suit is hanging on one of the hooks by the shower. It should've been removed when the rest of my clothes were, but the matron left it behind. Why?

I go into the kitchen and push the call button. The matron responds quickly, asking what I need. I lie and tell her my head is starting to hurt worse, so she says she'll be up shortly, but almost an hour passes before she finally enters the apartment.

"I brought you something stronger for the pain," she says, handing me a shot glass filled with a blue liquid.

I take it from her, but don't drink it. "Who are you?" I ask.

She looks at me, clearly puzzled by the question. "I'm not sure I understand," she says.

I go and close the front door. The woman begins to sweat and tremble, though she's doing a good job of trying to hide it.

"You left something behind when you collected my clothing," I say.

"Oh, I wasn't aware that I had. Do you need me to clean it?"

I walk around her, which causes her to shake more. I feel she's on the verge of collapse when I gesture towards the bathroom so she can retrieve the item. Once we're inside, I lock us in.

Twenty-Six

"Icarian isn't what you thought it was, is it, Cil?"

The woman's body relaxes, almost going limp. "How did you figure it out?" she asks, leaning against one of the walls.

"You left the suit behind."

"Still, that shouldn't have tipped you off," she says as she removes a necklace from around her throat, which causes her face to morph into the one I'm familiar with. Her hair color and length return to normal as well. "Comes in handy when you're hiding." She hands me the necklace. "Keep it. I have more."

"Where you'd get it?" I ask, fingering the smooth, shiny metal.

"The same place you got the suit," she says as she sits on the floor, her body completely at ease. "Did you know they have cameras in each room except this one?"

So that's how Jack knew I was alone.

"That doesn't surprise me," I say, sitting on the cool tile across from her and leaning back against the shower stall.

"Still, Max, how'd you know it was me?"

"You're the only one I noticed without a laurel tattoo on the side of your wrist," I reply. "Which means you haven't been here long. Also, I caught the look in your eyes down in the lobby yesterday when you saw me. You can wear a mask, but when you recognize someone your reaction is hard to hide. The others didn't look startled, but you did and that could only mean you thought I was elsewhere. Everyone else I know is either in the Outer Limits or dead. And you seem to easily move about the regions without any problems, so who else could you have been?"

She lets out a laugh, which causes me to laugh as well.

"So, now what?" she asks.

"I ask you a couple of questions, then I kill you," I say nonchalantly.

The laughter stops. "You can't be serious."

I swing the Kopis towards her throat. "I'm very serious."

"Why…why would you want to kill me, Max? I've done nothing but help you," she says, almost pleading.

"You're a Dracken traitor, Cil. You tipped off the Patrician on how to get into Pentras Tower, but you also told the Keepers about the plot to mutilate me. You've been playing both sides, but I can't figure out why."

"You're crazy, Max," she says, shaking her head and letting out a nervous laugh.

"Then tell me, how did the Patrician know what type of lighting was needed to read the directory in the lobby of Pentras Tower?" I ask. "You're the only one besides Lok who knows how to maneuver their way around the wristbands' programming. Also, you just said yourself that you got this necklace from the same place I got the suit and there's only one way you could've possibly known that: if you're actually a Dracken, one from the previous society that was destroyed by the Patrician." I lean in closer, the tip of the Kopis almost piercing her skin. "Tell me, Cil, how have you been kept alive all this time? That attack happened, what, about a century ago? That would make you ancient, yet you still look young. What did the Patrician promise you if you helped them?"

"Immortality," she hisses. "I told them that I could get them into Pentras Tower, but they couldn't wait any longer. When their plan failed, though, they finally listened to me. Only, my terms went up." Her eyes grow dark as she crosses her arms across her chest. "I was one of the researchers who helped create the technology the Patrician are seeking. When they arrived they threatened our society, said they would turn the world to ash if we didn't give them what they wanted. I began smuggling some of the items out, but the Patrician grew impatient. They dropped nuclear weapons on Pentras while I was traveling to one of their ships. The tower's defenses went into action, preventing anyone from entering, and the city was so contaminated that no one could get close enough to disengage them. The Dracken who survived retreated to the Outer Limits after securing the area with the dome. I was the Patrician's only link to the technology they craved."

"So, you traded your soul for living forever. Unfortunately, that's not going to pan out for you. But why help the Patrician at all?"

"Sometimes worlds just need to be scratched from existence," she says heatedly. "And this one needs to be turned to rubble."

"Tell me why, as it may cause me to spare your life."

"Wow, Max, you're as nuts as your parents," she says. "That's what their thinking was, too, and look where it got them. And you, for that matter."

"Wait a minute," I say, lowering the sword and scooting closer to her. "My parents wanted this place destroyed?"

"Yes, but not because of the Patrician. This world was heading for destruction before the Patrician ever arrived. They just accelerated the process."

"Then why?" I raise my weapon again, almost jamming it into her throat. "I'm tired of this bullshit, Cil. Just spit it out already."

"Fine," she hisses. "Because they learned the truth about what the Dracken were going to do. I helped them realize it, but that was only after they'd been exiled to the Outer Limits and you disappeared." She takes a deep breath. "The technology isn't only to assist the Dracken in moving from one world to another, but to leave inferiors behind to die. They were only going to transfer those they felt worthy of their superior society, which meant that millions of people would be left to succumb to the poison the world houses."

"You're giving me a headache, Cil."

"The Dracken need their technology to survive; it keeps the world from killing its inhabitants. If the Dracken take the technology with them, then those who aren't permitted to go will perish. The Patrician were offering a way out for those of us who were going to be left behind. If we helped them get the technology, they'd take us with them. We would be saved."

"They lied to you," I say. "I've seen what the Patrician have done to the worlds they invade. Nothing is left, including its people."

"Did the Dracken show you that?"

The pounding in my head increases the more we go around and around with this nonsense. "At this moment, Cil, I don't believe anyone. Including you."

"Suit yourself, but don't blame me when you get tossed aside by the Dracken when this is all over with."

"Too bad you won't be alive to see it."

I thrust the Kopis into her neck, almost severing her head. I clean the blood from the blade, hide the suit in the bottom drawer of the dresser, and use the call button. A new matron is sent up when I advise her that there's been an incident. Cil's body is removed and the bathroom cleaned without any questions being raised, which I'm thankful for. I have to change my clothes again due to the blood spatter, but this time I put the suit back on and cover it up with a dark blue jumpsuit. I belt my Kopis around my waist and look for an apartment number on the communicator.

"Change your mind?" Jack asks as he opens the door a few minutes later.

My Kopis slices his thigh, then I shove him to the floor and quickly close the door.

"What the hell is wrong with you?" he shouts, putting his hands on his leg to try to slow the bleeding.

"Tell me about the academy."

"What?"

"What were you all taught at the academy?"

"What does that have to do with anything?"

I tap my weapon against his other leg. "Tell me or your other leg will be just as useless."

He winces from the pain, blood flowing from his wound. "Get me medical attention, then we'll talk."

"I need a guarantee, then."

"Like what?" he asks through gritted teeth.

"You leave me the fuck alone. You even *try* to rape me again and I'll gut you."

"Fine."

I press the call button in the kitchen. Since his apartment is identical to mine I didn't need to ask where it was. His matron arrives swiftly and the two of us move him onto the couch, so she can begin mending his injury.

"Talk," I say, sitting on the coffee table, tapping his good leg with the Kopis.

"Garrett can have you," he says through spasms of pain. "Or is it Frey you're with now? Troy tells me you're quite the object of people's desire lately, so I wonder who's next for you."

I slide the Kopis up his thigh. "What did I tell you?"

"You're no fun," he mutters. He waits until he's mended and the matron leaves before continuing. "The Patrician run the academy, or at least they used to." He adjusts his position on the couch, trying to get comfortable. "We weren't taught much since it was mainly propaganda against the Dracken. What we did learn was that the Patrician are a people who absorb other societies. They didn't hide the fact that they've destroyed other worlds. In fact, they boasted about it, and told us that if we were to be loyal to them we needed to know our history… the Patrician history."

"And the Dracken?"

"We had the occasional student voice an opinion about what liars the Patrician are, but that was mainly because their parents were Dracken loyalists like Frey's father."

"What about your parents? Especially your father. Remember, he's the reason my parents are dead."

"Your parents' own ignorance is the reason they're dead," he says furiously. "Not because of my father. They just couldn't leave well enough alone. Our society was making great headway with the Patrician in creating an alliance with them to secure our existence, but your parents had to go and fuck everything up."

I'm half tempted to punch him in the face for being so naïve, but I need him to keep talking so I try to keep myself calm.

"What my father did was for our own protection, including yours," Jack adds.

He moves his leg slightly, checking its strength. The healing ointment has done its job, so he's able to put weight on the leg. He gets up and goes into the kitchen, but I stay seated on the coffee table. He brings a pitcher filled with a pale red liquid and two glasses. He hands me one, pours me a drink, and sits back down on the couch. I know better than to trust anything I'm given now, so I sniff at the drink.

Cinnamon.

"Nice try," I say, setting the glass onto the coffee table.

"Hey, you know I'm not going to give up, Max. You'll eventually see things my way."

"Have you always been this arrogant, or am I just lucky?"

He laughs as he pours himself a drink from the same container. "Not only does this stuff increase your desire, it also relaxes the hell out of you," he says, raising his glass then pouring the liquid down his throat. "Ah, now that's better."

"Why would you want to form an alliance with the Patrician? They obliterate worlds."

"And the Dracken aren't any different," he says, pouring himself another. "At least with the Patrician you're given a fighting chance. The Dracken are just cold-hearted individuals who only believe in the preservation of the worthiest. Of which there are few." He empties his glass, then set it down on the coffee table.

"So, what did the Patrician promise you if you followed them?" I ask.

"Whatever I want, which of course keeps changing every day. Like now, for instance. You're what I want the most, so what do I have to do to earn you?" he asks as he moves to the edge of the couch and begins massaging my thighs.

I'm about to run him through with the Kopis, when I stop myself mid-thought. I put the weapon off to the side, take his hands, and place them on my hips as I move closer to him.

"Get me to the Outer Limits without the Patrician or the Dracken finding out," I answer.

He smiles, but it's more from the alcohol than my request. "There's a way I can do that," he says, eyeing me up and down. "But I need some kind of security from you. What are you willing to give me now, so I know you're serious about this transaction?"

I think about that since it won't be a simple price. "I can give you a preview of what to expect," I reply as I climb into his lap, straddle his waist, and shove my tongue down his throat.

He has me on my back in seconds, his hands searching for the opening of the jumper. I push him back, move from the couch, and let him fall back down.

"There'll be more later," I say as I push the button to exit. The door slides open and I'm back in the elevator, ascending to my floor before he has time to recover.

Garrett rings the bell just as the sun is setting, but I don't turn on any lights since I don't want anyone to know I'm letting him in. Especially Jack.

"Why do you have it dark?" Garrett asks when he crosses the threshold.

"No privacy, remember? I don't want my life to be on display for all of Icarian."

The door closes and we sit on the couch. "Have you seen Jack? Troy has been looking for him for hours, but no one can find him."

"Nope. I haven't seen him since we got here."

Garrett pulls me to his side and starts to nuzzle my neck. "So, are you ready to tell me what happened earlier?"

"Forget it, it's been taken care of."

"You still don't trust me?" he asks, but his accurate observation doesn't stop him from pulling me down on top of him.

"Is this all any of you think about?" I ask, pushing myself up.

"What can I say? You're desirable, Max; and I want to enjoy you as much as possible whenever possible."

"Have you taken anything with cinnamon in it?"

He stops and looks at me, puzzled, but I can see the wheels turning in his head and then click when it finally sinks in.

"Shit," he says.

I move to the other end of the sectional while he adjusts his clothing.

"I warned you about it in Tarsus, and here I am bathing in it," he says.

"Bath salts?"

"No, body wash."

"I think this place is full of the stuff. That's probably why everyone is so into bedding each other. It's false desire," I say.

Dracken influence or Patrician? What a second. When Lok and Garrett warned me about it, they said that Leader Fallon had banned it. So, it's the Dracken providing this drug-like substance. Does that mean they really did create Icarian? If so, for what purpose? I bet Cil would have known, but there isn't any way to ask her now. Who's left from the original Dracken society? Is there anyone?

"Max, did you hear me?"

"Sorry," I say, shaking my head to clear it.

"Have you eaten dinner?"

I tell him I haven't, so he calls down to the matron and asks for our meals to be brought up. For this, we have to turn on the lights. The matron brings us our meals, but we only manage to get through half of it when the doorbell chimes. I get up and notice that it's Troy, but he looks agitated. I open the door and quickly close it after he enters.

"Did you find Jack?" Garrett asks, getting up from his seat at the dining room table.

"Yes, but there's an issue," Troy says. "And I need Max to come with me."

"I'm not going anywhere with you," I say, returning to the dining room.

"He's in trouble because of you!" Troy shouts. "You fucked with his head, Max, and now his life is at risk."

Garrett turns towards me. "What did you do?"

"The same thing everyone has been doing to me… manipulating him to get what I want, and I'd do it again to any of you," I say. "I'm tired of this damn puppet show. I just want this whole thing over with, and at this point I don't care who wins."

"Fine," Troy says. "Then come with me."

"I'm going, too," Garrett says.

"Well, I'm not going unarmed," I say.

I retrieve my Kopis from the sectional where I'd left it when I returned earlier, then slip into the bedroom and tuck the necklace Cil gave me into one of the pockets in my jumpsuit. We take the elevator down to Garrett's room, where he retrieves his bow and arrow. The lobby is bustling with matrons and citizens, as it seems Icarian's nightlife is a lot more colorful and entertaining than the daytime activities. We exit, cross the courtyard, and take the road behind the apartment building.

As the sun sets the sky turns black, displaying vast amounts of stars that I've never seen before. The air is too polluted in the Outer Limits and Tarsus had so many lights it washed the night sky out. I continue to stare up as we walk and notice two objects that appear out of place: one a colored globe, and the other a bulkier metal sphere. They're a great distance away, but it's obvious they aren't a natural occurrence.

Troy veers off the road about twenty minutes later and down a pebbled path leading into the middle of a field. It takes another ten minutes before I finally see a structure. It's oblong and covered in a domed roof made of small reflective panels. A small light hangs next to the lone door and Troy enters a code on a keypad by the light and the door opens. We step inside and before I know it someone knocks me down from behind. My head hurts from the impact and everything is blurry. I can make out Troy and Garrett scuffling by the door that's now closed. An image of my attacker slowly comes into focus as he gets closer. Jack kneels next to me, resting on his heels.

"How dumb do you think I am?" he asks. "You're just as treacherous as your parents."

He grabs my throat and lifts me into the air. I claw at his hands, but his grip only tightens. I try to reach for my Kopis, but I can't find it. Troy punches Garrett hard in the face, breaking his nose. Blood pours from the wound as Garrett collapses to the sandy floor, and Troy begins kicking him in the ribs that I hear crack.

"Enough!" someone shouts from behind me. "Jack, put her down."

He doesn't do it right away, so the man behind me has to tell him again. Jack drops me and I fall to the ground, suffering through a violent coughing fit as I try to get air into my lungs. As I scan the room looking for another exit, I realize that none of us has a weapon, not even Jack and Troy.

The older man who told Jack to let me go comes over to me, extends his hand, and helps me to my feet. "Weapons aren't permitted in this building," he says, noticing the look on my face. At the sound of his voice flashes of memory come back to me, but only for an instant and not long enough for me to hold on to.

"Who are you?" I ask, brushing myself off.

"Guy Larsen," he replies. "I haven't seen you, Mera, since you were three. My, how you've grown." He walks around me, sizing me up with his lustful eyes, just as Jack did, and it sickens me.

"You're just as beautiful as your mother was," Guy says. His hands brush across my back, then rest on my shoulder. "Oh, how the sun would turn her raven hair a dark purple. Tell me, does it have the same effect on you?"

"Get away from me," I say, swatting his hand off me.

"She goes by Max now, Father," Jack says.

"So I've heard. A new name for a new identity," Guy says.

"It's my only identity," I state angrily.

"We'll see about that," Guy responds, his lips curling up into a distorted grin.

He turns around and behind him is a small display sitting on a narrow, white pedestal, just like the ones in Pentras Tower. There isn't anything else in the room, which disturbs me greatly. He grabs my hand and pulls me towards it. I try and fight him off, but he's surprisingly strong. Garrett starts to get to his feet, but Troy is quick to shove him back down. Guy forces my hand over to the display, which lights up upon my approach. He takes out a small piece of broken glass, cuts my finger with it, and squeezes several drops of blood onto the display.

"Thomas, Mera," a female voice chimes around us. "Authentication confirmed."

The panels that make up the walls of the structure change from clear to milky white and the room is filled with light, but not blindingly.

"What is this place?" I ask, pinching my finger to stop the bleeding.

"It's the Icarian Depository," Guy says, gesturing to the walls. "It has all the records of Dracken history, dating back to when this world began. We've never been able to access it until now because we needed a direct descendent of the original society's leadership to gain entry and it took the Patrician years to realize who that person was."

"That's the reason I was selected to be in the *Litarian Battles*," I say. "Not because of the mutilation, but because if I won the game I would be sent here, another location the Patrician haven't been able to get into just like Pentras Tower."

"Jack was right about you, Mera. You are smart," Guy says.

I try to back up, but my path is blocked by Jack. "Don't call me that," I say angrily.

"In order to guarantee your victory," Guy says, ignoring my comment, "Leader Fallon had you removed from the orphanage and modified. It was the only way we could be sure you survived, since the Keepers had started changing the rules of the game almost daily."

"I thought you supported the Dracken," I respond.

"We go with whoever has the best offer," he replies. "And at this moment, since it's almost the end, the Patrician have made our loyalty to them very much worth our while. As soon as you transmit the information from this depository to Patrician Nine, and you get the technology we seek from the tower, this will all be over."

"And what happens to me?" I ask, crossing my arms across my chest.

"You live," Jack replies, pressing his body against mine.

I have a feeling my life will include being made Jack's sex slave, along with anything else the Larsen family desires.

"And what if I refuse? Killing me isn't an option for you," I say with an attitude.

"No, it's not. But killing Garrett is," Troy says, removing a blade similar to the one Lok has.

"I thought weapons weren't allowed in here," Garrett says through fits of pain.

"There's ways to conceal them," Jack responds.

They think threatening me with Garrett's death will work, so I start to laugh, almost hysterically.

"Go ahead, he means nothing to me," I say as I continue to chuckle. "But there's something you should know. He's an offspring of a Patrician leader, so I'm not sure how they'll feel about you murdering one of their own." I step around Jack and Guy, trying to put them between me and the pedestal. "So, I see no way of you winning this little showdown."

"She's bluffing," Guy says.

Troy advances towards Garrett; I feel my Kopis returning to my hand. I thrust the blade into Jack, a satisfying experience and one I've been thinking a lot about. I'm removing the weapon when I notice that Garrett's bow and arrow have also been returned to him. He fires, hitting Troy in the eye. I flip the blade around and hold it against Guy's throat.

"Any last words?" I ask.

"How is this possible?" Guy asks, a look of utter shock and disbelief on his face.

"You fucked with the wrong family."

I drag the weapon across his throat. Garrett stands and shoots one more arrow into Troy's body just to make sure he's dead. I wipe Guy's blood off my blade and use the jumpsuit to clean the blood spatter from the display. I sheathe my Kopis and begin calling up the various records. I have to look at the walls to see what I'm doing since the screen on the display itself is too small to read anything.

"What just happened?" Garrett asks, swinging his quiver and bow over his shoulders.

"You tell me, Garrett. You're the Patrician leader, not me."

"This is a Dracken building, Max. There's no way the Patrician could've been able to arm us."

"Yup, you're right. So what does that mean?"

"It means, Garrett, that you need to trust us," a voice booms around us.

I know who it is before even looking at the picture off to the side.

"Once you make the transfer, Max, you should be able to loop back to Pentras Tower," Hammond says.

"Transfer? What transfer?" Garrett asks, clearly confused.

"I'm moving the historical data from the depository to the computers in Pentras Tower."

"Why?"

"To preserve them since we need to destroy this building and everything in it," I reply.

"Transfer initiating," the female voice chimes.

"Why?" Garrett asks. "No one cares what's in this building except for Guy Larsen."

"Because the Patrician have taken over Icarian," Hammond says. "It's only a matter of time until they try to locate another successor to Max to obtain the information."

"Has Lok managed to break through yet?" I ask Hammond.

"No. We've managed to keep him at bay, but it won't be long until he figures out the pattern."

"Transfer is at fifty percent," the female voice announces.

"Will one of you please explain to me what the hell is going on!" Garrett yells.

"We'll do that upon your return to Pentras Tower," Hammond says.

"Transfer complete," the woman says.

"Loop now, Max. The Patrician have learned about your treachery, so you must get back to the safety of the tower as quickly as possible," Hammond says.

"What about the building?" I say.

"It's too late, you must leave now," Hammond says, then vanishes.

I grab Garrett's arm and loop us. I've never done this long a projection before and I barely get us to the plaza when all hell breaks loose. Bombs rain down from above, hitting the dome and cracking it in a few places. I quickly loop us towards the building and into the lobby.

"We need to find Lok," I say as I run towards the elevator.

"He might still be on the twelfth floor," Garrett says, almost crashing into me in his haste to get into the elevator.

We reach the twelfth floor, but Lok isn't anywhere to be found. His rucksack is sitting on the floor next to the work station, so he couldn't have gone far. We check the forty-ninth and fiftieth floors, but they're empty.

"You don't suppose he could be on one of the sealed floors, do you?" Garrett asks as we descend.

I hit the stop button when we're just on the opposite side of floor seven. I take Garrett's hand and loop us inside. The lights are on, which means someone is currently on the floor. I unsheathe the Kopis and hold it by my side as we step through the open security gate. The plasma table in the center is on, showing the Patrician bombing the dome. It's begun to crack in more places, but the glass is still thick enough to keep any of the bombs from penetrating… for now anyway.

"Hey," Lok says, popping up from behind the same computer bank he was at earlier. "I wasn't expecting you to be back so soon."

"Change of plans," Garrett says. He tries to sound normal, but the nervous shaking in his voice is giving him away.

"Um, okay," Lok say as he stands, and that's when I notice his bow and arrow are positioned in front of him, armed and ready to fire. "Where's Troy?"

"Dead," I say. "The Dracken killed him. We need to hurry and get moving on locating that technology the Patrician are looking for."

Lok aims his bow at me. "You said that a little too fast, Max. Since the Patrician are currently trying to shell their way into the Dead Zone I'm guessing something else happened. Are you going to tell me what it is, or do I have to shoot you first?"

"We don't have time for this," I respond.

I reach for Garrett's weapon, but Lok fires before I get a chance to grab it. The arrow cuts through my back, exiting out my side. I collapse as Garrett fires his arrow at Lok, hitting him in the chest. I look down, surprised by what I don't see. Blood should be seeping out of me, but it's not. I don't even feel any pain. My collapse was pure reaction to what I thought my body would feel, not actually due to an injury.

"You're not injured? How is that possible?" Garrett asks, kneeling next to me and examining the entry and exit holes in the jumpsuit.

I unzip the outfit, pull my arms out of the sleeves, and look at the suit. Not a mark on it.

"Is this the stuff everyone's been looking for?" Garrett asks, touching the soft material.

I nod. "We have to destroy it," I say, stripping the jumpsuit off and removing the necklace from the pocket. I put it around my throat and hope it doesn't change my appearance. It doesn't, so I must need to instruct it like I do with the suit.

"Destroy it? Are you kidding me?" Garrett asks, stunned "This would make us all impervious to harm. We could go anywhere, do anything."

"That's the Patrician in you talking," I say. "This technology is dangerous; it has to be destroyed."

I head towards the elevator with Garrett close behind. I push the button for the thirteenth floor, but the elevator stops at the eighth floor. We try descending, but it won't move down either.

I wonder…

I take Garrett's hand and loop us onto the eighth floor. We're met by a wide hallway covered in crisp white paint. A set of double doors looms in front of us, but without any handles, just like the doors for the Icarian apartments. As we approach a biometric reader drops down from the wall next to the doors, so I place my palm on the screen.

"Thomas, Mera. Access granted," the same female voice from the depository says from hidden speakers.

The room we enter is similar to the one we just left, right down to the door and the biometric reader.

"How many rooms do you think we have to go through?" Garrett asks.

"I don't know," I answer, placing my palm on the reader.

"Thomas, Mera. Access granted."

The door opens to a room void of color, only darkness. Tiny dots begin to twinkle around us as the door closes.

"What is this place?" I ask, scanning the room and noticing the floor is also dark with tiny dots.

"Where would you like it to be?" Hammond asks, stepping forward. His body is being projected into the room, but I can't tell from what or where.

"You're the Keeper," I state.

"One of them, yes," Hammond replies.

"How many of you are there?" Garrett asks.

"There are only a few of us left. The Patrician have made sure of that."

"So, what the Dracken said is true: you're the enemy of the Patrician," I say.

"Yes," Hammond says. "We've been fighting against the Patrician for many centuries. We were hoping to make progress in restoring the worlds they shattered, but we've been largely unsuccessful. Our hope was that, in saving Pentras and the Dracken society, we would be gaining an ally with the type of technology needed to defeat the Patrician."

"But the Dracken weren't who you thought they were," Garrett says.

"Yes," Hammond says sadly. "They aren't a giving or kind people. When they realized that the modifications the Patrician had done to Max would benefit them in retrieving their lost technology, they used her and anyone who followed them for their own means."

"Why?" Garrett asks, a confused look on his face.

"Because when Pentras Tower went on lockdown, it not only kept the Patrician from gaining access but the Dracken as well," I respond. "Their security was too effective. They needed someone from an original bloodline to penetrate the building, locate the information, and give it back to them. But wait a minute… Cil said she was one of the original researchers when this all started. How come she couldn't get in?" I ask.

"What she told you is a half-truth. Cil was old, but not a direct descendant of the original settlers to this world. The Dracken were so concerned about protecting their technology that they created an almost impossible failsafe, one that they hadn't thought all the way through. It wasn't until Leader Fallon hid you that the Dracken realized their mistake."

"So, they did intend to leave those they felt were beneath them behind to die," I comment.

"Yes," Hammond says. "Your parents were the last line of pure Dracken blood. While living in the shanties by the smelting plant, they learned the truth of their heritage. They didn't feel the same way as their ancestors. But Guy Larsen was determined to bring the Dracken way of life back. With him gone, the Dracken are no more."

"Except for Max," Garrett says.

"In a way, but she is much like her parents." Hammond smiles, which causes me to smile in return.

"Now what?" I ask.

"The Patrician will continue to attack this world until they get what they came for. You need to destroy it," Hammond says.

"How?" Garrett asks, stunned. "The building is built solid. The Patrician nuked the area and nothing happened to the structure."

"We need to get to the Outer Limits," I say, heading towards the door.

"Why? What's there?" Garrett asks, following me.

"Van and his explosives."

Twenty-Seven

We head back to the elevator, but instead of selecting the lobby I push the button for the thirteenth floor. This time the elevator moves. The doors don't open when the car stops because of the lockdown I'd put in place. The biometric reader emerges next to the floor selection panel, so I place my palm on it and the doors open. The lights turn on as I run over to the machines encased in the side wall. Sitting in neat piles behind the glass are at least one hundred suits, with more being created. I step through the entrance, take four suits, and exit. I hand one to Garrett and place the others into one of my pockets. While he's changing I step over to the virtual imager, tap on the display and hit the cancel button, which causes the machine to stop. When I return, the suit has changed to match Garrett's quiver and bow. He's a little shocked by the effect and wants to put his other outfit back on.

I tell him to leave his other clothes behind, as he won't need them for now. We get back into the elevator, but we don't start to descend until I reset the lockdown. When we reach the lobby, I loop us outside. The dome is slowly being destroyed, but there aren't any holes visible yet. I loop us until we're in front of the airlocks that'll lead us to the Outer Limits. I try looping us through, but because of the wristband the Patrician are stopping us from leaving the area.

"Now what do we do?" Garrett asks.

"We walk."

I slowly approach the airlocks, visualize in my mind what I want, and the suit immediately reacts. My exposed skin is covered and I easily move through the glass. Garrett does what I tell him and is beside me in a matter of moments. Once we're through both sets of locks the suits return to their normal appearance and I try to loop us – once again, unsuccessfully. The Patrician must have completely disabled my ability.

"Shit!" I scream.

"Now what? It'll take us hours to reach the main center of the Outer Limits," Garrett says.

"If you tell your arrow to hit my wristband it would, wouldn't it?"

"It should, yes," he replies. "Wait, you want me to shoot an arrow through your arm? No, Max, that's crazy."

"Well, what do you suggest? Lok is dead and the equipment to get into the wristband is back in Pentras Tower."

"But how do you even know you can resume looping if the wristband is destroyed? Isn't that what gives you the ability?"

"Remember what you told me right before our first time in the *Litarian Battles*? You said that maybe it wasn't just my hands that were damaged, and I think you're right. If the Patrician were desperate enough, and knew I was going to be placed in the Looper unit, why not give me that enhancement without the wristband?"

"Okay, well, I'm not shooting an arrow into you since there may be another way."

He waves for me to follow. A mile away from the dome is an empty carriage with two Aedox dead on the ground beside it, their weapons gone. Garrett climbs into the driver's seat while I get in next to him. He turns on the engine and we race down the line as fast as the motor will allow. When we reach the outskirts of the Outer Limits, smoke and flames fill much of the sky. People run around, fighting Aedox who are gunning other people down.

Garrett switches the lines when we get to a junction and moves us towards the second-level housing. We have to climb a couple of steep hills to get to the ridge the complex sits on. The buildings line up perfectly in several rows and they all look to be in the same condition the orphanage was in before it was destroyed. We change lines again, going down between the third and fourth sets of structures. Garrett stops the carriage and tells me to get out. We run to the last section of the fourth row, climb a few flights of stairs, and enter an apartment. The interior is covered in gray paint with black tiled floors, and only consists of one room. The kitchen, bathroom, bedroom, and common room are in the same confined space.

"I think the bedrooms at the orphanage are bigger than this whole place," I comment.

Garrett goes over to his bed and slides out a box full of tools and other random items from underneath. "Yeah, but it still beats the shanties."

By the lone window is a cinderblock shelving unit holding a small television, a few photos, and a dead plant. One of the pictures catches my attention, so I pick up the flimsy wood frame and have to look at the face carefully to make sure I'm seeing it correctly.

"Is this my mother?" I ask.

Garrett looks up from his task, but only briefly. "Yes," he replies. "The Patrician gave that to me in case I saw her and was able to see if she knew where you were."

I remove the picture from the frame and that's when I see it. A black dragon, just like Frey's, on the top of her left chest, just like mine. I tuck the photo into a pocket in the suit.

That would explain why seeing Frey's tattoo made me feel comforted. He got the same one my mother had. But why?

"Here," Garrett says, pulling me over towards the bed and having me sit.

He takes a thin set of pliers and tries to force it between the display screen on the top of the wristband and the rubber backing imbedded into my skin. I wince at the pain and he apologizes, but I tell him it's fine. It takes almost ten minutes before the two pieces finally separate.

"I can't simply cut the connection between the device and you because that'll kill you instantly. What I need to do is disable that portion of the wristband's programming," Garrett says as he reaches for his box of tools again.

He removes a small screwdriver, but it's not like one I've ever seen before. He touches the tip of the tool to one of the circuits, and along the side of the screwdriver a display describes that circuit's function. There are so many circuits in that tight space that it'll take him a while to locate the right one. Yelling pulls my attention away from what Garrett is doing since it sounds close. The building shakes as a bomb goes off.

"Do you think they're nuclear?" I ask as Garrett continues to work.

"I don't think so because they would've used them before now if they had them," he replies. "I think they may be afraid of killing someone useful, like you." He looks up and smiles at me.

"Where'd you get that tool?" I ask, trying to distract myself from the mayhem outside.

"I used it in the smelting plant. I was relegated to maintenance, so I needed this type of screwdriver to make repairs on the machines or to stop a specific action. Ah, there it is," he says.

Along the other side of the screwdriver are small buttons. He pushes a few, and the wristband's looping ability is temporarily deactivated.

"I can't permanently disable it," he says, replacing the casing over the wristband. "Hopefully the Patrician don't look too closely. I also disabled your locator, so they can't track you."

I kiss him deeply just as the building shakes again. This time, cracks appear in the walls and ceiling. I take Garrett's hand before he has time to put away the tool and try to loop, hoping my theory about me being modified is right. It works. Within seconds we're in front of the orphanage, or at least what's left of it. I walk up the steps to the front door and head inside. Only a few pieces of the exterior walls remain, and the top floors have collapsed onto the main level.

"Why'd you bring us here?" Garrett asks from the entryway, dropping the screwdriver into his quiver.

"I was hoping Brink would've brought the others here, but I guess he didn't."

I run to the grove just to be sure, but it's empty. My workbench is in ashes, but the wall surrounding the grove is perfectly intact. It looks like the Patrician bombs are designed to destroy only designated targets and not everything around it.

"Now where? We can't loop around the whole city," Garrett says, joining me.

"Headmaster Edom's mansion. Maybe they're there."

I take Garrett's hand and loop us to the hallway just outside the den. Aedox fill the room and Garrett and I are immediately fired upon, so I loop us to the upper level. Luckily the suits protect us from being killed.

We carefully walk towards the staircase, peeking around the corner to count exactly how many Aedox there are.

"I'll distract them while you loop," Garrett says.

"Fine, but wait a few seconds until after I loop."

He nods as I remove my Kopis and vanish. In the void, I hover above Garrett as he fires his arrows rapidly, striking a couple of Aedox before he's fired upon. I land in the back of the group, blade at the ready. Two Aedox fall before me, but I have to loop again since the others see what's happening and attack. I don't land but stay in the void while Garrett continues to shoot, but he's running out of ammunition. I project myself across the room, land, slice up two more Aedox, and loop again. Only four Aedox remain. I sheathe my Kopis while still in the void and land next to a dead Aedox. I remove his gun and fire at those still standing. Garrett steps on to the top of the landing when he sees there aren't any more.

"Here," I say, tossing him one of the Aedox rifles as he gets off the last step.

He takes another one along with some extra clips, so I do the same, placing the ammunition into one of the pockets. We begin scoping out the mansion one room at a time. We split up; Garrett starts on the upper level while I work my way down to the cellar where the carriages are kept, but it's empty. Garrett didn't follow me down to the cellar which he should've done by now, so now I go looking for him as well. I find him in the dining room and discover he's not alone.

"I was wondering what happened to you when the war started," Vernon hisses.

"You let the Aedox take me," I say, cautiously stepping towards him.

"I had to, dear," he says cheerfully. "You see, it was imperative that you get to Tarsus and the *Litarian Battles*. From what I've learned, you've done quite well. Leader Fallon will be so pleased."

Garrett points his gun at Vernon, pressing the barrel almost to his temple. "You're not going to get the chance to tell her you saw us."

"Don't be so sure," Fallon says, walking in from the kitchen.

The dining room fills with Aedox and Garrett and I are relieved of our guns. An Aedox tries to remove my Kopis from its sheath, but his hand goes right through it.

"Never watched the game, did you?" I say with a slight laugh.

The Aedox hits me in the back with the butt of his gun, knocking the air out of my lungs and causing me to fall to my knees. My hands are shackled.

"You've done well, Garrett," Fallon says approaching him. "You'll be greatly rewarded for your loyalty."

I glare at him, rage coursing through my veins as I'm hoisted to my feet.

"It wasn't me, Max," he says, pleadingly. "I didn't tell them anything. I'm with you now, not them."

"There's no need to keep trying to win her over, Garrett. She sees the real you now. After all, it was your tracker that led us here," Fallon says, placing her hand on his shoulder. "This will all be over soon."

"I can just loop out of here, you know," I say, arrogantly.

"Yes, but I don't think you will," Vernon says, rising from his seat and nodding to a couple of Aedox.

Frey is dragged into the room, blood caked along the side of his head. An Aedox has a gun pressed underneath his chin. He looks at me and smiles. I gasp at the sight of him, and choke on tears and bile. I step over to him, but the Aedox doesn't remove his weapon.

"I didn't know where you were," Frey says hoarsely.

"I've been looking for you," I reply, kissing him gently on the lips.

"See, Garrett, Max does prefer Frey over you," Fallon says.

Garrett's face flushes red and I can see the anger in his eyes.

"Where are the others?" I ask, turning my attention back towards her.

"They're with the Dracken," Vernon answers. "They'll all be dead soon."

"How?" Frey asks.

"The Outer Limits will be eradicated like Pentras was. Now," Vernon says, gesturing towards the door for the hallway, "shall we?"

I'm led out first, with Frey closely behind me. Garrett exits with Leader Fallon and Vernon, who are at the end of the line, which just affirms his betrayal. We go out the front door and are halfway across the yard when gunfire erupts all around us. The Aedox that was holding me falls, as does the one holding Frey. The remaining Aedox return fire while Frey and I drop to the ground and begin searching for the key to our shackles. I finally locate it, give it to Frey, and he unlocks me.

"Come on, I know how to find Brink and Van," Frey says, taking my arm as we stand.

"Not without Garrett," I say, shaking him loose.

I pick up a gun from a fallen Aedox and toss it to Frey, who starts to shoot at anything that wears an Aedox uniform.

"Why?" he screams to be heard over the battle.

"He has something the Patrician want, and I'm not letting him give it to them."

I unsheathe my Kopis and make my way through the crowd towards Leader Fallon, Vernon, and Garrett as they retreat towards the carriage entrance to the cellar. The doors swing open when we run through them and Frey shoots at Vernon, hitting him in the leg. He aims next at Leader Fallon and hits her in the shoulder. He's about to fire at Garrett when I stop him.

"Don't," I say.

"Why not?" he asks, his eyes looking through the sight on the top of the large weapon.

"Because it'll just go right through him."

"I'm not taking this off," Garrett says, pulling at the suit and smirking. "The Patrician will have their technology shortly."

His tracker still works, so they can loop him.

I charge and as he's readying his bow and arrow I cut into his arm, an inch above the wristband, severing it. He screams and collapses to the ground.

"You bitch!" he shouts, cradling his wound.

"See if they can find you now," I say through clenched teeth.

"Fuck you, Max," Garrett says, trying to stem the blood running from his arm.

I knee him in the face. "Kill them," I say to Frey, pointing to Leader Fallon and Vernon.

I get Garrett to his feet as the suit reacts to his injury and covers the wound. I'm not sure what more the suit could or might do, but I know we need to move fast to find the others. Frey joins us as we're making our way out of the cellar's back door.

"This way," Frey says, tapping me on the shoulder.

I practically have to drag Garrett with us. A few feet away we find an empty carriage, so I shove Garrett into the back and Frey slides in next to him while I take the controls. I have no idea where I'm going, but anywhere is better than being near the mansion. We're about a mile away when the bombs hit the structure, incinerating everything and everyone in and around the building.

"Where are they?" I ask Frey as I go by the factories.

"Brink said to meet him at the place where you two grew up."

"We were already there," Garrett says through spasms of pain.

I swing the carriage around and head back towards the orphanage. I have to change our lines several times to make sure we're on the correct one leading to it. I take us off the main line when we reach the alley and let momentum bring us to the gate of the grove. We hop out and enter the grove, but still no one is around.

"This is so damn frustrating," I almost shout.

"Chill, Maxy, it's all good," Brink says, emerging from the shelled structure.

"Where are the others?" Frey asks.

"Not far away. Come on, we'll go on foot," Brink says, and gestures for us to go back out the gate.

We hustle down the alley, Garrett now being carried by Frey and me. His color is fading, so perhaps the suit can only do so much for his injuries. We stop when something detonates a few blocks away. Brink looks around the corner of a demolished shop and signals for us to continue. We wind up almost at the complex for second-level housing when Brink directs us to an opening at the base of the steep hill. Heavy metal doors open as we approach. They're manned by heavily-armed citizens, but many have the dragon tattoo visible on their exposed flesh.

The doors close behind us as we enter a tunnel that's lit by small gas-fed lights that are secured into the metal that covers the walls. The air is stale and reeks of unwashed bodies. The tunnel finally empties into a large space filled with cots, boxes of food, and over one hundred people. Two men take Garrett from us to tend to his wound while Brink goes to look for Van.

"What is this place?" I ask, putting my Kopis back in its sheath.

"A refuge created shortly after Pentras was annihilated," a female voice answers from somewhere in the crowd.

Nan emerges from the fold. Frey raises his weapon, aiming it at her. Those around us immediately point their guns at Frey.

"No, don't," I say to Frey, placing my hand on the barrel of his gun.

"She's a Patrician. That's why she killed my father," he says, not lowering the weapon.

"She's not with the Patrician," I respond just as Nan is opening her mouth to speak. I turn toward her and smile. "She's a Keeper."

"What?" Frey asks, disbelief etched on his face. The weapon wavers in his hands before being lowering to his side.

"It's true," Nan says, moving closer to us. "How did you know, Max?"

"I thought at first you were with the Patrician, especially after you killed Avery. But then it dawned on me when I saw Hammond at the Icarian depository. The Patrician were looking for you, so if they were looking for you, and since you'd murdered a Dracken leader, I figured you had to be a Keeper."

Van pushes his way through the crowd and gives me a hug. "I'm so glad you made it," he says after letting go.

"You three come with me," Nan says. "Everyone else get prepared."

We walk past the cots and towards the back corner of the vast room. Brink joins us a few minutes later with news that they've been able to stop Garrett's bleeding. I lean against the wall and watch Frey hug his mother.

"We don't have much time," Frey says, releasing her. "The Patrician are going to nuke the Outer Limits."

"I know. That's why this shelter was created," Nan says.

"We need to get back to the Dead Zone," I say.

"Why?" Brink asks, seemingly disgusted by the idea. "We're perfectly safe here."

"It's not about safety," I counter. "I need Van and his bombs to destroy the contents in Pentras Tower."

"What are you talking about?" Frey asks.

I point to the suit I'm wearing and look around to make sure no one is in earshot of us. "The Patrician want the technology used to create this suit. If we don't get back to the Dead Zone and destroy it, they'll just keep trying until they have it. Once they do, all worlds are in danger. Not just ours."

"It's Dracken technology, right?" Brink asks. "Why not just give it back to them?"

I'm about to respond when Nan stops me by placing her hand on my shoulder.

"I'm sure that's Max's intent, Brink. Perhaps Van can take the suit Garrett is wearing so he can safely return to Pentras Tower."

I reach into my pocket to pull out the suits I'm carrying, but stop myself. Van leaves to get the suit from Garrett, while Brink and Nan discuss tactical maneuvers for getting us near the dome's entrance. I pull Frey away from the others, moving us off to the other end of the room near a couple of gas tanks that are feeding power to the shelter. Once we're alone, he pulls me close and kisses me deeply. I pull back, reach into my pocket, and pull out the picture of my mother.

"Does this look familiar?" I ask, tapping on the dragon tattoo she has.

"It looks just like the one I have," he responds.

"Who told you to get it this specific one?"

"Troy's father."

"Did he tell you why?"

"No, not really. I thought it was odd, but Guy Larsen was getting me into the game so I wasn't about to argue with him."

"Maybe he thought of it as a way to get to me, and when that didn't work, he had Troy use the Archives to jog my memory."

"He wouldn't have known you would be sent to the game."

"Sure he did," I say. "Leader Fallon told him, and Troy knew of the mutilation done to me long before anyone else did. The only way he could've known that was from Leader Fallon. She would never have talked to him directly, but it makes sense that she would tell his father, in order to ensure his loyalty to the Patrician." I slip the photo back into my pocket and remove one of the suits from the other pocket. "Here, put this on under your clothes, but be discreet about it."

He takes it, goes off to another vacant area, and puts the suit on. He returns just as Van does. I instruct Van to put his other clothes on over the suit, so it's not obvious he's wearing it. The three of us return to Nan and Brink, who've moved back to the main area with the cots. The four of us head back towards the entrance, but stop short of the guards.

"What about Garrett?" Brink asks.

"We'll take care of him," Nan answers. She turns her attention to Van. "Would you mind giving me a couple of your explosives?"

He looks puzzled at the request. "They won't work for you," he says. "They're designed to be used exclusively by me."

"You and the Keepers," she says with a smile. "We just never mentioned that part to the matrons."

He hands her two and cinches the bag closed.

Nan hugs Frey again, but this time with tears in her eyes. "I'll be thinking of you," she says to him.

"I'll be back," he replies.

I know what her intentions are, but I'm not telling Frey until I have to. He won't ever understand the sacrifice his mother is about to make, but I do. I hug her as well, holding on for a long time. I feel like I'm also saying goodbye to my own mother. Secretly I am, in a way.

The guards open the door and the four of us step out. The doors are sealed shut immediately behind us, so there's no going back now. I take Van and Frey by the hand. Brink takes Van's other hand and I loop us. I could loop us right into Pentras Tower, but something is telling me that isn't the way to proceed. We land a few seconds later just outside the mansion. Everyone has either scattered from the area, or is dead.

A massive explosion draws everyone's attention. The hill the shelter is under buckles and collapses, and flames erupt from exposed gas pipes. Fire eats away at the second-level housing, lighting up the evening sky.

"Mom!" Frey shouts.

I loop us again before he can run back to her.

Twenty-Eight

We're at the entrance to the dome when Frey says he needs a break, but I don't give him one and instead move us quickly through the dome and deep into the Dead Zone. He shakes me loose before I can loop us further and sits on the ground. The Patrician haven't ceased their bombing and the glass of the dome is almost cracked completely through.

"Why? Why would she do that?" Frey asks anyone who'll answer him.

"I'll tell you when we're back in Pentras Tower," I say, reaching down to help him to his feet.

"You knew?" he asks, swatting my hand away, anger heavy in his voice. He stands, grabs my arms, and squeezes them tightly. "You knew she was going to blow them all up? Why didn't you stop her?"

"She was saving us all, Frey," I say, trying to hide the pain that's flooding my muscles. "You have no idea what the Dracken were going to do."

"But I'm one of them, Max. So is Brink. So are you. This doesn't make any sense."

"Can we have this discussion someplace safer?" Van says, pointing to the drones that are moving in on us.

They open fire as we run. Frey and Brink fire back, using the Aedox guns they took from the shelter. Brink runs out of ammunition, so I toss him a clip from my pocket. I reach out for Van and Frey. They each take my hand and Brink grabs hold of Van and I loop us, but not before searing pain shoots up my arm. I can't hold on to Frey any longer and he falls out of the void just as we make it to the lobby of the tower. He falls hard onto the concrete steps while the rest of us tumble to the tile floor. I quickly loop back for him and get him inside just as the drones locate us.

I collapse to the ground in agony. A bullet has ripped clean through my forearm. Since the suit has short sleeves it didn't protect me. Van runs down to the medical supply closet, returning with some gauze and bandages. He puts pressure on the wound and I let out a howl.

"Explain!" Frey yells at me while Van works to stop the bleeding.

"Your mom wants you to live," I respond through the searing pain.

"I would've been all right. She didn't need to kill herself."

"Your mother is a Keeper and the Dracken know this. If the Dracken win this war, you'll be left behind with the others to die."

"What do you mean?" Brink asks.

I tell them what really happened to Pentras, that Frey's sister was correct in what she discovered, and the truth about the Dracken. "That's why your sister was killed, Frey," I say through spasms of pain. "She figured everything out just like my parents did when they were sent to the Outer Limits, but by then it was too late for all of them."

"The Patrician killed my sister," Frey protests.

"That's what your father told you, right?"

He looks contemplative. "Yes."

"Just a Dracken leader trying to throw suspicion onto the Patrician, Frey," I respond. "He's the one who turned your sister in to the Aedox. It's what Drackens would do to protect themselves."

He steps back, raises the gun, and fires at the displays behind the counter.

"Feel better?" Brink says when he finally stops.

"Shut up," Frey responds.

"I can't get the bleeding to stop," Van says. "We need to take her up to the surgical floor."

Brink and Van carry me to the elevator. Frey follows and presses the button for the seventeenth floor. We enter the first room we come to and Brink sets me down on a surgical table while Van scours the cabinets. He locates a contraption similar to the one used on my knee and the device is secured around my arm. I scream when I feel my skin being stitched back together. Van injects a painkiller into my neck and I start to feel drowsy. The room spins slightly.

"How long will it take to mend her?" Brink asks.

"About a half-hour," Van responds.

"I'll keep an eye on her, if you two want to find good locations for the explosives," Brink says.

Van and Frey leave, much to my disappointment. Especially Frey. He knows Brink's attitude towards me, so why would he leave me alone in a room with him? Is he that mad that he's willing to put my safety at risk? I finger the handle of my Kopis as Brink slides onto the table next to me.

"I think your boyfriend is mad at you, otherwise why would he leave the two of us alone?" Brink says, sliding closer. He starts to rub my arm then begins to tug on the suit. "I know Van is wearing one, and I'm sure Frey is also. So, why wasn't I given one of these high-tech outfits?"

"Because you're vile, Brink. I only want to protect those who mean something to me, and you don't mean anything to me."

He slaps me hard across the face. "You're still mine, you know," he says.

"The Dracken are dead, almost extinct, so whatever promises were made to you are no longer valid."

"That's what you think," he says furiously. "There are more of us out there and as soon as the Patrician destroy the dome we'll be raiding it in no time."

I try to remove my Kopis, but he's stronger than I am at the moment and keeps my arm pinned against the table.

"Who told you all of this?" I ask through clenched teeth.

"Tilda, of course. Who do you think promised you to me?"

"She wouldn't," I say, choking on tears.

He takes his free hand and caresses my cheek. "Oh but she did, Maxy. She knew who you were the moment Headmaster Edom dropped you off at the orphanage. Why do you think she was always so nice to you and no one else? To win your trust."

"She told you who I was?"

"No, not entirely. She only said you were someone who needed protecting. Someone who would make the Dracken whole again, and you've done just that, Max. United us."

"Where are they?"

"They'll be here soon," he replies. "Nan killed herself for nothing. Those in the shelter were simply followers, not the true Dracken… not like you."

He nuzzles my neck then begins to kiss my cheeks and then my lips. I grapple for my Kopis, but his weight is preventing me from getting a good hold of it. I feel the pouch for his Deer Horn knives and open it, grasp one, and slice him across the side. I push him off me and he lands on the floor, blood seeping through his clothes. I jump down from the table, push him flat onto his back, and place the weapon against his throat as I straddle him.

"Where are they now?" I demand.

He just laughs.

I cut him deep in the thigh. He screams and tries to wriggle out from under me, but my strength is restored.

"Tell me!" I shout.

"They never left," he says crossly. "You think they needed you to get them into Pentras Tower like the Patrician did? You're so fucking stupid, Max. They needed you to free them from the tower."

"There isn't anyone in this building but us."

"Are you sure?"

I think back to my encounter with them on the seventh floor. They used the monitor at one of the workstations to talk to me, but how? Is it possible there are others in here?

"You're lying," I utter.

"Did you ever watch the music videos back in Thrace Tower or at Frey's house?'

My expression changes to puzzlement.

"It was how the Dracken could communicate with the rest of us," he says. "Being stuck in this tower for over a hundred years, they kept evolving and advancing their technology. They're a part of everything now, but their failsafe prevented them from escaping. The Keepers placing the dome over the Dead Zone sealed the Dracken in. You were the only one able to unlock it all."

"You're crazy, Brink. You couldn't possibly know any of this. You're just making shit up."

He taps his wristband. "The Keepers and Patrician aren't the only ones with access to these."

I realize at that moment that it's not Brink talking, but a Dracken. "Where's Brink?"

"He's here, but not for much longer," the thing says. "The Keepers have done wonders, giving us a way to survive. If it wasn't for them, we would never have achieved our greatest scientific accomplishment."

"And what is that?"

"Immortality. With the wristband implanted in all the winners of the *Litarian Battles*, once the Patrician send them into the Dead Zone and you've disabled the security on the building, we'll choose the most valuable people and take over their bodies, just like we've done with your friends."

Frey and Van. That's why they left like they did and how Van knew what was needed to fix my arm.

"I'll stop you," I say, gripping the knife tighter.

"I'd like to see you try."

The blade cuts an inch-deep groove into Brink's neck. I know the Dracken will simply move back into whatever electronic device they're all hiding in until a new host comes into play. I need to find Van and Frey quickly, but don't know where they went off to. I remove the healing device from my arm, toss it to the floor, and notice that the wound is perfectly mended, no scarring. I go to the elevator and take it down to the eighth floor. I get past the two security doors like I did before and enter the dark room where Hammond was.

"Hammond!" I shout, hoping he can hear me from wherever he is.

The security door closes, locking me in the room. Hammond appears in the same spot he did before. "We know," he says.

"Where are Frey and Van?"

"They're lost to you now, Max. The Dracken have them under their control and the Patrician army is at the rim of the dome in Tarsus. There are only a few minutes left before it all comes to a head. We'll teleport you now to a safe location."

"No!" I yell. "I can do this. Just tell me where Frey is."

"Max, please, it's over. We've lost, but you can still be saved," Hammond says, pleading.

"Then I'll find them without you," I say, and loop up to the fiftieth floor.

I step towards the window as the glass of the dome explodes. Within seconds a deadly hail of shattered glass rains down onto the streets, and nothing left above us. I race to the other side of the room to look toward Tarsus. The city itself is just a small dot on the horizon, but I can picture the Patrician army flowing into the Dead Zone.

The Dracken are stuck in the building until the security failsafe is disabled. If they're in fact controlling Van and Frey, the Dracken can direct them on how to do that. Which would mean they're on the seventh floor.

I ignore the elevator and loop right in front of the gate separating the room from the elevators. Van is in front of the plasma display with his back towards me, his bag of explosives at his feet. I remove my Kopis and side-step around the area until I'm on the other side of the room, facing Van. He's so focused on tapping symbols on the plasma screen that he doesn't notice me approach.

"Where's Frey?" I ask, holding my Kopis up by my shoulder with both hands.

Van looks up, but I can tell it's not really him. "He's around."

"Van's dead, isn't he?"

"Yes, Max, he is."

"Then killing you won't hurt so much."

I jump onto the display, but Van is ready with one of the Aedox rifles. I instinctively tell the suit to protect me and it covers my entire body as bullets sail through me, but my Kopis doesn't do any damage to Van either since he's instructed his suit to do the same as mine. I change tactics and grab the bag as I fall to the floor. I sheathe my weapon and loop into the void then land next to the bank of computers that Lok worked on, arm a bomb, adhere it inside the box, and loop again.

Van has to chase me around the floor, but I'm much faster. The first one ignites as I'm activating one to place on the last of the four computer banks. Van is blown across the room and against a concrete wall, then drops. I secure the bag around my shoulder and loop over next to him. He doesn't have a pulse. I step over to the plasma screen and apply five explosives all around the table. I loop behind the security gate and smile as the room lights up like a candle. I know this will bring down the security for the building, but it should also destroy any remnants of the Dracken.

I begin looping up one floor at a time. Frey is collapsed next to the main console on the twelfth floor. I run up to him, turn him onto his back, and begin shaking him.

"Frey, wake up," I say. "You're stronger than they are."

I look for his pulse, but can't find one.

"Damnit, Frey," I whisper through tears. "Wake up." I pound on his chest, then finally just rest my head on it.

I stand, go over to the exact spot where I landed when I looped, and take a deep breath. I close my eyes, clear my mind, and pick my point in time… back in time. I visualize myself being on the seventh floor, landing just outside the gate, but that's not where I project myself. I take that same instant in time and picture myself on the twelfth floor, right where I'm standing now. The suit retracts to its normal design as I slip into the void. I open my eyes as time rewinds in front of me and I feel myself split as the past begins again. I'm much weaker now since I'm technically in two places at the same time.

I step out of the void and approach Frey cautiously. He's sitting at the console, just like Lok had, his fingers flying through the various configurations that change every few seconds, but he's solving the puzzles, which means he's been taken over by a Dracken. I stop just behind his chair, my breaths are coming out slowly since my energy is being mainly used by my other half.

"Frey," I say, my voice almost a whisper.

He turns, and recognition shows on his face, but it's short-lived. He frees his blade, knocks me to the ground, and holds the weapon high above his head.

"You can't stop us, Max," the Dracken says, using Frey's voice.

"Frey, I know you're there. You're stronger than they are. Fight back."

"It's too late, Max. Frey doesn't exist anymore."

"You're wrong. I saw the recognition in his eyes when he saw me just a moment ago," I say, getting weaker by the minute.

Now I understand why it's so hard to loop back in time. You're not as strong or as in control, and I've made myself very vulnerable as time runs out.

"Max?" Frey asks.

I smile at him. "Fight them."

He cringes as the conflict inside erupts. His hand holding the blade wavers, then firms up.

"He's losing, Max," the Dracken says, almost with a laugh.

"No!" I shout with all my effort. "Frey, listen to me. You have to win. You'll be dead in a few seconds. Please, you have to win."

The blade comes down, but falls through the opening in the rails around the walkway. Frey screams as his mind is torn apart and I feel myself slipping away since time is catching up. Frey gets to his feet, grabbing the sides of his head, then stumbles towards the elevators and collapses. I fade as the void pulls me back to actual time and find myself standing behind the security gate on the seventh floor once again, my suit still covering my entire body. I quickly loop back to the twelfth floor and kneel next to Frey, who's currently moaning.

"Frey," I say, cautiously reaching out towards him as the suit retracts from my hands.

His eyes flicker open and relief floods his face. He reaches for me and I hold him tightly.

"I thought you died," he says. "You were there and then not."

"I time-looped backwards."

He raises his head so our eyes meet. "I told you I didn't recommend doing that."

"I second that," I say, standing and helping him to his feet. "We need to destroy what we can. The Patrician are on their way now."

I go back to the main console, attach a couple of explosives, take Frey's hand, and loop us to the floor above just as the explosives go off. I instruct Frey to take off the suit, which he does while I secure the bombs to the imagers. He puts his other clothes back on, but I can't strip since I have nothing else to wear at the moment. I'll destroy my suit later, but I need to take care of the machine used to create them.

Frey and I go into the clean room where the suits are stored. I take the two from my pocket, then Frey's, and loop myself behind the plate-glass window separating the machine from everything else.

I drop the suits and the necklace onto the conveyor belt, take the remaining bombs, and stick them to various points along the machine. I'm not sure if the impending fire will destroy the suits since nothing else has, but at least it'll bury them. I set the timers for one minute, turn, and am about to loop back when I see him.

Garrett's arrow pierces Frey's chest. I scream, but no one can hear me. Garrett looks up at me after relishing his kill. His hand has been completely restored, but without the wristband. I step back, plastering myself against the machine.

"You won't win," I say, even though he can't hear me.

The blast is bright, almost blinding. I feel my body crash through the glass as it shatters, finally coming to a rest by the damaged imagers. My ears are ringing and my vision is blurry, but I'm alive. The suit retracts from my body. I never instructed it to protect me against the blast, but it did anyway. I look up and see Garrett standing over me grinning from ear to ear.

"We're the Patrician. We always win," he says.

He grabs me by the throat, brings me to my feet, and we loop. He throws me hard on to the metal floor when we reach Patrician Nine. I bang my head and the world spins. I start to feel as if I'm going to be sick when Garrett picks me up again and we exit the hallway into a massive observation room. I can see the ruined landscape of the Dead Zone clear as day. Parts of Tarsus and the Outer Limits are only slightly visible.

Garrett shoves me on to a couch, goes over to a communicator, and presses a button. "Nuke it," he says.

I stand and get close to the glass. Missiles fly towards the planet, obliterating it in a matter of seconds. Another wave is sent, this one shattering whatever remnants survived into tiny pieces. Just behind the shards is a smaller planet, probably Icarian. It, too, is destroyed, blown to dust. I retreat to the couch and sink down.

"How did I fail?" I ask myself.

"You didn't fail, Max," Garrett says, sitting next to me. "You did exactly what you were supposed to."

I look over at him since I'd been transfixed on the devastation. "How?"

He reaches into his quiver and pulls out the screwdriver. "All Patrician tools have trackers in them," he says, smiling. "Did you think they would actually let me die? They looped me a few seconds before the explosions ripped the shelter apart."

"I can loop away from here."

"And go where, Max? Your world is gone, and it'll be some time before we get back to the Patrician home world. Besides, I think the modifications done to you will be reversed before we even get there."

I look back out into space. I feel numb, withdrawn, and angry. I reach for my Kopis, but it's not there.

"That was taken from you the moment we got on board," Garrett says, inching closer.

"Just kill me. You have what you want," I say, grabbing and pulling at the suit.

He wraps his arm around me, pulls me in close, and whispers in my ear. "Your life will be spared, Max. Your reward for your loyalty is to be my mate for life. You'll never leave my side. You'll be placed in a high-ranking position, and once the modifications have been reversed we'll start a family."

He pushes me down on the couch, removes the suit, and forces me to submit. I try to fight him off, but I have no will left. A few hours later I'm removed from the observation room and taken to a surgical stall down on the medical deck where the wristband is removed, the scarring on my hands is mended, and my ability to loop terminated. I'm fitted with a silver ring on my right hand that signifies I belong to Garrett, but it also prevents me from harming myself by sending signals to my brain to counteract any self-destructive thoughts. I refuse to listen to anything anyone tells me about my new rank in the Patrician order. Garrett is awarded the rank of Commander, which will allow him to invade other worlds with the Dracken technology. I wonder about Hammond and if he survived, but Garrett tells me Hammond was trapped inside Thrace Tower and died when the planet was destroyed.

The Keepers are now extinct, the Dracken forgotten, and I'm now a Patrician.